"The story is rockin' from the get-go, and doesn't let up on the gas… This page-turner had me constantly chuckling at something!"

—*Drey's Library*

"*Kiss at Your Own Risk* simply blew my mind with its off-the-wall humor, bizarre and astounding world building, and a pace that kept me goggle-eyed… Whoever's story comes out next… will be an auto-buy for me. Thank you, Ms. Rowe, for a reading experience that truly was extraordinary."

—*The Long and the Short of It*

"Fast pacing, funny dialogue, and volatile characters makes for a crazy rambunctious story."

—*Smexy Books*

"A great, action-packed story full of powerful emotions that just drive the story forward. And the drive was WAY hot!!!! A winner for me, and one that I won't soon forget."

—*Seriously Reviewed*

"Hilarious, thrilling, incredibly interesting, and very well thought-out. This is not your typical paranormal romance."

—*Read All Over Reviews*

"I love how Rowe balanced the romance and the humor. This book always had me on the edge of laughter."

—*Books Like Breathing*

TOUCH IF YOU DARE

STEPHANIE ROWE

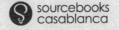

sourcebooks
casablanca

Published by Sourcebooks Casablanca, an imprint of Sourcebooks, Inc.
P.O. Box 4410, Naperville, Illinois 60567-4410
(630) 961-3900
FAX: (630) 961-2168
www.sourcebooks.com

Printed and bound in the United States of America
QW 10 9 8 7 6 5 4 3 2 1

For MIG, for showing me my path.

Chapter 1

SOMETIMES RESCUING A BUNCH OF ALMOST-DEAD warriors from black magicked pit vipers was just the kind of thing a man needed to help him forget the fact that he could not, for the life of him, figure out how to knit.

Jarvis Swain, the Guardian of Hate, ducked as the bright red snake launched itself at his throat, sprouting wings as it hit the air. He whipped his sword up just in time to de-fang it before it clamped its gums onto his jugular. "Since when do these suckers fly?"

He ripped the scaly mutant off him and tossed it out the door of the Hotel of Love and Healing, the pit of doom and despair where injured warriors were taken to recover or die after Angelica, Death's psychotic grandma, had tortured them until they were on the bleeding edge of death.

After a hundred and fifty years of incarceration, Jarvis and three others had escaped from Angelica's Den of Womanly Pursuits two weeks ago. They'd kicked Angelica's crazy-bat-shit-ass, saved a girl, and made a deal with Angelica's heir, Mari Hansen, to free the rest of warriors.

Two weeks post-escape, and Mari was stonewalling (so much for thinking Angelica's dethronement would make Mari become sane and reasonable) and the remaining warriors hadn't been released. Jarvis and his team of fugitives had decided to start plucking out the good guys one by one. First stop was the Hotel of Love and Healing. Any poor bastards still in there needed help—and in a big way.

Jarvis and his teammate Nigel Aquarian were rocking the sick bay rescue while their cronies, Blaine Underhill and Christian Slayer, played decoy with Mari and her assistants (no need to deal with a bunch of overly talented, lethally brainwashed, estrogen vessels of hate, if it could be avoided).

"These vipers aren't pure snake." Nigel flexed his hands, and two dozen three-inch knives exploded from his fingertips, careening across the cavernous room. Twenty-two vipes dropped to the cement floor, graphite blades winking in the centers of their murderous little foreheads.

Nigel might be an artist, but the man also had the aim of a Roman god. "Angelica cross-bred the snakes with ladybugs a few weeks before we bailed." Nigel's hands were charcoal black now, and ash was sloughing off his palms. "Bastard went right for my left nipple. Still healing from it."

"Angelica's a she-bitch-from-hell, but I gotta tip my hat to her vision. I always felt ladybugs had more potential than anyone gives them credit for." Jarvis thwacked another swarm of incoming vipers as he took inventory of the Hotel. Only six beds were still occupied, and every occupant was slow dancing so intimately with death that not one had even cracked an eyelid at their entrance. How many nights had he spent here, flipping off Death?

He swore as he remembered Death sitting on his headboard, waiting for him to finally give up. Those deadly shadows looming over his bed, daring him to accept the peace and relief they offered. Reminding him that if he decided to revive this time, he'd be back in the Hotel again, dying again, fighting for his last breath, *again*, in another week. A day. An hour. A never-ending cycle of torture, torment, and hell.

Jarvis saw the cleave marks in the first bed's posts, ones he'd left his last time here, when the pain had been so intense he'd left raw strips in the wood, clawed by his own fingernails. His grip tightened on his sword, and a bead of sweat broke out on his brow. "Coming home can be a bitch," he said quietly.

Nigel inclined his head in silent acknowledgement. "What do you say we retrieve these poor bastards and get the fuck out?"

Get the fuck out. Jarvis glanced toward the door. Yeah, still unlocked. They weren't trapped this time. They were in control now. They could leave whenever they wanted. He forced his grip to loosen and shook out his arm. "Let's torch the place on the way out."

Anything to wipe the nightmares from his soul. Nigel had his art. Blaine had his cross-stitching and his woman. Everyone on his team had something to cleanse the boils from their souls. But not Jarvis. The hell he carried inside him wasn't about to be placated by a session with a pair of lavender knitting needles and turquoise angora. He had no artistic reprieve, and he'd never be soothed by the tender touch of another human being, let alone a woman.

He could imagine it, though. He'd bet his ass it would feel like a fucking angel to have a female touch him the way he'd seen Trinity touch Blaine.

But peace was not for him.

He'd have to settle for torching everything that had ripped the marrow from his bones over the last one hundred and fifty years, in hopes that turning his aggression outward would keep the monster within from ripping him to shreds.

"Yeah, let's blow this place to hell," Nigel agreed. "Eliminate all evidence that it ever existed."

"Sounds good to me—" Jarvis swore as a reptile shot out from behind a pile of chains and went for his crotch. "These snakes must be female." He whacked it aside with his sword. "No male would fang a man's balls with a neurotoxin. Necrosis of the testicles is just not done between guys."

Nigel thudded him on the shoulder. "I'd protect your boys with my life."

They'd all done exactly that a thousand times already. It was why they were all still alive. And intact. "Back at you, my man."

"As always." Nigel took out another trio going for his own manly bits. "Plentiful little suckers, aren't they?"

"Breeding like rabbits. They have no idea what's coming now that we can fight back." Jarvis began to whip his sword over his head in a dizzyingly fast circle, channeling the dark energy of the room into his weapon. Adrenaline rushed through him at the realization that this really was different than it had been for the last two centuries.

He wasn't hog-tied and strung up by his balls, forced to take whatever hit came at him. He was in control now, and he was going to embrace every damn minute of it. He drew even more dark energy into the blade, turning himself from an ordinary combatant to one more lethal than any human being could comprehend. Stacking his sword with extra hate was kind of like the difference between sticking a match into a pile of newspapers or a stack of dynamite. Explosives were always an excellent choice when the lives of defenseless victims were at stake.

His blade began to glow with that heinous purplish mutant color. He smiled.

He casually nicked the wing of an incoming bug. It immediately exploded with enough force to take out ten more of its buddies and a chain-link chandelier. "Now that's what I'm talking about—" Then he caught sight of the poor sod in the nearest bed and noticed a shock of white blond hair on the filthy pillowcase. Mother of hell. It was one of his favorite newbies. "Pascal," he barked. "Get up. It's time to bail."

The kid didn't move, but a scaly beast dive-bombed the youth, fanged teeth going right for the pretty boy's charming dimples. "Hey!" Jarvis lashed out with his sword and bisected a snake a split second before its teeth sank into Pascal's face. "This kind of shit doesn't happen anymore," he snapped as he scooped the rookie up and threw him over his shoulder.

"I'll take him out," he shouted at Nigel. Granted, the kid was a disrespectful pain in the ass with more guts than strategy, but the kid's appreciation for life had helped keep Jarvis sane for the last fifty years. He sure as hell wasn't going to leave him behind to get turned into dinner for Angelica's pets. "You deal with cleanup."

"You got it." Nigel's palms began to smoke, and then dozens of micro-sharp knives exploded from his palms.

They shot across the room, hitting his prey with unerring precision. "This kind of action is good for my muse."

Jarvis paused as Nigel engaged the enemy in a full-scale assault. His skin itched with the need to unleash some of the hate festering inside him. "Next time, I get ass-kicking duty."

Nigel grinned. "Stop whining, and go rescue the kid. You know you love the hero role. It's your shtick."

"Shut up." Yeah, he'd taken the hit when Angelica had intended to kidnap his brother a hundred and fifty years ago, but that was his job. Protect his brother. It wasn't about the glory. Assigning him a hero complex was insulting as hell, and they all knew it. One of these days, he was going to behead the next one who said it.

Pascal's muscles began to twitch. Incoming torture-induced seizure? Jarvis lightly squeezed Pascal's shoulder, trying to give him comfort. "Easy, kid. We're almost out." Jarvis turned toward the exit just as the door flew open.

He whipped his sword into position, ready for murderous breasts and hostile mascara wands—

A cosmetic dentist's wet dream glided into the Hotel instead, and Jarvis relaxed at the sight of another male. As with all soulless bloodsuckers, the vampire was too thin to be taken seriously as a badass, and giving him a spray tan would be an act of mercy.

What was a vamp doing inside the Den? The undead were too emotionally fragile to make good subjects for Angelica's studies. They were going to be destroyed if they stayed. "Get out," Jarvis warned, striding toward them, ready to shove them to safety if they didn't respond. No more suffering. No more. No more. *No more*.

"This is not the place for men. These women aren't the ones you want to be using to satisfy the bloodlust thing."

The vampire held up a melodramatic hand with long, well-manicured fingernails and a way-too-stereotypical large black ring with a family crest of some sort on it. "I'm here for you, warrior."

"My soul's already got a lien on it." Pascal twitched again and let out a low moan of distress. Urgency tightened Jarvis's muscles, and he gripped the kid more securely. Pascal needed freedom, and he needed it now. "Call me on my cell next week. Kinda busy right now."

Twelve more tuxedo-wearing vampires appeared behind the first one. A baker's dozen of the undead. Arms were folded, shoulders were back, and chins were raised loftily in that "I am so much better than you" disdainful look they must practice diligently as soon as they were converted.

Jarvis raised his sword and let it burn with his poison. "Get out of my way." He kept his voice low. A promise of no mercy—

The lead vampire's eyes flashed red, and his fangs elongated. "My Lord, you are not going anywhere." Behind him, his cronies went caveman: fangs as long as tusks, skin like stale marshmallows, eyes going cherry-bomb. Battle stance for hemoglobin junkies.

Under normal circumstances, thirteen parasites with big canines and bad fashion sense were no match for two magically enhanced ex-torture victims with serious attitude problems. Odds were with the good guys. But throw in a nearly dead kid fading fast on Jarvis's shoulder and his buddy occupied with a bunch of rabid pit vipers?

Well, shit.

—∿∿—

Not that there's ever a really good moment for a woman to find out she doesn't have the cojones necessary to be a murderer, but *now* had to be one of the top ten most inconvenient times for Reina Fleming to make that discovery.

Seriously. It was D-day. Her sister was going to die in forty-eight hours. There was *no time* to discover the save-your-sister-plan Reina had been working on for the last eight years was fundamentally flawed. It had taken almost a decade to orchestrate this moment. Was it *really* possible that she was going to blow it?

No. It wasn't.

It was simply pre-harvesting jitters. This was going to go perfectly.

Reina took a calming breath as the werewolf whose soul she was supposed to harvest trotted down the ramp of the chicken house. His toenails clicked on the splintery wood, and each little tippety-tap ripped another hole in the hope dying inside her—

No. You're going to be fine, Reina. Don't panic.

"So, there he is. The big baddie you're going to drop kick into the Afterlife to get your promotion to Reaper." Trinity Harpswell, Reina's dearest friend and world famous black widow killer, held up her iPhone, comparing the picture on it to the four-legged chicken snatcher in front of them. "Same beady eyes, torn right ear, and a star-shaped wand burn on his left hip. Maxwell Smart has sent more fairy godmothers to the Afterlife than the entire Disney franchise. He deserves to do some late night bonding with Satan. Go to it, girlfriend."

But Reina couldn't get her feet to move. She just stared with increasing dismay at Fur Face as he sat down and began licking the feathers from his front paw.

Trinity shoved her doomsday black hair out of her face and shot Reina a frown. "What's wrong?"

"He looks like Roger." The single-use disposable sickle Death had given her to cleave Max's unwilling soul from his murderous little body dropped from her fingers and thudded to the crusty dirt of the chicken playground. "I wasn't expecting that."

Trinity retrieved the sickle from the chasm it had cleaved in the ground. "Roger? Who's Roger?"

"A werewolf puppy I rescued when I was six. He slept on my bed for a year until he healed enough to revert back to his human form." Roger was the only living creature she had ever managed to save. That one success had been the nugget of hope she'd clung to as she buried loved one after loved one. Seven sisters and her mother. All dead. Everyone she loved except her youngest sister, Natalie. And if Reina didn't harvest this pooch's soul, Natalie would soon be dead, too. *Oh, God.* "I can't fail her—"

"You're not going to." Trinity slapped the handle of the sickle into Reina's hand. "As Death's most promising assistant, you've carried more than a million souls to their final destination, and you hand out popcorn whenever someone dies. This is your *thing*!"

"I know, but it's different to rip an unwilling soul from a living body. Not the same thing as guiding a soul to its final destination after the person has already died." Failure to cleave meant Death wouldn't promote her to Reaper. No promotion meant she wouldn't have the power to switch her sister's soul to a living body when hers finally quit in forty-eight hours. "Dammit! It feels like murder!"

"It's not murder. You're simply fulfilling a basic tenet of our existence, which involves guiding souls to the Afterlife." Trinity set her hands on Reina's shoulders and squeezed. "You're just panicking because this is your last chance to save your only remaining family member from the horrific death that has claimed everyone you love."

Her last chance. "Oh, God." She took a breath, trying to control the desperation building inside her. "You really think I can do this?"

"Think deedub payback, and that should fire you up."

Reina's fist tightened around the embossed leather handle of the sickle. "I hate deedubs." The demonic leprechauns of hostile origin had stolen everything from her when they'd attacked her family that awful Valentine's Day so many years ago. She'd done everything to protect her loved ones from the gradual onset of those awful deedub symptoms, but each family member had eventually succumbed.

And now it was Natalie's turn. Her sweet, loving, baby sister had no one to help her except Reina, who had failed to save anyone else in their family. Reina fisted the sickle, but her fingers felt numb. Like she couldn't work them. "Come on," she whispered. "You can do this—"

"Hey!" Trinity grabbed her shoulders and yanked her close. "It you don't do this, your sister will die a really brutal, horrible death. Every last person you have ever loved will be dead, all because you weren't able to kill one deserving serial-killing monster. Can you live with that? Can you? Because I think it'll eat at your gut, gnaw at your soul, chip away at your heart until you're a broken shell of a woman who can do nothing but mourn for a chance to do it again, an opportunity you will never, ever get."

"Oh, God. That's horrible." Reina felt like someone had chained a cement block to her heart and tossed it in the English Channel where her sister, Jeanine, had drowned so happily on her sixth lap. The blackness of the night sky became too oppressive, the dripping of the rusted faucet by the henhouse seemed to mock her loneliness, and her mother's bracelet felt cold, heavy, and dead on her wrist. "You're really good at that."

Trinity nodded grimly. "It's not easy to bring a friend from a place of love and empathy into a pit of utter despair and misery, but I do my best."

"Well, you did it. I feel like my soul is being crushed." Reina put her hand over the searing pain trying to rip through her intestines, and black death powder spewed from Reina's fingertips. "Look at that," she said, unable to keep the hope out of her voice. "I've got my mojo back."

"Go get him, sweetie. I know you can."

Reina faced Max and flexed her hand. More powder spewed out, caking the ground by her feet. Dust that would knock him out long enough for her to harvest his soul.

Max paused mid-lick of his testicles, then he leapt to his feet, hackles up, saliva dripping from his jaw, yellow eyes narrowed with lethal hostility.

Reina braced her feet. "Bring it on, big guy."

Max charged, and suddenly the fifty yards between them didn't seem like all that much room.

Ignoring her urge to run away screaming from a werewolf in full attack mode, Reina let her vision go black and gold, and a mucky, filthy aura was visible around Max. Fantastic! He might have cute ears, but he was one of the bad guys.

One with really big teeth who was closing fast.

"This is for all the girls who didn't get their dreams granted because you ate their fairy godmothers." Reina wiggled her fingers, and the lethal black powder shot out and hit the wolfman square in the muzzle when he was less than a yard away.

But Max didn't fall to the ground into happy naptime, dreaming of sugarplums and candy canes, like he was supposed to after getting hit with death dust. Instead, he body slammed her in the chest. She yelped as the sickle flew out of her hand and she skidded across the rocky dirt. Max pounced on her and plunged his teeth toward her throat. "Yikes!" She misted out of his grasp and reformed several yards away.

Max spun around, searching for her.

"You're sure you're doing the powder thing right?" Trinity asked.

"Of course I am! I've dusted millions of people. I can knock out a giant from two miles away." Well, slight exaggeration, but still. "I know what I'm doing—"

Max located her and then launched himself at her, baring teeth bigger than, oh, her head?

She tried to mist away… but this time nothing happened. "Oh, crap!"

He knocked her down, snarled, and then slammed his

teeth down on her jugular. She gasped as his teeth broke the skin. Good lord! Women found men with fangs a turn-on? Painful, not sexy, in case anyone was wondering.

"Reina! Mist out of his grasp!" Trinity hauled on his tail, but he didn't release his grip.

"Trying." Reina summoned enough death powder to Agent Orange an entire continent and then unleashed it right into Max's face from point-blank range.

There was so much spillage in the air, her own eyes began to burn, and Trinity started coughing. But good old Max just tightened his grip on her throat, and Reina began to get dizzy. The night sky began to shift out of focus. It was almost impossible for her to die, but it sure felt like Max had figured out how to do it—

There was a sudden burst of pink light, and Max collapsed on top of her. He twitched once and then began to snore.

Okay, she knew she hadn't done that.

"Are you all right?" Trinity crouched beside her.

Reina pressed her hand to her neck and winced. Her skin was raw and frayed. If he'd actually ripped her throat out… she wasn't sure she could heal that. "That was close. Thanks for taking him out." She looked around for her sickle. He was down. Had to take his soul.

"Me? I didn't do it." Trinity pulled off her sweatshirt and pressed it to the geyser springing from Reina's neck. "I thought it was you."

"No." Reina stared at her friend in dismay. "If neither of us did it, then it must have been—" She bolted upright just as the wooden wall of the chicken shack began to glitter like a disco ball. "Oh, no."

Trinity followed her gaze, and she bit her lip. "That's not the fantastic timing we were hoping for."

"You think?" Reina scrambled to her feet as a tall, dark-haired man in a black tuxedo stepped out of the shimmering slats of the henhouse. Yep, it was Death, the power monger who had privatized death and turned it into the most profitable business in existence.

He was shaking his head in disgust. Perfect. Fail the big promotional test and have her boss there to witness it. Always a good plan.

Death squared his arms over his chest as he watched her frantically brush the dirt off her pants. He always responded much better to her when she was sexy. Having dirt, blood, and dog hair all over herself wasn't going to gain her wiggle room.

"Not laudable, Fleming." His deep voice rolled over her, and he sounded immensely unimpressed.

"The granules must have been past their expiration date." She pressed Trinity's sweater to her throat, trying to stem the bleeding. *Come on, throat. Do your healing thing already.* "I used enough to—"

"It's not the quantity of the weapon." Death tapped his forehead. "It's about the intent. You have to become simpatico with the powder."

Reina blinked. "Simpatico? What do you mean?"

"You have to want it to work."

"But I did—" She suddenly remembered the only other time her dust hadn't knocked out a target: when she'd tried to take down Jarvis Swain.

She still remembered the way he'd loomed over her, threatening her, crowding her with his bulk and his ominous presence. She had tossed dust at his imposing form and expected him to drop. He hadn't. She could still feel the tug in her soul when she'd realized he wasn't going down, that she couldn't hurt him. That his wall of muscle, domination, and strength was stronger than she was.

For a split second, she'd felt intense pleasure and excitement that there was a male who she didn't have to be careful around. And then that rush of decadent sensation had been chased away by the fear of what it meant: that she could not stop him. Ever.

She thought of Jarvis's dark eyes, of the turbulent danger that lurked in their depths, or the anguish that edged his voice, and awareness rippled through her. Awareness of the man, of his soul, of his inner strength that had enabled him to survive... and then she remembered the way everyone moved away from him, the sense of darkness that seemed to dim the light in the room whenever he walked in.

Yes, Jarvis was incredibly sexy, with broad shoulders that dominated his space, and he looked at her with such potent sexuality that she had to peel off layers at the mere thought of that sensual stare; however, he was also dangerous, deadly, cold, stubborn, and terrifying. There was no chance she would have failed to drop him because of some inner desire to have him erect and in her personal space, despite Death's claim.

No, definitely not. She'd wanted the death dust to work on him, and he'd had some sort of immunity, most likely the result of one of Angelica's brutal experiments. It wasn't her. It *wasn't*.

"If you want the target to be taken down, the dust works. Every time." Death folded his arms over his chest, and he really didn't look like he was kidding.

Hmm… that was disconcerting. "I must disagree. I wanted to take out both Max and Ja—"

"You have it, or you don't, and you clearly don't." Death shot her an impatient look. "You're fired."

"What?" She gaped at him. "You can't fire me—"

"Of course I can. I'm Death. I can do anything I want." Then he turned and disappeared through a nearby tree trunk.

"Wait!" Reina ran after him, smacked right into the tree, and bounced off it. No misting ability? No wonder she hadn't been able to mist away from Max. Death had taken her power away! Which meant… "Holy crap. He really fired me."

How in God's name was she going to save Natalie *now?*

Chapter 2

"DUDE!" A YOUNG VAMP WITH RED HAIR AND FRECKLES shoved his way to the front of the pack of pointy-tooths who had apparently ditched all sense of self-preservation and decided that blocking Jarvis's exit was the smart thing to do. The Berkeley wannabe had been boxed out by the other vamps so Jarvis hadn't noticed him before, but he was noticing him now. Hard not to. He was wearing a hot pink tie-dyed T-shirt, Birkenstocks, and a herd of macrame bracelets halfway up his forearm. "You gotta help us! Rocco's like going down big-time, and you're the only one who can save him."

Jarvis swore at the look of raw terror on the kid's face. The fledgling couldn't be more than twenty years old, still with enough humanity to retain the carrot top and think it was just fine for the Holy Undead to use words like "dude," or admit to caring about something other than being stoic and dull. A face with the unabashed guile of someone who'd put his heart out there for his buddy and was in the process of having it crushed.

Son of a bitch. "Shit, kid. I wish I could help you, but now's not the time. Come find me in a year—"

"A year? He'll be dead!" Sylvan grabbed Jarvis's wrist before Jarvis realized he was going to make a move.

He'd forgotten how fast vampires were. Hadn't run into one since he'd been kidnapped. Maybe he should find a couple as sparring partners. Might be nice to actually get a challenge.

"Seriously! Look at him!" Sylvan pointed frantically toward the door. The pack of vamps split, revealing a rent-a-wreck bloodsucker being dragged along by his wrist. The poor bastard was dirty, wearing a tie-dyed T-shirt and torn jeans no sane vampire would allow within a mile of his refined palette. The decrepit creature was so pale he made the others look like they'd just spent a month in the tropics with baby oil. He was bleeding from an impressive wound in his chest.

Jarvis didn't like to see anyone like that, even a vampire. "Your buddy get staked?"

"Dude, yeah, by his girlfriend."

Anger stirred inside Jarvis at that hellish fate of an innocent. Why in the hell would any man turn his back on a woman?

Maybe his teammate Blaine had found a woman who didn't torture him, but Blaine was too caught up in salvation and poetry to think straight. What was the point of learning not to trust women if a man threw his lot in with the first non-Den woman he met? No chance Jarvis would do that. He had a brain, and he liked to use it.

Then the image of a certain auburn-haired gal flashed in his mind. There was one woman he'd met who was different. Reina Fleming had courage. Her blue eyes were the same color as the delphiniums Christian kept in their common room, and her sensual lips would make even the most cynical warrior believe there was a God.

Yeah, she was female all right, but she'd also impressed him with her loyalty. She'd stood by Blaine's new woman, no matter what cost, and he liked that.

But just because that kind of loyalty was noteworthy, it didn't mean he was going to be dropping trou and letting her line up her sights on his jewels.

Unlike the poor bastard in front of him who'd let a chick near him with a wooden instrument o' torture.

Pascal groaned and shifted suddenly, nearly wrenching himself out of Jarvis's grip. Chat time over. Getting Pascal out of the Den was critical. "Sorry, Sylvan, but there's nothing I can do." He jerked his head toward Nigel, who was finishing off the last of the lady vipers. "Artist boy over there is the healer, but you're gonna have to get in line—"

"No!" Sylvan slammed his palm into Jarvis's chest and sent him crashing against the wall.

"Shit!" Jarvis used his body to protect Pascal as they hit the stainless steel wallpaper. He swore as the metal burned his skin, eating away at his strength and defenses. Mother of hell. He never thought he'd have to feel that stainless attacking him again. He fucking hated that metal.

"You will be at ease." Damien laid his hand on top of Sylvan's head. The kid blanched (impressive feat for a vampire), then Damien chanted something in an ancient language. The youth's face went blank. Utterly expressionless.

The fangbanger had mindrolled his own kind? Disgust surged through Jarvis. If a man couldn't count on his peeps, he had nothing.

He shoved himself off the wall, gritting his teeth at the burning in his cells as the stainless began to invade his body. Mother of hell. He wasn't going down that road again. "You have one chance to get out of my way, and then you're toast." His hand twitched around the handle of his sword. "I hope you choose not to move."

Damien immediately dropped to one knee and bowed his head. At the flick of his wrist, all the vampires behind him followed suit. All except Rocco-the-staked, who had slumped to the floor and was reciting random and awkward poetry about broken hearts and true love. The only other one not genuflecting was Sylvan, who was still standing there like a zombie.

Well, hell, it was against his ethics to behead someone who was bowing before him. That was too much like taking out a bunny rabbit who'd rolled over for a belly scratch. Jarvis lowered his sword in disgust. "Get up."

Damien kept his eyes on the mold growing between the cracks in the cement. "My Lord, we humbly request your assistance with Rocco. He is the son of our leader, Abraham. If he returns from his sabbatical and finds his son died while in our care, we will all suffer greatly."

Pascal groaned and twitched again. Jesus. What was wrong with the warrior? "You guys can heal yourself, so get on it."

"Rocco does not desire recovery, so his body must obey." Damien still didn't lift his head, wouldn't even look him in the eye. "We've had three interventions, but Rocco keeps returning to his woman. After she staked him two days ago, it broke his soul, and he is trying to die."

Jarvis snorted. "Tell him to toughen up." Was this what regular males were like? Wanting to die because some chick had blown him off? Try a hundred and fifty years in the Den. No tears in torture-land. Almost made him appreciate Angelica for forcing him to man-up. No chick would ever reduce him to blubbering tears and a willingness to give it all up. Not even Reina.

Shit. Why did he keep thinking of her? Ever since he'd had her pinned to the floor for a little private discussion, she'd been shoving her way into his thoughts. He barely knew her, had spoken to her maybe a handful of times, but he'd had her breasts wedged up against his chest, and her body had been warm and soft when he'd been on top of her. He'd been reliving that feeling ever since it had happened. When he'd finally convinced her he wasn't the enemy, and he'd felt her whole body relax beneath him, he'd felt like a king for getting her to trust him.

And for that moment, that brief instant when she was under him, he'd had a chance to experience physical intimacy with a woman who wasn't trying to kill him. That moment, feeling the warmth of her body against his, those deliciously feminine curves molded to his body... shit. He'd never forget that sensation.

Reina had baggage, and she trusted no one except her friend Trinity, and then she'd let go and stopped fighting him. When he'd realized that he'd given her relief and diffused some of her tension, given her a moment of peace... Hell. He'd felt satisfaction unlike anything he'd ever felt in his life.

He'd felt like a man, and no woman had *ever* made him feel like a man before. Women made him hurt, they invoked his antipathy, they haunted his nightmares. But never, ever had a woman brought words of comfort and soothing to his lips. And he'd liked it. For that split second, for that instant, a part of him had come to life that he'd never met before.

Had the connection been real? Had he imagined it? Half the time, he was sure it had been some devious female trick, and he was ready to take out Reina the next time he saw her. But sometimes… sometimes…

"Toughen up? You insult us with that suggestion." Anger flashed in Damien's eyes, jerking Jarvis back to the present. "You think we have not tried every method known to us to help the boy find the will to live? Words mean nothing when the soul is broken."

"Yeah, broken souls are a bitch," he acknowledged. He'd helped bury too many warriors whose souls had been broken by Angelica. There was no hope for someone who wanted to die. "Sorry to hear that." And he was.

Because there was no sense in wasting time on those who'd packed it in. He focused on the ones who fought to survive. Like Pascal, who was now groaning constantly, interspersed with occasional shrieks of pain. There was something stirring inside him that was not good. "Nigel. What's your status?"

"Almost ready to blow this place." Nigel came up beside him. Slung over his shoulder was a heavily tattooed warrior Jarvis recognized as Isaiah Hawthorne, the toughest son of a bitch Jarvis had ever met. Nigel was carrying a second inert form in his arms. Jarvis swore when he saw them. No man should be reduced to that. Ever.

He grabbed the victims from Nigel. "No one gets left behind."

Nigel met his gaze, and Jarvis saw the same hardness in his teammate's face. The scars from revisiting their old hell, and the relentless determination to end it. Now.

"Never," Nigel agreed, before turning and sprinting back into the room to retrieve the last three men.

Jarvis balanced one warrior on his free shoulder and the second on his left hip, keeping his sword hand free. "We're taking them out together. Now."

"My lord." Damien had retreated back to his subordinate serf imitation. "We humbly request the assistance of the Guardian of Hate to imbue our dear and beloved friend with the blackest of emotions so that he is consumed with bitter bile that will drive him to hunt down and attack Sarah Dutton, drain her blood, rip out her heart, and destroy her so she no longer walks this earth."

Dutton? Where had he heard that name before? Ah, now he remembered. It was a gathering of women who did shit like what had been done to Sylvan. Women who'd be a perfect fit in the Den.

"I like your dedication, Damien." Nigel hoisted a seven foot male who was little more than blood and skin onto his left shoulder. "Not every brokenhearted teenager has friends thoughtful enough to turn him into a homicidal maniac."

"Rocco won't even drink blood or have sex right now," Damien continued.

Sex. The word made Jarvis's skin crawl, as it had ever since Angelica had taken him and the others into her personal hell and begun the warrior's lessons on proper lovemaking. That was one place he wasn't going. Not ever again. Having a female beneath him with ice picks in his nuts was just not the stuff wet dreams were made of. Now, if a woman was as soft and pliable as Reina had been that day, well—

"Do you realize how Rocco's lack of sexual desire and bloodlust will break his father's spirit?" Damien demanded. "All he does is recite poetry about broken love."

"Hey, don't underestimate poetry." Nigel picked up the last warrior, a freakishly thin male who couldn't have been more than eighteen. "Tapping into your artistic side is critical for a man to be sufficiently badass and violent."

"Yeah, it looks like the poetry is serving him well." Jarvis saw he had about thirty seconds before Nigel would be ready to leave, so he leveled his sword at Damien. "Release Sylvan's mind. I'll speak only to him."

Damien was there to save his ass from getting whipped by his leader. Sylvan was there out of loyalty to his friend. The latter was the only motivation worthy of response.

Damien flicked a finger, and Sylvan suddenly returned to consciousness. "Dude! You going to help us?"

Jarvis lodged the tip of his sword under Sylvan's chin and forced him to stand tall, like a warrior. "I admire your loyalty to your friend. Keep it up."

Sylvan beamed. "Gee, thanks, Lord Hate. That's really nice of you to say." The neophyte pulled his shoulders back and puffed his chest out a little.

Nice. He liked to see that attitude in the kid.

Nigel snorted in amusement. "Lord Hate?"

"Stay clean, kid." Jarvis ignored Nigel's bark of laughter. "Hate's bad shit, and you don't want to mess with it."

Especially not now. Jarvis had kept hate locked down for a hundred and fifty years, but if the vamps had tracked him here, that meant he was leaking. Yeah,

theoretically, it was helpful to learn his recent testiness
was because he was finally losing control of a noxious
toxin that could blow up the entire world, but he'd rather
have discovered he was just cranky from lack of battle
and knitting—

Pascal suddenly unleashed a scream of holy hell and
ripped himself out of Jarvis's grasp with a strength no
almost-dead warrior should possess. Claws erupted
from his fingertips, and he launched himself at Sylvan.

Sylvan screeched, fanged out, and threw himself
at Pascal.

"Shit!" Jarvis lunged for Pascal as he jammed his fist
into Sylvan's chest. Sylvan shrieked like a raven with
a hangover, turned into a bat, then tail-whipped Pascal
across the face so hard that the warrior's head snapped
back like a freaking rubber band.

Pascal howled and leapt into the air.

"Oh, hell," Nigel said. "He's going to go scaly,
isn't he?"

Wings exploded from Pascal's back, scales erupted
over his body, and acid-laced spines exploded from
him, shooting in all directions. Welcome to the party,
dragon boy.

"Stop, fledgling!" Damien lunged for Sylvan, but the
two youths were already across the room, knocking each
other around like a couple of playground bullies.

Hormonal supernatural badasses were difficult
enough, but when one had been tortured into insanity
and the other was terrified his friend was about to die, it
made the situation a little more unpredictable.

"They're both pretty quick. I like their potential."
Nigel stashed the injured warriors into a protected

alcove behind a stainless steel weapons vat as Pascal began shooting acid-spiked spines all over the place. "You know, I had a bad feeling when Angelica let Pascal play with acid last month. I felt he was a little hotheaded for that kind of weapon." Nigel ducked as one nearly took his eye out.

"It's war!" Sylvan screamed, and all the other vampires shrieked in response. Eyes turned red. The temperature in the room dropped about sixty degrees as the undead prepared for war.

Lemmings.

"No!" Damien howled his orders, "Everyone down!"

Impressively, not a single one obeyed. Not every leader had that little control over his insanely murderous team.

Jarvis tore across the room toward Pascal, ducking his head against the onslaught of spines. Pascal's eyes were pitch black, pulsing with pathological hate. That's what this was about? Hate?

Son of a bitch. He'd infected Pascal with his hate and set off a frenzy among the vamps. How had that happened? Yeah, his skin could be toxic if he wasn't paying attention, but he always kept it under rigid control and he never, *ever* lost his shit enough to infect people unlucky enough to simply be in his presence. What the hell was going on?

"Nigel!" Jarvis barked the command. "Get over here! Take Pascal. I can't touch him." His fingers flexed with the need to shut the kid down, but contact with him would make it worse. He hated feeling impotent. And he detested knowing that he was poison to those he wanted to keep safe.

"Take care of the bloodsuckers, Hate Boy." Nigel was already running toward Pascal. "I'll get the newbie."

Jarvis whipped out his sword, set his weapon to a notch below dead as a doornail, then hit a vamp right in the chest. The undead dropped like a load of cement.

Jarvis took out another one as Damien raced over to check on his downed comrade, but apparently the thing was still alive, because Damien nodded, then went off to start taking down the others. Excellent. Team effort, everyone.

Thirty seconds later, it was nap time. Clean-shaven ghouls were unconscious and bleeding all over the floor, and Damien was breathing hard (who knew vampires even breathed? Learn something new every day). Nigel had knocked out Pascal so he couldn't throw spines anymore, and the place was ready for tea and brunch. Pascal was still in his stuff-of-nightmares form, and his body was twitching, but he was sleeping like a man who'd just serviced a dozen women and a flock of angels.

"Well, I'm impressed, Jarvis." Nigel slowly stood up, stretching his back. "Didn't think you could infect an unconscious man with enough hate to wake up him from a coma and put him in full attack mode. You're kinda like LSD for the uninitiated."

Jarvis eyed his friend, searching for a sign that his buddy was about to get on the hate train. "You feeling okay?"

Nigel pulled out a sketch pad and a pen. "Give me two minutes, and I'll be as good as a pansy in a patch of sunshine." He glanced at a nearby bed, visibly stiffened, then chose to sit on the cement floor instead. He crossed his legs and began to draw.

Lucky son of a bitch. Right now Jarvis would give his left arm for five minutes of the kind of peace that Nigel found in his art. Maybe he'd try knitting one more time. Worth it to take the edge off the adrenaline racing through him right now... then he scowled at the fury that rose deep inside him, as it always did when he thought about taking on the most hellaciously frustrating pastime ever created. Knitting was the last thing he needed right now.

He rolled his neck, trying to ease the restlessness in his body. "You okay, Damien?"

The bloodsucker was on his knees, his eyes were red, and his fangs were out. "Give me a sec."

Damn. If he'd even gotten to an emotionally vacant bloodsucker with a thousand years of self-control... impressive, as Nigel has said. But not in a good way.

Nigel's pen was flying across the page. "So, I'm guessing that the fact you accidentally caused this brouhaha isn't a good thing?"

"Yeah." The stream of blood gushing from Pascal's side had gotten stronger. Nothing like turning into drooling dragon-boy to interfere with healing. "But as long as it's only leaking outward, we're okay. It's when it starts to affect my own sanity, that's when we really have a problem."

Nigel shoved his sketch pad into his back pocket and gave Jarvis a long look as he began to pick up the warriors again. "What's the deal? You going down? You need my help?" He set the warriors back down and took root in the place they'd been so desperate to leave. "I'll heal you. Right now. Right here. I'm not letting you detonate."

Jarvis shook out his shoulders. "All I need is ten minutes with my brother, and he can clean it up." Yeah, he hadn't seen his brother since Jarvis let himself be taken in Cameron's place a hundred and fifty years ago. But the Guardian of Love would be there for him. As a brother. As a Guardian. As the only freaking being on the planet that could ease some of the hell inside Jarvis—

Jarvis suddenly noticed a sharp tingling in his palm. He looked down, then stiffened. There, at the very tip of his lifeline, was a tiny black star. The first signs of hate taking over his body.

He clenched his fist and swore. Every Guardian was eventually destroyed by the hate. Fifty years was the usual life span, and he'd already gone a buck fifty. He wasn't ready to die. But even his brother couldn't stop this slide.

Nigel narrowed his eyes suspiciously, as if he knew what Jarvis had seen on his palm. "How long do you have until you go insane and destroy the world if you don't find your brother?"

"I'll be fine." Jarvis unclenched his fist. Maybe it couldn't be stopped, but he could slow that train down to a crawl. His brother could help him. Now that he was out of the Den, Jarvis had the liberty of going after Cameron, and it was clearly time to get on it. As soon as he had the Hotel's occupants safely stashed in his place—

"Lord Hate." Damien's eyes flashed. "You owe us now. Infect Rocco with hate so he can be happy again someday."

"Hell, are you blind? You don't want me." He grabbed his sword, letting the heat of the handle burn into the mark on his palm. "Take Rocco to my brother. The Guardian of Love can help the girl fall in love with him and—"

"The Guardian of Love was indisposed," Damien interrupted. "You were our second choice."

"Indisposed?" Jarvis stiffened. Cameron was so in love with his abilities that he never turned down a chance to show off. "What are you talking about?"

"He informed us that he had abdicated," Damien replied.

Jarvis's tainted palm began to burn. "What are you talking about? The Guardian of Love can't abdicate." That's why there was a Guardian of that damned emotion, and that was why Jarvis had taken the hit for his brother two centuries ago. Because love needed to be protected. "Love needs constant attention or it *dies*."

Damien crouched beside Rocco and laid his pale hand on the boy's cheek. "That appeared to be his plan. He had a bonfire flaming on the edge of the lake with blue flames spelling out the words 'Death: I am ready.'"

"Bloody hell." What had happened to his brother while Jarvis had been incarcerated? Was it impossible for *anyone* to be safe without Jarvis there to protect them? Both Jarvis and the entire world were fucked if Cameron went AWOL. "Nigel! Take care of Pascal and the others." He broke into a sprint for the door. "I gotta go find Cam."

Chapter 3

"Cameron!" Jarvis sprinted up the grassy hill toward the metal shack he'd called home nearly two hundred years ago. "Are you around?"

There was no answer. Just his voice bouncing off the cliffs he and Cam had spent so many hours shimmying up when they were kids. An unfamiliar emotion swirled through Jarvis at the sight of the home where he'd last seen his family. The last place he'd been where anyone had touched him in kindness.

Fuck that. He didn't need to go there. He was a warrior, not a melodramatic pansy, no matter how hard Angelica had tried to turn him into one. He had his team, and that was all he needed.

Jarvis bolted across the clearing to the shack and ripped the aluminum door off the hinges. Nothing inside but two cots and a pile of clothes in one corner. His dad's guns were racked up on the west wall. And, of course, the framed letters of commendation for all the slippery bastards his bounty hunting dad had tracked down.

Pride thickened his throat. *Nice job, Pa.*

It was his dad who'd had Jarvis out on the shooting range at age two, who'd dropped Jarvis on his head from a height of twenty feet at age three, who'd taught him how to retrieve burning coins from a campfire with his bare hands simply by believing he could do it.

His dad had given Jarvis the skills to survive Angelica, and it was right that his dad had gone on to such success.

"Maybe your brother's going on a walkabout. You know, finding his meaning in life." Blaine Underhill III, the insanely love-sick warrior who'd spearheaded their escape from the Den two weeks ago, poked his head into the shed. When Blaine had heard about Jarvis's quest, he'd hauled ass to catch up to Jarvis and provide that team support they all prided themselves in.

It was the first time Blaine had been more than a hundred yards away from his woman since they'd hooked up, and Jarvis was well aware that only some serious concern about Jarvis's future would have dragged Blaine away from her. He'd been surprised when Blaine had caught up to him, but it had felt damn good to know that Blaine was still his teammate even when he was shacking up with a woman. Trinity wasn't going to destroy Blaine, and Jarvis was glad as hell about that. He grinned at the lover boy. "You sure you remember how to function without Trinity holding your hand?"

"She's having a girls' day. Reina's in some sort of trouble, and Trinity had to help her." Blaine shrugged. "Figured I might as well save you instead."

"Reina's in trouble?" Jarvis looked sharply at Blaine, his grip tightening around his sword. "What's wrong?"

"No clue. Trinity wouldn't tell me, so I figure it's a female thing." Blaine rolled his eyes. "I know we were trained to go those places, but I'm happy to pretend I have no clue about girl things."

Jarvis's blade began to glow, and dark anger pulsed through him. "What if it's not a female thing? What if they can't handle it?"

"You questioning my ability to take care of my woman?" Blaine held up a fist, and a ball of flame appeared in his hand. "Because I'd have to kick the shit out of you for that."

"I'm not worried about Trinity." Jarvis kicked aside the cot with a little more force than he'd intended. "But who's got Reina's back?"

"Reina?" Blaine's eyebrows shot up, and he extinguished the flame. "The woman works for Death. I think she's got things covered."

"She's not as tough as she pretends she is." After all, she hadn't been able to knock him out, had she? What if she ran into something else she couldn't handle? He'd felt the tension she carried in her body, and he knew she wasn't as together as she liked to pretend. Reina was afraid. Of what? He suddenly needed to know. *Now*. "She's not like us. She needs protection."

A slow grin spread over Blaine's face. "Shit, man, you've noticed she's a woman, haven't you? With one rocking bod, too."

Jarvis stopped in surprise. Was that what it was? Hell, no. He was too fucking smart for that. "I'm just watching your back. If something happens to Reina because you didn't interfere, your girl will ride your ass to the end of hell and back."

Blaine paled. "Shit. You're right. I gotta get back there."

Jarvis nodded and relaxed his grip on his sword. Next stop, Reina. They would make sure she was all right. "I'll go with you."

Blaine nodded in acknowledgment. They were always a team. No one went it alone. Which was why Blaine didn't take off to go after his woman right away, but looked around the shed instead, albeit with more impatience than he'd had two minutes ago. "Where's your damn brother? Saving the world, one love bug at a time?"

"Cam's not motivated enough to go on an international tour. He waits for the adulation to come to him. He's got to be around here." Jarvis ducked back outside again, feeling even antsier to find his brother, take care of business, and get the hell out and help Blaine find Reina. And Trinity, of course. He knew what Trinity and Reina were like, and the odds of them being involved in something that was more than they could handle weren't as low as he would have liked. "Cam!"

Again, no answer.

Just the distant roar of the waterfall he and Cam used to play in. How many times had his dad held him underwater, teaching him how to push past his limits, to reach beyond what every cell his body was screaming at him that he couldn't do?

The old man had cared enough to nearly drown Jarvis thousands of times, while poor Cameron had been off weaving daisies into crowns for the raccoons and making googly eyes at the neighbor's girls. His dad had long given up trying to bless Cameron with the ability to be a man, and Jarvis felt a sudden pity for his little brother, left behind without any of the skills a young boy should have. What kind of life would Jarvis have had if he'd been left with love as his only tool to survive?

He shuddered at the thought. Yeah, hate was a bitch, but he'd take that over lolling with the butterflies any day of the week. What could love get you anyway? A stake in the heart by your girlfriend, for one. Thank the gods of hell he didn't have to worry about that soft emotion infiltrating his body, even if it did seem to agree with Blaine.

It wasn't his cuppa, and he was good with that.

"Can you sense Cameron?" Blaine asked. "I thought you guys were connected."

"Yeah, we were, but it's been a long time." Jarvis closed his eyes and tried to attune himself to his brother's frequency, but he was too tense. Too much energy bouncing around. "I'm on edge. Can't do it."

That wasn't a good sign. A quick inspection revealed there was a second tiny star on his palm now, beside the first one. He closed his fist. "Damien said Cam had been using a bonfire to contact Death." The sky was blue in all directions. "Can you pick it up?"

"Fire? Now you're talking, baby." The skull and bones tattoo on Blaine's chest began to smoke. Blaine was three-quarters flames, and he had a special bond with anything smoky and hot. He closed his eyes, then pointed to the southeast. "That way."

"Eagle Vista." Jarvis headed in that direction, vaulting easily over a crumbling stone wall at least ten feet high. How many times had he struggled to climb that thing when he was a kid? And now, after being ruthlessly mutated, he could jump it easily. What a man he'd become. Pa would be proud.

Jarvis burst out of the woods and saw his brother. Cam was sitting in the water, arms draped loosely over his knees. Fish were jumping into the air in front of him, and a dove was perched on his bare shoulder. His hair was long and shaggy, mud was caked on his back, and his beer belly hung over the waistband of his jeans. He'd gone to hell, but he was alive. "Cam!"

His brother didn't turn.

"He's talking to someone," Jarvis said. "Can't see who it is."

Jarvis shaded his eyes as he jogged toward his brother. With the sun setting behind Cam, he hadn't seen the other person at first (raise your hand if you think it's a bad sign that he'd failed to notice an entire *person*), but now he could see the dark silhouette of a man standing in front of his brother. The broad shoulders, the tuxedo, the dark hair... "It's Death." Jarvis unsheathed his sword. "Hey!" he shouted. "Get away from my brother!"

Death turned sharply toward them, then he held up his palm. A stream of black dust exploded toward them.

"Oh, shit." Jarvis raised his sword to block the particles, but they parted around the blade. They smacked Jarvis in the chest and flung him backward. He landed hard on his back, and icy coldness crushed down on him, sucking the air out of his lungs, the strength out of his body.

Blaine was down beside him, utterly still. Face gray.

Jarvis fought to breathe as Death helped Cam to his feet. The death dust had put him a thread from the cold permanence of eternal night.

Jarvis pictured Angelica: her blonde hair, oversized rack, her hourglass figure, and the cold ruthlessness of her eyes. The red hot emotion of hate ripped aside the cold grip of death, surging fire into his muscles and life into his body. He lunged to his feet and hurled his sword at Death.

"Oh, please. You bore me." Death flicked his hand

in Jarvis's direction, and the sword screeched to a halt in midair, then turned and slammed itself right into Jarvis's gut.

"Jesus." He sank to his knees and yanked the sword out, gasping as the poison from the blade raced through his body. Hello? Rule No. 1 of Battle Skills for Beginners: Never get your own weapon turned on you. Had he learned nothing in the Den over the last one hundred and fifty years? The fact that Death was predisposed to never lose a showdown was no excuse.

Blaine stirred beside him and groaned. Fire began to lick at Blaine's chest as he fought back from the precipice as well.

Jarvis fumbled for his sword, fighting to get his numb fingers to function as Death led the Guardian of Love toward a cluster of pine trees. Jarvis palmed the donut-hole in his gut as he struggled to his knees. "Cam," Jarvis croaked. "Don't go with him."

Cam turned his head toward Jarvis. Gone was the child-like awe of his own magnificence, the impish smile of irresponsible troublemaking, and the irrepressible joy of self-adulation. In its place was a haunting emptiness. Sunken cheeks. Hopelessness.

Holy hell. Love was *dying*. If Cameron died, he would take love with him, and that was just not a good thing for his brother, for the Guardian of Hate, or for the world in general. "Cameron Swain, get your ass over here right now—"

His brother dissolved into millions of black particles and was gone. Taken by Death, who was the one being in existence Jarvis had no chance of defeating or even subverting.

"Mother of hell," Blaine groaned. "You're screwed. You'll never get him back from Death."

"No, I won't." Jarvis couldn't help the stupid-ass grin of anticipation as he gripped the wound in his belly. The surge of interest at the twist that had just been thrown at him. "But there's one woman who could work a little deal with that scythe-bearer."

Blaine raised his brows, a sudden knowing look on his face. "Dude, you didn't need to get your brother kidnapped by Death to have a reason to talk to Reina. We could have just done a double date."

"Fuck off." Jarvis shoved himself to his feet, stumbling as the poison raced through him. "I don't want to date her. I just want her help."

Blaine sat up and rested his arms on his knees, trying to regain his strength. "Got news for you, buddy. Reina's dealing with some serious personal shit, and she doesn't like you. There's no way she's going to help you."

"She has no choice." Jarvis sheathed his sword.

"That woman always has a choice."

Jarvis grinned, thinking again about that moment when he'd had her underneath him. When he'd sweet-talked her into seeing his side. "Not when it comes to me."

———⁓———

Reina raced up the marble steps to the Castle of Extreme Opulence, praying she was sliding in before the "Fired: Do Not Admit" tattoo showed up on her forehead.

She flung open the front door, and a quick inspection of the ornate, three-story, twin staircase foyer revealed that the Death wasn't present. Dammit. She needed to find him before—

Linneah Nogueira, Death's willowy executive VP and HoneyPot Queen, threw open the French doors and strode into the reception area. "Reina? I thought you'd been fired."

Oh, crap. Reina faked a relaxed, slightly confused expression even as her heart began to thud. She couldn't let Linneah stop her. She had to get to Death. *She had to.* "Good morning, Linneah. It's nice to see you." Reina sauntered oh-so-casually toward the long hallway that led toward the executive office suites known as the Hallows. "Did he really say he'd fired me? He's such a tease. Is he in? I owe him an espresso."

Linneah's lovely smile didn't falter, but she began walking toward Reina. "I'm so sorry, my dear, but I can't let you go back into the Hallows. I shall be happy to escort you outside—"

Plan B: *Run*.

Reina bolted across the lobby toward the offices. She hip checked the doors open, then hit the panic button just inside the hall. The doors slammed shut behind her, and she heard the rumble of the black magic locks that Death's grandma, Angelica, had installed. It had been a gift on Death's hundredth birthday after some local devil worshippers had thought it would be a lark to see if they could steal a pair of Death's underwear for their team unity bonfire.

Apparently, a man's skivvies were one of those things a grandmother considered sacred, because Angelica had put protecting her grandson's banana hammocks on top priority. Next time a tighty-whitey thief tried to co-opt

Death's silk unmentionables, they'd find themselves trapped in the Hallows with no way out.

Or, in an entirely foreseen adaptation of a brilliant technology, the leader of the HoneyPots would find herself trapped outside the Hallows with no way in, while a certain ex-Guide made a break for her boss's office.

There was a thud as Linneah crashed into the door, and a muttered curse, but Reina didn't slow down. Linneah would have the HoneyPots on her within seconds.

Reina ran past her office. Her twenty-four-carat white gold nameplate with embossed emeralds was no longer on her door. He'd already removed all signs of her existence? She stumbled, her legs suddenly clumsy as fear gripped her. *I'm so sorry, Natalie. I swear I will fix this.*

The air suddenly reverberated with Linneah's shrill "calling all sheepdogs" whistle, and then there was the clatter of spiked heels pounding the marble as HoneyPots abandoned their tasks and went into hunting mode. There had to be at least a dozen pairs coming after her.

The women Death hired to service him in assorted ways might be talented at sexual favors, but he'd also trained them well in the protection of his castle. Women in general could be ruthless, but these particular ones? Let's just say that getting caught by women defending the man who was their link to money, power, and orgasms wasn't a particularly fantastic way to spend the afternoon.

Reina glanced at her watch as she skidded around a corner. Two minutes past eleven. At least she was getting her timing right. Death always sucked down his quadruple espresso at eleven o'clock, and guess who was the only one who could get his temperamental machine to work?

That's right. Say hello to the caffeine goddess.

The massive Brazilian pine doors of her boss's office were shut, and Death's vehement epithets were easily audible through the wood. Sweet! He was entering caffeine withdrawal, and she was the only one who could provide relief. Leveraging his caffeine addiction into a second chance was her only hope.

It had to work.

She jammed her fingers into the Swarovski crystal globe that locked and unlocked the doors in the Hallows. The moment her hand was inside, lavender mist began swirling, but there was no Open Sesame. "Hey, sweetie." She leaned closer to the pale purple fog and wiggled her hand. "I've been bringing you M&Ms every day for the last nine years. Just open the door, okay? One more time—"

Sharp pain suddenly hit her palm like a thousand razor blades. She yelped and jerked her hand out. Dozens of razor-fine quills were lodged in her skin. Oh, come on! After nine years of bonding, it treated her like a pariah just because some arrogant bastard had wrongfully fired her? "You could have just said 'No,'" she hissed.

She gritted her teeth, fisted the spines, and then yanked them all out in one motion. She screamed with pain and wedged her hand between her thighs. "Minor setback," she gasped. "Nothing I can't manage—"

"Reina." The doors were flung open to reveal Death in all his tuxedoed glory, sporting a gold-laced cummerbund and bow tie. "I thought I recognized your shriek of pain." He was wearing his platinum scythe cuff links and a shirt artfully decorated with diamond bling, but his ashen face and trembling hands kind of blew his Me Dominant Male image. "Make me some espresso. Now."

The clickety clack of stilettos got closer, and the tip of an alligator pump came into sight around the corner. "Sure." She stumbled to her feet and squeezed past Death into his office, her damaged hand hanging limply by her side. *Don't think about the pain. Don't think about the pain.* Shoot. She was thinking about the pain.

"I've got her," Linneah shouted as she rounded the corner, her gown sweat stained and torn.

"Reina is green-lighted." Death flipped the door shut in Linneah's startled face, then leaned against the interior of the door, as if he were too exhausted to hold himself upright. "Where have you been?"

"Where I have been?" Blood was oozing onto the floor, and Reina's hand felt like a dozen poisonous spikes had been shoved through it. Oh, wait. It had. "You fired me, remember?"

"Of course I remember. Don't insult me with such inane questions." Death strode across his plush carpet to the wall that sported a ten-foot mural of Cupid.

According to Castle gossip, it was the first painting Death had commissioned when he'd bought out the Grim Reaper three hundred years ago. He dusted it by hand every day and wouldn't trust anyone else with its care. Reina had often found him in an admiring thrall, staring rapturously at the three-foot cherub with rosy cheeks who was casting arrows on assorted lovers, all of whom were engaged in various intimate and acrobatic positions.

Maybe it was all the naked couplings depicted.

Maybe it was the implications of how great sex would be if Cupid helped.

Maybe it was professional admiration for another being that wielded complete power over something basic to the human experience.

No one knew why he loved it so much, and the big man wasn't talking.

The austere and ruthless magistrate tapped Cupid's harp. The instrument vanished, revealing a harp-shaped cabinet. Inside were shelves of glittery bottles and jars, a medicine cabinet for the rich, famous, and magical. He shot an impatient scowl at Reina. "I said, where have you been?"

"Sorry, I must have missed the memo that said I was still in charge of your coffee even after getting wrong-fully terminated." Yeah, probably not the best choice to be flippant with him, but she was in too much pain to be polite. "You need me. I want a second chance." Her legs began to tremble, and she eased down to the Oriental carpet. She tried to bend her lavender-tinted fingers, and they didn't move. That couldn't be good.

"Have you learned nothing in the nine years under my ruthless and brilliant tutelage? My reputation as a domineering businessman does not allow for second chances." Death selected a star-shaped bottle shimmer-ing with golden dust. "Make the coffee, Fleming."

"The coffee." She willed herself off her knees and made her way across the room, still fighting not to start screaming in pain and dropping to the carpet in convul-sions of misery. Cradling her injured hand to her chest, she tugged open the cabinet and grabbed the five-pound bag of beans.

Then she walked over to a full size bronze sculpture of the original Grim Reaper, complete with black cloak and weapon. She kicked the handle of the creature's scythe, then stepped back as a bronze urinal exploded out of the wall.

Death narrowed his eyes. "How did you know about that?"

"I pay attention." She opened the bag of beans and tipped it precariously over the glittering man-toilet. "It'll take you years to find out who my supplier is for these beans. You'll never survive the withdrawal. Give me another chance, or the caffeine takes a hit." She couldn't keep her gaze from wandering over to the collection of scythes above the massive fireplace. Death had acquired them when he'd bought out the Grim Reaper, and they were the real deal. Which one would he use on her?

Death glowered at her. "Why you arrogant little female—" Then he suddenly burst out laughing, showcasing his high octane pearly white smile. "I can't keep up the facade anymore. You're threatening my prized beans with urine! That's beautiful! You've got game, girl! You have surpassed my expectations, which really weren't that high to begin with, of course."

She stared at him in stunned surprise. "What are you talking about?"

"Nice work, Fleming." He smacked her on the shoulder so hard she lost her balance. Her injured palm collided with the statue, and pain ripped through her. The room began to spin, spots began to dance in her vision, and she slithered down to her knees. Dammit. She didn't have time to get hurt!

"I need a second chance," she croaked. "Now."

Ignoring her request, Death crouched in front of her, took her wrist, and flipped her hand over. "This should help." He thumbed open the bottle he'd taken from the harp cabinet and poured a pulsating gelatinous substance onto her injury.

Her skin began to burn, a tingling sensation like a thousand gnats tangoing on her skin. Which was entirely possible, given that she was in the office of the grandson of one of the most powerful black witches in existence. And then the pain dissolved. Just like that. Gone. "That's incredible."

He beamed at her. "Excellent. I've never tested it before." He clapped the lid shut. "And I was referring to my expectations with the werewolf situation. It was a test."

Reina sat up and flexed her hand. No pain. Hurrah. "You mean, Max was a test for something *other* than to see if I could harvest his soul?"

"Of course. I would never give you such a linear, simplistic assignment. I am so much more complex than that." He set the bottle back into the wall, then tossed the coffee at her, still grinning. "Put the beans down and we'll talk."

She caught the package. He was acting way too friendly and conspiratorial for a guy who was still firing her. She was kind of thinking that now was the time to deliver the goods and see what was up. She cautiously hoisted the coffee and walked over to the machine. "So if I'm not getting another chance, then what? A new assignment?"

Death's gaze was fixated on the beans. "Yes. Of course. That's the whole point."

Her boss never, ever went back on his word. He believed that a man's success was only as good as people's ability to trust him to deliver on his promises. Ironically, Death was one man you could always, always have faith in. So she punched the button, dropped the coffee in, adjusted the seventeen different dials to get it exactly as he liked it, then hit start. "Okay, so explain."

"Of course." He picked a six-inch, pale pink mug off his desk and stroked his finger fondly over the diamonds encrusted along the rim before handing it to her. "If you'd harvested the werewolf, you would have failed."

She slid the cup into the machine. "You didn't want me to take his soul?" After all her emotional trauma, she wasn't even supposed to have harvested Max? Hello? Anyone want to sue for intentional infliction of emotional distress? Completely brutal... and... fantastic! Who knew that total failure could result in complete victory? "So, then, what—"

"I made sure you selected a target that would remind you of someone you loved." He picked a blueberry scone off a silver tray on his desk. As always, it had been delivered to coincide with the eleven o'clock caffeine hit.

"Why?" Her stomach rumbled with hunger. She'd been so stressed about her first harvest that she hadn't been able to eat for the last twenty-four hours.

"If you'd killed him, it would have shown me that you valued killing more than those you love. That's not the kind of ethics I want in my staff. The power to kill is seductive, and I need someone who isn't going to get sucked into the high of killing and start running around killing willy-nilly. I need someone who understands the importance of each and every harvesting, and who has the self-control not to kill for the sheer pleasure of it."

"So, I don't need to harvest anyone?" *Please, please, please, let that be the case.*

"Of course you do."

Of course she did. She grabbed a chocolate torte. Sugar reinforcements needed. She shoved the whole thing in her mouth… Damn. It was *good*.

"Just not the dog." He took a bite of his pastry and sighed with delight. "Mother of pearl, that's the best scone Vladimir has ever made." He hit the speakerphone on his desk.

Linneah answered on the first ring. "Yes, sir?" She sounded out of breath and a little disgruntled.

"Give Vladimir a raise. This scone is brilliant."

There was a pause. "But—"

"You're fired. No one contradicts me in this office." Death released the button and took another bite as he gave his attention back to Reina. "And then you passed the second test by coming back here and getting in my face to give you another chance. Sometimes it takes that kind of tenacity to get a hit."

"I'm extremely tough." Total lie, but that was okay. If Death's delusion helped her case, she wasn't going to enlighten him that she was desperate, out of hope, and horrifically traumatized by the thought of her sister dying. She grabbed a lemon torte. Not that desserts would solve the situation, but sometimes a good hit of sugar made things seem better.

Death shoved another pastry into his mouth and made a grunt of rapture. "Do you know who Augustus is?"

She bit into the decadent delicacy. Mmm… so good. "Augustus? The assassin who killed more than three thousand immortal beings in the last year alone? The one who wiped out that whole camp of ancient vampires in less than ten minutes? *That* Augustus?"

"Yep." Death sat down in his luxurious desk chair and stretched his long legs out as he helped himself to a croissant. "I have investors willing to pay over five million dollars to see him taken out of action, as long as it's done by this Friday. So, get on it."

She froze mid-chew. "You want *me* to harvest *his* soul?" The odds of her going after Augustus and coming out alive were… um… zero. He was unkillable, and he could dispatch immortal beings with less effort than it took a cow to mow some grass. If Reina tried to snatch his spirit, he'd kill her first. Ten times. Before she had a chance to sneeze.

Death raised his brows, a challenge in his tone that told her that this was her only chance. "You can't do it?"

No way on earth could I possibly do it. You're insane to even think so! She managed an arrogant shrug of her shoulders. "Of course I can. I was just clarifying. You know, given the confusion last time about what my actual goal was supposed to be."

"Now your other task…" He grinned, his eyes sparkling. "This is the really fun one."

"More fun than harvesting Augustus? Impossible." Was the universe not in support of her overcoming her abysmal track record at saving those she loved? Because it sure seemed like the entire cosmos was against her, and if so, it would be good to know. Or maybe not.

Maybe she was just better off not knowing some things. You know, things like that could be a little overwhelming to cope with.

The lemon torte that had been so delicious moments ago? Nothing but dry, bland sandstone in her mouth. The brewing coffee stung her nose. The blueberry scones looked like moldy piles of mud. Okay, so losing control of the positive attitude here.

"I'm so excited about this other project." Death grinned, and his eyes began to glow with excitement that, weirdly enough, she wasn't really sharing. "I have this special project I'm working on. It—" The machine beeped that the espresso was ready.

Death ripped the mug free of the machine and chugged its contents. He slammed the empty cup down and took a deep breath. When he looked at her this time, his eyes were sharp and alert. "I'm launching a new Reaper this weekend."

"You are?" She was supposed to be the next Reaper. He hadn't had a new one in almost a hundred years. "You promoted someone?" How was that possible? None of the other Guides were even a fraction as good as she was.

"Nope. External hire."

"External?" Well, wasn't that typical? Bypass the employee that had been doing great work for years in favor of some glitzy external hire? It couldn't be Augustus, since Death just told her to kill him. Napoleon? Or the vampire triplets who'd taken out three of Satan's minions while they'd been eating donuts the other day? Jarvis? He might not be an official assassin, but he was certainly deadly enough. She frowned as she thought of the warrior. No, no, he might be on the edge of something dark and deadly, but he wouldn't become an assassin. She was sure of it. His soul was too... pure wasn't the right word. But she knew he had a solid core that would withstand any malevolent temptation, even Death's most lucrative offer. Jarvis was good. Scary, deadly, most likely insane, but good in his soul.

But even without the inclusion of Jarvis, there were thousands of internally recognized killers-for-hire who would up the cache of Death's business. Was cache his new thing? Because she had no cache at all. "Who is it?"

He grinned and waggled his fingers. "Uh, uh, uh, no sneak peeks, Fleming. It's monumental. I am going to be the talk of the world, even more so than I already am, impossible as that may sound. It's not every day that a company makes a new hire of this caliber. It's going to change the way people look at death forever. It creates new options, opens a whole new market. Great stuff." He giggled.

Reina blinked. "Did you just giggle?"

"No." He immediately scowled. "We'll have the first official soul harvesting on center stage, in front of a very esteemed guest list. Some key reporters and media representatives."

Reina frowned. "Who is he harvesting? Or is it a she?" If it were a she, that cut down the list of possibilities. There were only five or six really glamorous female assassins who were sufficiently successful to impress the king of eternity.

"Tsk, tsk. It's a secret." He winked conspiratorially. "Linneah will organize the details of the festival, but you're in charge of arranging the donation of souls and finding the investors. It's worth about three billion dollars, so that's your minimum target. If you can get more than that, it'll impress me."

"Three billion dollars?" Yeah, of course. Because she had so many contacts in the death-for-hire business. She could wrap this up by lunchtime. "Listen, I think maybe—"

"Money and soul harvesting are all I care about, and this is your chance to show you can deliver." He leaned forward and tugged on her chin, forcing her to look at him. "Impress the hell out of me, and I can make you the richest, most powerful female in creation."

But if she failed him, her sister would die.

No! Natalie would not be the seventh Fleming female to die. Reina might have failed to save everyone else she loved, but this time she would find a way. So what if she had to divest a highly decorated assassin of his soul, find investors and victims for a harvesting, just to appease the overly demanding bastard who was so stingy in doling out the power she needed to save her sister?

No problem.

She could handle it. A fun challenge. She liked death, right? It inspired her. This was up her alley. There was surely a way to stay positive, find the solution, and save her sister, right? Of course there was. No one failed to save their loved ones seven times in a row. Six had to be the limit. It was her time to triumph. "So, I have all my powers back, right? Like misting?"

Death cocked his head. "I think the youth have become too dependent on misting. I'll give you two more mists, and that's it. Use them wisely."

"Only two?" Because she just wasn't getting enough of a challenge in life.

"Yes. I like to see how innovative you can be. Creative thinking is critical to succeed in business." Death scrawled a note on a pink sticky and handed it to her. "Here's Augustus's home address. Don't fail."

"Of course I won't." But her hand was shaking as she took the note. How on earth was she going to pull this off?

Chapter 4

WHEN REINA SAW THE LINE OF MEN OUT THE DOOR OF Scrumptious, the chocolate cafe she and her sister owned in the Back Bay, which was the classically elegant section of Boston, she knew her timing was going to suck.

"What's with the crowds?" Trinity asked as they squeezed past some rowdy men comparing boxes of condoms they'd apparently purchased from the specialty store down the street.

"We're launching a new product today." Although the desserts they served were magnificently delicious, that wasn't why Scrumptious had been so enormously profitable since they'd opened their doors six months ago.

It was because of Natalie's special talent: her power of suggestion. With a few well-chosen and clever words, Natalie could use her Mystic talents to get a man to propose, a fourteen-year-old to decide to wear a suit to school, or a librarian to vault onto a luncheon table at the Ritz and start singing the national anthem. But as wickedly potent as she was, when Natalie used chocolate to increase the suggestibility of her subjects, she was positively hypnotic. The fact that Natalie's specialty was the more salacious side of life made her especially in demand.

The sisters' new product was going to rock the town of Boston. Unless, of course, Natalie freaked out over Reina's news and accidentally made every man in Beantown impotent, undersized, and inconveniently flaccid. "I'm worried about telling Natalie about my getting fired. She's been such an emotional wreck lately—"

A shrill shriek of absolute delight jerked everyone's attention to the front of the store, and Natalie leapt up to the ceiling, plucked a napkin off the fan, and vaulted back down with a gigantic smile on her face.

Cold dread made Reina halt. "Did you see that move? Did you see the joy in her face?"

"She couldn't have done that ceiling leap yesterday." Trinity looked stricken. "And she looks so happy. When did she get happy?"

"It must have been the last twelve hours. I just saw her yesterday and she looked haggard and depressed." Reina felt like someone had just slugged her in the stomach.

The curse of the deedub: The closer the victim got to death, the better she felt and looked. The deedubs loved the irony of feeling your best before kicking the bucket, and they'd been known to hover around a victim's family, laughing as loved ones started to say things like, "Wow, she looks great! Maybe she's getting better!" only to have their jaws drop when their dearly beloved ended up in a head-on collision with death.

Reina had already been down that road with seven sisters and her mom, and she'd learned to dread that happy expression and those well-toned biceps. Well-toned biceps belonged only on warriors like Jarvis, thanks so much.

Natalie saw Reina and waved furiously, her formerly limp, light blond hair now a rich head of luxurious golden curls. "Hey, girls! Come on in! It's going great!"

"You think she has less than twenty-four hours now?" Trinity asked. "I mean, she looks really good."

"Maybe it's not that bad. Maybe she's just psyched about the product launch." *Please let it just be natural euphoria.* Reina shoved her way through the crowd of boisterous men. "Hey, Nat. How are you feeling?"

"Hi, girls!" Natalie shot them a high octane grin as she grabbed the next customer by the lapels. "You will give your wife seven orgasms tonight because you will know exactly where to touch her and how to touch her to drive her wild."

The cop grinned. "Awesome!"

He was already running for the door by the time Natalie turned toward Reina, her cheeks flushed and her eyes sparkling with delight. "Oh, God, Reina, it's awful!"

Reina's heart sank. She'd seen that look too many times. "You feel good?" The question stuck in her throat, like sludge coating her voice.

"Fantastic." Natalie held out her hands, and all the calluses from years of work with chocolate were gone. Just smooth, perfect skin and long, gorgeous nails. "Did you realize the John Hancock tower has 1,632 steps? I ran them six times before work this morning. Took me less than fifteen minutes."

Reina's head started to pound as she touched her sister's skin. Terrifyingly perfect. "Two weeks ago, you thought exercise was for people who were being chased by the devil."

"I know." Natalie lowered her voice and leaned close. "I thought I saw a deedub this morning."

"You did?" Dear God, were they haunting her sister already? Hovering nearby so they could bask in the horror of her upcoming demise?

"I'm not sure. He looked like a normal kid in a

baseball hat, but something about him…" Natalie sighed. "I don't know. I'm probably wrong."

Reina exchanged glances with Trinity, who was already scanning the crowded store for a kid in a baseball hat. "But how do you feel emotionally?"

"I can't stop laughing, and I'm completely exuberant." Tears filled Natalie's eyes. "I feel so joyful and sexy and strong, I don't know what to do!"

Reina hugged her, holding on as tightly as she could. Afraid to let go. "We'll get through this, I swear. We'll get you feeling insecure and moody again, I promise."

Trinity had her hand over heart and looked like she was going to cry. Trinity had been there when Joanie had entered a contest for cage fighting dragons. Sweet Joanie, who had spent her life playing with butterflies, had become a dragon cage fighter in her last few days, dragged into the feeling of invincibility by the deedub poison.

Each Fleming female had been consumed by her wellbeing until she'd pushed herself so far that she'd died. It was how the poison worked, making the body so strong while eroding the boundaries in the mind until there was no sense of restraint or limitations. A suicide drug.

And if Nat was feeling jubilant already… "Should we lock you up?" Reina asked.

They'd constructed special cells in the basement of the Fleming family home to keep the sisters from hurting themselves as the deadline neared. But the poison wouldn't be stopped forever. All it did was buy them time. A day, an hour, a minute? It was always different.

"Oh, no. Not yet. I can't go in today. Not with the launch of the virility balls."

Natalie pulled back.

Reina reluctantly released her. What if this was the last time she ever got to hug her sister? "It's not worth your life—"

"Natalie!" Gina Ruffalo, assistant chef extraordinaire and the angel who'd been thrilled to offer her body for Natalie's soul switching, tapped Natalie's shoulder. "The men need you. You can't leave a man hanging with his masculinity at stake."

Gina was a little moody and elusive, but she was the key to Natalie's life, so the girls put up with her. Gina was desperate to get back to heaven to reunite with her true love, who had inconveniently died during their first romantic interlude. As a disenfranchised angel, Gina was immortal and banned to the physical world, so she had no chance of joining lover boy, unless she got her soul switched into a doomed body.

Reina had met Gina when the gal was trying to find a way to kill herself, and it had been a perfect match from the first moment. Give Gina a body that was about to die, and give Natalie one that would live forever. A perfect switch. If, of course, Reina could get the powers to actually make it happen.

"I want to work today," Natalie pleaded with Reina. "I'm still terrified of how happy I am, so that's good, right? Working gives me something to fight for."

Reina bit her lip. "Are you still afraid of dying?"

Natalie nodded. "Totally. Freaked out as hell."

Reina sighed with relief, so glad it wasn't just her own hope that made her see genuine terror in her sister's eyes. "Okay, but—"

Natalie squealed with delight. "Thank you, Sis!"

She flung herself on Reina, hugging her so tightly Reina felt like her ribs were going to snap, then jumped back and swept a tray of desserts off the counter. "The release of the new Dark Chocolate Virility Balls is going fantastic."

"Virility balls?" Trinity raised her brows. "What man could say no to that?"

"None, apparently." Natalie handed two decorated balls to the next male in line. "We've had a queue out the door all morning."

Reina watched her sister chat cheerfully with the client. Yeah, it was probably good not to cause her sister additional stress by telling her what had happened with Death, but at the same time, Reina needed help. Big time. "Nat? I think we should talk—"

"I can't last long enough to get my girlfriend off when we have sex." The customer stole Natalie's attention before Reina could cough up the bad news. "I tried baseball and politics and I still go too early. I'm afraid she's going to leave me—"

"It's no problem. I can help." Natalie handed him the balls. "Eat."

"Yeah, okay." The man took a breath, shoved his construction hat back on his head, and then he slammed both balls into his mouth.

"The moment you become romantic with your girlfriend, you will develop an erection," Natalie instructed as the man began to chew his balls. "It will last until she has an orgasm. When you feel her climax, your body will release and you will have a fantastic orgasm as well."

"That's awesome," Trinity whispered to Reina.

"That's so much better than impaling men on acid-laced pokers every time they fail to pleasure a woman the way Angelica did to the men. Blaine still has flashbacks when we make love sometimes."

"She did that to all of them?" Empathy for Jarvis tugged at Reina's heart. No wonder his icy blue eyes were so laden with darkness. Blaine's entire team carried the weight of a hundred and fifty years of hell in their souls, but Jarvis's pain was greater than the others. Darker. His torment gave her the chills, but at the same time, it made her want to reach out and hug him until his anguish went away.

Jarvis was dangerous on a level she couldn't fully comprehend, but she would never forget the way he'd cradled her face with his hand so she wouldn't bang her face on the floor when he'd tackled her to keep her from jumping out the window. He was so huge and so tough and so dangerous, and yet his touch had been so gentle, so tender, so soft.

She could still feel the muscled hardness of his body against hers. In that one minute, for the first time in her life, when she'd been pinned beneath him, she'd felt like the world wasn't trying to rip her feet out from under her and send her crashing into hell—

"Reina? You okay?"

Jarvis's image vanished from her mind. "Yeah, yeah, fine." What was she doing fantasizing about Jarvis? She had no time for personal pleasures, and even if she did, Jarvis was bad news. Even his friends looked at him as if he were tainted. She had no time to be doling out comforting hugs to men who were three slaps and a tickle from going over to the dark side. She had a sister to save, an assassin to harvest, and investors to recruit, after all. A full schedule.

"Excuse me. I'm late for a meeting and can't wait any longer." A man shoved his way to the front of the line.

He was tall, well-muscled, with short dark hair and a gorgeous double breasted suit. His eyes were dark and hooded, as if he were hiding secrets no one wanted to hear about, and a small scar marred his left cheekbone. He was money, he was elusive, he was danger, and he was raw male. He was exuding so much sex appeal she felt her own body tighten, and all she could think about was Jarvis. His hands on her body, running all over her—

"Oh, dear lord," Trinity whispered, her voice throaty and rough. "I need to find Blaine. Right now."

The man held up a pair of virility balls. "Who's helping me with these?"

"I am." Natalie stepped up to the counter.

The man's gaze fell directly on her full and gorgeous breasts. He swore under his breath. "Isn't there anyone else who can assist me?"

"No. Just me." Natalie's pulse began to throb visibly in her neck. "My name's Natalie Fleming."

He gripped the marble counter, his tanned forearms flexing. He was muscular and corded, almost as much as Jarvis…

Oh, crap. Why was she thinking about Jarvis? But she couldn't help it. Her mind was in the gutter big time, and it felt wonderful. She could practically smell that dark, woodsy scent he carried with him. His skin hot to the touch, stretched taut over his muscles… "Trin? Are you feeling weird right now?"

Trinity was bracing herself on one of the counters,

and her face was flushed. "You mean like, if Blaine were here, I'd rip off my clothes and ride him 'til the sun went down, even though the room is packed with about a hundred strangers? That kind of weird?"

Reina's lower belly was throbbing, a deep, rhythmic pulsing that was the same as she'd experienced that moment when Jarvis had had her pinned beneath him, his weight heavy, dominating, so male. "Yeah, like that."

Trinity wiped her hand over her forehead. "Is it the virility balls?"

"No, they only work on Dullets. Humans with no magical ability."

"You're dangerous to my self-control," the man said to Natalie, dragging his gaze off her breasts. "I need to shut it down."

"Shut what down?" Natalie breathed, her voice so throaty that Reina felt her own thighs begin to ache.

"Sex." He shifted restlessly, as if he could barely contain the energy rushing through him. "I can't kill any more women with sex. I've been celibate for three months, and I can't hold off much longer. It's got to change." He set his hand on Natalie's and ran his fingers up her arm. "And you're making it harder. My God. You're captivating."

"You kill with orgasms?" Natalie echoed, her voice trembly.

"Holy shit!" Trinity gripped Reina's arm. "It's the Godfather. I heard he was in town."

Reina rubbed her palm over her belly, trying to ease the tension. "The Godfather? The man who has orgasmed over a hundred women to death?"

"Yes," Trinity whispered. "I've heard he has such an

effect on women that they can orgasm simply by being in the same room with him. Of course not everyone is susceptible, but as long as she's within kissing distance of some dirty thoughts, a woman's got no chance against him."

Jarvis flashed in Reina's mind again. This time he was naked and hard. He descended toward her, his eyes intense and dark. Then he took her in a devastating kiss. His mouth was demanding and hard, a warrior who would throw her up against a wall and take what he wanted. But his arms were cradling her, protecting her, giving her safety even while his lips were so hot and—

"I heard it's worse if he touches you," Trinity said.

"It is?" Reina realized Godfather's fingers were trailing down Natalie's arm, touching her bare skin. They were leaning so close to each other. A sex murderer and a girl on the edge of a deedub death? *Holy crap*. Reina grabbed her sister's arm. "Nat! Get away from him—"

"Let go of me. He's a client." Natalie jerked her arm free and sent Reina slamming back against a bookshelf. Boxes of chocolates tumbled down on top of her.

"Reina!" Trinity raced over. "Are you okay?"

"We have to stop her." Reina shoved a box off her. "She's going to think she can survive his orgasms and die, just like how my mom tried to get it on with a succubus on meth."

Natalie's attention was riveted on the Godfather. "I've never tried to lower a man's virility."

His mouth was inches from hers. "Try," he whispered.

"Yeah, okay." She gripped his balls in her palm. "Eat."

He slipped the chocolate spheres in his mouth as Reina scrambled to her feet. "He's Magick, Natalie, it

won't work on him. You can't make him less dangerous." Was he Magick? He had to be. No ordinary human
could orgasm a hundred women to death, no matter how
sexy he was.

The Godfather shot an annoyed look at Reina, and
she felt her insides melt. Suddenly, all she could think
of was how it would feel to have Jarvis's lips working
their way down her spine. Over her hips. On her belly.
Then lower, and lower. He would slide his tongue inside
her, and—

Trinity fell to her knees with a groan. "We've got to
get Natalie."

"I'll get her." Reina closed her eyes and willed herself
to think of Jarvis's haunted eyes. Of the monster within
him. Of the trepidation that clawed at her gut when she
saw him watching her. Her body went ice cold, and the
relentless sexual need consuming her eased enough for
her to access her raw fear of the man who was about to
kill her sister.

Grasping onto that terror like a lifeline, Reina
sprinted across the room and jerked Natalie out of the
Godfather's grasp. "Get out of my store," Reina ordered
him. "Now!"

"No." The Godfather vaulted over the counter and
headed right for Natalie. "I'm taking her."

"Yes, take me." Natalie started struggling and Reina
knew she wouldn't be able to hold her for long.

"Natalie! Don't do this!" Reina felt her own muscles
begin to tremble, responding to the vibes he was giving
off. One more minute, and she was going to drop to the
floor in an orgasm and be screaming Jarvis's name while
a beast carried her sister off into the sunset.

Her sister was going to die, and there was no way she could save her. She felt it in her heart, in the depths of her soul. This man was her sister's fate. Augustus didn't matter anymore, because her sister's time to die had just arrived.

Jarvis had about one second to commend himself for tracking Reina down so efficiently, and then he caught the scent of arousal. Instinctively, he went for his sword. After one hundred and fifty years at the merciless and not-so-doting hands of Angelica and her apprentices, a room that smelled like sex was a room that meant pain, torture, and women who thought foreplay meant jabbing toothpicks in his nuts.

"Jesus." Nigel came to a dead stop beside him. "It feels like the Pit of Sexual Pain and Pleasure." He white-knuckled the doorway. "I'm already traumatized enough by bad sex. I'm going to have nightmares tonight."

"I hear you, buddy." Jarvis surveyed the room and saw the women were down on their knees behind the counter, hunched over like they'd just been sucker punched. Shit. Was she hurt? "Reina!" He tore across the room, shoving his way through the men crowding the door.

One was leering at Reina and Trinity like they were pole dangers in a seedy bar, and Jarvis slammed the butt of his sword into the bastard's head as he went past. "Learn some manners," he snapped as he vaulted the counter and landed beside the girls. "Reina. I'm here."

She looked up at him. "Jarvis?"

He froze, shocked by the raw lust in her eyes. Jesus.

No one had ever looked at him with such raw, un-abashed, pure wanting before, especially not Reina. His body responded instantly, and he started to reach for her. To haul her against him and kiss her until—

His fingers brushed the ends of her hair, and the sensual feel of her silken strands shocked him back into awareness, and he jerked his hand away. No one would use sex as a weapon against him. Ever.

"Bye, bye," a woman's voice sang out. "Love you all!"

Reina paled. "Natalie." She tried to lurch to her feet, and Jarvis caught her arm as she stumbled.

He could feel the heat of her skin as she fell against him. The woman was oozing pheromones worse than a leopard in heat. He immediately released her and stepped back, needing space, needing distance from the almost unstoppable urge to throw her down right on that floor and lose himself to the passion she was emanating. Who in God's name had made her so hot? And why was he responding like this? Women tried to seduce him all the time, and it never worked. But now? Jesus. All he could think about was how her hips would feel under his palms. What her lips would taste like. "What the hell have you been doing?" he demanded. "And who got you in this state?" Because he had a very strong urge to behead that bastard right here. Right now. Twice.

But in complete lack of reciprocity, she managed to restrain herself from unzipping his fly, and instead she was running out the door.

"Natalie," she shouted. "Get back here! God, Trinity! Help!" She misted out of sight. Instant vanishing.

"Shit!" He'd lost her already. Was that her weapon? Turn him into a giant hard-on so he couldn't think,

and then bail on him? If he wasn't so strung out by
the blood rushing to his lower regions, he'd be impressed with the success of her plan. No woman had
the ability to get him to think about sex. None except
Reina, apparently.

Jarvis crouched beside Trinity. She was still hunched
over, exuding sex as thickly as Reina. But it wasn't turning him on. He actually just wanted to keep his hands
off her, which was how it should be. Him, in control.
Woman, not. "Where'd Reina go?"

She pointed out the front window. "She went after
her sister, Natalie. They must be on the street outside.
Bring them both back, Jarvis. Please!"

"I will." He shoved his way through the men, who
were now clamoring for assistance and yelling some shit
about virile balls.

Jarvis reached the sidewalk just as Reina appeared
across the street, directly in front of tall, suited man and
a well-stacked gal who had to be her sister, Natalie.

"Nat!" Reina lunged for Natalie, who sidestepped
Reina and flung her to the side. Reina crashed into a
parking meter with a thud that made anger rise fast and
hard inside Jarvis.

"Hey!" He bolted across the street, sword out. No one
messed with the people in his life, and Reina was his,
both because she was the best friend of Blaine's woman,
and because he needed her help.

He swept Reina off the curb, tucked her against him,
and then grabbed Natalie's wrist. Her eyes were glowing too brightly and her skin was hot. Too hot. Almost
reminded him of Blaine's, but he wasn't buying that this
chick was made of fire the way Blaine was.

Hell, no. This woman exuded sex on a level he'd never run into in his life. But it couldn't penetrate the ball of hate that surrounded him. Immune as always. Except for that moment when Reina had looked at him. He'd felt that, and in a big way. Didn't like it. But at the same time, it felt good as hell to feel like a male.

"Hey." The man stepped up, and his eyes were flashing. "She's mine."

"You don't get to have her." Reina braced her hand on Jarvis's waist, then she waggled her fingers at him. Death powder spewed out and hit the guy squarely in the face, but nothing happened.

Well, hell. Jarvis had seen Reina drop Nigel on his artist-boy-ass with that powder, and this guy hadn't blinked. Who was he?

Natalie ripped her arm free of Jarvis's grasp with strength he wasn't prepared for (hadn't he learned not to underestimate women by now?). "I love you, Reina, but I have to do this." She lowered her shoulder and charged.

The intent on her face was clear. She was going to hurt the woman he'd come to recruit. The woman who had, for the first time in his life, turned him on with real, honest-to-God desire. "Screw that." He whipped his sword around and butt checked the handle of his sword into Natalie's head. She dropped instantly on the pavement and didn't move.

Oh, shit. Women didn't usually like when you knocked out their loved ones. "Uh, sorry, Reina—"

But in an entirely unexpected turn of events, Reina looked at Jarvis with utter relief on her face. "Thank you!"

As she knelt beside her sister, Jarvis felt like the king of the world. Yeah, he'd saved the girl. Rock on. He grinned and cheerfully levered the point of his sword at the other man as he reached for Natalie.

"Don't even think about it," Jarvis said. "Leave." His fingers twitched on the sword. "Or stay and fight. I'd be down with that." Well, not really. He had a feeling that if he let go a little bit, he was going to lose it all. But that didn't stop the hate monster inside him from wanting to engage.

The man glanced at Natalie, then eyed the sword with its black, glowing blade. He inclined his head in capitulation. "I defer." Then he turned and stepped into a limousine that was waiting by the curb.

The sleek silver car roared and then slipped out of sight around the corner.

Jarvis sheathed his sword. "Okay, Reina. Let's go."

"Hey, sweetie," Reina said softly.

He stiffened at the tenderness of Reina's voice. Women who spoke like that were never to be trusted. Sword up, he turned sharply, only to see she was stroking Natalie's cheek, cradling her the way a mother would hug a small child.

His sword dropped at the tenderness of the moment. There was no guile in that embrace. Simple, pure tenderness. For a moment he was too shocked to do anything but stare. The corners of Reina's mouth were tight, tears were glistening in her eyes, and her shoulders were shaking. With relief? Agony? Terror?

He took a step toward her. Wanting to help her. To ease her pain. He had a sword. He could kick the ass of anything that was scaring her. He was good at that. Really good.

"Hey, Natalie," she whispered, her voice trembling. "It's going to be okay. I'm here for you."

The pain on her face was soul-deep anguish. It was so different than the pain when a warrior got his foot spliced by a half-demon succubus. It was real, worse, so deep he could almost feel it in his own gut. He reached out to touch her, not even sure what he was trying to do—

Then something hit him in the back of the head and he was out.

Chapter 5

REINA LOOKED UP AS JARVIS TEETERED FORWARD AND toppled over, landing beside her with a thump. For a second, she was too surprised to move. Seriously, it wasn't every day that a towering hunk of manliness went belly-up on Newbury Street for no apparent reason.

Had the sight of female bonding been too much for his scarred and tortured soul to handle? A late afternoon sugar crash? Or was it some Pavlovian response to something Angelica had drilled into him? Not that it mattered. Even the tall, dark warriors harboring undefined black souls were supposed to always be on their feet and ready to defend, preserve, and protect. "Um, Jarvis?"

She patted his unresponsive cheek, then she noticed the five pointed pink star protruding from the back of his head. "Jarvis!" She threw herself over his inert from instinctively, trying to protect him.

She knew who carried pink stars. She knew who killed with pink stars. She knew who *assassinated* with pink stars. *Please let me be wrong.* Cautiously, so ridiculously terrified of what she might find, she sniffed.

Rotten bananas.

"Hello, my dear," a well-cultured male voice drifted over the afternoon air.

She scrambled to her feet, and there he was, less than ten yards away. Augustus. *Not Good.*

The world's most well-decorated and highly sought after assassin was every bit as scary as she'd thought he would be. At least two inches over the five foot mark, his skin was crusty, and a half-smoked cigar was dangling from the left side of his mouth. A tattered cowboy hat was askew on his balding head, a few gray hairs were protruding from his chin, and his purple velvet slippers seemed to be a sign of impending insanity, which was never a good thing when it came to professional killers.

He smiled, a thin, nasty smile that would have made the nearest cockroach run for cover. "Reina Fleming, I presume."

He'd come for her? "Oh, I'm so sorry. Reina died ten minutes ago. You just missed her."

But in a horrifically unfair state of affairs, the ultimate bad boy had enough brain cells to realize she was lying. "I heard you wanted to kill me."

"You did?" She'd gotten her assignment less than two hours ago. If she was still alive to text after Augustus left, she would let her boss know that his impenetrable safeguards had been violated… hmm… had Death himself leaked the news? Was he setting her up to fail?

Of course he was. That would be just like him, wouldn't it? Hadn't he told her that he was far too complex for a linear, simplistic assignment? Anyone with the ability to comprehend the blatantly obvious would know that she had no chance against Augustus, so if Death had sent the ultimate black sheep after her, then it meant he was trying to get her fired in the most permanent way.

Men could be so despicable sometimes. Weren't women supposed to be the ones who were plotting, circuitous, and resourceful, and men were simply supposed to put their heads down and charge? Hello? Had someone failed to copy her on the gender reversal memo?

"Of course I know you need to kill me," Augustus said. "Do you think I would dominate my esteemed profession if I didn't have an extensive underground network of people willing to betray others to keep me alive in return for a payoff so paltry it insults their intelligence?" He ripped open his black satin shirt to reveal an unexpectedly well-muscled chest and a black tattoo in the shape of a chicken over his heart. "I'm busy, so I thought I'd make this easy for me. We'll do it Old West style."

Oh, this did not feel good. "Do what?" she asked warily. She poked Jarvis with her toe, but the menacing hottie didn't budge. Was he dying? Fear edged at her, and she risked a quick glance. His chest was moving. Still alive. Relief rippled through her, and she nudged him again. "Jarvis," she whispered. "I need you."

No response.

She did a quick look around to see if anyone else could help her, but the street was eerily empty, as if every living creature had sensed the need to stay away from the purple slipper killer. All the wannabe studs who'd been queued up outside Scrumptious? Gone. Where were the male heroes, huh? What happened to rescuing a damsel in distress? No wonder these studs needed virility balls. Any man who took off at the sight of the perennial all-star assassin was not a real man.

Not that she needed a man to rescue her, of course. It was simply an observation. But hey, if there was a man who *wanted* do to the hero thing and help her, well, why not contribute to his ego and self-esteem? As a woman, wasn't it her girly duty to help build up the testosterone level in every male who had the potential to, you know, save her life? A man like Jarvis.

She quickly knelt beside the warrior in question, pulled her sleeve over her hand to protect it, then yanked the star out of his head. She lightly tapped his shoulder. "Jarvis? Can you hear me?"

Augustus pulled out another pink star and lodged it under her chin. "To your feet, my dear."

She stood, her heart racing. Yeah, some people might say, hey, how convenient that she didn't have to search for Augustus. But her sickle was back at the store, and her death dust was so useless she hadn't been able to coax even a yawn out of the Godfather, so she wasn't feeling the love for the fortuitous turns of life. The odds in a mano a mano with Augustus weren't exactly skewed in her direction under the best of circumstances, but right now? She was bottoming out, in a big way.

Augustus grinned. "We're going to have a gun fight, modern day style."

Let's see… no sickle, no time to prepare, and trying to kill Augusts when he was ready and waiting? Not such a good plan. "Listen, I appreciate the offer, but this isn't a good time. My sister—"

"Hey," Augustus interrupted. "The focus should be on *me* right now. Not your sister." He tossed his shirt onto the street and flexed his muscles. "My therapist said I'm not enjoying my work as much as I used to, so he's instructed me to find more joy in my day. I'm starting with you."

Crap. She needed to stall him. As soon as Trinity

finished multiple orgasming, she'd be out here and could bring the sickle and advice. Trinity had killed a lot of people. She'd know what to do. "Really? You're not enjoying being an assassin? But you're so good at it."

"I know I am, but I'm letting the grind get to me." He loosened his gun belt so it sat lower on his hips. "How does one lose the passion for something so near and dear to one's heart? Is it the pressure of staying at the top? Of surpassing my annual income each year? Of setting another record for the most consecutive number of years receiving the Assassin of the Year award?"

"You hate killing?" Well, wasn't that dandy news. If Augustus couldn't stomach knocking out souls before their time, how was she supposed to be okay with it?

He shoved the weapon into his left holster then set his hands on his hips. "I wake up every morning, look at my list of people I need to kill, and I just want to roll over and go back to sleep." He pulled out another pink star and tossed it carelessly into his right holster, clearly not taking the time to savor the moment. "My therapist suggested going back to my beginnings and trying to rediscover the joy of killing, so I'm giving it a try." He snapped the holsters shut. "Ready."

Ready? Uh, oh. "I don't think—"

"Hey!" Trinity shouted, and Reina turned to see her friend running down the sidewalk toward her.

"One hundred paces. Then we draw." Augustus began marching down the street.

"Trin!" Relief rushed through Reina as her friend neared. "Tell me you brought the sickle."

"No, I didn't realize he was out here." Trinity bent over to catch her breath as she eyed Augustus's speedy progress down the street. "I'll never make it back in time. Knock him out, and then we'll get the sickle while he's passed out."

"I don't know if I can. I couldn't even knock out the Godfather."

"Oh, come on! Now is not the time to suffer a crisis of confidence! You heard Death say that the powder only works if you're simpatico. You need to get in alignment!"

"Fifty!" Augustus yelled, his bare shoulders gleaming in the afternoon sunshine.

"I'm not ready to die." Reina's hands started to tremble. "Maybe I should just run away. Give myself time to prepare—"

"Hey, Sis, you can totally do this. I believe in you. Death is your thing."

"Nat?" Reina whirled around and saw Natalie was sitting up. Her relief at seeing her sister conscious faded when she saw how her sister's eyes were sparkling. She looked way too happy. "Shouldn't you be a little worried right now?"

"Seventy-five!" Augustus shouted.

"I'm giving up living in fear." Nat hopped to her feet cheerfully. "After a lifetime of being terrified of dying, it's a relief not to have my stomach churning with fear, angst, and general misery. I want to feel good."

"Dear Saints alive," Augustus yelled. "The girl gets it! It's all about enjoying the ride!"

Nat waved at him. "I do get it, and it feels great," she shouted back.

Oh, God. Like she needed to have her sister bonding with the man who was about to murder her. That was just the ultimate insult to an already bad day. "Nat—"

"Does being miserable and terrified keep bad things from happening?" There was the weight of extreme heaviness behind the cheerfulness on Natalie's face. "No, but it destroys the quality of time you do have left. I feel good for the first time in my life, and I like it. I don't want to be terrified anymore. I still want to live, but I'm not going to resist the joy and delight in the meantime."

Damn. That almost made sense.

"Eighty-five," Augustus shouted. "My name is Augustus," he called to Natalie. "May I take you to dinner sometime? I'd love to find out how you developed such a fantastic attitude."

"I got bitten by a deedub. Dinner's a maybe," Natalie said easily. "I might be dead."

Fat chance of that. Nat's death sentence ended now, no matter what Reina had to do to make it happen. The bad guy was distracted, the good girl was talking about her upcoming demise, and the superhero sister was going to step up.

"Dead?" Augustus sounded aghast. "But I need you! You can't die now!"

Augustus was too far away to risk powdering. She had to mist close to him and strike before he noticed she was there. She'd already used up one of her two allotted mists (saving her sister from orgasm central had been well worth it), so this was her last one. But it was the right moment. Augustus was upset, engrossed in her sister, and this was the best chance she was going to get.

"You must change your plans!" he shouted at Natalie. "I forbid you to die until I have gleaned all pertinent information from you about how to enjoy life!"

Reina let her eyes go gold and black. The street shifted into black and white vision, and she flexed her hand. Black death dust filtered through her skin and filled her palm.

"Ninety! I mean ninety-one." Augustus was barely paying attention to the Showdown at High Noon. "How can I get bitten by a deedub?"

Reina flexed her palm. *You are one with the powder.*

"The effects of a deedub bite are mixed," Natalie explained. "You'll be happy, but then you die."

"Oh, I won't. I'm immortal," Augustus said. "How do I find a deedub?"

Reina misted. She reformed right behind him, unleashed the powder at him—

He whirled around, whipped his hand into his pocket, then thrust the pink star at her neck. She had no time to duck—

A sword whipped past her face and then the star clanged against the flat of Jarvis's blade where it was guarding her jugular.

The star bounced off and landed in the dirt with a hollow thud.

"Jarvis!" Disbelief and elation rushed through her. Not only had Jarvis revived from a deadly pink star attack, but he'd actually come to rescue her. "Thanks—" Her relief died as Jarvis stepped up beside her and she looked into his eyes.

They were solid black, haunted and deadly. She was looking into the soul of the monster she'd always known was there. Only now, it had come out to play.

Jarvis shoved Reina behind him as Augustus went for his second star. Her defender moved so fast she didn't even see his hand move, but suddenly Jarvis's sword was hilt deep in Augustus's chest.

Well, that was probably a good plan for stopping a lethal assault. Who needs impotent death powder when there are long, sharp implements around?

Yes, Jarvis had monster eyes, but he'd turned them against her assailant, not her. Trouble, tormented, but somehow, in those depths, finding a place to protect her? No one ever protected her. She was always trying to keep others safe and failing miserably. To have him jump and take some of the pressure off... her chest tightened. It was a gift. She'd never touched him on purpose before, never dared to reach out. But suddenly she didn't feel so afraid of him. She wanted to connect to that part of him that had cradled her face and saved her life. So, she reached out to touch his arm—

Jarvis moved out of her reach before she could make contract. Disappointment and embarrassment flooded her cheeks, and she jerked her hand back. Had he moved on purpose? But when she looked at him, he was focused on Augustus, and she got no answers from his expression.

"Bugger that!" Augustus clutched his chest as he staggered backwards. "How in the name of all that's deviant and miserable did I not see you recover?"

"You were cocky." Jarvis's voice was hard. Brewing with some very scary stuff, which was fantastic. Scary stuff was needed when taking on Augustus, and she hadn't exactly figured out how to corner that market. "That kind of shit doesn't work on me very well." Jarvis jerked his sword out of Augustus's rib cage, streaks of blood on the blade.

Reina stared at the blade, her stomach turning at the evidence of death and violence, the world her boss was trying to force her into. Stabbing people was different than handing out confetti when a soul was finally freed from the constraints of their physical body. It wasn't her thing. Really wasn't.

Jarvis wiped the blade on his jeans with a casualness that spoke of an utter lack of concern for violence and killing. He simply wasn't bothered by it, and she clung to his ease, got comfort from it. Maybe it wasn't such a big deal, this whole killing thing. Maybe it would all be okay. Maybe?

Augustus peered at his body as his torso turned gray and streaks of black began racing up his throat toward his head. "Good Lord, man, what do you have in that thing?"

"Hate." Jarvis's response was matter-of-fact, but his grip tightened on his sword, almost imperceptibly.

Reina was startled by his response. What kind of answer was that? Yes, sure, he was all tormented and stuff, no doubt, but *hate*? That didn't make any sense. Not for him. Not for a man who'd pulled himself out of a pink-star-stupor to save a woman he barely knew.

"Hate?" Augustus stomped his foot in fury. "Like I need hate in my life right now! I'm trying to find my passion and love again. What kind of a bastard are you?"

"The worst kind." Jarvis pressed the sword against the assassin's throat. "You have two seconds to get away from Reina, or you're toast."

Something jumped in Reina's heart at his threatening tone. He was protecting her. Really and truly. Not just saving her life, because maybe any warrior would feel the need to stop a woman from being killed. Right now, there was no overt threat from the debilitated assassin, but Jarvis was still pushing him back, defending her space as if he had taken her safety on as a personal mission.

No one ever stood between her and harm. It felt weird... and marvelous. Like this cool breeze rippling over her skin, clearing a humid, oppressive weight from her body after a lifetime of living beneath the smog. Instinctively, without even thinking it, she touched his back in silent thanks, and this time she made contact.

His muscles were taut, and his body pulsed with energy and heat. The connection rippled down her arm, and she felt a sense of rightness, of absolute perfection in that moment.

Jarvis glanced over at her, his eyebrows nearly shooting off his forehead in surprise. At being touched? Did no one ever reach out to him? That was so sad.

But he didn't move away, and her hand continued to rest on his back, a silent connection between them.

"You can't kill me," Augustus proclaimed, pulling his shoulders back, as if he wasn't turning into a piece of wrinkled black licorice.

"No?" Jarvis cut off one of Augustus's chin hairs with a flick of his wrist. "You sure about that?"

Blackened lines were spilling into Augustus's palms. The wrinkled angel of death was as immortal as they got, and one strike with Jarvis's sword had poisoned him. Exactly how dangerous *was* Jarvis? Slowly, she pulled her hand away from his back.

"Back off," Jarvis said quietly to the assassin. "And I mean it."

"Oh, fine. I'll be back when I'm recovered." Augustus snapped his fingers, and his chariot landed beside him, the six winged horses as majestic as ever. "I'll get her when you're not around."

Jarvis smiled with what could only be called macabre pleasure. Chills ran down her spine. "Then I'll have to be around," he said.

"She has to sleep." Augustus climbed into his ornately carved black and gold carriage.

"I'll sleep with her."

Um, hello? The residual tingling of the Godfather Effect was too recent for that kind of remark. She took a step back, suddenly wanting space. It was too much, the decadent fantasies she'd had of him combined with the lethal and deadly vibes he was sending out.

"She has to shower." Augustus grinned. "Somehow I think our little warrior woman will remove your testicles before she'd let you in there with her."

Both men turned to look at her, and she felt her cheeks heat up in denial. "I'm not an ice princess," she snapped, suddenly feeling embarrassed that Jarvis might think that she was.

Not that she cared what he thought about her sexually, but at the same time, she couldn't help wanting to make it clear that she wasn't defective. Yeah, okay, maybe she hadn't dated since that miserable bastard had ditched her in a brutal move that eviscerated her soul due to her phobia of having those she loved leave her. But that didn't mean she would never put herself out there again. She was just busy right now, you know, saving her sister and all. Someday, co-ed showers would be a part of her life again. Just not *now*, and not with a man who was so dark and dangerous that he would be the very, very last one to trust to stick around if she happened to get too emotionally dependent on him.

Jarvis shrugged. "I'll take my chances on the shower." His words were slow and drawn out, and there was no mistaking the thoughtfulness in his expression.

She swallowed, her throat suddenly tight. The way he was looking at her made it very clear he was looking at her as a woman, visualizing her naked with water streaming over her breasts and down her hips and to other more interesting parts of her body. Her skin felt hot, and he kept staring at her, making her feel even warmer.

Jarvis's mind was clearly in the gutter now, and the thought of it made all sorts of sweet nothings run through her body. Damn the Godfather for getting her all worked up. Jarvis was not the kind of man a girl with intelligence, important plans, and a well-developed sense of self-preservation fantasized about. He was not the man to come out of retirement for, and certainly not at this pivotal time in her life. She needed to focus, get her job done, and *then* think about being a woman.

"I'm going to go heal this paltry insult, and then I'll come back and kill you all," Augustus said, jerking her attention back to the enormity of the problems in her life right now. The sexual high vanished, replaced by the cold tendrils of fear digging into her stomach.

Augustus climbed into his carriage. "Except for you, my dear," he said to Natalie. "I'll give you massive amounts of money for two hours of your time. Call me. We'll do tea." He doffed his hat at Natalie and cracked his whip, then the vehicle leapt into the air and disappeared into the horizon.

She stared at the spot where it had disappeared, halfway dreading that it would reappear. That there would be no respite.

"Interesting son of a bitch." Jarvis sheathed his sword, pulling her attention back to the present.

Jarvis was taking himself off the offensive. The threat was over. Augustus was really gone for the moment, thanks to Jarvis, a man she never thought she'd be indebted to for doing something nice for her. She started to thank him, and the words died when she saw his hard expression. It was her first good look at him since he'd swooped in on his devil broom and… yikes. On many different levels.

His blue eyes were darker than she'd ever seen them, and the air around him was rippling, as if he was burning with heat. His leather jacket was bunching over his shoulders, and his jeans were hanging low on his hips. His sword was jammed in a scabbard on his back.

She hadn't seen him in several weeks, but he looked so much more tortured and dangerous than last time. He was studying her intently, like a panther about to pin her to the floor and end any freedom of a choice she thought she had. Her stomach tightened with the sudden urge to flee for her life, her sanity, and her womanly virtue.

"Jarvis!" Nigel jogged up. "You okay, man?" He stopped a careful distance away, as if he didn't want to get too close. Resignation tightened Jarvis's features, a recognition that his own friend, an immortal warrior who was unkillable, wouldn't risk getting near him.

For a moment, her heart shifted with unexpected sadness for him. For her, there was nothing more terrifying than the prospect of winding up alone in this world, and there Jarvis stood. Alone. Even while standing beside friends.

"Reina." Natalie touched her arm.

She was surprised by the look of sanity on Natalie's face. "You're better?"

"A little. When Jarvis stabbed Augustus, all my hate for the deedub who bit me jerked me out of my happy place."

Jarvis was watching Natalie with an impassive expression, but his eyes were turbulent with regret. Hate was really his internal demon? That made no sense. Jarvis was scary, dangerous, and aloof, but hateful? Never. No man who lived on hate had the loyal friends he did, or stood up for women he had no reason to protect. Jarvis wasn't hate, no matter what he claimed.

"I can already feel myself getting more relaxed," Natalie said, "so I think I'm going to be going back to my lala land soon. Before I do, we need to talk."

"Oh, Nat—"

"Here's the deal. I don't want you to die. Seeing you like that, almost dead, scared me." Tears filled Natalie's eyes. "If you get yourself killed trying to save me, when I'm going to die anyway, well, what's the sense in that?"

"You're not going to die—"

"I am! No one survives a deedub attack. I've been going along with your rescue attempt because I was terrified, and because I wanted to give us both hope, but if you could feel the intensity of the power building within me…" Natalie flexed her hands, and muscles rippled in her forearms. "There's no stopping it, Reina."

"We have to try—"

"No!" Natalie shouted her denial and slammed her

hand over Reina's mouth. "Stop talking, and listen to me! I don't have much time!"

Reina nodded once, regret heavy in her heart as her sister began to slip away again. The real Natalie was gentle and soft-spoken. Warm. Not this muscle-bound tough girl.

"You're supposed to kill Augustus to save me, right?" Natalie took her hand away, allowing Reina to answer. "So, let's see. How well did that go?"

Reina shifted, aware that Jarvis and Nigel were listening. Was there a need for the warriors to know exactly how inadequate she was? "I wasn't ready. Next time I'll kill him—"

"You won't! You'll wind up in a thousand pieces on his therapist's coffee table! And even if you don't, how are you going to find investors willing to pay three billion dollars for an assassination by Friday? And you have to find the victims too? All that, just to have the *chance* to save me? You really think that's going to work?"

Jarvis tapped his sword against his boot, and she jumped at the thwack. On edge, much? "Well, yes—"

"Let it go," Natalie said. "This is the first time in my life I've felt happy, and honestly, it feels really good. I'm going to die either way, but if I'm worrying about you getting killed on my behalf, I'll die the same miserable person I've been my whole life." Natalie took Reina's hand and pressed her palm to her heart. "If you love me, if you have any mercy in your heart, you'll stop trying to save me, so I can use these last few days to experience an inner peace I've never had in my whole life. Would you really deny me that?"

"What kind of request is that?" But Reina could sense her truth and knew the request was coming from the sister she loved, not the demented happy-pill-girl.

"It's my death bed wish. Everyone gets one."

"You don't!" Natalie was sane enough to know what she was asking. Could she really deny her sister? Yes. Yes, she could. Sometimes the role of family was to deny loved ones everything that was important to them.

"You don't get to refuse a death bed wish," Natalie said loftily, her voice becoming infused with that awful cheeriness. "It's against the rules." She poked her finger into Reina's shoulder. "You will stay alive and let me go to gallivanting into the Afterlife. And you—" She pointed at Trinity, who was now hurrying down the street toward them. "You will help me get a date with the Godfather. I'm not going to pass from this world by falling into a crevasse on Mount Everest like my sister. That's such an underachievement. But death by orgasm? Think of all the stories I'll be able to tell in heaven."

In a weird and entirely inconvenient way, Reina actually sort of got what her sister was saying. Body-exploding orgasms hadn't had a significant role in her life, and the thought of a really, really great orgasm was incredibly tempting… But, on the other hand, the big O was not a reason to die. "Nat, I can't let you go after the Godfather. Remember, you said you wanted me to lock you up to keep you alive as long as possible—"

Natalie went into a martial arts warning stance worthy of a bad karate movie. "Don't keep me from my dreams, girlfriend."

Reina blinked. Since when did her sister know how to get lethal with her hands?

"Hey, Tae Kwon Do Girl, don't forget that today is your big product launch," Trinity said, easing up next to Natalie. "You'd be so bummed if you jumped ship without properly launching the balls. The men of Boston need you, and you're their only chance."

Natalie glanced toward the store, and naked longing for her business flashed across her face. Reina felt her breath catch at the evidence that her sister was still in that body, fighting to hold on.

"That's true," Natalie admitted. "I've been working so hard on those balls. But —"

"No buts." Trinity took her arm and pushed her gently in the direction of Scrumptious, past Nigel and Jarvis, who were not even bothering to pretend they weren't listening to every word of the discussion. "Finish out today. Cement your legacy. We'll go after the Godfather tomorrow. You have plenty of time to get your life snuffed from you by a well-muscled ecstasy factory."

Natalie shot a suspicious look at them both, but she was already taking a step toward the store. Yay for workaholics pursuing lifelong professional dreams. "You promise?"

"Swear. I can talk Reina into anything, including allowing you to die amidst shrieks of pleasure." Trinity nudged her. "Go. I'll catch up."

Natalie nodded and sprinted off down the street, calling to the men who were beginning to emerge from doorways, now that Augustus was gone and it was safe for them to come out. Wimps. Nothing like Jarvis, who'd marched right out into the fray the moment things had gotten dangerous.

He had folded his arms across his chest, and he had

a smug look on his face. Like he'd just come up with a plan that he liked, one that made him the king of the world. God, she envied that kind of confidence. What she'd give for one minute of believing that she could accomplish whatever she wanted.

"I'm back," Natalie shouted as she ran into the store.

"Nice distraction, Trin, making her think about work instead of being ready to grab her." Reina started after her sister, fisting her hands. She could do this. She could be like Jarvis. "Now we have to lock her up. Let's tackle her by the flour barrel—"

"Wait!" Trinity pulled her back. "You can't deprive her of work. Let her be."

Reina's stomach dropped. "What? You're going to honor her death wish?"

"Of course not, you nitwit. She needs to be behind the counter today, to focus on something else for a while. After work, I'll prey on her trust of me and lure her into her cell. Then I'll betray her by locking her in there."

"Thank God." Reina closed her eyes with relief. "For a moment I was worried you thought I was a bad sister to refuse her death wish."

"Are you kidding? Death wishes are for manipulating the dying person into doing what you want. I'll go get her locked down, and you take care of Augustus."

Oh, Augustus. Big swallow of fear.

Trinity's fingers tightened on Reina's arm, and she leveled a hard gaze at her. "But don't you dare get yourself killed, or I will knock you off myself."

The front door slammed shut and Natalie danced past the store window, wiggling her hips for all her customers. "I should go check on her," Trinity said. "I don't want her to get too horny and slip out the back door. The lure of great sex can be powerful." She released Reina and hurried over to the store. She paused on the threshold. "Be smart, but make it happen. There's no time to fail again."

"I know." Oh, she knew. But failure was what she knew best, at least when it came to things that mattered.

Like this.

Chapter 6

JARVIS HAD REINA EXACTLY WHERE HE WANTED HER, AND IT felt good.

He hadn't had the upper hand with a female in, oh, about a hundred and fifty years. His quality time with the chicks usually ended with him skewered, stuffed, skinned, and trying to remember why he bothered to keep reviving each time Death offered him an invite to a happier place. Being upright, intact, and in control of a woman was a significant improvement over his old life.

And Reina Fleming was all woman, that was for certain. He'd never have thought he'd turn to a woman for help, but Reina was different. She had grit, and he liked it. He grinned, remembering her surprise when she'd tried to dust him several weeks ago, and it hadn't worked. Had she backed down? Nope. Not for a second. She'd been on a mission to protect Trinity from him, and the fact she'd suddenly found herself unarmed hadn't deterred her for a moment. Reina might be female, but she understood loyalty to others, and that made her different than any other woman he'd known. And that trait was what had brought him to her door and shoving a sword through the heart of the man trying to do her harm.

"A morally ambiguous situation," Nigel said thoughtfully. "I can't say I agree with your decision, Reina. Your sister has a good point."

Reina started, as if she'd forgotten they were there, then she looked over at them. As always, her gaze went first to Jarvis, even though it was Nigel who had addressed her.

He stiffened at the intensity of her scrutiny, at the way she seemed to see into the depths of his soul. The flash of empathy, and then the retreat, the subconscious (or conscious) understanding of exactly what bad news he was.

What was with the way she looked at him? No matter how many people were in the room, or how far away they were from each other, he always found her watching him.

He didn't like that kind of interest from women. It always ended up with him being strung up by his balls to a stainless steel wall and fending off new and creative ways to peel the skin off his body.

Her eyes widened at whatever expression she saw on his face, and she quickly averted her gaze, turning to Nigel. "What do you mean?"

Well, hell. Jarvis didn't like her looking at someone else. Didn't like it much at all. Nigel shoved himself off the Hummer he'd been leaning against and strode across the sidewalk toward Reina. "I mean—"

"He means, fuck what your sister wants." Jarvis felt a smug sense of satisfaction when Reina looked sharply at him. "You make the call on how you respond to the shit life throws at you. No one else does."

Relief flickered across her face. "Thank you for saying that. I appreciate the support, especially when my sister is so good at making me feel like I shouldn't try to save her."

Before he realized it, he grinned at her. "You're welcome."

She stared at him as if he'd grown a rat out of his forehead. "I've never seen you smile."

Did he have a bad smile?

Then she smiled back, and he felt like the sun had just come out. God, her smile was magnificent, an expression of an inner truth, not some artificial attempt to manipulate him. He grinned back. "You should smile more," he said. "It's nice."

"It is?" Her smile widened, and her cheeks took on the most appealing flush. "Thank you."

He took a step toward her. "You're welcome."

"Okay, enough with the romantic flirting for remedial learners," Nigel interrupted, breaking the moment. "What I actually was going to say that although you have a right to get your ass kicked if you so choose, it's up to your sister to decide if she's ready to die."

Reina frowned at Nigel, all of the light and beauty gone from her smile. All that was left was frustration and tension. "That's not really helpful."

Nigel grinned. "I'm not trying to be helpful. I'm just observing. Your sister is an intriguing juxtaposition of assorted emotions. She's conflicted, and it shows on her face. She interests me." He pulled out his sketch pad and pen. "Hold that expression. It's a fascinating look into the anguish that love can cause. Brilliant."

Love. The word was like a knife blade in the kidney. *Shit*. There was going to be serious anguish in this world if the Guardian of Love didn't get pried out of Death's grasp. There was no time to get distracted by a woman's personal issues. Men had missions. Men had goals. Men were human, even when they weren't. Women were machines of torture. Instruments of pain on a merciless mission. At no time was it appropriate to forget that and actually develop empathy for one of them.

He got it, Nigel got it, and after a nearly fatal mistake, Christian got it too. But Blaine? Different story, though it seemed to be working out for him.

Honestly, Jarvis didn't get Blaine's fascination with Trinity and the way he got all soft over her. Didn't get that about women at all. Hell, Jarvis couldn't even be bothered with sex anymore. Ended up not being worth it, because the minute the orgasm hit him, he couldn't keep his shields up and all his hate spilled over into the female. And then the woman always turned into a screaming banshee and tried to kill him, which sucked when they were Angelica's black magicked apprentices. Not their fault they went insane on him, but still. Not exactly fun. He could keep his barriers up if he didn't go over the top, but sex without the orgasm... well, what was the point of that? He already had enough torture in his life.

But Reina... something about the slope of that delicate nose and the curve of those sexy collarbones almost made him want to try one more time.

If, of course, he was a stupid fool who didn't know what was good for him.

But he had to admit that when she'd put her hand on his back a few minutes ago, his body had responded like a hot poker in the fires of hell. He'd wanted to whip around, haul her against him, and kiss her until they both exploded from the heat.

Which was something he didn't do and didn't even think about. But the truth was, he hadn't been immune from her since the start. From the first moment he'd seen Reina, he'd dug her thick, auburn hair and the way she liked to wear it twisted up in a sexy knot on top of her head, with all those strands spilling down around her face.

Maybe he liked her hair because none of the women in the Den had hair with that tint of red in it. Or maybe he was as tactile as Angelica always accused him of being (badass warriors were not tactile, thanks so much), and the thought of spinning his hands through her hair was appealing as hell. Didn't really matter. Fact was, he was not going to succumb to temptation and mess with those locks.

He might believe Reina could help him manipulate Death, but trusting her for the kinds of things a woman and a man did together? No chance. No female got that kind of trust from him.

She set her hands on her hips, and he saw her summon strength and drop the worried, vulnerable look that had been making him get a little weird. Instead was a determined, thoughtful expression that bespoke a relentless drive to fulfill her mission. "I don't suppose either of you know someone willing to ante up three billion dollars and a victim for an assassination festival this weekend, do you?" Her tone indicated that she was expecting a resounding no.

Jarvis grinned. *And now the bait gets dropped.* "As a matter of fact, I do."

"You do?" She looked so startled he almost laughed out loud. "You must have misunderstood. I meant—"

"I know what you meant," he interrupted. "You need someone willing to fork over big bones in return for the harvesting of someone's soul. I can give you the target and the payor."

She blinked. "But—"

Damn, this was fun. "And Augustus?" He folded his arms over his chest and had to work to keep the smugness out of his tone. "You did a smashing job killing him. You need help with that too?"

"You were eavesdropping?"

"Of course. It's the best way to figure out how to manipulate you."

Reina's eyes narrowed. "You're going to manipulate me?"

"Yeah." He waited. Just because it was such a pleasure to be in charge of a woman. It was a new experience, and he was going to milk it for everything it was worth. A once in a lifetime opportunity would not go unappreciated.

She flicked her hand at him impatiently. "Well, go on. Fill me in."

"You help me, I help you."

She was already shaking her head. "I don't have time to help you. I have issues that I—"

"Jarvis could deliver for you, you know." Nigel flipped to a new page in his sketchbook. "You might want to rethink your hasty dismissal of his offer." He checked the sun and then moved to his right several feet before starting to draw again. "Jarvis isn't real friendly with women, so if you've got a chance to get his help, you might want to take him up on it before he returns to his usual, sullen, woman-hating self."

She glanced toward the gilded front window of Scrumptious before giving Jarvis a wary look. "What do you want?"

He grinned and almost started rubbing his hands together. Looked like he was going to have to buy Nigel
a drink after this for his assistance. Nigel might be as
anti-female as he was, but he sure knew how to manipulate them with a few well-chosen words. Nigel had a
finesse none of the rest of them had bothered to acquire.
Why waste the effort? Nigel could do it for them if it
was required. "Death took my brother," he told Reina.
"I need to take him back."

Reina shoved her bangs off her face, her movement
restless and agitated. "I'm kind of on thin ice with him
right now. I can't really risk my position."

"Fine." He wasn't going waste time begging. He had
her where he wanted her and she'd figure it out sooner
if he just left her to work it out.

Jarvis headed toward the cross street where his car
was parked. He'd already made it to the corner when
Reina finally spoke up. "Wait."

He looked back over his shoulder. "Yeah?"

"You really know someone? You'll help me with
Augustus?" She sounded so doubtful it pissed him off.

"Hey." He strode back across the bricks toward her.
"I don't make many promises, but when I make them,
I keep them. Hell, yeah, I'll help you. What kind of
question is that?"

She jerked backward, and he realized suddenly that
he was reaching for her, ready to grab her.

Shit. He dropped his hand. The last thing he needed
was to taint her up by touching her and infecting her
with his hate. Jesus. He was getting edgy. One comment
questioning his moral integrity had set him off? What
did he care what she thought of him, or whether she

understood exactly how good he was at what he did? Since when did a woman's opinion matter to him? It didn't. But for some reason, one flicker of doubt from Reina felt like a full assault to his manhood. He needed her to realize how great he was, and that was seriously messed up. Reina was getting to him in a way he couldn't afford.

"Jarvis?" Reina was looking at him warily, and he felt something twitch inside him. Something he didn't like.

Hell, he was outta here. He had to go find a fight. Sparring practice. Anything to bleed off the negative energy amassing inside him.

Jarvis turned sharply and headed straight for his car. He had to get away before he went over the edge. The hate was building, the monster was coming, and being around Reina was stripping his self-control. He needed to get out of there, and now.

He was nearly sprinting by the time he reached the corner.

———

"Questioning a warrior's abilities isn't always a wise thing." Nigel offered the unsolicited advice to Reina as she watched Jarvis heading away from her. "We tend to get offended. Might want to rethink that approach."

Jarvis was leaving. It was a relief, but at the same time, she felt like a piece of hope had just been ripped out of her heart. She took a step in the direction Jarvis had gone. He was dangerous and unpredictable, and he wanted her to risk her job in a way she absolutely couldn't afford, but he'd said he could help. Could he really? Would the payback destroy her dreams, or was he her chance to succeed? He was powerful enough to do it. She knew he was. But was she strong enough to survive him? "Do you know who he's talking about? The people who would pay for a soul harvesting?"

Nigel didn't look up from his sketching. "I have an idea."

"So, you help me." She gave her full attention to Nigel. He was a lethal warrior, but he didn't scare her like Jarvis did, despite his leather pants and impressive muscles. Maybe it was the pale pink rose tattooed beneath his cheekbone. Maybe it was because Nigel's obsession with his art gave the illusion of him being in control. Either way, Nigel didn't unsettle her the way Jarvis did, so working with him would be so much smarter. Granted, Nigel didn't compel her either, but that was good, right? She had no time for compelling men. "Will you? Please?"

His pen kept flying across the page. "Nope."

She fisted her hands in frustration at his careless dismissal. Didn't he understand how important this was? "But why not? He left. I'm sure he doesn't want to—"

Nigel tapped his pen against his tattoo and studied her. "It's like how you don't date your buddy's ex. He made the offer. You're his property now."

"What?" She was horrified, but at the same time a thrill of excitement went through her. "I don't belong to anyone. I just want to save my sister. Jarvis—"

Nigel gave her an interested look when she cut herself off. "Jarvis what?"

"Scares me," she admitted.

He nodded. "Smart girl. He should." He leaned the pad against his chest and studied her. "But what should scare you more is what will happen if you don't help him. Forget what he can do for you. If you don't help Jarvis, nothing else will matter. *Nothing*."

A chill rippled over her, and she rubbed her arms. A warrior of such strength needed *her*? It scared her to think of Jarvis facing something so dangerous he couldn't defeat it himself, but at the same time, to think that *she* could help him… it was empowering. A gift. Exactly the thing she'd strived for and failed at with every member of her family. She'd tried to help. She'd failed them. Could she really make a difference with Jarvis? "What do you mean?"

"He's a good man." Nigel's face grew deadly serious. "Honorable. Without him, many of us would have died long ago." He leaned forward. "He honors you by asking for your help and offering you his assistance. You should get down on your knees and bow to him. He's that fucking good." A blade suddenly appeared in Nigel's hand. "I will not let anyone betray him," he said. "Ever."

Reina stiffened at Nigel's intensity. Where was the easygoing art guy? "I wasn't going to betray him. I just—"

Nigel looked down at the blade. Surprise flashed across his face, then he closed his hand and the knife disappeared, as if it had never been there. But they both knew it had. "He's leaving." Nigel pointed his pen down the street. "You're losing your chance to team up with the best fucking warrior alive."

Jarvis was pulling up to the intersection in a black Escalade. Leaving. Right now. She had no time to process or evaluate! How could she possibly agree to a deal she didn't even know the terms of? "I don't—"

Jarvis revved the engine and began to drive away.

Nigel grabbed her arm. "Go to him. *Now*." Then he shoved her in Jarvis's direction.

Damn all men! Make her an offer she couldn't afford to refuse, with terms she couldn't afford to accept, and then give her zero time to decide, look for other options, or to have some other sane kind of response. Decision made under duress, anyone?

Duress or not, she knew she couldn't risk losing her one chance. Her choice had been made. She ran, and Nigel saluted her with a pleased grin.

She didn't bother to respond. She just hauled ass down the street, praying she would make it before it was too late.

He was just pulling out when Reina leapt out in front of his truck and slammed her hands down on the hood. As she knew he would, he jammed on the brakes in time to avoid crushing her, then he gestured for her to get off his SUV.

"I accept your offer," she shouted.

Jarvis checked the rearview mirror, then shifted into reverse. What? He was bailing on her? She raced around to the side and yanked open the passenger door. "Wait—"

"Back off." He shifted back into drive.

He was actually going to take off without her? Fat chance of that! She grabbed the door handle and swung herself into the truck just as he peeled out into the street.

He stopped the vehicle. "Get out."

She wedged her body into the plush leather seat. "No. You made an offer and I accepted it."

"It's rescinded."

"Why?" She slammed the door shut, grabbed the seat

belt, and snapped it closed. She must be losing her mind. Locking herself in a car with a man who terrified her? Brilliant move, truly brilliant. But at the same time, it felt good to stand up for herself, to grab onto hope and refuse to let go. She hadn't had real hope in a long time, and the idea of Jarvis adding his resources to her battle was desperately appealing.

Jarvis took his sunglasses off the glistening dash and slapped them onto his face. "Out."

"Why? You need my help—"

"You were a poor choice." The air inside the truck was getting heavy and thick, like it was a hot humid August day, but it was May and only fifty degrees.

She rolled down the window. "If you want help with Death, I'm your only choice." Okay, twilight zone moment here. What was up with *her* trying to convince Mr. Scary Guy to help her after he'd offered and she'd said no?

"We always have more than one choice." His voice was low. "If you open your mind, there are always an infinity of possibilities."

"Not for me." She touched his arm, and he jerked away from her, nearly crawling out the window. Wow. Talk about a one-eighty. Last time he hadn't moved away at all. Had she developed some horrific communicable disease in the last three minutes? "You said you could help. I don't have any other choices. You think I want to work with you and risk my boss's ire? If I had any other options I would!"

Slowly, he turned his head to look at her. She couldn't see his eyes behind his shades, but she still shivered. His jaw was rigid, and there was a lethal energy rolling off him. With deliberate slowness, he pulled his sunglasses off his face.

His blue eyes were now a bottomless, dangerous black. "Run."

Oh, three cheers and a toast to that idea. Unfortunately, despite what he claimed, a girl didn't always have access to an unlimited plethora of fantastic choices. "I can't. I need your help."

"You endanger me. And yourself."

His voice had an edge that would scare even the toughest badass on the planet. And in case anyone was confused about the facts, she was not tough. She was a softy who just wanted the people she loved to be safe. That was it. Nothing more. "How could I possibly endanger you?"

He made a snarling noise and leaned toward her so quickly she didn't have time to get away. His face was an inch from hers, so close she could smell the most delicious scent of woods and man, and she could see the muscle ticking in his jaw. The heaviness of his energy pressed at her, making her skin hot and clammy.

"I don't react well to you," he gritted out. "You edge my control."

"What did I do?" She leaned back further, aware of his chest so close to hers. Of the width of his shoulders boxing out all the space in the front seat, trapping her, stealing her air. The door dug into her shoulders. All she had to do was pull the handle and slide away.

But she couldn't. She needed him. Saving her sister was more important than hiding from him. And plus… there was something about him crowding her that felt good. Which was insane, of course. Except she knew it wasn't. He might be stalked by hell itself, he might demand that which she couldn't afford to give, but he'd already had chances to hurt her, and he hadn't. He'd saved her, and no woman in her right mind would fail to think that was an appealing trait in a male.

"I don't know why you unsettle me," he gritted out. "But I can't afford to go over the line right now." He shook his head once as if to clear it. "You. Must. Leave."

There was torment in his eyes. Lines of pain around his mouth. Tension in the cords of his neck. And suddenly he didn't seem like a monster anymore. He seemed like a man in agony. "Jarvis." Before she could think about the fact that it was one of the less intelligent moves she could make, she laid her hand on his cheek. "I'm sorry for your pain."

He sucked in his breath, and she thought he was going to jerk away, but he didn't.

He went still under her touch. His gaze was riveted to hers, and she saw the shock on his face.

His skin was hot, as if he were burning up from fever. She moved her hand to his forehead. "Are you sick?"

He closed his eyes and leaned into her touch. "Your hand is so cool," he whispered, disbelief raw in his voice.

A man who was shocked by the comfort of human touch? Well, not that she was entirely human anymore, but close enough. She put her other hand on his cheek, not afraid of him anymore. Just wanting to ease his pain, as she'd done repeatedly over the years for her sisters and mother, as they got sicker and more terrified of their future.

Until, of course, they reached that nefarious end, turned into advertisements for GNC health food centers, and lost their ability to feel anything but an über-high.

At which point, Reina's loving support had become unwelcome and annoying.

But Jarvis needed to be touched. She could sense it in every fiber of her soul, and her spirit yearned to give him comfort. She framed his bristly face with her hands and rested her forehead against his. The position, with his face against hers, was so intimate, a connection between lovers, between soul mates who had no boundaries between them. She felt the world go still, like all the hell chasing her faded, until all that was left was the sensation of his skin against hers, of his presence wrapping around hers, of her own reaching out for him.

It was a moment of utter stillness, of peace, of having the most intimate connection with a tortured man who could protect her against the world. His skin was still burning up, but it seemed to be slightly less likely to give her third-degree burns. She was easing his pain, or maybe she simply wanted to believe she could give *someone* relief from the hell that stalked him, after a lifetime of failing to succeed to save anyone. It didn't matter whether it was real or not. In this moment, it was a gift of peace that she would never let go. "This feels good," she whispered. "I—"

"Shit!" Jarvis jerked back suddenly, out of her grasp. His hand went to his sword, and before she'd even moved, he had the tip of it at her throat.

Well, excellent. That was exactly the feel-good kind of feedback she'd been jonesing for.

Chapter 7

JARVIS HELD THE SWORD STEADY, WAITING FOR REINA TO descend into the hell-o-hate and decide that he had to be castrated, disemboweled, and other fun stuff. He'd gone skin to skin with her for several minutes, when the hate had been so thick in him he'd barely been able to see. Her mind would snap within moments. He shouldn't have touched her. He knew better.

But when she'd laid her palm against him, he'd literally lost his mind for a minute. Her caress had felt so good, and she'd simply wiped the monster away. The relief had been instant. He'd been so shocked by the sensation he'd been unable to force himself to pull away in time.

"What's with the sword?" Her eyes were still a rich blue, her cheeks still a healthy pink. Her mouth hadn't compressed into that thin line of aggression, and her hands were palm out, in a gesture of "I'm not going to hurt you, please don't slice my head off."

Not that he was buying it. Some women were very, very good at hiding their intentions until the barb ice pick was already lodged in assorted soft tissues. But hell, she sure looked normal. "How do you feel?"

"Unappreciated."

He lowered the tip a fraction. Made no sense, but he wasn't feeling any aggressive vibe from her. Just that same sense of peace and warmth he'd been getting from her, tempered with a shiver of wariness. But no aggression. Was it really possible? No, it wasn't. It couldn't be. There were no miracles for men like him. "What else are you feeling? Cranky? A little violent?"

"No, just confused. It's not every day a man goes through as many personality changes as you have in the last ten minutes." She cocked her head. "Is it that time of the month for you?"

She was teasing him? Yeah, it was the desperate humor that emerged when you're scared shitless, but not the kind of jokes chicks made right before they went for his jugular. He leaned closer and passed his hand just above her heart. Warmth beat from her skin, not coldness, no tingle of black magic. "You're not feeling angry toward me?"

"Angry?" Her gaze flicked down toward the blade again. "Um, no. I must admit, though, I'm not feeling quite as warm and fuzzy as I was a few minutes ago."

"Ah! I knew it." He raised the blade again, feeling smug that he'd been right. But there was also an unfamiliar prick of disappointment in his gut. For that split second, he'd started to think that he could actually touch her, that she could touch him, and he'd be damned if that hadn't sounded like a hell of a good idea. It wasn't something he'd ever considered, or even bothered to want, but that one second of thinking he'd found it only to realize he hadn't... Not that it mattered. It was better that way. He liked his life just fine. "The hate will fade as soon as you get away from me," he told her, repeating the same instructions he'd given so many women over the decades. "Just get out of the car and—"

"Oh, so now you're invalidating my emotions?"

He blinked. "Invalidating your emotions? Shit, woman, I'm *Hate*. It's not an emotion. I'm a fucking curse."

"You think I'll stop being annoyed you pulled a sword on me if I leave? That I'm not capable of generating my own aggravation? That the only way I could dislike you is if you messed me up?"

She should be insane by now. Attacking him. He didn't understand why she was psychobabbling to him instead of stabbing him. "What are you talking about?"

"I'm trying to tell you that my emotions don't work that way, and you can't simply dismiss them. You have to apologize, express your appreciation for who I am, and put the sword away. That's how it works between adults." She eyed him. "Or are you going to kill me? Because if you are, then I might take your advice and leave you alone."

"I don't engage in first strikes against women," he snapped before he could think to take advantage of the opportunity to lie and give her a reason to remove herself from his presence. He narrowed his eyes, trying to figure her out. Why wasn't she going AWOL on him? "I'm merely going to keep you from attacking me."

She made a small noise of aggravation. "Why would I do that?"

"Because you hate me." What part of the Guardian of Hate did she not comprehend?

She stared at him, then burst out laughing.

Laughing.

He was too stunned to react. He couldn't understand it. How could she be laughing? Violent aggression he was ready for. Delighted, whimsical laughing was beyond his ability to process. He hadn't heard genuine, innocent, female laughter in his whole life. And it sounded *good*. God, it sounded good.

"Jarvis, you have a serious complex. I mean, yes, holding me at sword-point isn't endearing you to me, but why would I hate you? I'm not like that." Her eyes were dancing with amusement, but there was a sadness in her expression that made him uncomfortable. "I've never met anyone worth hating. Sure wish I could manage it, because it would make my assassination attempts a lot easier if I could hate the person I was trying to kill, but it's just not my thing."

She laughed again, and he felt the honesty in her voice and her tone. There wasn't anything dark festering inside her. She really wasn't going to the dark side, even though she'd fondled him for well over a minute.

The woman was immune to him. He couldn't shake her. Couldn't contaminate her. Couldn't tap into a dark side that she didn't even know she carried. *Holy crap*.

Cautiously, he lowered his sword, still waiting for the sudden shift that would take her from woman to a double X assailant. Not quite trusting it to be true. That there was a woman, a passionate, loyal, courageous woman he could touch. He had to be wrong. He had to be.

But all he saw was a look of relief in her eyes as he sheathed his blade. No flare of excitement as she took advantage of the opening and leapt at him. She simply relaxed in her seat.

He didn't get it. She'd eased his hate, and she hadn't been rocked by such close contact with him. Yeah, his evil twin was still swirling inside him, but her touch had taken the edge off enough to give him his control back. How? And why hadn't she been brought down?

If her touch could keep the monster at bay, then maybe he could afford to be in the same room as her after all. For the mission, of course. It was strictly professional. "Okay," he said. "Here's the deal. I'll work with you as long as you promise not to piss me off." Regardless of what her touch did, if she eroded his self-control by taunting him, even accidentally, they would all be screwed.

But the feisty female was already shaking her head. "I can't promise that, and why would I?"

"Because if you piss me off, I can't promise not to kill you." And the rest of the world.

She cocked her head with sudden understanding. "You really do have a monster inside you." It wasn't a question. It was more of a statement of "oh, well, that explains everything."

"No monster. Just me." As fantastic as it would be to be able to attribute his dark side to the external application of evil juice, he was hate. Why else would he be the Guardian of it? It was a match made in heaven.

She nodded. "Okay, I'll try not to aggravate your inner alien. I'm actually glad to know it's not *you* that's the scary one, just some demon-like predator roaming inside your body."

He scowled, and he felt darkness bubbling around inside him again. The beast didn't like to be argued with now? Fantastic. It was bad enough to be the Hate Hotel. But having it become overly sensitive was just not adding fun to the game. "*I* am the monster."

"Okay, fine. Whatever you say." She reached over and patted his cheek, and he caught her hand and pressed it to his face. Her skin was warm, her touch gentle. He'd never been touched in kindness before, and it felt amazing. He took a breath, letting the feel of her skin fill him. And just as before, the sharp edge smoothed, and he was able to take a breath, as if an anvil had been shifted off his chest.

She smiled. "I like that."

He forced himself to release her hand, not daring to hold it any longer, but all his instincts were screaming at him to hang on, because this moment might never happen again. It was most likely an aberration, a heartbeat in the wind, a hiccup in his hell. "What do you like?"

"Giving you peace."

Yeah, understatement of the year. He could sit there with her hand on his jowls for the rest of his life and never move again. Which was just weird. He'd never been able to sit still for anything, but Reina's touch made something inside him quiet. Which was good. He could focus again, and that was what he needed for this mission.

He started the engine again. "Don't get too comfortable. It's not going to last." A reminder for both of them.

She ignored his warning as he shifted into gear. "So, we have a deal? You help me?"

"And you help me."

She bit her lip and looked at him. "As long as it doesn't endanger my sister."

He pulled out into traffic, dodging an aggressive cab driver. "That's fine. I don't care about your sister."

Her face became shuttered, and she looked out the window. "Well, I do."

"Well, hell. I didn't mean it like that. I just meant I had no interest in endangering her."

She shrugged. "I know. It's fine."

But it wasn't. He could see she was almost ready to cry. *Hit a woman while she's down, why don't you, big guy?* Hadn't he just listened to that whole conversation with her sister? He knew what was up and he'd still made a callous remark. Crap. Hadn't he learned a damn thing in Sensitivity Training for Warriors 231? He knew better, and he'd still blown it.

He swore under his breath as he swerved around a double parked Mercedes. What was he supposed to do now? He'd been taught to give flowers and foot massages when he was an insensitive boor, but he was pretty sure if he offered to lube up Reina's feet, it wouldn't go over all that well, though the idea did hold some appeal…

How was he supposed to team up with a female? A team was only as good as the partnership. He knew how to insult Nigel into putting the sketch book away. He knew how to threaten Blaine into healing himself from the edge of death. He was fantastic at interpreting Christian's grunts. And he was great at sparring with any of his teammates to let off steam and get each other fired up.

But he had no clue how to make a female better, stronger, and tougher. What was he supposed to do about the weepy look on her face? Was he supposed to punch her in the shoulder? Make a joke about getting her balls hacked off by Angelica? Give her crap about how Angelica was winning in her desire to make a bunch of blade-wielding saps out of them all?

That'd work for the guys. But Reina—

Jarvis looked over at her and saw that the V-neck collar of her shirt had slipped to the side, revealing the edge of a black lace bra. She was wearing a gold chain so delicate he knew he'd break it if he so much as breathed on it. From the links dangled a jade pendant that nestled softly between her breasts.

The recently neglected part of his body that always reminded him he was a man, despite years of Flower Arranging 101 or Advanced French Braiding, twitched and then stiffened.

Ah, hell. This partnership was never going to work.

Because he knew only how to team up with men. Women were enemies, always the ones to distrust. He didn't know how to work with one. Screw it. He was finding another way to access Death. He would—

Reina looked over at him and smiled, making those rosy lips of hers curve up in a way that made him want to yank her right onto his lap and see how long he could kiss her before she hated him. "I'm glad you're helping me," she said with an earnestness that made him shift in his seat. "Without you, I know my sister would be dead in another day or two. With you on my team..." She gave him hopeful, tremulous smile. "For the first time, I feel like I have a legitimate chance to save her. So, thank you."

Bloody hell.

Angelica had Pavloved him and the other men into being useless when a woman looked at him that way.

He was stuck with her, wasn't he? He looked down at his palm. Five stars were there now. Ten minutes of being around her and more stars had appeared.

Best guess? They had less than twenty-four hours to save his brother, the world, Love, and her sister, or they were all dead.

And not in a good way.

———〜〜〜———

Reina couldn't help it.

Ridiculous, she knew.

But she couldn't stop herself from wanting to touch Jarvis again. She'd made a difference to him, if only for a moment, and she wanted more of it.

Jarvis looked over his shoulder to change lanes, and she tapped the back of his wrist with her index finger. He jumped. "You need to stop that."

"Why? Doesn't it feel good?" Because it felt amazing to her.

"Yeah." Jarvis was silent for a moment, and then he seemed to make a decision. He swung the truck off the street and peeled into the woods beside the road.

"Where are we going?" Reina grabbed the armrest as they bounced over the rough ground, driving farther and farther away from circulation. From people. From escape. Hmm... suddenly she was remembering with vivid clarity her prior concerns about the monster within. Was she really feeling warm and snuggly enough to head off into a secluded area with the man who sported eyes of bottomless pits of hell?

"I need to show you something." He finally stopped the truck deep in the woods. No houses. No people. No one to come to the aid of a maiden in distress. "Come on." Jarvis slammed the truck into park, then got out and threw the door shut behind him.

The keys were still in the ignition. She could leave if she wanted to. Did he scare her that much? Yes, of course... and then she thought of the anguish in his face and the way his whole body had shuddered with relief when she'd laid her hand on his cheek. She recalled his tormented expression as he fought down the beast that haunted him, and she felt her heart soften.

The answer was no. Jarvis Swain no longer terrified her. He was a man in pain, and she could help him. So she opened the door and joined him amidst the isolation of pine trees and shrubbery.

He was standing silently, his sword at his side, surveying the surrounding forest. His brown hair was wafting slightly in the faint breeze, and his muscles were flexing in his sword arm, as if he were preparing for battle. "Hear that?"

All she heard was the rustle of leaves, the chatter of squirrels, the creak of branches. Forest sounds. Sounds of comfort, but instead of feeling a peace, goose bumps popped up on her arms. "What am I listening for?"

"The birds."

There were only a few chirps and tweets, not as many as she'd expect. And then even those quieted. The squirrels went silent, and even the trees became still, as if they'd gone into hiding, just like the men on Newbury Street. Had it been Jarvis who had driven everyone away before, not Augustus? "Is that because of you?"

"Yep." He raised his sword and began whipping it in a circle over his head. The air began to thicken, and she heard a loud humming.

Her hair began to blow in a sudden, unnatural wind. The sadness in her heart began to lift for the first time in years, as if the sun had come out inside her soul. The leaves became more verdant, the flowers became brighter, and the birds began to sing, louder and louder, as if the entire world was feeling the same glorious relief she was, as if a mantle of doom that she hadn't even noticed had suddenly been lifted.

Then Jarvis hurled his sword. It cut through the air with a shriek, the blade glistening as it raced in and out of the shadows. It slammed into the trunk of a huge oak tree, the blade sinking almost to the hilt.

Jarvis turned toward her, and his eyes were blue again. Not as pale as the first time she'd met him, but definitely blue. No longer black. It made him look human, handsome, and alive, and she relaxed.

He bowed deeply. "The Guardian of Hate, at your service."

She frowned. "The Guardian of Hate? What does that mean?"

"It means I'm the only thing between a world of peace and a land where everything and everybody destroys each other. I just pulled the hate out of myself and my environment, which includes you. How do you feel?"

"Better," she admitted. "My heart feels lighter." Her relief at the happy feeling in her heart began to fade, replaced by the dull thump of trepidation. Why did she suspect they weren't heading toward a blissful conclusion to this experiment?

"I put the negative energy from you and the immediate vicinity into the sword, and then into the oak." He nodded at the tree. "Watch. This is what the world becomes without me in it, or if I lose my ability to contain the hate."

A small, black circle was surrounding the blade, as

if the tree had created a target around it. The bark was decomposing, and she could smell the rotted contamination stripping the tree of its vitality. "What's happening to the tree?"

"Just wait."

The circle grew larger and larger, like an insidious black plague that had taken root in the trunk. There was a high-pitched wail, as if the plant was screaming in agony, and then the leaves turned brown and shriveled. They wafted gently to the ground, crumbling as they fell. "Did you do that?"

"Yeah. I'm poison." The ground turned black, and then the taint began to creep across the soil toward them. Saplings shriveled, ferns crumbled, bugs took to the air with a frantic buzzing. Faster and faster it spread, gaining speed, destroying everything in its path. "Oh, *shit*," he muttered. "I need to stop that." He grabbed her around the waist and tossed her easily on top of the car. "Don't get off, no matter what!" he ordered.

"But—"

He sprinted across the clearing and grabbed the sword. The moment his hands touched the handle, his whole body went rigid. Smoke began to rise from his palms.

"Jarvis!"

"Stay there!" He jerked the sword out of the tree and plunged it into the soil. The blade glowed, and a horrific grating noise ripped through the air. The sun seemed to disappear, dark shadows crept off the tainted soil and up his legs, like the demons of hell were sucking him into the earth. She realized he was harvesting the hate out of the earth and back into his body, and it was killing him.

"Jarvis!" She leapt off the truck. The moment her feet hit the ground, she felt like fire was burning through the souls of her feet.

"Stay back!" He shoved his sword deeper into the earth, his whole body trembling.

She fought across the ground, but it was draining her dry. Her body was aching and screaming, agony was bleeding at her head. Her chest constricted until she couldn't walk anymore. Until her body wouldn't work. She fell to her hands and knees. "Jarvis!"

He let out a loud battle cry and ripped his sword out of the ground. There was a keening scream, as if he'd broken the earth in half, and then all the torment vanished from her body. Immediate and complete release.

Jarvis braced his hands on the ground, his skin mottled with black just like the soil had been. He'd stripped the hate out of the earth and put it in himself, poisoning himself to save everything else. "Jarvis!" She leapt to her feet and ran toward him.

His eyes were demon black now, and his face was twisted with anguish. "Don't touch me," he rasped out. "I can't contain it—" He caught her as she fell into him. "Reina, I'll destroy you if I touch you—"

"Oh, God." He was on fire! Okay, yeah. Wrong decision to ignore his warning to stay away! She struggled to get out, but his arms closed around her, crushing her against him.

"Holy shit," he gasped.

Her skin was burning, her body screaming to get away. "Let me go!"

"I can't." He grabbed her hair and yanked her head back. "We're fucked."

And then he kissed her.

Chapter 8

THE MOMENT HIS LIPS TOUCHED REINA'S, JARVIS KNEW HE had to have her. Had to take her. Not for relief. To destroy her. It was the beast talking, acting, taking her. Not him. But he didn't care. Didn't want to stop. Because he wanted her, too. Any way he could get her.

She fought against him, and the monster inside him grinned. The hate would come alive inside her. It always came. It was time for hate to win, for the world to succumb to the way life should be.

Reina suddenly stopped struggling. She flung her arms around him and began to kiss him back.

The kiss froze Jarvis. Her lips were cool like the soothing balm of the waterfall behind the cabin he'd grown up in, and the turmoil inside him began to quiet almost immediately. He became aware of her hands in his hair, of her fingers rubbing gently along the back of his neck.

He focused on her touch, on her kiss, on the sensation of her lips moving against his, using her existence as a map to find his way back to sanity, to control. He concentrated on the feel of her breasts pressed up against his chest. On how cool her body felt against his. He breathed in the taste of her.

She felt amazing. The way she was kissing him back: no desperation, no anger, just pure, unabashed passion. No one had ever kissed him like that, not for this long. It always turned dark and hateful within seconds. But her kiss was still untainted, still clean, and it felt magnificent. She was chasing the monster away. As he began to find his way back, as he reclaimed control of his body, he softened his grip on her hair and cupped her head, angling for better access, kissing her now because he wanted to, because it felt like someone had wrapped him up in angels and music.

Her lips parted beneath his, and he groaned as he brushed the tip of his tongue over hers. She tasted like strawberries and woman, like the warm sunshine when it heated him after a grueling torture session. He tightened his grip on her, and then she made a small noise of discomfort.

He immediately pulled back and searched her face. Regret pulsed through, guilt that he had risked her by kissing her for so long. There had to be limits to what she could withstand from him. "How are you?"

Her cheeks were flushed, but her eyes were bright blue. Not murky and tormented. Her ponytail was askew, and stray locks dangled, making her look like a woman who'd been thoroughly kissed, not a crazy killer chick about to attack.

She blew a tangled tendril of hair away from her face. "There's a lot of different ways to answer that question, actually. What exactly are you referring to?"

He stroked her face, unable to believe her cheeky tone, the sparkle in her eye. She was a mirage, an illusion he'd created out of his own insanity. "How do you not hate me right now?"

"Hate you? I told you, I'm not a hater. Not my thing." She picked up a handful of brown dirt and let it trail through her fingers. "It's clean again." She looked behind him, and he knew what she would see. "The tree is healthy. Green leaves." She frowned at him, not with fear, but with the studious inspection of someone trying to figure him out.

He realized it was the first time she'd ever looked him without even a hint of wariness. Which was ironic given that he'd just lost his shit.

"Tell me what happened." She fingered a lock of her hair that was dangling loose, then she pulled out her ponytail holder and shook out her hair.

He forgot for a second what he was going to say, fascinated by the way the afternoon sun lit up the strands. "Your highlights are gold with a hint of copper. Reminds me of a fawn that used to live near our house, when it would dance in the field with its mother."

She went still, her fingers tangled in her hair. "What?"

"I had to learn colors in Art Appreciation," he muttered. What kind of sappy shit was that? What kind of warrior talked about fawns gallivanting?

Man up, Jarvis. He noticed his sword was lying on the ground several feet away. Hadn't even realized he'd dropped it? No wonder he was going the artsy-fartsy tenderfoot route. He picked it up and fisted it, focused on his badass weapon instead of highlights and hair texture.

She touched the blackened burn marks on his wrist. "It hurts you when you harvest hate like that, doesn't it?"

He watched the diseased spots fade beneath her touch. "I don't understand how you ease it."

"The hate?"

"Yeah."

"Is it gone?"

"No." He held out his palm to show her. There were so many stars now, they were too clustered to count. The tangle was about the size of a quarter. "Hate is taking over the host. It happens." Maybe it wasn't her fault it was happening so fast. How could she push him toward hate and pull him back at the same time? Maybe it was just his own desperate ride that was hauling his ass toward death and destruction, and she was slowing it down.

She touched the stars, and his hand tingled from her touch. "What do you mean?"

He closed his fist. "The Guardian lasts only for so long before hate destroys him. Most Guardians explode after about fifty years."

"Explode?" Wariness was back in her face, and he didn't like it. He wanted that trust again. It had felt good, dammit.

"How long has it been for you?" she asked.

"One hundred and fifty-five years."

Her skin paled. "So, you're going to die soon?"

"Explode. Yeah."

"Dammit!" Reina immediately pulled her hand back.

The moment she broke contact, it was like a dark cloud descended on him, and he recognized it as the way he always felt. He'd never noticed that he lived with that pall shrouding his existence, not until this moment, when it came back after having given him the first respite of his life.

The miasma of doom felt suffocating, and he wanted to leap to his feet and slash it with his sword until it dissolved. He wanted that lightness back that Reina had given him. He began to reach for her, then he saw her stricken expression, and he forced his hand to drop to his side.

"What is with me attracting people who are going to die? I mean, come on! Are you serious?" She stood up, grabbed her hair, and twisted it into a slightly frantic bun. "That seals it. After I save my sister, I'm going to do some serious work on my karma to figure out what's wrong with me."

He rolled to his feet and slid his sword into his scabbard, grinding his teeth with the effort of keeping himself from seeking her comfort and her touch. "It's not you. It's me. I'm the one with the problem."

"No, it's me. I bring people who die into my life." She released the bun, and it immediately fell down. "Dammit." She started twisting it again. "I'm sorry, Jarvis, but I can't give you my heart anymore."

"Your heart?" His hand shot to the handle of his sword. "I don't want your heart!" Mother of God! Since when had hearts been a part of this deal? He was just talking about a feel-good kiss!

"Oh, come on." She gave her hair an extra twist, wrapped her elastic around it, and then released it. "You're such a guy! Don't freak out. I didn't mean it *that* way." Her hair began to slide free again. "I'm not in love with you, but I'm the kind of person who opens my heart to people. Anyone who comes into my life. But I have to take it back with you. I can't do this again. I really can't." She touched his arm as her hair tumbled back down. "Please, don't take it personally, but I have to set limits, or I'm going to break. I don't have time to break right now, you know? I have too much to do."

He went still under her touch, afraid to dislodge her now that she'd finally reached out and he'd gotten what he wanted. The woman didn't love him, so that was cool. All was well. They understood each other, and it was copacetic. So, it was time to beef up his partner's emotional well-being. "Nothing's going to break you."

"Hah! I'm a woman. We fake it all the time. Didn't you know that?" She twisted her hair up again, but when she released it, it all fell free again. "God! I can't even get my hair right! How am I supposed to save my sister, and now you, if I can't even get my hair out of my face?"

"I don't need to be saved. Just my brother." He noticed that her hands were shaking violently. No wonder she couldn't do her hair. His trip AWOL might not have given her a penchant for destruction, but he'd shaken her up. "Hey, it's going to be okay." He smoothed her hair back from her face. "I'll do your hair. Turn around."

She pushed his hand away, distracted and tense. "What? I don't need you to do my hair—"

"Yes, you do. A woman's self-esteem is often linked to how she feels about her hair, and I can help with that." He grasped her by the shoulders and turned her so her back was facing him, putting her in proper hair-styling position. "I aced Advanced Hair Styling and became a part-time instructor for the new kids on the block."

She looked back over her shoulder at him, clearly too surprised to argue. "You're a hair stylist?"

"No, I'm not a stylist," he snorted. "I can do hair. It's not the same thing."

As he started to reach for her hair, he had a fleeting thought of what the other guys would say if they saw him doing hair. There would be extensive ridicule and substantial derision. He paused. But if it helped with his mission, that was still manly, right? War was always manly, and it testosteronized any wimpy actions like hair styling or emotional analysis.

So there. He rubbed his hands and looked around for a proper set-up. No chairs, but the nearby stump would put her at just about the right angle for him to maximize his talents. He gestured to the wood, as he took her elbow and guided her across the mossy ground. "Sit."

For a moment, she didn't move, confusion marring her lovely features. Then she sat, putting herself at his mercy.

He couldn't quiet his anticipation as he took his position behind the glorious auburn tresses cascading over her shoulders. Right now, this moment, was almost worth the torture he'd gone through at Angelica's hands.

And when he sank his hands into her magnificent tresses and felt the silken strands glide through his fingers, he knew this moment hadn't made the torture *almost* worth it.

It had definitely been worth it.

Reina was still trembling when Jarvis scooped her hair off the nape of her neck. His touch was gentle and tender, almost a caress. His fingers were warm, like he was burning with the fire of a man who could bring down the world, but his touch was so light and delicate. An oxymoron. A decadent delight.

He ran his fingers through her hair, combing the strands by hand. A light tug as he snagged a tangle, then soothing gentleness when he carefully unwove it. His touch was of infinite patience, of the most delicate precision, of luxurious pampering.

She closed her eyes as a shudder rippled over her. A tremor of release, a relaxing of tension and fear, a gift of soothing.

Then she noticed the crumbled remains of the incinerated leaves blowing across the ground, the carnage from Jarvis's demonstration. Oh, right. He was going to *die*. How could she forget that?

She hugged herself, feeling a chill that wasn't in the air. "So, what exactly happens when you do the fireworks imitation?" Maybe she'd misunderstood. Maybe exploding wasn't as bad as she thought.

"The hate spills out all over everything. Kind of like a nuclear plant blowing up, from what I hear." His fingers stroked over the sides of her head, smoothing the bumps, untangling the ends with his fingers. So gently. So tender.

She wanted to turn around, throw herself into his arms, and let him consume her. Touch her as if she were a princess, protect her with his ferocity, and to clear all the hell out of her life. Excitement pulsed through her at the idea, and desire rushed to her lower body at the thought of losing herself in him.

But she couldn't do it. She wouldn't do that to herself. He was *dying*.

The insects were beginning to return to the land that had been DOA just a moment ago. She watched a yellow jacket circle cautiously over a flower, as if uncertain whether it would fry his little legs if he landed on it. "So, the nuclear explosion of hate would be bad." She unclenched her hands that were tucked in her lap, then asked the questions she always asked, the one she'd had yet to make happen in her own life. "Is there any way to save you? And the world?"

"Me, no."

Of course not. That would be too easy to have there actually be a way to save him. Evading Death couldn't be easy just once, could it? "What about the world?"

"The world, yes, if my energy can be transmuted." He shifted to her other side, lightly tugging through the snarls. "Love and hate are both emotions of hot passion, which means they generate heat energy. Energy cannot be created or destroyed, but it can be changed. You've heard of the fine line between love and hate, right? I'm the bad twin."

"That's not a very positive and self-affirming way to regard yourself." She turned to look at him. His eyes were dark blue, and he had an aura of contentment she hadn't sensed about him before. He almost looked human... Except, of course, for the dark streaks on his wrists disappearing under the sleeve of his leather jacket, and the black tangle on his palm.

His gaze went to her mouth.

She forgot what she was going to say. She suddenly could think only of the way he'd kissed her. Of that dark fury he'd begun with, of the aching need that had filled him at the end.

He lightly tugged her hair to force her to turn forward again. "If I'm near the Guardian of Love when I snap, he can harness the hate and hold it in abeyance until a new Guardian is tapped. If the Guardian of Love isn't there when I go, that's when things get ugly."

His fingers caught another tangle, and he deftly

cleared it. How many women's heads had he fondled to become so good at it? Oh… yeah… that wasn't a helpful thought. No need to start getting possessive over a man who was soon going to explode. "The Guardian of Love is your brother? That's who you need to get back from Death?"

"Yeah."

"Wow. Nigel wasn't kidding when he told me I needed to help you. Death will never want to release the Guardian of Love. He has a serious crush on Cupid." Yeesh. She couldn't afford to cross Death like that, at least not until her sister was saved. "How long until you—" She waved her hand, not quite wanting to put the ugly truth into words. "You know. Do your thing? A week or so?" That was all she needed. Just a week.

"I don't know. I've never exploded before."

Of course not. That would be too convenient if he had. She toed the dirt with her foot. "And I suppose everyone else who has exploded before you isn't willing to talk about it?"

He began to twist her hair, his hands smoothing her hair so effortlessly. "No. Weirdly enough, they don't seem to stick around."

"Decidedly thoughtless of them." The question of the day: How did a warrior manage to have velvet hands? It had always seemed a little oxymoronic to see burly Blaine sitting in his man-cave-chair with his cross-stitching. She'd never quite gotten why it made Trinity want to race across the room and leap into his lap.

But she understood now. There was something appealing about a really big, really tough, battle-scarred Guardian of Hate doing something so intimate and delicate. Her girly parts just wanted to sigh and fall into his lap.

"So, explain your situation." Jarvis's voice was deep, rough, so different from the way he twisted his fingers so delicately through her tangled strands.

And there went the snuggly feeling. "My sister is dying from a deedub bite." Tension shot through the left side of her neck. Her muscle cramped up from her ear right down to her shoulder.

He began to knead the knotted muscle. "Deedubs attacks are rare. How did she get bitten?"

"She's a Sweet. All my sisters and my mom are." She winced as he dug into the knot. "Sweets have a special affinity for all things chocolate related." Every superstar pastry chef, the founder of Hershey, the entire Swiss chocolate industry... all of them were Sweets. Great heritage if you want a biz in the dessert industry. Not so great if a deedub happened to get within sniffing distance, what with their chocolate addiction and the twisted mind that a thousand years in hell will do to a brain.

"I know what a Sweet is. Angelica tested a few deedubs on me once, but they wouldn't attack because I'm not a Sweet." He leaned forward and nuzzled her neck.

She froze at the feel of his warm breath on her skin. "What are you doing?"

"You don't smell like chocolate."

"I'm not a Sweet. I have a different father. My sisters' dad died before I was born, and my mom had a one-night stand with a chef from Hershey's. I was the result. Before the attack, I hated the fact that I wasn't a Sweet. My family were all such geniuses when it came to creating magic with chocolate, and I couldn't even tell the difference between Swiss and Belgian chocolate until I was six." Her mind flashed back to that night so many years ago. "But in the end, it saved my life. I was the only one he didn't want."

"Who didn't?"

"The deedub." And suddenly she was back at that moment. "We were sitting around the table, one of those rare nights when all seven of my sisters were actually home. There was a knock at the door." God, she still remembered the creak of the floorboard when her mom had opened it. "His eyes were glowing gold, his hair that bright red." Her mom had shouted a warning, that awful, awful warning that they'd never thought they'd hear for real. "Everyone ran for the trap door, the one that led to the safe room."

His hands stilled on her shoulders. "They didn't make it?"

"My mom... her scream when it bit her. I'd never heard such a sound of agony and disbelief. My sisters... me... we all froze... watching the blood run from her neck."

Jarvis began to stroke her hair.

She leaned into his touch, trying to use his caress to keep her from falling into the abyss of her memories. "And then he tossed aside his Yankees hat and howled. The sound was horrific. It broke us all out of stupor and we ran. My sisters for the trap door, me for the unicorn horn above the mantel. We kept it there in case of an attack, because they were supposed to be the most effective, you know?"

Jarvis continued to slide his hands through her hair.

"No unicorn horn is going to stop a deedub in a chocolate frenzy. You needed someone like me."

"Yeah, well, we didn't have you." How fast she'd run for the fireplace. "By the time I grabbed it, he'd bitten everyone except Natalie. I plunged it right into his chest. That was my job. To save them. We all knew it wouldn't go after me."

"Didn't work, did it?" His voice was quiet, almost regretful.

"No. He just grabbed me, sniffed me, and then threw me aside. I was still in the air when he attacked Natalie. I blacked out when I hit the wall, and when I woke up, he was gone, and everyone was down." Her whole family. Strewn over the floor like discarded Tootsie Roll wrappers. "And in the twenty years since, they've all died. One by one." Her neck muscle twitched again.

"Except Natalie." He pressed his thumb into her neck. "And you have a plan to save her?"

"Yes." She balled her hands into fists, refusing to think of the past. Only of the future. How this time was going to be different. This strong, powerful warrior was on her side now. "I'm going to switch her soul into the body of our friend Gina, but I have to become Reaper to be able to do it. But to get promoted I need to harvest Augustus's soul. You saw how that went. I can't even get the powder to work anymore—"

"Ease down, sweetheart." He laid his palms against her temples and pressed lightly. His tone was calm, and his utter lack of concern made some of her tension ease. "We'll figure out Augustus. I'm not worried."

This was a man who had survived hell for a hundred

and fifty years, and he'd revived from death a thousand times, or more. He knew how to win. And he was on her team now. She took a breath. "Okay."

"That's better." He cupped the curve of her shoulder, and warmth began to penetrate through her skin, loosening the knot. The heat from his hands made her feel like she was lying on a beach, letting the hot sun heal her soul. The heat of hate, she knew now. Didn't stop it from feeling wonderful.

"And my investors?" she asked. "And the target?"

"Taken care of with one visit after sundown tonight. Easy." He snapped his fingers. "Do you have an elastic?"

She handed him the pale pink band she'd selected this morning. She'd selected pink as a reminder that she was harvesting souls in the name of love, hoping that would help her get over her issues. Obviously, it had been a brilliant tactic.

He began to wrap the holder around her hair. Why did it feel so good to have a man's hands in her hair? Or was it just Jarvis?

He finished the bun and dropped his hands. "All set. Feel better?"

Reina touched her hair and was surprised to feel a complicated looping and twisting of her hair. She shook her head, and the updo stayed in. She smiled and realized she did indeed feel better. "Yeah, I do." Was it because of the hair? Or because he had spent the last five minutes giving her some seriously wonderful TLC?

He nodded with a smile of smug self-satisfaction. "Women always derive a lot of their self-confidence by how they feel about themselves physically. Hair's a big one." He tapped his temple. "The best partners learn what gets their teammates in a fighting state of mind. The hair seemed to be a good strategy for you." He tucked a stray tendril behind her ear, giving her hair the scrutinizing inspection an artist might give his masterpiece. "I hate to give Angelica credit for anything, but…" He shrugged and dropped his hand. "Seemed to work. I'll keep that in mind."

Keep it in mind? Did that mean he was going to do it again? Her stomach did a little jump of excitement. She got stressed all the time. Maybe he should take up residence in her hair and—

Hello! What was she doing thinking it was sexy that he not only knew how to do a woman's hair, but actually admitted it? She had no time for sexy, especially when it came to Jarvis. The man could destroy entire forests simply by breathing, and he'd literally brought her to her knees when she'd been burned by the earth he'd contaminated. As an added bonus, he wanted her to go against Death, when she couldn't afford to piss him off.

And on top of it all, the man was going to explode, sooner rather than later.

That was way more than three strikes.

No more sexy thinking about him. Business partners only.

Jarvis brushed a fleck of dirt off her shoulder, as if he couldn't quite keep himself from touching her. "First stop, the Castle of Extreme Opulence."

"Oh, no, let's take care of my things first." If she helped him and got caught by Death before she'd saved her sister, it would jeopardize everything. See? She was thinking clearly again. Go her.

But Jarvis shook his head. "We can't meet with my

investor until nightfall, so let's go find my brother and clear my shit up." He fisted his hand, the one with the black tangle on his palm. "I'd hate to explode before we had a chance to take care of your sister."

She bit her lip. "You think you could go soon?"

"Anytime, babe. I've never been down this road before." He turned and headed toward the truck. "Cameron might be able to give me more time."

She watched him stride across the clearing. "You want more time?"

"Hell, yeah. I'm free man now, sweetheart, and I want to enjoy it." He reached the Escalade and opened her door. "Your chariot, my dear."

Oh, come on! Like it wasn't bad enough that she liked him and he was going to explode, but he actually *wanted* to live, too? She couldn't handle that pressure. Not again.

This would never work. She was already under so much stress she couldn't even put her own hair up in a bun, and apparently she'd lost all ability to powder anyone, let alone Augustus. If she started worrying about Jarvis dying, then what? She'd be so freaked she'd be useless to anyone, especially Natalie. "This won't work. I can't team up with you. I can't."

"Let's go." Completely ignoring her protest, he left the car door open and strode around the truck to the other side. His body was so well-muscled, and he moved swiftly and efficiently, a man who was used to precise execution in everything he did. He was fast, dangerous, and smart, everything she needed to accomplish the impossible.

She couldn't afford to find someone else to help her.

She needed him, and she needed him now. How come her only chance to save her sister was also the biggest threat to doing just that?

Chapter 9

DEATH WAS TWO STEPS INSIDE THE DOOR TO THE DUNGEON of Temporary Situs when he heard the mournful sound of the harp reverberating through the cement walls. Holy hell and high water. The Guardian of Love was playing his harp again!

He barreled down the circular stairs, nearly skidding out on the first turn when the top stone twisted under his foot. Damn rotting dungeon! The terms of the purchase and sale from the Grim Reaper had banned Death from structurally altering the classic dungeon in any way that made it less depressing, scary, and miserable.

At the time, Death hadn't really cared. All he'd wanted was his own business, and Lord Grim (as he'd insisted on being called) had worked the death business into such a hole that it was available for a bargain price. Death had leveraged his ass off to get it and had agreed to any terms that would lower the price to within his range.

But three hundred years later, the crumbling stone steps were treacherous as hell in dress shoes. But if he made any improvements, the son of a bitch could take the entire business back for the original purchase price. Given that it was now worth about three hundred billion dollars more than when he'd bought it, Death wasn't all that high on that idea.

The harp drifted up louder and more mournful.

"Cameron! Stop it!" Death reached the last cell on the right and raced inside.

The Guardian of Love had his head inside the strings of the harp, and he was sawing at his throat with the strings, trying to decapitate himself.

"Hey!" Death jammed his knee into Cameron's back, yanked the harp off his head, then headlocked lover boy onto the handwoven Oriental carpet he'd had brought in for his new guest (Lord Grim had forgotten to ban decor). "Did I not make myself clear that you could not play that harp?"

Cam was struggling, trying to get to the instrument. "I love my harp. She calls to the essence of my soul."

"It turns you into a blubbering suicidal embarrassment to love." Death tossed the harp into the hallway and slammed the door shut. "You're like a woman and chocolate. Get some self-control, man."

The bright yellow tulips he'd brought down yesterday had opened. The two humming birds he'd imported were happily dive bombing the feeder, their buzzing filling the air. The waterfall was bubbling cheerfully over the stones, and little blue fish were swimming merrily around, occasionally leaping out of the water for the sheer joy of it. "How are you not in a good mood? I did a brilliant job creating an oasis of peace and harmony."

He was delighted he'd had the foresight to lock Cam up instead of succumbing to his whiny requests to sleep in the guest wing last night. After yesterday's trip back to the homestead to retrieve Cameron before he succeeded on his mission to die at his home, Death wasn't taking any more chances with his most precious commodity.

Cameron sank into the luxurious armchair and pressed his forehead to his hands. The tux Death had given him was wrinkled, and he clearly hadn't bothered to use the monogrammed gold razor that was still sitting on its silken towel next to the rusted spigot oozing brown water. "I can't do this. I just want to go home and—"

"Kill yourself?" Unacceptable. He would not let love vanish from this realm just because the Guardian was some manic depressive sap who couldn't see goodness if it had breasts and belly danced on his face for hours. Death pulled out the ottoman and straddled it. He leaned forward, invading Cameron's personal space. "Hey!" He kept his voice sharp. "What do you want most in the world?"

Cameron sniffled, like a freaking pansy. "To die."

Death smacked Cameron on the side of his head.

"Ow!" Cameron looked up with a scowl. "Don't hit me."

"What else do you want?"

Cameron narrowed his eyes. "Nothing—"

Death smacked him again, and this time Cameron nearly fell off the chair. "World peace, you dimwit. World peace!"

"Oh. Right." Cameron rubbed the side of his head and sat back up. "I forgot."

"Well, remember it, because you're going to make it happen. You're about to change the world as it exists. Remember?"

Cameron sniffled. "That thing this weekend?"

"That thing this weekend is going to make us both billions of dollars, give you a purpose in life, and create world peace." Or close enough on that last one. "Where's your excitement? You were all fired up about this last night."

"I just feel a little weepy today." Cameron plucked the silk handkerchief from his tux pocket and blew his nose like a girly girl.

"Cameron." Death yanked the handkerchief away and shoved it back in the sap's pocket. "Men don't cry. End of story." Death pounded his fist against his chest. "We hold all our emotions deep inside, even love."

"Prentiss! Where are you?" A desperate male voice rang through the dungeons. "I need help!"

Death ground his jaw. A visit from the amoral, womanizing, black magic witch who abandoned him for over three hundred years was not what he was in the mood for right now. "I'm in a business meeting, Napoleon. Make an appointment."

"Your real name is Prentiss?" The Guardian of Love started to laugh. "That's even less manly than Cameron."

"Shut up." Death sighed with resignation as the door to the prison cell turned a pale gray, and then the world-renowned assassin walked in.

Then he took one look at his grandpa, and he sat up. "What happened?" Napoleon was always meticulously adorned, but his suit was so wrinkled it looked like he'd been wearing it for a month. His usually pristine black hair was jagging past his ears, messed up, and shaggy. The laces were missing from his right shoe, and he smelled like he'd slept in a sewer.

Napoleon sagged against the door, as if he was too exhausted to stand any longer. "I've lost her."

"Her?"

"Angelica. Your grandmother. My wife. My true love. I've lost her."

"Oh. That." Disgusted, Death sat back down and returned his attention to Cameron. "So, let's go over the plans for this weekend—"

"Did you not hear me?" Napoleon strode across the room, grabbed the beanbag chair from the corner, and plunked it down between the two men. "My truest, most wonderful sprite has been plucked from my loving arms."

"I'm the Guardian of Love." Cameron sat up. "I am very insightful when it comes to that emotion. This woman. You love her."

"Oh, yes." Napoleon whipped out his BlackBerry. "Let me show you pictures."

Death snatched the phone away from his grandfather. "When you walked out on Gram three hundred years ago, you lost the right to love her. If she's locked you out of the Den, then that's your own problem." He still couldn't look at his grandfather without remembering how the narcissistic bastard had walked out on him and Gram. With Death's parents long dead due to one of Napoleon's experiments, the old man had been the only father he knew, and the son of a bitch had taken off.

"I want to see the pictures of his true love." Cam plucked the phone out Death's hand. "This man is clearly experiencing love. Let it blossom."

"He only loves her because he can't have her," Death snorted.

"Oh… I understand now." Cameron slumped back in his chair and let the phone slither away. "This is an example of the miserable, hopeless, destructive side of love. Did I tell you what happened to my father after my mother died? It was a dark night, years after my brother had vanished. I—"

"Stop!" Each time Cameron told that story of how his father killed himself after his woman had died because he loved her too much to live without her, the grief nearly did Cameron in. Cameron had been perseverating for a century on how love had stolen his family, and he'd lost the will to do his job.

But not for long.

Death was going to clean this mess right up.

"Angelica didn't lock me out of the Den," Nappy sighed. "Augustus has her. He's using her as bait to keep me from my duties."

"Augustus has Gram? Why didn't I know about this?" But he knew why. He'd been 24/7 on suicide watch with Cameron for the last two weeks while he'd tried to find a way to resurrect his will to live. "Go get her back. Now."

"I can't find her!" Tears began sliding down the old man's face.

Cameron plucked Death's handkerchief out of his tux pocket and handed it to Nappy. "I thought you said men don't cry." Cameron shot an accusing look at Death.

"Real men don't. Napoleon is a spineless, amoral bastard." Gram could hold her own against Augustus, but being locked up had to be chafing at her. He was going to have to get her back.

Nappy blew his nose into Death's handkerchief. "I'm a real man," he announced. "I've assassinated over one million people with black magic. How is that not manly?"

Cameron raised his brows at Death. "Yeah, how is

that not manly? I think that's manly." His eyes began to glisten and he began weeping into Death's handkerchief. "Life is hard, and it's okay to let that pain fill us."

"Both of you, pull yourselves together!" Death strode across the cell to the well-stocked bar. He grabbed a bottle of Knob Creek bourbon and three crystal tumblers. He slammed them down in front of the wusses, filled them straight up, and handed them out. "Drink."

Cameron took a sip, then wrinkled his nose. "I think I just blew up my throat."

Napoleon tossed the glass over his shoulder and didn't flinch when it shattered against the cement wall of the dungeon. "You have any Chardonnay? I would love a glass."

Cameron set his glass down. "Oh, how about a white wine spritzer? That would be great. Prentiss? Do we have any?"

"The name is Death." He grabbed a bottle, popped the cork, and filled two wineglasses. He shoved the girly drink at them. "Here. No spritzer. Deal with it." There were limits to what he could permit to be imbibed in his presence.

"Oh, delicious." Cameron inhaled it. "I love this vineyard."

"I do as well." Nappy was still sniffling as he took a long drink of the wine.

Death chugged his glass of man-juice and refilled the bourbon. "I already have an assassin after Augustus. He should be taken care of shortly. You just go find Gram and rescue her. Surely you can manage that?"

Nappy shook his head. "I have no idea where she is. I am at a great loss."

"I can bring lovers together." Cameron crossed his legs and swung his foot. No socks with dress shoes? The boy needed work. "It's what I do."

"I don't know if she loves me," Napoleon sighed. "Prentiss is right. I did fail to honor her as she deserved."

"Love is so destructive." Cameron sank back into his chair. "I don't know why people think love is so great. It's a recipe for heartache and—"

A light knock interrupted Cameron's soliloquy. Before Death could refuse entry, the locked door opened and a thirty-something ponytailed brunette in jeans, Keds, and a fitted T-shirt slipped inside. She had flour on her cheek, white paste in her hair, a blueberry stain on her toe, and she was carrying a large silver tray of what appeared to be pastries.

She had a pert little nose, a spattering of freckles, and she wasn't wearing any makeup at all. Fascinating. He'd forgotten what color a woman's lips actually were. Sort of a dark rose, with a hint of violet, and—

She set the tray down on the coffee table, and the clank of the silver hitting the wood jerked Death back into consciousness. She'd infiltrated the cell before he'd reacted. What kind of devil spy was she? "Identify yourself."

The intruder gave a cheerful smile. "My name's Anna Gusman. I'm your new pastry chef."

Ah… well, that explained the utter disarray of her appearances. Chefs were allowed the liberty of their own style in concession to their artistry. "Where's Vladimir?"

"Apparently, he eloped with the dish girl."

Ah. That explained the incredible array in his office earlier. It had been far outside the scope of Vladimir's talents. "Did you make the scones this morning?"

She brightened. "I did. Did you enjoy them?"

"Did I enjoy them?" he echoed in disbelief. No one ever questioned Death, and she should know it. Clearly, she hadn't been briefed on Castle etiquette.

"I apologize for my grandson's rudeness." Napoleon took Anna's hand and pressed his lips to the back of it. "My name is Napoleon. I'm a world famous black magic witch specializing in assassinations for hire, and I'm extremely virile."

Anna plucked her hand out of the old man's. "Nice to meet you, Napoleon."

"Back off, old man," Death growled. "You're pining over your wife, remember?"

"Ah, I am married, to a lovely woman who hates me." Napoleon bowed his head. "My grandson, however, is not, although he is apparently quite virile as well. I assume from your appearance that you are one of the rare women who work here who isn't planning to have sex with him?"

"Sex with—" Anna's gaze flicked to Death, and he had a sudden vision of getting in a naked food fight with her. She would laugh if he got pancake mix in her hair. He knew she would. She would laugh, and it would be this magical, lighthearted sound, not the calculating practiced laugh of all the HoneyPots—

"My fiancé wouldn't be so happy with me dallying with the boss."

Fiancé? "Unaccepta—"

"What are these?" Cam leaned over to peer at the tray.

"Lemon tortes." She picked up a croissant and tapped it against Death's staff. "And one special croissant I created this morning just for you. I think you'll like it."

"For me?" Death caught a whiff of that buttery

decadence, and his mouth started watering. He took the dessert, and his fingers brushed against hers. He waited for her sharp intake of breath, the sudden flush to her cheeks, the delight in her eyes, but got nothing.

Instead, her watch beeped, and she glanced at it. "Gotta go. More buns in the oven. Nice to meet you all." Then she turned and jogged out of the room, flipping the door shut on her way.

What? She'd just walked on him without a single flirty look? What kind of woman did that?

Napoleon leaned back in the beanbag chair and helped himself to the box of cigars on the coffee table. "Well, how about that, Prentiss? A woman who doesn't want to get into your pants or your wallet. I like her."

"She's engaged." Death scowled. "It's against my rules for any woman on my staff to be married or have a significant other. I require total loyalty."

Napoleon opened the pressure-sealed cigar box. "I think you like her, my boy."

"Your opinion doesn't matter to me." What was he doing wasting time thinking about a woman anyway? He had a business to run. "Let's get back to the matter at hand. Cameron, we need you to find Gram." A man without a career with a man without a will to live. He was giving the boy a new career on Saturday, but until then, maybe hunting down Gram could keep him busy. "Help my grandfather find her."

"You'll loan me the Guardian of Love to find Angelica?" Nappy's face illuminated like the bright sunshine on a Florida day. He dropped the cigars and threw himself at Death. "Oh, Prentiss! You give me hope! I was out of resources!"

"Don't touch me." He sidestepped the hug and Napoleon crashed into the floor-length mirror behind him. The bastard had killed his parents, nearly broken his grandmother's heart, and left them all. To give him joy… well… it just felt crappy.

But he was willing to make the sacrifice to save Cameron. And his grandma, of course.

"Cigars all around! We're going to find her!" Napoleon shoved three cigars in his mouth and lit them all. "I can't believe it!" He was radiating, literally glowing. Because of love. Because of the chance to find his woman.

Death had to respect love like that. Hell, he wasn't going to be able to hate his grandfather nearly as much, was he? "You see that, Cameron? You going to help him find his true love, or are you going to let it die?"

There was yearning on his face. Desperation. "I could do that, I think."

"Excellent." Death slammed his hand down on Cam's shoulder. "This will be good therapy for you before this weekend. Get in touch with your inner love child. Enjoy it."

Cameron slammed the lemon torte down and stood up. "Let's go! I can do this!" He started running for the door.

"Cameron. The clothes."

Cameron stopped and looked down at the rumpled tux, at the food stains on it, the yellowed shirt. "What's wrong?"

"No man who works for me dresses like that." He pointed Cameron to the supply of custom tuxes. "Clean up, my good man. You'll feel better."

"But—"

"Now."

Cameron shrank a little as he scurried back toward his clothes, but Death didn't regret his tone. Nothing made a man feel better than a nice tux. And Cam needed all the help he could get.

Death leaned toward his grandpa and lowered his voice. "Gramps, I'll let you take Cameron out of here to help you find Angelica, but he's suicidal so don't leave him alone for a moment."

"Suicidal?" Napoleon glanced over at Cameron, who was now humming "Stop in the Name of Love" while surfing his armoire. "My specialty is killing people, not keeping them alive. What if I screw up and then love ceases to exist on this planet? I don't want that kind of responsibility."

"World peace!" Cam was standing on top of the armoire, sporting a D&G suit, slicked back hair, and polished wing tips. "I will give peace to all."

Death clapped his hands. "Excellent." He nudged Napoleon. "Applaud."

Napoleon slapped his hands together a few times. "World peace? What's he talking about?"

Cam leapt off his tower, sashayed over, and bowed low before Napoleon. "What do people fear most in life, my king?"

Napoleon frowned. "Me, of course."

"Dying!" Cameron pulled off one of the diamond earrings Death had loaned him and dropped it in the wine. It sank to the bottom. "This is what happens to the soul when it is consumed by fear. It drowns. Fear begets violence, hatred, and other destructive emotions, and the fear of dying is the most destructive emotion of all."

"That is true," Napoleon acknowledged. "People are terrified when they see me coming for them. It's a lovely ego boost."

Cameron dropped a cork into the wine. "See how it bobs? That is the human spirit when it is supported by love. Bouncing through life." He laid his hands on either side of the glass, and the goblet began to glow hot pink. "If I am the one to take their souls, I could fill them with love at the moment of their demise, transforming death into a glorious experience. Gone will be the fear of dying, leaving people free to enrich the world with love, laughter, and well-being." He removed his hands and the jewel was now floating on top of the wine beside the cork. "And we have world peace."

Death felt glee beginning to bubble up inside him. No matter how many times he heard it, the plan was still masterful. "Think of the cash cow, Gramps. Now people can pay me for early termination of loved ones without guilt. Drunken Uncle Al who has stripped the family coffers with his gambling problem? Now the family can off him and know that Al finally found love. It's brilliant. It will change the Death business forever. I'm projecting an increase of thirty percent on early terminations by request."

"I'll be incredibly wealthy, magnificently powerful, and highly sought after by people other than weepy teenage girls." Cameron raised the now-glowing diamond. "And we will have world peace."

"I must disagree with your mercenary tactics to earn money." Napoleon blew a smoke ring. "Love isn't about killing. Love is about—"

"About leaving the woman you love for three

hundred years? Killing your own daughter in an experiment and not caring?" Death grabbed his grandfather by the shirt, his muscles trembling with the need to shake the bastard. "Is that what love is? Because that's crap, Gramps, and you know it." He lowered his voice. "If you take away Cameron's dreams and render him suicidal before I can give him meaning in life, I will hunt you down and rip your soul out of your body in the most inhumane way possible. I will *not* allow love to die or be destroyed. Turning him into a murderer is the only way to save him."

Napoleon stared at him, a shocked look on his face. "My God, boy," he whispered. "This has nothing to do with making a profit off the youth, does it? You're doing it to save love for the world."

Death scowled. "It's always about the money."

A slow grin spread across Napoleon's face, a look of utter pride. "Of course it is, my boy. Of course it is."

"You have no right to be proud of me."

Napoleon's grin got bigger. "If you're making this call with your heart, then maybe you're right that it'll work." He nodded at Cameron, who was now gallivanting about the room. "Okay, I'm in. World peace it is."

"You're in?" Cam skipped across the room and dropped to his knees before Napoleon. "It is a great honor to work with a man who teems of anguished loved as thickly as you do." He beamed at him. "I treasure your participation in my future."

"Let's go, my boy." Napoleon stood a little taller and herded the youth toward the door. "Now that you're going to be an assassin, you need a mentor. As it turns out, I'm available—"

The door shut behind them, and Death smiled, satisfied that they wouldn't have to return there. Cameron had a mission.

Love would never go back to what it was.

And it was good.

Chapter 10

"You know, I'm pretty sure breaking into my boss's office isn't one of the top ten ways to assure my promotion." Reina paced restlessly beside Jarvis in the hall outside Death's office.

"It'll be fine. I'm an unstoppable force." Jarvis rapped on the door, but he could already sense the lack of emotion in the room. Every living thing gave off heat energy, and Jarvis was the man who could pick it up.

He watched Reina as she moved around, and he saw the worry lines in the flawless skin of her forehead. When she'd been in his arms, standing down the monster in the woods, she'd seemed so strong, a tiny bundle of courage and power.

But right now she looked delicate and breakable. He hadn't noticed how tiny her wrists were, or how small her hands were. He wasn't used to thinking of women as vulnerable, but as he watched Reina, he realized that as tough as she was, she needed his protection. He stood taller and set his hand on her shoulder. "Hey, sweetheart. I've got this under control, and there's nothing to worry about—"

She started to protest, and he laid his finger over her lips to quiet her.

"But if it makes you uncomfortable or nervous to break in," he continued, "feel free to stay outside while I do my thing. It'll only take a couple minutes."

Reina had gotten them into the Hallows, but he could access Death's office himself. He understood the importance of her place by Death's side, and he wasn't going to jeopardize it, but she didn't trust him enough to believe it. It bugged him that she couldn't trust him, but he also respected it. The woman had a goal and she wasn't going to let him derail it. He suspected that she'd turn him in before letting her sister die, and although that technically would be a violation of the concept of team, he actually liked it. Loyalty was good, and for that, he wasn't going to push her past what she could deal with, not when he could take care of it for her.

She set her hands on her hips. "But what if he finds you in there and kills you?" she demanded. "Who will help me then?"

"First of all, he can't kill me. Hate's the only thing that can bring me down." He pulled out his sword and brandished it to remind her of exactly what he was armed with. "However, it's good to know you aren't concerned with my fate for self-serving reasons," he teased, trying to get her to relax. Did she have no sense of the capable hands she had entrusted herself to?

"I can't afford to piss him off right now." She looked over her shoulder for the hundredth time. "Can't we pick a less risky choice?"

"I like this one. It's going to be fine. Trust me." Realizing now that the only way to get Reina to relax was to get the whole thing over with, Jarvis reared back to slam his sword though the wood—

"No!" She caught his arm, and he allowed her to stop him. "He'll freak if you ruin his doors. Let me do it."

She plunged her hand into a goblet of purple mist. The doors immediately opened.

He grinned at her. "Nice job."

She was too tense to smile back, so he caught her arm and gave her a reassuring squeeze as he guided her inside.

Jarvis stepped into the office, and he liked the room immediately. The dark wood was fantastic, and the twelve-foot desk with its carved, twelve-inch legs and extensive computer system were as rugged as it could get. Throw in the maroon carpeting and walls, and the framed cigar display above the well-stocked bar... "A man who works in a place like this could easily afford knitting without losing his masculinity."

Reina shot him a look. "You have a knitting obsession?"

"Hell, no. I detest knitting. It was just a random observation." Jarvis noted the hidden door behind the wet bar, the marble condom dispenser beneath the three framed Picassos, and the keypad on the wall beside the bookcases loaded with Otherworld law books. He planted himself behind the enormous desk and began tapping on the computer. "It'll take me only a minute."

"Do you wish you could knit?"

"I can knit. I just choose not to." He bent his head and focused on the computer, not wanting to engage in a dissection of his failings as a knitter.

"You're good at hair."

"Better at killing," he muttered, though he was sensing that he'd fallen too far to fully redeem himself. After all, the woman was still sporting evidence of his hair talents.

But she didn't press it, and he was fully aware of her

watching him restlessly as he worked. He knew the moment her energy finally shifted from the coldness of fear and worry, to the darker, warmer energy of determination and resolution. He knew she came within seventeen inches of him as she walked past him and opened a tall mahogany cabinet. He caught her tangy scent of citrus, mingling with the vanilla coffee beans in the cabinet. He heard her soft sigh as she filled the espresso machine, the clink as she put the mug in place. "That's my excuse if he finds me in here," she said. "Making his coffee."

He got past the first safeguard on the computer. "Fear is debilitating. You need to ditch it."

"You think? Tell me how and I'll do it."

He got past the second level of protection. "Make yourself indispensable to him, so he can't afford to fire you. Then you can lose the fear that you're going to sneeze wrong and lose your job."

"The possibility of getting fired isn't what is making me so tense."

He got past the third one and shot a curious look at her. She was standing at the coffee cabinet, her arms folded defensively across her chest. The posture made a nice little crevice between her breasts, one that he couldn't quite help but notice. "No?"

"Getting fired is just a failure along that road. Failing to save my sister is what really scares me."

Ah, yes, he knew that. A big weight for her to carry. No wonder her shoulder looked so small. "It starts in the mind." The fourth security mark fell. "Believe you'll succeed, and you will. Piece of cake."

She raised her brows skeptically. "Just like that?"

"Just like that." Of course it would be easy. He was an

immortal warrior, and he'd already saved her life twice. She made him feel powerful, and that made him more powerful. The damsel would be plucked from the jaws of hell by the fancy immortal warrior, so he could plunge to his hateful death with redemption and salvation. A good ending for everyone. He punched one more key, and then a big heart appeared on the screen with the words, "Welcome, My King." He grinned. "And we're in."

"You are? Really?" She shut the cabinet. "You must be good."

"Yeah, I am." Damn, he liked that she boosted his ego. Every man needed that from time to time. He whistled cheerfully as he whizzed through the files. Now that he was in, it took him less than five seconds to find the file on his brother. "Got it."

Reina braced her hand on the desk and leaned over Jarvis's shoulder to look at the screen, close enough that he was able to get a full frontal of her scent. He inhaled, inviting the smell of strawberries and sunshine to fill his soul. He could practically feel it cleansing the darkness inside him. "You smell a hell of a lot better than Nigel."

She stiffened. "Jarvis—"

"This is my brother." He pointed to Cam's name on the screen, trying to cover up the compliment that he'd obviously screwed up. Didn't women like for men to notice when they smelled nice? He could have sworn that was one of the early lessons in Intro to Chivalry.

Not that he was trying to compliment her as a woman. It was just that partnerships worked better if everyone felt like they could kick ass. Reina clearly wasn't in that mindset, and it was his job to get her there. But apparently boosting up women was more complicated than trying to kill a cockroach on meth. Why hadn't complimenting her scent made her happy? It was even the truth. She did smell good, so light and sweet, almost as if she were an ethereal fairy, barely flitting past him, in some dress made of scarves so delicate that they would disintegrate if he breathed on her—

"Cameron Swain? That's your brother?" Her breasts were brushing against the back of his shoulder, the faintest touch, but he could feel it even through his thick leather jacket. She reached past him and tapped the screen. Her nails were a pale shade of pink nearly the same color as the fuzzy socks he'd been trying to knit before their escape.

Did she like that color? Almost made him wish he'd finished the socks so he could give them to her. You know, for team bonding. He gave his buddies a shot in the head with his sword. Reina might like the socks better.

"It says here that your brother first arrived at the Castle three weeks ago." She was skimming the page, reading the shorthand more quickly than he would have been able to decipher. And her breasts were still pressed against his back.

Jarvis tried to concentrate on the screen and not on the tightness of his jeans. "What does the red skull next to his name mean?"

"It means it was an attempted suicide."

Okay, that was a real crotch-loosener. "Cam tried to kill himself?" Shit. *What are you doing, Cam?*

"Yes, but it looks like Death intervened before he could succeed." She smiled reassuringly at Jarvis, showcasing the sweet and gentle nature that didn't fit a woman who was being forced to manage assassinations for profit. His hand twitched with the need to touch her cheek, to whisk her away from the hell she was facing and protect her soul.

Which was crap. He was the Guardian of Hate, remember? All he did to other souls was taint them and screw them up. Yeah, Reina had been immune so far, but who knew how long she could resist. He wasn't her prince. He was her demise.

"Love is Death's Achilles' heel," she continued. "I caught him once sparing someone who was supposed to die, because the man's wife was so heartbroken over the loss of her true love. I'm sure he was furious that the Guardian of Love was trying to kill himself."

"He's not the only one." Jarvis shifted in the chair, jonesing to go find his brother and knock some backbone into him. "If Cam kicks the bucket, it won't matter what happens to me." He scanned the screen, beginning to grasp the shorthand. "Says he's in the dungeon. Can you get us in?"

"Yes, of course—"

"Well, let's go." Jarvis shoved the chair back and headed for the door.

But Reina parked herself in the vacated chair and stared at the computer screen with a worried expression.

Something was wrong.

Of course there was.

Because there wasn't already enough hell to deal with.

"My name is in your brother's file. I want to know why." Reina was aware of Jarvis's restlessness to get to his brother. It was apparent in the tension in his bunched shoulders, in the way he was gripping the doorframe with his callused hands, as if it was taking all the self-control he could muster not to haul her out of the office and down to the dungeons.

But he managed not to kidnap her. Instead he studied her with his hyper-vigilant, blue-flecked eyes, as if trying to decide how seriously to take her concern.

"I'm only linked to people who are about to expire, and only when I've been selected as their Guide," she explained. She clicked on the code Death used for her, and it took her to her bio page. Date of hire. A list of every person she'd used death dust on, including the failed attempt with Jarvis. He knew every move she'd made during her nine years working for him. Uh oh. What if he figured out her plans for Natalie?

Jarvis went still. "My brother is scheduled for Death?"

"That wouldn't make sense. Death would protect love. I want to know what's going on and why we're connected." She clicked on a "conflict-of-interest" button, and then saw a list of everyone in her family who had died. Their photos. Dates and time of death. How they died. Who Guided their soul. It was like being smacked in the face with her worst nightmare, and she clenched her stomach against the sudden shock. "My family," she whispered. *Oh, God, I miss them.*

"What's on that screen?" Jarvis was already striding back across the room. "What happened?"

"They're all here." Every memory. Beating at her. She couldn't hide. Couldn't forget. Couldn't pretend it hadn't all happened. Not with the list before her, tracking all their demises.

"Who?" Jarvis moved up beside her, then swore when he saw the monitor. "Your family?"

She tapped the screen, her hand shaking. "My mom. Paula Fleming. I was eleven, and she went joyriding with this gang of biker werewolves. I was running after them, screaming at her to come back, and there was all this dust and this exhaust and then they were gone and—" She swallowed. "She died trying to leap across Lover's Canyon on the leader's bike. Apparently, he was on the other side, naked, and she was trying to get some action." She could still remember standing over her mother's grave, her whole body shaking with disbelief, of raw emptiness, of abandonment, of sheer unadulterated terror that the nightmare had begun. She'd been so cold, nothing had been able to get her warm, not for days and days. "I couldn't stop it. I couldn't help her. None of them. They all left me—"

"Hey, babe." Jarvis crouched beside her and rubbed her back with a tenderness that tightened her heart. "I'm sorry."

"And that's Arlene." She pointed at the picture of the cheerful redhead, with all the freckles and the bright blue eyes. "It was right before she snuck off to try to break the Guinness World Record for kissing length. She picked an incubus and suffocated. I mean, come on. Why would you do that?" But she knew why. Because the deedub messed with everyone's mind. "I tried to convince her to go for popcorn popping, but she wouldn't. I mean, if she'd done that, maybe I would have had time to find a way to save her, but she—"

"Listen." Jarvis parked himself on the edge of the desk, partially blocking her view of the monitor. His face was soft in a way she'd never seen before, and his eyes were understanding. He laid his hand on her cheek, his touch warm and gentle. "I know it sucks when people you care about die. I get it. I buried a lot of friends while I was in the Den. It's hell."

"It is." She couldn't help the sudden tears that flowed at his understanding tone and she wanted to bury herself in his chest. She wanted to stop being brave. To end the charade of pretending it was okay, that life went on.

As if understanding her unspoken need, Jarvis held out his arms. She accepted the offer, and he enfolded her in the protective shield of his body. His chest was hard, but his heart was beating softly, pulsing with warmth and humanity. He was alive. He was holding her. She wasn't alone, not anymore. "I was supposed to save them," she whispered. "I didn't. I failed them—"

"Stop," he snapped as he shoved up his sleeve and held out his arm. On his skin was a tattoo of a black serpent, dotted with hundred of black skulls where its scales should have been. "See the skulls?"

She nodded numbly, her heart grieving with the weight of decades of self-recrimination and loss. "Yes, but—"

"Each one represents a recruit I mentored while I was in the Den who died while under my protection. Two hundred and seventy-one of them." His voice was hard. Unyielding. "I couldn't save a single fucking one of them. And since that was my job, I did actually fail them. Your only job was to love them, and you did that."

Oh, God. He'd been through it almost three hundred times? Her heart cracked even more, but this time it was for him, for his pain, for his own sense of failure. She laid her hand over the serpent. She felt the weight of his own agony pressing down onto her. He understood. He really did. "I'm so sorry you had to go through that—"

"My only reason for existence is to protect those under my care, and I screwed it up. I betrayed the very reason I am alive." Violence rolled off him in hot waves. "No one else dies under my protection, and that includes the entire, fucking world that'll suffer if Cam goes down and if I explode before he's there to clean it up. Get it?"

Her heart tightened for the pain in his steely voice. For the tautness in his muscular shoulders. For the determination in his eyes, the absolute refusal to allow himself to fail on a major scale. "But how do you know it ends now?" Because she could feel his strength rolling off him and his conviction that it wasn't going to happen again. "How can you be so sure that you won't fail again? And again? And again—"

He put a finger over her lips, his touch almost more of a caress than an order of silence. "Because I won't allow it. Now that I'm out of the Den, I'm in control of my life again, and I say who and what dies around me. I decide now."

She searched his face and saw he spoke the truth. "Just like that? You just believe it and that's enough for you?"

"Yeah." He thumbed her cheeks. "Take all your love and turn it into power, not fear and weakness."

"It's not that easy." She gestured at the screen. "My family is on there and it's just a matter of time until…" Natalie's picture flashed on the screen. "Nat?" she whispered, terror stealing her voice. Little words appeared beneath it. "Soul: Natalie Fleming. ETD: Friday, May 3rd, 11:01 PM. Death by Orgasm. Guide: Not Assigned."

"She's been scheduled." She couldn't get any air. Couldn't make her lungs work. Couldn't swallow.

"Hang on there, babe." Jarvis grabbed her hips and spun her away from the computer. He crouched between her knees, his voice urgent and demanding. "Stay with me. You're in control here."

She grabbed for his shoulders, hanging on desperately. "I thought this plan would work. I really did. And I'm too late. I can't—"

"That's bullshit. You can. It's not done." There were black flecks in his eyes, haunting him, chasing him, just like the deedub poison chasing her sister.

"And you're going to die, too." Oh, God. "I can't deal—"

"You're a warrior, for hell's sake." Frustration wrought his voice. "Warriors take a hit and keep on going—"

"A warrior?" She stared laughing, hysterical, awful laughter. "I'm not a warrior. I'm a failure. Every time it counts, whenever it matters, I fail—"

He swore and then yanked her close. "Tell me what to do to help you pull yourself together," he ordered. "Tell me."

"I don't know!" He was right, he was right. Panicking was accomplishing nothing. She had to snap out of it, had to—

The screen flashed again, and this time the words "Confirmed" appeared across the top of her sister's picture. "I'm too late—"

Jarvis swore, fisted her hair, and then kissed her.

Chapter 11

REINA FELT INSTANT RELIEF IN HER SOUL WHEN JARVIS kissed her. It wasn't simply the warmth of his lips on hers. It wasn't just the way his fingers were tunneled through her hair. It wasn't only the heat of his ribs as he wedged himself between her legs.

It was the absolute, utter tenderness of his kiss.

The kiss in the woods had been violent, hot, carnal.

This time, his lips were soft, a light kiss on the corner of her mouth, on the bud of her upper lip, a tender nip on her lower lip.

It wasn't about knocking her down and dragging her onto his lap. It was a kiss of respect, of honor, of wanting, yet not ravaging, of trying to tempt her back into sanity and peace. Of trying to show her that there was good in the world, in herself, and in those around her. Of giving her something to believe in other than failure, death, and loss.

He was giving her beauty, purity, connection, and her heart bled for more. For something to hang on to, to propel her to pull herself together one more time and believe that this time there could be a happy ending.

He moved closer, pushing her legs apart as his torso forced between her thighs. The heat from his body was intense, hotter than a man, hotter even than Blaine, Mr. Fire Guy. His left hand was on her hip, holding her still, his right hand buried deep in her hair. She was trapped, and it felt wonderful because his strength made her feel safe. Like she wasn't alone anymore. Like he was there for her.

Her body shuddered, and then peace rippled over her, and hope flared in her heart. *It could be different this time.*

Jarvis broke the kiss and pulled back, his black-flecked eyes searching hers. He hadn't released his grip on her, hadn't moved from between her legs. His eyes were smoky and dark, brimming with a sensuality that made her body tighten.

For a moment, neither of them spoke. The silence between them grew, and he thumbed her lower lip. Her heart began to race, and she caught her breath. The expression on his face was pure desire, a passion that comes from the calling of his spirit, from the man, not the beast. It was a look of intimacy, of a yearning to tumble her onto the nearest set of silken sheets and spend hours luxuriating in the burning ardor between two people who'd gone to hell, and somehow pulled each other back to sanity, to humanity, who had awakened each other's hearts.

Then he let out his breath and dropped his hand from her face.

Disappointment and loss surged through her, and she had to stifle a cry of protest, a request for one more moment, one more intimacy, one more caper in his arms. "Jarvis—"

He grinned, a satisfied look flashing in his eyes. "That worked. You're not panicking anymore."

"What?" He'd gifted her with that incredibly romantic and tender kiss just to calm her down, just to help her heart recover? She should be annoyed and disappointed, but she couldn't summon the emotions. She was feeling too peaceful to get annoyed by the fact he'd kissed her just to calm her down. His kiss had eased her pain, it had given her hope, and she was going to cling to it. "Thank you."

"It's my job as your partner. No thanks necessary." He shifted his grip in her hair, sifting softly through the strands, apparently not quite ready to break the connection. "I hate to admit it, but Angelica seems to be right about women."

She smiled at his thoughtful tone, as if he was trying to assimilate all the information about how to work with a female. "It wasn't just the kiss that calmed me down."

"What?" He cocked a brow. "I'm a fantastic kisser. The chicks all gave top marks even with the fact I poison them."

"You're a great kisser?" She grinned, her heart actually light enough to dance a tiny bit, and it felt wonderful. "It wasn't long enough for me to make that call."

Challenge flashed on his face, and he reached for her. "Well, let me—"

"Oh, no. I'm not ready for that." She pulled back, out of his reach, laughing at his grunt of aggravation. "It was the whole protector thing, not just the kiss. That was the beauty of the kiss."

His eyebrows shot up. "I don't create beauty."

"You did. For me." She traced her hand over his serpent, not wanting to ruin the afterglow of the experience by dissecting it. "I'm glad I'm somewhat sane now, so thanks." Then she saw Natalie's face on the screen, and unsettled fear rippled over her. "I can't believe she's been confirmed—"

"Don't knock yourself out about it." Jarvis rested his elbows on her thighs, clearly very content to remain between her legs. He'd given her something to treasure, and that was still in the air, creating an intimate connection between them. "I had Guides sitting by my side at least a couple hundred times while I was in the Den, and I ditched them all. Confirmed doesn't mean shit until your soul says hasta la vista, baby."

"Oh, that's good to know." She imagined Jarvis fighting to stay alive while a Guide loomed over him, waiting to take him. How awful. Is that what it would be like for Natalie? Strange shadowed beings waiting for her to die... "Oh! I just had an idea" She leaned past him and began typing on the computer. "I'll make myself her Guide, and that way if it comes down to the last minute, I'll be the one there to take her and we can do the switch. I could stall if I needed to." She hit enter and sat back, watching her name flash next to her sister's. "That feels so much better. Insurance policies are good."

Jarvis grinned. "I like that thinking. Excellent backup plan."

She smiled back at him. "Thanks for clearing my head. I appreciate it." She paused. "It's nice not to be doing this alone."

His smile faded and the room suddenly felt hot. Small. She became aware of him between her thighs in a way she hadn't been before. Suddenly, the connection wasn't about innocent reclaiming of hope. It had turned hot and dangerous. Passionate. There was a look in his eyes that made something throb low in her abdomen.

He slipped his hand beneath the hem of her shirt. His palm was warm against her skin. "I'm not used to being able to touch people," he said quietly. "I bring out the hate in everyone."

The look of awe on his face made something tighten in her throat. "You can touch me whenever you want. I like touching." Oops. Her voice sounded a little too breathy. "You know," she added, "team bonding thing. It helps you focus, right? Calms your mind."

He said nothing, but his hand moved across her belly, his fingers tracing her ribs. So slowly, so precisely, as if he were absorbing every moment, as if he were experiencing it for the first time in his life.

And he probably was.

"It's okay," she whispered. "I'm not going to flip out. You can touch me." She knew she cleared his head the same way he'd given her peace. It was good to have a partner with mental clarity. That was why she'd offered. Because it was smart. And, yeah, well, okay, it felt good, too. Really, really wonderful.

"I want to know why you work for me." He moved suddenly, grabbing her hips with both hands and yanking her against him. "Why do you ease the noise in my head? How come I don't wreck you?" He cupped her face. "When I touch you, I can think again. The monster's still there, but it's not trying to fuck with me." He leaned closer, until his lips were a breath away from hers. "And when I kiss you," he whispered, "I feel like myself. I didn't know what that felt like until now."

This time, it was going to be a real kiss. A kiss of passion. A kiss between a man and his woman. She could see it in the darkness of his eyes, in the intent on his face. A kiss that was only about following the raw, unfettered desires that made him a man.

And yes, it was stupid, inane, and crazy, but she desperately wanted him to kiss her. Really, really kiss her. Because she knew it would make her feel alive in a way she hadn't dared to feel since her family had started dying on her. She laid her hand on his cheek, felt the roughness of his stubble beneath her palm. "Yes," she whispered. "Kiss me."

His grip tightened in her hair and he leaned forward—

"What in God's name is going on here?"

Reina jerked back just as Death's gleaming scythe came hurtling across the room, right for Jarvis's head.

"No!" Reina leapt up from the desk as Death stormed into his office. "Don't kill him! He's with me!"

Jarvis whipped out his sword and intercepted the scythe a split second before it would have lopped off his head. Hooray for men whose minds had been cleared with some hot touching with a female!

Death vaulted across the room, swept the scythe off the floor, and slammed it toward Jarvis's heart. Jarvis blocked it again, and the two men went into looming-predator mode, muscles flexing, blades pressed against each other, each of their grips strong and secure, glaring at each other over the locked blades.

"You are fortunate I averted my swing," Death snapped.

"I'm fortunate I'm faster than you are," Jarvis replied easily, having no trouble going from passionate would-be lover to badass warrior in an instant. His muscles were bulging, his legs braced in battle stance, and his face was utterly calm. He exuded confidence, aggression, and utter control. And this man, this incredible warrior, was on her team.

They really had a chance.

"If I had powdered you, you'd be dead," Death said. "The fact you're still living is my choice, not your paltry battle skills."

Jarvis inclined his head. "Just because you got me once doesn't mean it'll work again. I'm extremely difficult to kill."

"I'm *Death*. I can kill anyone merely by thinking about it."

"Okay, guys!" Reina paused to punch the start button on the espresso machine, hoping to distract her boss. "Death, meet Jarvis Swain. Jarvis, this is Death. We're all friends, so put down the weapons, please."

"If I relinquish my blade," Death said calmly, "it puts me in a defenseless position against a warrior with a tainted sword. I cannot agree to such an asinine action."

"And if I sheath my blade, which I agree is heavily tainted." Jarvis shoved harder against Death's blade. "It puts me in a defenseless position against a man who gets his jollies out of mowing off people's heads before their time."

"Honest to God, do you really think it doesn't affect me when the innocent must fall beneath my blade?" Death made a noise of exasperation. "Does everyone on this forsaken planet think I have no compassion and no understanding of love? I have feelings, for hell's sake!"

Jarvis leaned more of his weight into his sword. "If it's any consolation, I'm completely fucked when it comes to love myself."

Death leaned closer, inspecting Jarvis closely. "You speak the truth."

"Yeah."

"Sucks a bit, doesn't it?"

Jarvis shrugged. "It is what it is."

Death studied him. "You may live for the moment." He abruptly dropped his scythe and Jarvis nearly fell over when the pressure was released from his sword.

Reina sank down in a chair in relief. Everyone was alive for now. Which was convenient, since she needed both of these men in major ways. Not that she was really worried that either of them could be stopped or hurt, but how would a battle between two immortal warriors end? She glanced at Jarvis, thought of his impending demise, and a cold chill rippled over her. It was too soon for his ending.

It would always be too soon, she realized.

Her boss turned toward her, still fondling his staff with too much enthusiasm. "What are you doing here, Fleming? My office is off-limits when I'm not here, and never do you allow access to anyone I haven't pre-approved—" He paused suddenly and sniffed the air.

"I was getting you coffee."

"A complete lie." Death was already striding across the office toward the espresso. "You are a naughty girl for trying to use caffeine to distract me." He stopped suddenly and looked at his computer. "You were in my system," he said quietly, a lethal undertone. Death's entire body went rigid, and his fingertips turned black.

Oh… shit…

"I did it," Jarvis strode forward. "I was looking for—"

"My sister," Reina interrupted. Yes, it made her go

all snuggly and warm that Jarvis would step up and
try to protect her from Death, but the man had no idea
what made Death tick, and she did. She had a chance
of sweet-talking their survival. He did not. Weren't
they partners for a reason? Who had the insider knowledge with Death? Yes, that would be the girl. "I think
Natalie's going to die soon, and I wanted to see if she
was in there."

Death looked at the computer, where Natalie's face
was still grinning on the monitor. Hallelujah! Sometimes
being faced with your greatest nightmare came in extremely handy.

Jarvis glared at her, shooting her a silent reprimand
for taking the blame, and she smiled back at him. It felt
good to have someone trying to help her. It really did.
It made her stronger, and that was a brilliant feeling.
Maybe that's what Natalie had meant when she'd talked
about not wanting to walk away from the feeling of
power and invincibility that the deedub curse gave her.
It felt so much better to be courageous than afraid, and
Reina had Jarvis to thanks for giving her that boost.

Death leaned forward and studied the screen, then
looked up, his eyes gentler than she'd ever seen. "She's
the last of your family."

Reina felt her throat tighten, and she shoved her
hands in her jeans, not wanting him to see her pain. He'd
take advantage of it, she was sure. "Yeah, well, yes."

Jarvis threw his arm around her shoulders and tucked
her into the curve of his body. She leaned into him, accepting his strength.

Death narrowed his eyes thoughtfully. "You love her."

Reina raised her chin, emboldened by Jarvis's

support. Plus, she knew Death respected love, so hiding it wouldn't help her. "Of course I do."

"Well, then." Death sat down in the chair and began typing. "We can't have you suffer like this. This is wrong."

Reina's heart started to race. Was it this simple? "Are you going to take her off the list?"

Death laughed softly. "My dear, you know I can harvest someone before their time, but if someone's time has come, I can't stop it."

"But you can! I've seen you—"

Death flung up his hand. "I have *never* interfered with preordained death. To do so would violate my oath to Lord Grim." He gave her a meaningful look that commanded her not to dare contradict him. "And why bother? When the soul reaches the Afterlife, it's happy time anyway. So, why torture a soul by keeping it here when it's ready to go? Ridiculous." He waggled a finger at her. "Keeping her here would be only for the benefit of those left behind, and you, of anyone, would know that's not a good enough reason."

Desperation made Reina shove away from Jarvis and grab Death's desk. "But she doesn't want to go—"

"If she didn't, then she wouldn't. It's that simple." Death tapped his temple. "All our power is up here. She believes she's going to die, then she does. She believes she won't, and she doesn't." He jerked his chin at Jarvis. "Just ask him. The boy's circumvented me more times than the entire vampire community."

Jarvis shrugged modestly. "I had things to do."

"Exactly." Death started to type again. "But I do understand the pain of losing someone you love." Shadows haunted his eyes. "So, I'll put you on personal leave for

the next forty-eight hours. That way you can spend these
last two days with her. We'll deal with your promotion
afterwards. Seems rather callous to be worrying about
your job when your sister is dying, don't you think?"

Reina's stomach dropped. "Oh, no. Don't put me
on leave—"

"And that's simply cruel to have you listed as her
Guide. I'll change that." He hit the keys a few more times.

"Wait, no!" Reina leapt forward. "I want to be there
for her! If some stranger takes her—"

"Oh, you'll be there, but you won't have to take that
final step of cleaving her soul from her body." He shut
off the monitor. "We already know you have a problem
with that, so what makes you think you could do it to
your sister? The poor dear would be hovering between
worlds, stuck because you couldn't make yourself bring
her over. Is that what you want for her? I think not." He
grabbed her shoulders and hugged her. "I won't let you
throw away your love for your sister. Embrace my gift."

She fought to get free. "I do love her, but the only
way I can handle her death is to work—"

He set her back and eyed her. "Love is a gift, Fleming,
and if you piss it away then you aren't the person I want
working for me. Take the holiday, and don't come back
until Monday. If you come back earlier, you're fired,
and this time for real. Got it?"

Oh, *shit*. "I'm not pissing it away. You don't understand love—"

"Oh, now you want to accuse me of being an insensitive beast, too?" Death shoved back from his desk so
hard his chair slammed into the wall and left a mark in
the molding.

"Death—"

"No." Jarvis's arm slid around her throat, pulling her back against him. His voice was low, his breath warm against her ear. "Stand down, babe. Now is not the time."

She gripped his forearm. "But if I can't work, I can't save her—"

His arm tightened, anchoring her against his chest. "You press it now, and you cut off all your options. Be strategic."

Death whirled around to face them. His eyes were deep black, roiling with fury.

She'd never seen him this pissed. He never lost control. Ever.

"And you." Death jammed his index finger at Jarvis. "What the hell are you doing in my office? You know better than that."

Jarvis thumbed her lower lip with his thumb, a tender gesture to the outside observer, but a silent order to keep her mouth shut. "I need to speak to you about Cameron Swain. I understand he is a resident here."

Reina leaned her head back against Jarvis's shoulder, her mind frantically trying to come up with a plan. Anything. What was she going to do? She didn't have a backup plan for being taken off duty!

Death's eyes narrowed. "I don't know anyone by that name."

Jarvis stiffened behind her, and she felt his body begin to heat up. "It's very important I speak with my brother. It's official business about the fate of the world."

Death's eyebrows shot up. "Why don't you give me the message? If I see him, I'll pass it on."

Jarvis shook his head, and she felt him shift. His

muscles were tight, his breathing was getting stronger. He was getting angry at Death for evading. The monster was taking over. Not what they needed right now. "I'll pay you ten million dollars to hand him over to me," Jarvis said.

"Hah!" Death laughed. "One-time sums are not what a company is built upon. I am about long-term strategy."

"Twenty million."

Death yanked his skull and crossbones mug out of the machine. "Insult me with another offer and you die."

"Thirty million."

Death rolled his eyes and sat down at his desk as he idly flipped the scythe free. "Honestly, do people not take me seriously when I threaten death? Do I look like a pushover? I do have my name for a reason."

"Wait." Reina pulled free of Jarvis's arms. "The truth is that Cameron is Jarvis's brother. Jarvis is dying and he needs to see Cameron before he dies—"

"Oh, for hell's sake. You think that just because your story worked on me that I'm so soft that any little story about love between brothers will knock me around?" He took a long drink of coffee and sighed with delight. "The complexity with which I make decisions are far beyond the ability of ordinary beings like yourselves to comprehend." He pointed his scythe at Jarvis. "You want to burden your brother with your own problems, and it has nothing to do with whether you love him." He raised his brows. "Do you love? Do you, young man?"

Agony ripped across Jarvis's face, making his eyes even darker. "I don't have that capacity."

Death inclined his head in respect. "I admire that

honesty. For that, I allow you to live." He spun the scythe around on his fingers. "On two conditions: You leave my dwelling and never return. The second is that, since you have clearly already tried to burden my star Guide with your own problems, you reverse that and instead assign yourself as her bodyguard for the next two days and make sure she does not work or return here. Learn about love from her. She's got the goods." He cocked his head thoughtfully. "In fact, return here on Monday morning with a ten page dissertation on what you learned about love from Fleming and her sister. Got it? Otherwise, I'll kill you."

Jarvis narrowed his eyes, and she could see the wheels turning his mind. Well, that was good at least. He was the self-proclaimed God of the Infinity of Choices. Let him come up with another option.

In the meantime... She sat down in Death's guest chair. "I do love my sister," she said. "And that's why I need your understanding here. It's really, really important for me to be her Guide, and she has specifically instructed me to keep going with my career so she doesn't need to worry about me when she dies. Continuing to work is necessary for my own sanity, but also as my gift to her—"

"Which is why I'll let you come back on Monday instead of taking a six-month grieving leave." Death tapped his cheek thoughtfully. "But that does mean I need to find someone else to take care of the harvest of Augustus..."

"I'll do it." Jarvis set his hand on Reina's shoulder. "And in exchange you'll bring Cam to me."

"I will do nothing at your command," Death snapped.

"For your information, your brother is already on his way to find Augustus with my grandfather. I'll have them take care of the assassin. Gramps would like it anyway."

"Cam? You want Cam to kill Augustus?" Jarvis's hand went to his sword. "Love is only as pure as the vessel it's in, and if Cam murders, that'll blow love to pieces. End of the world chaos. He can't—"

"Oh, give me a break." Death snorted. "Why would I make the Guardian of Love a killer? He is simply using his love skills to help my grandpa find his true love."

"You lying son of a bitch." Jarvis reached across the table and grabbed Death by the lapels. "Where the fuck is my brother?"

"Jarvis!" Reina grabbed his arms. Hello, warrior guy! Strategic error to threaten Death. "Let go!" She could feel the heat rising from his skin, and she knew it wasn't Jarvis calling the shots. It was his beast.

Death's eyes were glowing black. "You are now on my short list, Mr. Swain. Surely there is someone who will pay me good money to harvest your soul. Once I find them…" He snapped his fingers. "Then it becomes worth my time to kill you."

Completely undaunted in a totally badass and insanely bullheaded way that was so not the cool, calculating warrior she knew he was, Jarvis tightened his grip, his own eyes getting darker by the nanosecond. "Tell me where my brother is before I—"

"Be off, both of you now." Death grabbed a totem pole from the back of his office. "Catch." He hurled it at Reina's head.

"No, don't touch it. It's wood and he can send us away through it—" But Reina's warning was too late.

Jarvis caught it a split second before it plundered through Reina's skull. The post brushed against her forehead, the room turned fuzzy, and Jarvis's face became blurry.

And then they were gone.

They'd just been exiled.

Chapter 12

OF ALL THE DECIDEDLY INCONVENIENT INVENTIONS, TINTED limousine windows had to be one of the most aggravating ones.

Natalie set her hands on her hips as she surveyed the string of limos lined up outside the Symphony Hall. Mostly black, a few white, all of them gleaming and shiny. All of them with tinted windows keeping her from finding her target.

Somewhere in that line was the Godfather, but she had no idea which one. And she didn't have much time to figure it out. Trinity would know by now that Natalie had vaulted out the bathroom window, and it would take a three-second Google search to find out that the Godfather was attending the private benefit by Elton John at Symphony Hall tonight.

Natalie's phone rang and she looked down. Trinity. She declined the call but knew her friend would be closing in fast. Desperation pulsed through her, an almost frantic need to find the Godfather. It didn't make sense, but she couldn't stop it. She'd been drawn here by an invisible cord, hauling her down here faster than she could even conceive.

Her phone beeped. A text from Trinity. *Your soul wants to live. Don't let the deedub poison mess with you. Tell me where you are and I'll help you. Don't make the same mistake all your sisters and your mom made. CALL ME.*

Her mother. Her sisters. All gone.

Another text. *You don't want to die, Natalie. You don't!*

Oh, God. Trinity was right. Natalie didn't want to die like them. She wanted to live, she wanted a chance to have a life like a normal person. She wanted to wake up to the sunshine and not wonder whether today was the day when she went over the edge. She didn't want to die naked and exposed in the arms of some stranger just because he could hypnotize her burdensome libido with the snap of his manipulative and deadly fingers. She hit send and put the phone to her ear. "Help me, Trinity," she said, unable to keep the panic out of her voice. "I'm losing it!"

"Tell me where you are. I'll come right away."

"I'm—" Natalie froze as a tall figure stepped out of one of the limos further down the way. He was in silhouette, but his shoulders were broad, and he was tall, so tall. Awareness pulsed deep in her belly and then he stepped under the white theatre lights.

The Godfather.

Dread filled her at the same moment that excitement ricocheted through her. "Oh, no," she whispered. "It's too late. He's here."

"Who? Where are you? Talk to me, Natalie!"

But she couldn't concentrate on her friend. She let the phone drop by her side and turned toward the man who was going to kill her. She wanted to run, tried to scream, but all she managed was one step backwards and a low moan.

His gaze was fixed on her, and there was such heat in his eyes she felt her own body ignite. He strode toward her, purposefully, not even noticing the people who had to jump out of his way to keep from being plowed down.

She knew he wasn't responding to her. He was caught in the glare of her deedub glow. This wasn't real. It was a charade, a deadly game.

He stopped in front of her. He was wearing tails, and his dark hair was slicked back from his tanned complexion. "Natalie. You came."

Stating the obvious was incredibly erotic when done by a man whose clothes fit him better than a supermodel's, by a man whose voice made her girly parts tremble. But she managed to shake her head, fought for sanity, struggled for salvation. "I shouldn't have come. I need to go." She managed another step back.

"Natalie? Who's that? Where are you?" Trinity's frantic voice echoed over the phone. "Nat!"

The Godfather took her wrist, and she stopped retreating, unable to tear herself away.

All she could do was watch in terrified anticipation as he spoke into her phone. "I promise I'll take good care of her."

"What? Who is this?" Then there was a pause. "Oh, shit. It's you. Don't do this—"

The Godfather shut off the phone and slipped it into his pocket. He held out his arm. "Would you care to accompany me into the gala?"

"No, God, no." *Run away! Run away!* The voice in her head was distant, screaming desperately…

And then it was gone.

Replaced by a burning need she couldn't resist. Didn't want to resist. Couldn't think of a reason to resist.

"I would be honored." She slipped her hand onto the Godfather's proffered elbow. The material of his suit was so soft, so silky, as if it had been handwoven by a dozen angels and blessed by a rose. A rose. A pink one. Like the one on Nigel's cheek. *Nigel*.

His dark eyes flashed through her mind, the way he'd leaned against that Hummer, drawing her as she'd woken up after Jarvis had gratuitously knocked her out. She recalled with perfect clarity that moment she'd seen Nigel watching her, as if he saw her in a way no one else did. Not the erotic temptress, not the well-stacked diva, not the terrified wimp who lived a life of fear, but someone else, someone strong and courageous. She'd never met him before that moment, and yet she knew he'd seen a truth inside her that no one had ever bothered to see, even herself—

"Excellent."

She jumped as the Godfather's deep voice jerked her out of her revelry. She cringed as he set his hand over hers to escort her down the red carpet. She fought to hold Nigel's image in her mind, but with each additional moment of contact between her and the Godfather, it got more and more difficult, and everything else began to fade until all that was left was the man by her side.

The Godfather didn't seem to notice the cameras, the microphones, the press screaming questions about who she was. He just bent his head so he could whisper in her ear. "And after the concert, would you consent to accompany me back to my hotel for some champagne?" He lightly brushed his lips over her cheek. "You're too dangerous to my goals of celibacy and keeping women alive." He nuzzled the curve of her neck. "It would be best if you declined."

He caught her chin and turned her face so her lips met

his. The kiss was electric, and she felt her overly zealous hormones leaping at the contact. Her soul understood the threat, but the poison coursing her veins was stronger.

She swallowed, fighting to clear her mind. Struggling to remember the name of the man with the pink rose tattoo who had watched her so intently. Trying to think beyond the electricity sizzling through her body, the fire so powerful and so strong she knew it wasn't normal, wasn't safe, wasn't right. "I decline. I accept." God, what was wrong with her? "Let me go."

"I can't." The Godfather gripped her hair, anchoring her against him. His breath was hot, his eyes intense. "You drain me of all logic. I'm not safe with you. I don't want to kill again. You can't come to my hotel with me. Get away from me."

She swallowed. "Yes, yes, get away. You don't want me. It's the deedub poison."

"I sure as hell don't want you, but I can't resist you." He kissed her again. Hard this time. Deeply. Forcefully. And she felt herself melt into him, drink in all that he had to offer. Her body convulsed and a sudden orgasm burst through her. She clung to him as her body shook, and his arms anchored around her, holding her so close that he absorbed every shock with his strong body so thoroughly that no camera would be able to tell what had just happened.

It was the action of man well used to handling that situation. A man who would ruthlessly add her to his list of lovers who had succumbed to his charm. A notch on his lethal bedpost. She had to run from this stranger, this man who was nothing but sex, who was preying on her erotic side, on the poison racing through her brain.

For a long moment, they stared at each other, and then her heart began to thump again, responding to his call.

And the bastard heard it. She saw the struggle in his own eyes, and then he silently held out his arm again.

She fought it, lasted for almost two seconds, and then she took his arm.

They walked into Symphony Hall.

Together.

Toward a future that was as horrific as it was ravenously decadent.

And neither of them could say "no."

Jarvis misted out of a wooden fireplace right behind Reina. He caught her as she stumbled over a pile of laundry that had apparently escaped a large antique basket masquerading as a hamper. He couldn't believe he'd just been drop kicked out of the Castle. "Where are we?"

"We're in my condo in the South End of Boston."

"Son of a bitch." He slammed his fist into the wall, fury rising hard and fast. He'd been so close to Cam, and he'd gotten deported like a piece of baggage.

Luggage was not something he'd aspired to when he'd broken out of the Den three weeks ago. "We need to get back inside. Now."

"We can't. Not until Death's gone." Reina yanked an assortment of lingerie off a drying rack, but not before he got a good look at a black lace thong, red silk bras, and a camisole in light pink that was the exact color of those damn socks he'd never finished. "The dungeon is right below his office," she said. "He'd sense us and kill us."

"How far below?" He was accustomed to lingerie being used to heighten torture and force responses he wasn't in the mood to give. But the way Reina tossed it out of sight indicated it was for her, and her alone, and he liked that. Liked it a hell of a lot better than what he was used to. Tension raced through him at the thought of what lingerie had been used for against him, and he had to ball his fists to keep from charging over there and shredding it with his sword. Jesus, he was a mess. He was furious, edgy, and unable to think.

"A hundred feet. Through stone. It runs the length of the building." She hip checked the drawer door shut, her face dismayed as she surveyed the clothes, books, and general carnage strewn across the bedroom. "But Death said that he was with Napoleon searching for Augustus—" Her eyes widened. "You're getting that look that gave me nightmares the first time I met you."

Of course he was. He'd just missed out on finding his brother, he'd lost his shit with Death and made a strategically asinine move that had gotten his ass booted, and he was skating the far edges of his control. Where was the warrior he'd spent one hundred and fifty years training to be? He was an expert in standing down the poison boiling inside him. It was time to get it back in control. His sword clenched in his fist, he surveyed the room restlessly, needing anything that would help him. "You got any knitting needles and yarn?" Hell, he'd try anything.

"Knitting needles? No, sorry." She stalked over to the bed and grabbed a book titled *Living with Fear*. "But I can give you exercises so you stop freaking out about your life."

He closed his eyes, fighting off the urge to stab the book. Stabbing reading material? Seriously? *Keep in control, Jarvis.* "I don't think that book's going to keep me from exploding, but thanks."

Reina sat down on the bed, her shoulders sagging. "Look at this room. It's a total wreck. I didn't even notice until you walked in." She gestured at the disarray. "There was a time when I took care of my things and my life."

Jarvis forced himself to look at her room, tried to think about something other than the darkness trying to get free of its walls.

Reina's puffy white quilt was covered with books and her laptop was in the middle of it. It was the bed of someone who hadn't taken the time to sleep much lately. In fact, her whole room was the lifestyle of someone who hadn't taken care of herself in a long time. And he knew why. Because she loved her sister.

He tried to focus on her, knew that she needed help. He wanted to say the right things to calm her. "The chaos indicates you're smart enough to spend your time fighting for what matters, instead of wasting time adhering to society's useless mores about what a home should look like. Speaks to your power."

She stared at him in surprise. "You're serious?"

"My place is a shithole. Haven't picked up a damn thing since I got out of the Den. I've got more important shit to take care of." He flexed his hand against the burning in his palm. "Your place doesn't bother me. I like what it says about you." Focusing on Reina felt better than thinking of himself, but it wasn't enough. Still wasn't enough.

"It's not the same thing. You can live in a hellacious mess because you're a guy." Reina pulled a hardbound book called *Poetry for Sisters* out from under her bottom and tossed it on the floor. "As a woman, the first time a man shows up in my room in years, I'd like it to be more like a den of seduction and passion than an advertisement for a makeover show on TLC."

He raised his brows at the sudden thump in his gut. "Seduction?" Every cell in his body was now focused entirely on her. Yes, yes, seduction. Sex. Intimacy. That would work.

Her cheeks flushed. "I meant, hypothetically speaking. Not specifically in this situation…" Her gaze inadvertently went to his chest. "I mean, not that I'd even know how to seduce you, anyway."

He shoved his sword into his scabbard and rubbed his hands in anticipation. "No problem. I know how to seduce."

Her fingers tightened in the comforter, gripping it a little too tightly, like a woman suddenly hit with unexpected desire. "Well trained in it?"

"Extremely." He began to walk toward the bed, deciding that perhaps he was not as resentful of the years of brutal training in the Den. After all, Angelica had been right about the hair thing, and the kiss… Shit. With Reina, he could actually touch her long enough to seduce her.

A long, luxurious lovemaking session with Reina? He moved closer to the billowing mattress of decadence and grinned as Reina lifted her face toward his in a subconscious invitation. She didn't try to move away or stop him, and his muscles tensed in anticipation.

How clear would his mind be after making love to

Reina? The few kisses they'd shared had been like an angel shining down into his soul What if they connected all the way? Could his insanity even survive it, or would it vanish forever?

He still didn't understand the effect she had on him, but he was smart enough to take advantage of it. An hour of loving so he didn't do something asinine like assault Death again? So he could think strategically enough to make the right choice to find his brother and reclaim the balance of love and hate in the universe? So he could feel the peace in his heart long enough to save the world? Seemed smart as hell.

He eased down beside her. The bed shifted under his weight, tilting her toward him. She let herself roll in his direction, not stopping herself until she was resting against his shoulder.

For a moment, neither of them moved, the tension so tight he could have snapped it with a flick of his finger. He could feel her breath on his face and could see the rapid tick of her pulse in her throat as she lay beside in him her bed, tangled in the sheets.

Slowly, with more self-control that he would have thought he possessed, he lightly thumbed the ends of her hair between his fingers. Pleasure thrummed through him as he played with her hair. Testing her. Testing him. Seeing if it would help his mind. Seeing if it would help hers. Anything to help them win this battle. Anything to bring a sense of peace and tranquility to the restlessness trying to make him crazy.

Reina angled her head toward him, an invitation for him to continue. "You know, there was a day when my place looked nice. I just…"

"I don't care about your place." He brushed his lips over the nape of her neck. The feel of her skin against his… something so right pulsed inside him. Yes, yes, this was what he needed. Her. Touch. Sensuality. Passion.

She went still, and her hand rested on his chest. Not pushing away. Not pulling him toward her. Uncertain, and so tantalizingly feminine. "What are you doing?"

"Testing a theory." He kissed her neck again, longer this time. Tasting her skin. "What were you going to say?" *I want to have you inside me. I can't take another minute without being intimate with you.*

She leaned slightly, so her shoulder was pressing against his chest. "I haven't thought of anything except saving Natalie for so long, I've forgotten what it feels like to care about anything else. Like keeping my room clean." She flopped back on the bed, her blue eyes intent on his face. "I don't want her to die."

"I know you don't." He braced one arm over her and shifted his hips so he was facing her. "What else do you care about?" *Me? Getting naked?* "The room really doesn't matter, Reina, and you know it."

"I know, I know. It's meaningless." She raised her face to his, revealing the most endearing expression of vulnerability, and he couldn't stop himself from kissing her forehead. "I'm so afraid of failure that I can't even powder anyone anymore." She wiggled her fingers dejectedly. "I've lost my mojo."

"Your mind is too noisy." He laid his palm on her stomach and could feel the agitation of her energy, the heat of love mixed with the iciness of terror. "Too much fear. Too much distraction. You need a quiet mind."

"I hate feeling afraid." She laid her hand on his

cheek, and her hand was cold. She searched his face for answers, held onto him as if he were her anchor toward courage and sanity. "Tell me how to ditch the fear, Jarvis."

He shoved aside a book on *Stories of Survivors: A Collection of Life Affirming Memories from People who Shouldn't Still be Alive*, and stretched out beside her. He moved closer so his body was against hers, and his tension eased. Yes, this was right. Sometimes the best action to take was to slow down and regroup. "I don't know how to release fear," he said. "It's not a useful emotion, so I don't allow it in the first place. I allow only useful thoughts into my head." Or at least, that had been his modus operandi before the hate had taken over.

She eyed him. "But aren't you afraid of exploding?"

"Afraid, no? Pissed off? Hell, yes." Anger surged through him at her question. Mother of hell. He wasn't ready to explode. He wasn't ready to lose his shit and bring down the world around him. The peace he'd gotten from touching her faded, replaced by the throbbing hate of himself and of his path. He swore and yanked her shirt up, then moved closer so his torso was against hers. The skin to skin hit him hard, and he lost his breath for a second at its intensity. He felt something inside him come alive, trying to fight its way through the sludge to the sunlight. It was his sanity, his humanity, his ability to think. *Come on, baby.*

She made a small noise of surprise, then rolled onto her side, so she was facing him. She splayed her palms on his chest, and he breathed in the feel of her hands on his body.

"This feels so good," she said.

"I know." He slung his leg over her hips and hauled her closer. Wishing he didn't have jeans on. Needing to feel the skin of her legs against his thighs.

She pulled his arm around her. Fear seeking protection. He could provide that, because he needed her focused as well. The two of them together were worth shit if both of them were too insane to think right.

He rested the back of his hand against her breast. His entire left palm was black, as if he'd been stained by the darkest of night. He swore at the sight of his tainted skin. No wonder he felt like hell. The shit was coming for him, and it was coming fast.

She saw his hand, and her skin grew cold again as she took his hand in hers and looked at the evidence of his impending doom. "I hate this," she whispered. "I hate that you're going to die."

Something shifted inside him. Anger. Fury that she could be suffering like this. He fisted his hand, his palm burning. Shit. Since when did he let emotions take him like this? He was becoming unstable and distracted by emotions that were too hot to be helpful. "It is what it is."

"I know." She rolled onto her back again and covered her face with her hands. "I can't believe she's going to die, too—"

Jarvis growled and rolled on top of her, pinning her to the bed. No way could he allow her to turn away from him. He needed her, and he needed her now. He couldn't allow her to withdraw. He caught her face and forced her to look at him. "Don't turn away from me," he growled.

She went still, her face softening as she looked at him. "Your eyes are black again."

"You're pissing me off." His muscles were tight,

twitching. More hostile thoughts poured into his mind, the negative energy feeding off itself. He couldn't stop thinking about how Death had cut him off from Cam. The son of a bitch was so fucking arrogant he wouldn't even listen. Jarvis had been so close, and he'd gotten his ass booted—

Reina laid her hands on his cheeks. "Stay with me, Jarvis."

He fisted her hair, knowing he wasn't being careful, but he didn't care. He was too desperate, clinging to the one chance he had to accomplish his goals. Reina was his only hope, and he couldn't lose her. Couldn't lose what she could give him. "You clear my head, but not enough. I need more. Do you understand?"

She went still beneath him, sucking in her breath. "So, what do you need me to do?"

"Make love to me."

Her skin flushed. "Are you kidding? We don't have time and—"

"I don't know what it is, or how you do it, but I need your help. I'm running out of time, and you give me time." He paused, trying to keep his shit together, trying to think. Trying to think of how to explain it. Of how to convince her. "I swear I'll protect you. I'll help you save your sister, if you'll just keep me sane long enough to find my brother."

"You're using me for sex?"

He tried to remember what the right answer would be. He'd been taught to seduce, he'd been taught all the poetry, all the words of seduction. But he couldn't remember any of them right now. He couldn't think of anything but the darkness marching toward him. "I just need you." His voice was raw, hoarse, not his voice. He was trembling, something he never did. But he knew she could give him relief from the hell that had been chasing him his whole life.

He tensed, waiting for her to lash out at him. To unleash some torture weapon at his testicles for being so crass, for putting his own needs above hers and yet he couldn't stop the words. He was so angry about Cam, furious that Reina was facing such hell, hating himself for letting everyone down, pissed he was going to explode before he could fix everything, disgusted he was going to fuck them all because he was so mentally weak he couldn't even hold onto his sanity long enough to make a single sane battle decision.

"Jarvis—"

He grabbed her hair, saw her wince of pain, and hated himself even more. And still he couldn't shut up. "I'm losing my mind, and I need the peace you can give me. I just need to bury myself inside you. I know I'm a bastard. I just can't do this without you. I—"

She wrapped her arms around his neck, pulled him down, and kissed him.

Chapter 13

THE MOMENT HER LIPS TOUCHED HIS, REINA KNEW THIS KISS was different.

Jarvis was on the edge, like he had been in the woods. But that time he'd been violent, spiraling, a stranger plunging into a magical spring in hopes of finding abatement from the violence within.

This time, there was a raw need within him, but it was more personal.

This time, he was kissing *her* and not simply something that could give him relief.

She could feel it in the way he held her so tightly, protecting her even as he kissed her with a fierceness that made her whole body scream for more.

She kissed him back. His body was crushing her against the mattress. He was a heavy, well-muscled warmth shielding her from the world. She slipped her hands under his shirt, felt the strength in his shoulders and the scars on his body.

He growled under his breath, then ripped off his shirt. His eyes were black, pulsing with dark energy as he grabbed the hem of her jersey and tugged it upward.

Her heart began to thud as he pulled it over her head. Was she really going to give her body over to him?

His eyes flashed and he pushed her back down, covering her body as he kissed her again. A slow, luxurious kiss now, with less frenzy and more precision. A man who was coming back into his mind, who was beginning to think again, a man on a mission to seduce.

"Yes," he whispered, breaking the kiss to work his way down her neck. He licked the swell of her breast, and she couldn't suppress her gasp.

Dear God. What was she doing? She couldn't open herself like this to him. What would she do when he died? "I can't—"

He pulled back, searching her face. His eyes were no longer solid black. There were flecks of blue. Dark, midnight blue. His face was serious, no humor. It was the face of a warrior preparing to go to battle.

This was who she needed. He was here. Holding her. Touching her. Making promises to her. And just like that, the fear that had been dogging her for a lifetime dissolved. Her body shuddered, a thousand tensions in every cell finally letting go. She didn't have to fight. Didn't have to fear. Didn't have to swallow down the terror eating away at her. Because somehow they became so much more together than they were by themselves.

Jarvis pulled her bra to the side. His mouth closed over her nipple, and she arched her back at the intense sensation rippling through her.

She wanted the feeling of strength he gave her, and she wanted to empower him the way she'd never been able to empower anyone who mattered to her. So what if he was going to explode? So what if he was going to die?

This moment wasn't about the future between them.

This moment was about how they could join together to could create their separate futures they both wanted. They were a team, for now, and that was more than she'd ever had before.

Jarvis nipped at her breast, and she closed her eyes as his hand went to her jeans. The button flicked open, and his fingers slipped beneath the waistband, moving closer to—

The tunes of the song "I Believe I Can Fly" exploded through the room, and Reina jerked upright, nearly up-ending Jarvis onto the floor. "My phone!"

Jarvis shoved her back down. "I'm not done," he said. "I need more."

Her heart thudded with excitement at the dark expression on his face, at the bulge of his triceps as he pinned her shoulders to the bed. His need for her, his determination to have her, and his raw, manly attitude were all evident in the aggressive stance of his body. A man who would not accept less than he wanted. And she had the power to soothe that savage beast in a way no one else could?

She was sheer, magnificent power. It was the most incredible sensation to feel that strength pulsing through her. She could help him. She could handle her own life. She was strength. And he gave it to her.

She grabbed his shoulders and yanked him down. "Then take me now, and make it worth both our whiles."

Heat flashed in his eyes. "I never do anything that's not worth my while."

And then he yanked off her jeans.

Jarvis stared in disbelief at Reina's naked body, momentarily overwhelmed by the beauty on display for him. So much skin. An oasis of salvation. She could save him. Not for good. Nothing could stop that. But she knocked his beast on its ass long enough for him to find Cam and save the world.

She held up her arms in invitation, and he kissed her. Deeply, with all the passion and fire racing around in him. She tasted like angels and sunshine, like all the nourishment his soul needed.

With a growl, he yanked off his pants and tossed them aside. Boxers followed, and then he eased himself down on top of her. The moment his thighs hit hers, soothing warmth pulsed through his soul, taking the edge off the monster. The beast was still inside him, still fighting to get out, but Reina was giving him the tools to hold it off.

He hooked his knee between her thighs and shoved her legs apart. He should do foreplay. It was proper. It was the manly thing to do. But he was so desperate for relief, his mind was screaming for the clarity that was teasing him. Seduction would come second. First, he needed to survive, he needed both of them to survive beyond this moment and—

"Dammit!" Reina jerked upright. "That's the second time!"

He stared at her, totally confused. "What is?" Had he already made love and not noticed it? Was he so fucked up in his mind that he couldn't even tell? Or was she on her second orgasm? He was good, he knew that, but that good?

"My phone."

"Your phone?" He became gradually aware of that same damn song blasting again. "You need to answer the phone? Now?"

"Yes." Reina wriggled out from under him and raced across her room, her beautiful, amazing, fantastic body moving in the wrong fucking direction. "If it's an emergency, we always call back a second time."

Jarvis face planted into the bed, groaning as the overdose of blood to his cock was crushed beneath him. Frustration, disbelief, and dark fury raced through him. "Reina. Get back here—"

"It's Trinity!" She grabbed the phone. "Trin? What's wrong?"

Jarvis fought to regain control of his body, of the hate now dancing gleefully in his soul, laughing at his desperation. Chaos was descending on his mind—

Reina went sheet white, and she fumbled for the back of the chair. "Oh, God. What happened?" She missed the chair and started to fall.

Jarvis grabbed her before she hit the floor, swearing at how cold her skin was. Shit. Right back where they'd started. Both of them a mess. He swept her up, sat down on the bed, and pulled her onto his lap so her legs were around his hips.

She grabbed onto him, as if as desperate for his touch as he was for her. He pressed his face to the curve of her neck, breathing in the feel of her body against his. Any relief was good. Any relief was better than none. Jesus. He was fucked without her.

"Where is she?" Reina's voice was wrought with disbelief, with agony, with fear. He wrapped his arms tighter around her and pulled her close, trying to infuse her with his strength.

"I've got your back," he said quietly.

She sat back, and trust evident in those big blue eyes. The moment he saw her expression, a smugness smacked him upside the head. He might be a big ball of the ugliest, most destructive, most immature emotion on the damn planet, but he could rock her world.

Reina punched the speaker button on her phone, and Trinity's voice echoed out in the room for him to hear.

"Natalie went out the bathroom window," Trinity was saying.

"The window is only six inches in diameter," Reina replied with a frown.

"Not anymore."

"Oy." Reina leaned her forehead against Jarvis's chest. "She's getting too strong. We're not going to be able to keep her."

"Yeah, well, you got any big strong men who could wrestle her to the dirt around you?" Trinity asked. "Because that's what we need. I can't hold her anymore."

Jarvis flexed his arm, showing his muscle.

"Yeah, I do, actually." Reina cocked her head and tapped his biceps thoughtfully, a spark of hope gleaming in her eye. "She didn't happen to leave a note as to where I could find her, did she?"

"She's with the Godfather."

"The Godfather?" Reina's fingers dug into his arm. "Where?"

"I Googled him, and it looks like he's on the list of VIPs who are attending that Elton John fund-raiser tonight. It started a half hour ago."

"Dammit! She could have found him and left already." Reina swung her leg off Jarvis and he felt a ripple of aggression at the loss of her contact as she raced across the room. She set the phone on the dresser, pulled a pair of black lace underwear out of the drawer, and slipped it on. "I'm going to head over there now—"

"Oh…" Trinity paused, her fingers clicking across a keyboard. "Augustus is also on the guest list."

Reina paled. "Augustus?"

Adrenaline surged inside Jarvis. "Son of a bitch." He yanked his jeans on. "My brother will be there looking for him."

"Jarvis?" Trinity's voice crackled over the phone. "You're there?"

"Yeah." He shoved his boots on, his mind racing. If Cam was there, this could all end now. Cameron could contain the hate when it exploded, protect the world. *Hot damn.*

"Reina's not ready to face Augustus," Trinity said. "Don't let her go."

"Don't be ridiculous." Reina tugged a light blue shirt over her head, moving as quickly as Jarvis to get dressed. "Of course I need to go after her."

"You can't put even a butterfly to sleep, let alone Augustus. Let Jarvis take this one, sweetie. If you get yourself killed, you can't save Natalie."

Jarvis saw doubt flicker in Reina's eyes, and he got pissed. Here was a woman strong enough not to be poisoned by his touch. A woman so full of love that she was immune to the hate spewing from him. "Fuck that." He walked over and picked up the phone. "We're coming in together. Reina's a warrior, she's not going to shy away from her opportunity to make things happen."

A brilliant smile flashed across Reina's face. "I can do it, Trin. I swear. I won't screw up again."

"Oy, I can't let you deal with this by yourself. Maybe I can help. I'll see you there." She hung up.

Reina bit her lip nervously. "I—"

"I've got your back. And in case I do detonate, I've got friends." He pulled out his phone and hit the speed dial for his team leader.

Blaine answered on the first ring. "You find your brother?"

"Symphony Hall. Cam's there, in the protection of Napoleon. Augustus may be attending as well."

Blaine swore. "Ever since Augustus tried to kill my woman, I haven't liked that man. I don't know if I can be polite."

"Well, your fiancée is on her way there as well."

There was a crash from Blaine's end of the phone. "Exposing herself to that assassin is not part of our agreement. Shit, man, don't fall in love with a woman. They'll break you. Too independent."

Jarvis grinned. "How soon can you be there?"

"Twenty minutes. Christian and Nigel are in the sick ward with the warriors we rescued, but I'll see if I can grab them." He paused. "You find Reina? She helping you out?"

Jarvis looked across the room at Reina, who was down on her knees, searching under the bed for something. He could see black lace peeking up from her jeans and a small mole on her lower back. "Yeah, she is."

"Nice job." Blaine paused. "How are you?"

Jarvis knew what Blaine was asking, but he couldn't give his teammate the answer he was seeking. "Gotta go. See you shortly." He disconnected over Blaine's protest as Reina scooted backwards, dragging a metal case out from under her bed.

She dropped it on the quilt and flipped the locks.

"What's that?"

She lifted off a purple velvet covering and set it on the bed. "My sickle."

Inside was a gleaming metal blade with a black onyx handle. "It's what I'm going to use to cleave Augustus's soul from his body." She tentatively brushed her fingers over the handle, as if testing to see if it would blow her hand up. When it didn't, she grasped it and lifted it out with so much trepidation he half expected the thing to burst into flames and consume them all. "Only Death gets a scythe. Supposedly, sickles are easier to handle with the shorter staff, but they're also slightly less powerful."

Jarvis watched her flip the blade into the handle, compressing it down to a weapon about the side of her forearm. He was too used to seeing women with weapons of pain, torture, and violence, and he didn't like seeing Reina with one.

Made her seem too much like the women he hated.

Then he saw the worry in her eyes, and suddenly all he wanted to do was protect her from the very thing she held in her hand. From the task she had in front of her.

But if he did, he'd be taking away her one chance to save the person she loved most. She would never forgive him. He had to let her become the woman she didn't want to be.

She tucked the blade into the back of her jeans. "Trinity was right that I don't have a great track record with successful reaping." She grabbed a set of car keys off the computer desk. "You don't have problems with violence do you?"

He laughed as he took the keys from her hand. "Can't say I do."

"So, will you help me get in the mental mindset I need to succeed? I need help."

He palmed her back to guide her out the door, copping a quick feel. Teaching a woman violence didn't sit well with him. Nothing like a couple centuries of in the Den to make a guy appreciate a woman with a soft side, like Reina. He didn't want her to become like the women in the Den. Fury began to swirl inside him, anger at the choice she was making, at the one she was asking him to back.

"Jarvis?" She glanced back at him as she ran down the hall toward the front door. "I thought we were a team."

He saw the question in her eyes, the first hint of distrust. Shit. She was the first woman who'd looked at him as something worthy, and she was the only one who didn't hate him.

He couldn't take any kind of negative vibe from her. She was all he had to make him feel there like there was a shred of decency inside him. He grabbed her hand and let the feel of her touch ease some of his anger. "Yeah, sure, I'll help you become a murderer."

She let out a breath of relief. "Thank God."

Yeah, that.

⸺ ⁓⁓ ⸺

Natalie couldn't focus on the tinkle of piano keys, or the melodic tunes drifting across the hall toward her. She really didn't care what brand of suit Elton was wearing, or who his date was for the evening, unlike some of the other gossiping patrons.

All she could think of was the Godfather.

The way his arm was resting against hers. The way

his black hair was slicked back. The strong set to his jaw. The way her body tightened every time he looked at her—

He turned his head slowly, caught her looking at him, and something darkened in his eyes. Without a word, he took her hand, stood up, and headed down the floor-lit aisle, right in the middle of Elton's song.

She followed him. She'd never been caught in a man's spell like this. The way his body eased across the wood floor, the firmness of his grip against hers. He hadn't asked her to leave. He hadn't requested. He'd simply taken her and she'd gone.

They reached the maroon leather doors and he shoved them open, his silent gaze intent on hers.

They stepped out into the hall where staff were lingering or rushing past with trays of wineglasses. He leaned close, his cheek brushing against hers. "I think it's time to leave. Unless you wanted to hear more singing?"

Her cheeks felt hot. Burning. "I wasn't listening."

He smiled. "Excellent." He led her down the hallway, toward the front doors, toward his limo, the car that would take them back to his hotel and—

A tremendous bouquet of pink roses was on the table beneath a portrait of a past conductor. Pink flowers, like the one on Nigel's cheek. *Nigel*.

She stopped. She became aware of the voice in her head screaming at her to run. To hide. *Run, Natalie, run*.

But she couldn't make her body respond. She was in a murky haze, a bastion of confusion, hooked by the siren's call. All she could do was feel the longing for this stranger.

The Godfather suddenly pinned her to the double

brass railing. Her body began to tremble in anticipation of what this magnificent specimen could give her.

"I don't want to kill you." He nuzzled her neck. "The chocolate must work. You have it, right?"

No, no. That wasn't right. She wanted to be tested. To prove she was all that. "No chocolate."

He swore and stepped back, his face pinched with fury and tension. "No chocolate? You were going to make it safe."

She set her hands on her hips. Safe sex? What was the point? Wasn't she here for the opposite? To push all boundaries? To see how far she could fly? "You can't hurt me." Something in the depths of her mind shouted that yes, actually, he could hurt her, but she ignored it. Little whiners weren't meant to be acknowledged.

"Yes, I will." The Godfather shook her lightly. "I've sent hundreds of souls to heaven, and I'm done. I won't be that playboy anymore."

"What?" His words should make sense. She should listen. She should walk away. But she couldn't remember why. Nigel would know. Why wasn't he here?

Not that it mattered. She didn't need him. "I want you to make love to me. I want you to rock my world."

His eyes darkened. "Natalie—"

"Look at me!" She held out her arms. "Do you really think you can kill me?" She felt brilliant. She felt marvelously strong. "Sex can't kill me."

The Godfather swore. "You don't understand what I'm like—"

"And you don't understand what I'm like." She grabbed the front of his tuxedo and tugged him close. He melted toward her like a man in a trance. "I can handle you." She knew she could. She was the wind. She was the mountain. She was the mother earth. "Do you really want to learn to hold back, or do you want a woman who can handle all you have to give?"

Longing flashed in his face, and she knew she'd struck his truth. He didn't want to fake who he was. "Oh, baby, you have no idea what I have to give."

"Try me. You can't hurt me."

His hands tightened on her hips, and he pulled her so close she could feel his erection pressing against the front of her jeans. Heat convulsed through her, and a sudden orgasm shook her to her core. He didn't take his gaze off her, didn't release her as the tremor wracked her body.

He just waited.

It subsided, and she took a breath. Her heart was racing, her blood thudding through her veins, but she felt strong. Stronger than she ever had. Nothing could stop her. Nothing at all.

One dark eyebrow went up. "You're okay."

"Of course I am."

Anticipation suddenly gleamed in his eyes, and he fisted her hair. "Be careful what you offer, my love, because I'm unlike any other man you've ever encountered." And then he kissed her, and she knew he was telling the truth.

Her entire body was on fire, and tremors were racing through her. His mouth was magic, a seduction of fairy tale lore. His hands on her back, the heat of his body melting the T-shirt from her body. She gripped his upper arms, felt the hard core of his muscles flexing beneath her hands, and her body lurched with excitement.

He cupped her breast and bit the side of her neck.

Another orgasm was coming. Like a tsunami building within her. Dear Lord, what would it be like to make love with him? How many times could he make her cross that threshold?

"Excuse me, sir." A cultured voice was suddenly right next to her. "But I'm afraid you'll have to relocate this activity."

The Godfather swore and pulled back, and the wave halted, poised at the crest, ready to tumble. She pressed her face to his chest, fighting the intense pressure rushing through her, desperate for release.

"My apologies." The Godfather hooked his arm around her waist. "We'll be on our way." His touch sent her over the edge, and the orgasm rushed through her like an electric shock.

"Dear God." Her legs gave out and she started to go down.

The Godfather caught her and guided her to the floor as the tremors hit her.

"Is she okay? Shall I call an ambulance?" The young man who spoke was wearing a black suit and a white tie. He had an aura of authority about him. He was attractive, with broad shoulders and a strong jaw.

But his eyes were cold. Calculating. A man's face that belied the youthful appearance. Raw fear rippled through her, and she felt her neck throbbing where she'd been lethally bitten so many years ago. "It was you," she whispered. "You're the one." The deedub had come back to enjoy her death. "Bastard!"

He grinned and saluted her as he stepped back. The Godfather caught her chin and forced her to look at him. He searched her face. "You okay?"

"Let me go! We have to stop him!"

"Stop who?"

"Him!" But when she sat up, the man was gone. Just a few patrons sipping wine by the draperies. "But—"

The Godfather grabbed her shoulders and shook her. "I need to know if you're okay!"

"Of course I am! Don't I look okay?" Shit! What was she doing? She was walking willingly to her death? She leapt to her feet and started to run for the front door.

"No!" The Godfather slammed her against the wall. He was radiating excitement. "You're the woman I've been searching for my whole life. You're coming home with me. Now."

Raw terror rippled through her. He was no longer resisting her. He was going to take her, and he was going to kill her. "No, no—"

His mouth crushed down over hers. She fought him off, trying to picture Nigel in her head. A man who didn't want to kill her. A perceptive artist who would see past this crazy persona and feel her truth—

And then Nigel was gone from her mind. All that was left was a screaming need for completion. For pushing the boundaries. For becoming the powerful woman she'd never been before. Her hands softened on the Godfather's shoulders, no longer fighting. Inviting.

"This is so exciting." The Godfather was grinning like a kid who'd just gotten a new puppy. "I can't believe I've found you! They say there's a partner for everyone, but I'd given up." He grabbed her hand and led her out the front doors.

Oh, yes, this was what she wanted. This was right.

"I've tried immortal women, vampires, incubi, succubi, fairies, angels, you name it. No one could handle me. And look at you! Two orgasms in less than a minute, and you didn't even pass out." He yanked open his limo door and tossed her on the seat. He was on top of her instantly. "I cannot *wait* to ravage you."

She touched his face, her heart swelling with appreciation. "No one has ever treated me like I'm tough. Thank you." After a lifetime of being afraid to walk to the mailbox, she felt as if she could fly. He was looking at her as if she could withstand a hurricane, and it made her feel like she actually could.

"And never in my life have I met a woman who enabled me to be who I really am." He kissed the flat of her palm. "Thank you, my dear Natalie, for embracing who I am. There's no fear in your eyes when you look at me."

She smiled. "And there's no worry in your eyes when you look at me." It felt so right to have him seeing her as strong and powerful. The Godfather saw her the way she had always wanted to be, and it made her almost believe it was true.

"Just raw, unadulterated appreciation and desire." The Godfather locked her hands over her head. "And now, it is just about us." His mouth descended on hers—

He flew out of the car and landed on his ass on the sidewalk.

Natalie jerked upright. "Did I do that?" Dammit! She'd thought he was man enough to handle her—

"Nope." An ostrich cowboy boot slammed down in the doorway, and a wide leather belt with a spur for a belt buckle came into sight. "I did." The intruder grabbed her ankle and hauled her out of the car. She hit the pavement and skidded across it, landing next to the Godfather, who was coughing and trying to pry a pink star out of his throat.

A pink star? She whirled around as a hunched man in tails and a sleek, black fedora slammed the car door shut and turned to face her.

He might be clean.

He might smell of Polo instead of rotten bananas.

And he might be wearing an Armani tuxedo instead of crusty jeans.

But those merciless black eyes were the same, and the way they cut into her drove chills through her spine. "Well, if it isn't my idol, Natalie Fleming, the gal with the best attitude on the planet." Augustus bowed deeply. "Welcome to my game, princess. You've just become a player."

Chapter 14

REINA'S AWE OVER HER FIRST SIGHTING OF RED CARPET WAS slightly tempered by the fact that Augustus was dragging her sister over it, toward a carriage drawn by six white, winged horses.

Natalie was fighting hard but Augustus's progress didn't appear to be at all impaired by the fact he'd chosen to abduct the Incredible Hulk with breasts. Nearby, Trinity was facedown on the asphalt, not moving.

Jarvis whipped the steering wheel to the right and Reina's sweet little Prius ducked between two limos and careened up onto the sidewalk, sending red velvet rope and brass posts flying.

"Hey!" Police officers came running as Jarvis threw open the door. Lights flashed as photographers whirled toward them, snapping pictures.

"I'll get Augustus," Jarvis commanded. "You take care of Trinity."

"Trin!"

She gave a weak wave. "Go get her," she mumbled. "I'll be fine in a second. Didn't quite manage to stop him."

"I need to get Natalie." Reina dove out of the car and raced across the cement toward her sister, but they were moving too fast. She'd never catch up before they reached the carriage. "Nat!"

Her voice was drowned out by the click of cameras and the shouts of the policemen closing in on Jarvis.

Hello? There was an abduction going on and they were worried about a little reckless driving? Okay, yeah, Augustus was flashing some badge with a star on it, but come on. Anyone could see that her sister was not some deviant that warranted a bounty hunter after her.

Her sister fought harder, and Augustus jerked her head, eliciting a howl of agony from Natalie.

Bastard. You don't get to hurt the people I care about. Reina's fingers began to tingle, and black dust began to spew from her fingertips. Hot damn! Nothing like seeing the jerk hurt her sister to provide the right motivation.

"She's mine!" A Tarzan yell echoed across the night, and the Godfather sped past Reina, wielding a stolen camera tripod over his head. "You do not take her from me!"

Okay, the Tsar of the Next Coming might be her sister's death wish, but he got big time points for trying to save her from big, bad Augustus. He swung the tripod at Augustus's head, but the assassin ducked, grabbed the tripod, and then slammed it over the big G's head.

The Orgasm King slumped to the pavement like a textbook patient in need of Viagra. Dammit! What good was he if his only skill was turning her sister on in a lethal fashion?

Natalie screamed for her fallen boy toy and ripped herself out of Augustus's grip in a sudden surge of "female must protect her lover" strength.

"Keep running, Nat!" Reina yelled.

But her sister fell to her knees beside the tongue tango expert. "I'm here, baby, I'm here."

Well, damn. Stopping to moon over a new flame wasn't going to be one of the building blocks of a successful escape, now was it?

Augustus grabbed Natalie by the ear and hauled her back.

"You're close enough, Reina," Jarvis shouted. "For God's sake, dust him now!"

Just do it. Yeah, baby, she was feeling the fire right now. She could take him down from a football field away. Easy. She wiggled her fingers to unleash the powder at Augustus and his head jerked up. His eyes widened, and she realized he hadn't noticed her until that moment. "Too late!" She unleashed the dust and it hit him square in the face.

He grabbed for his star and reared back to throw it, and then he got the biggest look of surprise on his face, tipped over, and went to sleep.

Right there.

On the street.

Sound asleep.

"Holy crap." Trinity stumbled up beside her. "You did it."

Reina was too shocked to do anything but stare at the snoozing bad guy. "I can't believe it." Yeah, Natalie was passed out beside him, due to Reina's apparent inability to target precisely, but she was okay with that kind of spillage. If she could keep Natalie knocked out for the next week, maybe they could keep Hormone Girl alive long enough to *really* keep her alive.

"Finish it," Jarvis ordered her. "Right now!" He had seven policemen at sword point up against her car.

"Wow. That's really sweet." Trinity nodded toward Jarvis. "Not many men would risk a lifetime in prison just so a girl can murder someone."

"He is pretty sweet," Reina admitted. Then she

noticed that his sword was deep purple, like an angry sky before a deadly tornado unleashed its rage upon an unsuspecting town. That couldn't be a good sign. "Sweet and deadly."

"Ohh…" Trinity put her hand over her heart. "Just like Blaine. That's such an appealing combination in a man."

"Reina," Jarvis warned. "Harvest him already. It's not that easy to keep all these cops at bay without causing them permanent damage."

"Yeah, okay. I'm on it." Reina slipped the scythe out of her back pocket and unfolded it.

"Stop!" A cop raced toward her, his gun right at Reina's heart. "Down with the weapon or I'll shoot."

Three more uniforms raced over to line up beside the first one. Feet spread, guns up, faces all too serious. Oh, come on. People never noticed when she was there to redirect a soul, but apparently wielding an ancient farm implement in an offensive manner was worth noting. Maybe it was time for a little chat with Death about giving his Guides invisibility skills *before* they actually became Reapers.

"Drop the blade," the officer shouted again.

"I can't do that." A milky white film was drifting up from Augustus's inert form. His soul was the lily white of purity? It should be black. How could he have an innocent soul? Oh, damn it, all! Like this wasn't difficult enough for her already!

Trinity eased up beside her, hands up in an "I don't have a weapon" stance. "You don't have time to get arrested, sweetie. Ditch the blade, talk your way out of it, and let's get out of here. We'll find Augustus later."

"Take him now," Jarvis shouted. "You won't get a better time. I'll take care of the cops."

Natalie groaned, and Trinity knelt beside her. "She's coming out of it," Trinity said. "And she's muttering something about how she's never going to be able to use her Pocket Rocket again after meeting the Big G."

"Oh, crap." Reina was out of time. The moment Natalie awoke, she'd be sucking face with the Sultan of Climax, and the pinnacle of all deaths would be shooting right toward them. She reared back to throw the scythe, and there was a loud crack and pain thudded into her shoulder.

She stumbled, and the scythe flew out of her suddenly numb hand. "Holy crap." Agony, anyone? Blood oozed from her shoulder and down her arm.

"I hit her," a police officer yelled.

She'd been shot? Seriously? Had they not heard about the immortal thing? Or the complete liberty of Death and his peeps to reap souls? Without her, souls would be causing traffic jams, stealing from dumpsters, sleeping in alleys, and doing all the other things that those poor homeless unfortunates were stuck doing.

"Reina!" Jarvis's frantic shout echoed over the din.

The concern in his voice was so sweet and endearing. "I'm okay. Just a flesh wound." But one that hurt like a mother! "I'm immortal, remember?" Or close enough.

"Immortals feel pain." Jarvis slammed the flat of his blade into a cop's head. One down. Six to go. "Hang on. Let me just clean these guys out of my way—" Another shot and then Jarvis was bleeding from his shoulder as well.

"Jarvis!"

"No problem, sweetheart, but I appreciate the concern." The bullet popped out of his shoulder and clanked on the ground. Well, that was handy. She should really develop that skill.

"Drop the sickle so they stop shooting," Jarvis commanded as he thwacked another cop and then whipped his sword around to block two more bullets. Then he was hit three more times, and blood was streaming from his chest. "I'll take care of Augustus for you."

Oh, how sweet was that? Not many men would be willing to murder for a girl. "Thanks, but it has to be me." She focused on Augustus's milky white soul.

"The Godfather's up!" someone shouted.

The Man of Endless O's was crawling relentlessly toward Natalie.

"Oh, no, no!" Trinity grabbed Natalie and dragged her toward a potted geranium on the other side of the sidewalk. Trinity's mom had the ability to transport anyone through vegetation, and if Trinity could get them over there, her mom would be able to suck them out. But the Godfather was moving too fast. "Stay away!" Trinity yelled. "This is one girl you're not going to get your woody into."

Reina whirled back toward Augustus, raised the sickle, and another bullet sent agony cascading through her left leg. She yelped with pain as her leg gave out and she crashed to the ground. The sickle spun out of reach on the sidewalk. "Oh, crap." They weren't going to let her get to Augustus, were they?

Suddenly there was a ferocious war cry and Nigel came leaping over the heads of the press. "I'm here, babes!" His palms were smoking and he unleashed dozens of tiny blades that hit guns and cameras with unerring precision. He paused when he saw Trinity dragging Natalie across the pavement. "Is Natalie okay? I can heal her."

"She's fine." Reina tried to stand up, but her legs gave out again. "I just knocked her out."

Nigel started toward Natalie, then spun around when the cops started shooting at him. Blades flew from his fingers, intercepting every bullet before it hit him.

"About time you bastards got here," Jarvis said. "Too busy getting your nails done?"

"Too busy trying to find Christian. Lover Boy appears to have taken off." Blaine leapt on top of the Godfather's limo, lifted his arms to the sky, and a wall of fire burst from his shoulders. "We need to find him after we finish here. Something's not right with him."

Blaine unleashed fiery lasers at the cops, their guns glowed red hot, and then all the officers were all screaming with pain and throwing their sizzling weapons down onto the pavement, including the ones who'd been using Reina for target practice.

Taking advantage of the involuntary disarmament, Reina began to drag herself toward her sickle, trying really hard not to think about all the bullets in her body. Yes, they wouldn't kill her, but they really did hurt. But she still had time for a happy ending. Augustus's soul was still outside his body. It wasn't too late. If she could just get there—

"Thanks, man." Jarvis leapt over the heads of the thronging media trying to pick the metal blades out of their microphones. He reached Reina's side as flames exploded from the pavement and shot fifty feet into the air, isolating their small group inside a twenty-foot circle, courtesy of Blaine. The scream of reporters, the click of cameras, the shouts of the cops, all went silent. No sound except the roar of flames, the crackle of blue fire, the smell of asphalt burning. She knew Blaine and Nigel were outside the circle, dealing with the cops, but inside, it was a separate world. The flames had created a boundary of protection, so they had to deal only with Augustus and not the interference of humans.

The heat inside the barrier was intense, but not as hot as it should have been. As in, she wasn't melting and her skin wasn't blistering.

"Blaine's controlling the heat." Jarvis grabbed her sickle then scooped her up. He cradled her against his body, squeezing tightly, as if he were relieved to feel her alive. Reina took a deep breath and let herself lean against him, taking a moment to regroup as he held her.

"Blaine can't hold the circle for long." Jarvis carried Reina across the carpet toward Augustus. The assassin's soul was fainter now, and she knew he was pulling it back into his body. She had seconds left to cleave it.

Jarvis set her beside Augustus and squeezed her waist for encouragement. "Do it."

The Godfather reached Natalie. "Hey, baby, I've got you. Come to me, sweetheart."

Natalie stirred, and her eyes flickered open. "You're okay?"

"Yeah, for you." He bent his head and kissed her, and suddenly Natalie was kissing him back so fiercely, the pavement started to melt beneath them.

"Down, boy, down!" Trinity kicked at the Godfather's pawing hands. "For God's sake, wait until you can get

a hotel room. Reina! Would you take out Augustus already so Blaine can drop his circle? I need to get to the plant so my mom can get us out of here."

"Yeah—" Reina felt panic start to build. Dammit. She needed to focus. Needed to clear her head—

Jarvis took Reina's face in his hands, forcing her to look at him. "Sometimes, the purest thing you can do is murder someone," he said. "You're doing the right thing."

She saw the truth in his eyes and clung to it. He believed in her and in her choices. He might be a warrior who had no problem with killing, but he was ruthlessly loyal and the protector of others, and if he thought she was doing the right thing, then she saw.

She took a deep breath and accepted his support, let it settle in her heart. "You're right, I know you're right." She looked at Augustus's soul, and in the white mist, she saw the faces of all the women in her family, all the ones she'd ever loved, who had all died. They had been innocent. Natalie was innocent. And it was time for the innocent to win.

And she knew she could do it.

She grabbed the sickle from Jarvis and swung it as hard as she could. The blade hit the base of the white smoky fountain and bounced off. "Oh, no—"

"You're almost halfway through." Jarvis pointed to a crack in the vanilla funnel. "Hit it right there again, and it'll be good."

"Okay." She gritted her teeth, tried not to think about what she was doing, and reared back to swing. And as the blade came down, she was hit with the horrifying, delightful, magnificent, self-loathing knowledge that she was going to reap her first soul.

The pleasure of seeing Reina achieving her goal was somewhat diminished by the raw agony in her eyes. Jarvis wasn't used to women who so clearly felt bad about inflicting pain, death, and hell on others. Who knew that kind of anguish in a female's eyes was such a turn on?

He was adding it to his list of "must haves" on his online dating profile after he exploded and went to the Afterlife. Assuming they had dating there. But hell. What woman could compare with the reality of Reina? Her courage, her passion, and her love for her sister? No one. Reina was it. His only moment in the sunshine, and he was going to enjoy every damn minute in her presence.

He smiled encouragingly at her, supporting her in the endeavor of her heart. "Lovely job, sweetheart." He grabbed the soul and held it out, like a ribbon, for Reina to cut.

She took a deep breath. "Okay." She brought the scythe down with impressive force for a woman who was so horrified by what she was about to do. The blade was inches away—

She suddenly dropped the scythe and collapsed to her knees. "Oh, my darling, Augustus! I'm so sorry I almost hurt you."

Jarvis blinked at her abdication. "What are you doing?"

She wrapped her arms around Augustus and pressed her cheek against his chest. "Oh, sweet man, tell me you're okay. I could never go on if I knew I stripped the world of a man of your lethal capabilities. You're magnificent, and I cherish your spirit and the challenge you bring to my life." She kissed his forehead. "When you recover, please let me buy you dinner."

"Reina!" Jarvis grabbed her arm, trying to pry her off the crusty old man. What in hell's name was going on? Yeah, she was a softy in her heart, and he'd been half-expecting her to drop the scythe, but going on a hug-fest with the scumbag made no sense. Had the man hit her with some magic spell or something? "Let go of him—"

"No!" She pushed Jarvis away and focused a loving, adoring gaze on Augustus. The kind of dotty expression one might expect when a woman looked up on a cute little puppy or a newborn baby. It was pure, unabating *love*. For Augustus? Jealousy ripped through him, and he unsheathed his sword, sudden rage burning through him. He recognized it as hate, and he embraced it, sending it all onto the sniveling bastard who was stealing his woman's affection and love when all he deserved was her antipathy and—

Love? *Love?* "Holy crap." There was only one being on this earth that could force Reina to love a man as despicable as Augustus. The Guardian of Love. Jarvis grabbed Reina away from Augustus and tucked her protectively against him, then vaulted to his feet. He shielded his eyes against the smoke, searching for the man he knew had to be there. "Cameron!" he yelled. "Where are you?"

Out of the flames stepped the Guardian of Love.

His brother had never looked so good.

And that was a very, very big problem.

Cam strode past the flames, wearing an Armani suit, slicked back hair, calf-leather shoes, and a huge ass diamond in his ear. Cam, a vegan who wore only synthetic materials so no plants or animals would be harmed in the creation of his wardrobe. Cam, the man who would spend hours stretched out in the mud so he could be one with the song of the bullfrog.

Cam was now a player. A money-grubbing sophisticate who had clearly abdicated from the lifestyle and morals that had made him worthy of protecting love.

Cameron was studying Natalie and the Godfather with great interest, and hadn't even noticed Jarvis. Again, not an indication that his brother was in alignment with his spirit. "Cameron!"

But his brother didn't hear him and walked closer to the dating duo, a fascinated look on his face.

"There you go," Reina crooned to Augustus, hanging over Jarvis's arm in an attempt to get closer to her new crush. "Your soul will be back in a minute."

"Shit." Reina was going to lose her chance. No way was he going to let her down. She'd worked too hard for this moment, and he was going to give it to her.

Jarvis grabbed Reina's sickle and blasted it through Augustus's fading soul. A deafening scream filled the air. The weapon turned silver and then disintegrated in his hand as Augustus's soul slipped back into this body.

"Oh, no! The sickle!" Reina lunged for the particles, but they sifted through her fingers and disappeared. The sickle was gone. Utterly destroyed. Her face was stricken. "I can't get another one. I can't reap a soul without it."

Oh, *shit*. He'd screwed up. "Reina, I'm so sorry—"

Searing pain suddenly ripped through Jarvis's body and he staggered. He looked down at the hand he'd used to wield the sickle and saw that the skin was blistering and sloughing off. "Jesus."

"You've been poisoned." Reina grabbed his hand and flipped it over so she could look at it. He expected her touch to provide relief like it always did, but there was nothing. Just more pain, and the beast within continued to get stronger. He was too far gone.

"No one can wield a Death weapon except for an authorized person," Reina said. "It helps prevent theft and the unauthorized use of our reaping technology. Nigel! Help!"

Jarvis's body was throbbing so much it kind of reminded him of the time Angelica had tested radioactive acid on his skin to see what his pain threshold was. "Mother of hell."

"I got this one covered." Nigel burst through a break in the flames. "The doctor is in." He glanced at Natalie in the Godfather's arms, and his face darkened. "That girl deserves better," he snapped.

"Nigel!" Jarvis barked. "Get your ass over here!"

Nigel jerked his gaze off the ravenous couple and crouched beside Jarvis and grabbed his hands. He frowned as he studied Jarvis's rapidly disintegrating skin that was turning into a ghastly shade of green. "Fascinating. I've never seen this before."

"He's been infected with death." Reina knelt beside him. "We need to get it out of him."

"I'd agree that would be a good plan." As Nigel began to work on him, Jarvis hunched over, struggling to contain the hell ripping through his shields, stripping him of everything sane, of everything human, of everything living. Hate began to build, filling the vacuum left behind by the death sweeping his body. "Cameron," Jarvis gasped, his voice hoarse. "It's time."

Napoleon burst through the flames that were clearly a defense only against humans. Blaine was getting soft. Never the same after he'd been murdered by his own girlfriend, apparently. "There you are, you wife-stealer!" Napoleon sprinted across the clearing and shook Augustus's limp shoulder. "Tell me where Angelica is!"

Jarvis fought for consciousness, barely aware of Reina and Nigel working him over. "Cameron," he snapped. "For hell's sake, it's me. Your brother."

Cameron's gaze finally flicked to Jarvis. He blinked. "Jarvis?"

"Yeah, man. I'm going over the edge. Help me out."

"Help you?" Cameron strode across the clearing in the fire and crouched before him. "You son of a bitch. You left us."

"I sacrificed myself to save your life. Angelica wanted you." He gritted his teeth against the fresh onslaught of pain. "Took me instead. So you could be free."

"Free? Is that what you call it?" Cam squatted as Jarvis's knees buckled. "Free to watch my own father go off the deep end, terrified for his favorite son? His love for you broke him. The more I tried to save him, the more he wanted to die. I was alone at age eight, you heartless bastard!"

Jarvis's stomach began to burn. His lungs seared. He couldn't breathe. The pain was everywhere, the fury, the self-loathing. "Dad's dead?"

"Yes, he is, brother dear. He tried to fill his heart

by finding true love. He married the most wonderful woman, and then she died, too, and that was it. Too much loss of those he loved. He killed himself."

Jarvis grabbed his brother's shirt and yanked him down. "Why didn't you save him? Why didn't you fill him with love, you son of a bitch?"

"Love was what killed him!" Cam shoved Jarvis off him. "Don't you get it? Love broke him! Love kills, big brother. Love doesn't save."

Shit. How had this happened? Everything was supposed to have worked out when he protected his brother. But he'd fucked it all up. He was supposed to save and protect his family, but somehow they'd all lost without him. His dad dead? Cameron insane? Jesus.

Pain knifed though his gut and he doubled over, gripping his stomach as the hatred spewed through him. Reina set her hands on his forehead, and he fought to concentrate on the coolness of her touch, but he couldn't access it. Things were raging too wildly inside him. Couldn't control it.

"But my new mentor has shown me the light." Cameron leapt to his feet and raised his arms above his head. "I accept that love kills," he shouted. "I kill!"

Reina grabbed Cam's arm. "Guardian of Love," she shouted. "Save your damn brother, now!"

"No!" Cameron began to hula dance in time to the crackling of the flames that Blaine was still holding up. "Let the hate explode! Let it fill the world! It's not going to hurt anything. Fear is what destroys the world. Love saves it. I am love, I am death, I am everything. I am world peace!"

Jarvis fought to make sense of what his brother was

saying, but his mind was scattered. His brain was snapping under the onslaught. Blind hate. Mindless rage. Fighting to take him. "Cameron," he gasped. "World peace starts with saving the earth from me."

Reina grabbed Cam's wrist and tugged hard. "Hey! He needs your help! Stop the hate!"

Cam flung her to the side, and Reina stumbled over her sister and the Godfather, who were still making out. She landed on her knees with a yelp of pain that eviscerated the last shred of humanity still within Jarvis.

Jarvis swore and grabbed for his sword. He ripped it out of the scabbard and had it at his brother's throat, fury coursing his body like he'd never felt before. "Never touch her like that again." Pain was bleeding through every pore of Jarvis's body, he could feel the poison racing through him, but it couldn't stop him. He was too angry. Too crazy.

Nigel moved up beside him. "Stand down, Jarvis," he said quietly. Calmly. "Pull your shit together. You can do it."

"Back off," Jarvis snarled. It was too late for Nigel to save him. He would poison Nigel if his teammate tried to touch him. "Get away from me."

"See? You fear that I'm hurting her. That's what drives the world. Fear of loved ones dying." Cameron grabbed the blade of Jarvis's sword, and the sword began to glow black with hate. What the hell? His brother wasn't taking away the anger? "Think of it, brother. What if Death came in the form of love? It becomes a gift." Cameron held up his hands, as if he were painting a mural in the sky. "Death no longer becomes something to fear, and without fear, we have peace on earth."

He bowed. "Love's assassin, at your service. Pleased to save the world. Launch, Friday night at midnight. Tickets are on sale for a hundred thousand per head."

Jarvis stared at his brother, sudden realization plunging through the disabled rut of his brain. "You're the assassin Death is launching this weekend." Son of a bitch. Cam was the one he'd promised to help Reina find investors and victims for. He shot a sharp look at Reina, who was struggling to her feet. "Did you know this?"

"No, of course not—" She caught his glance and her face paled. "Your eyes are so black. You've got to stop." She reached for Jarvis, then Augustus grabbed her ankle and hauled her back toward his carriage.

A new, lethal fury arose inside Jarvis at the sight of that bastard hurting his woman. He shoved his ranting brother aside and sprinted toward Augustus. "Leave her alone." The snarl coming out Jarvis's throat was foreign, a noise in the distance.

Augustus whipped out a pink star. Jarvis knocked it out of the air before it hit him. It careened across the area and smacked Cam in the chest.

Cam sucked in his breath. "Oh, dear lord, almighty! That really hurts!"

"Stop!" Napoleon leapt in front of Jarvis. "You can't kill Augustus before I've found Angelica." Napoleon hurled something small and black out at Jarvis, and amber smoke filled the air. Rich, luxurious, decadent filth that caked Jarvis's lungs. A black magic spell?

He didn't care. He didn't stop. He had to find Reina. He had to prevent Augustus from taking her.

He charged forward, swinging blindly, recklessly abandoning all the strategic thought he'd been trained in. He barely heard Nigel shouting at him to cease. He scarcely felt the swing of his weapon as he thrust to where Augustus had last been.

But he felt the moment his sanity completely snapped and he became the monster he'd been fighting against his whole life.

Oh, yeah. He felt *that*.

Chapter 15

YOU KNOW, THERE WERE TIMES WHEN IT MADE A GIRL FEEL snuggly to have a man lose it at the sight of her in danger.

When that man was the Guardian of Hate and he was emerging out of a black cloud with a look on his face that said there wasn't much left of the man, well, there wasn't exactly time to enjoy the moment.

He jammed his sword through Augustus's chest, and the assassin dropped Reina, stumbling as Jarvis yanked the sword out and reared back for a second strike.

"Trinity!" Nigel tackled Jarvis from behind. "Take him with you! He's going over the edge. We need to get him out of here."

"I can help him." Reina could see Nigel was losing the containment battle. Jarvis was too strong and too insane. "Go heal Cam before he dies. I'll take care of Jarvis."

"You can't—"

"I can! Just help me get him to the plant." Reina threw herself against Jarvis. He bellowed and his arms snapped around her. His grip was tight, almost smothering her, and she fought for breath even as she wrapped her arms around him. "Take us, Trin."

"Blaine!" Trinity shouted. "Let me out!"

The wall of flames split, opening a path to the geranium. "I need to get Natalie," Trinity said. "Can you knock them out again?"

Reina powdered the nearly copulating duo and they

both passed out, the Godfather facedown on Natalie's half-exposed breast, her hands frozen in his hair.

"Damn, girl, I'm so glad you have your mojo back." Trinity shoved the Godfather aside and dragged Natalie across the pavement. "Hurry! The flames are getting lower. Blaine's running out of steam."

Jarvis hooked Reina under his arm, raised his sword, and charged Augustus. Jarvis's skin was burning, sizzling, crackling with fire, and he hadn't appeared to notice that Augustus no longer had Reina or that the assassin was sitting on his butt, trying to heal the sword wound. He was going for the kill anyway, and that would deprive Reina of the chance to cleave Augustus's soul properly.

"Stop, you crazy fuck!" Nigel jumped in Jarvis's path and braced himself for the charge. "We're not letting you die, you bastard!"

"I'm ready. Bring him over here." Trinity was at the geranium with Natalie.

Um, yeah, sort of hard to do when she was being carted along like arm candy on a murder mission. She punched his ribs. "Jarvis! Stop!"

But he didn't. Couldn't. He was too far gone.

Blaine leapt over the wall of the flames and landed beside Nigel just as Jarvis plowed into them. The two warriors held their ground and threw Jarvis off them, somehow managing to avoid being plunged to death by the sword. Jarvis careened backwards. He regained his balance and prepared to launch himself at them again.

"Mother of hell." Nigel fisted his blades. "He's gonna go. Fuck!"

"No! He's not going to explode!" Reina shoved

her hand into his face and blasted him with her most deadly powder.

He swore, then dropped to the sidewalk. Unconscious, and still intact. Holy crap. It worked on him? Wow. When a girl got her mojo back, she really got it back. Nothing like fearing the loss of the one man who'd made her come alive in the last twenty years to make a girl step up.

"Nice work, Reina." Blaine and Nigel hauled him toward Trinity and the geranium. "Get him out of here."

Reina rushed over as his friends dumped him next to Trinity. "I've got him." God only knew how long the dust would hold him. She needed to be there when he woke up. "Go help Cam," she told them. "He can't die. And please, detain Augustus for me. I need to kill him."

"Both Jarvis and Natalie need my healing." Nigel took up residence next to Natalie. "I'm going with you."

But Blaine looked right at Reina. "Can you really take care of him?" His question was loaded with threat of what he would do if she was wrong. Loyalty to his friend that would be enforced at all costs, no matter how much his fiancée loved her.

She met his gaze. "Yes."

He nodded once, accepting her words as truth. "We stay behind." He jerked his chin at Nigel. "We need to clean up this mess."

Blaine turned and headed off after Cam, but Nigel didn't move. He just stood there, staring, his face wretched as his gaze flicked between Natalie and Jarvis.

Reina was shocked by the anguish on his face. Where was the cool, collected artist who was never rattled by anything? Was it all a facade? Because right now, Nigel looked like a warrior haunted by hells that had no words.

Reina touched his arm. "I swear I can do more for him than you can. The best thing you can do for him is to save Cameron, right?"

Nigel swore under his breath. "Yeah, yeah." But he didn't move. He just stood there.

"Touch Jarvis," Trinity ordered Reina. "We need to all be connected when my mom transports us."

Reina grabbed his hand and reached for her friend. The women touched fingers. "Now, Mom," Trinity said.

Reina had a split second to see Augustus racing toward her, and she went sick with the thought that she didn't have her sickle anymore.

And then they were gone.

Reina hurried down the stairs to the basement cells the Fleming family had erected years ago to contain family members racing toward their deedub high.

She peeked in at Natalie, who was still safely asleep in the first cell. Two hits by death powder in less than five minutes was taking its toll, and Reina was okay with that. Why hadn't she thought of it before? Keep Natalie asleep and she couldn't escape, right?

It was Jarvis she was worried about.

Reina slipped down the hall to the farthest enclosure. Jarvis's arms were chained above his head, and he was still unconscious. Trinity had insisted that he go under lockdown until the men got back, because the two women alone would never be able to contain him once he woke up.

Reina didn't like it. Not after his years of imprisonment. And she didn't think the chains or cell would hold anyway. As soon as they'd gotten him locked up, Trinity had gone upstairs to track down Blaine and Nigel and find out what had happened after the women had left.

Jarvis's hands were a dark purple, and his body was twitching even in its comatose state. "You do not have permission to die yet," she commanded.

He twitched again, and the purple crept up his wrists in sheer defiance of her orders.

That was it.

She was going in.

She grabbed the handle of the heavy steel door, braced her left foot on the wall, and hauled as hard as she could. Her muscles strained and sweat trickled down her brow, but it finally creaked open.

She stepped inside the cell, into a sauna that was at least twenty degrees hotter than the hallway. The hot emotion of hate was changing his environment, bleeding off him. She could feel it pricking her skin, like millions of invisible thumbtacks. "Jarvis?"

His body began to twitch and his eyes flew open, blind and unseeing. His eyes rolled back in his head and his body began to convulse.

"Jarvis! It's me! Reina—"

An inhuman shriek of such horror, such suffering, and such *fury* ripped out of Jarvis's throat. He fought the chains, screaming as if he were being skinned alive. Blood streamed from Jarvis's wrists and ankles as he yanked at the chains. He charged and was jerked off his feet by the chains. His head slammed back against the steel with a brutal crack.

"Stop it! This is not the way for you to go!" She bolted across the cell and threw her arms around his neck, pinning herself to his writhing body as he staggered to his feet again. "You're not hate!" she shouted over his screams, nearly losing her grip in all the blood. "You're still in there! I know it!" She wrapped her legs around his waist, clinging to him as he bellowed again, clearly not listening to her sage and loving advice.

She grabbed his hair, forced his face down to hers, and kissed him.

He didn't even notice. He wasn't even holding onto her. He was still fighting his chains, battling for freedom, trying to rip the world apart. Hello? Where was the ego-inducing fall-on-his-knees response to her kiss?

He was being consumed by hate, but she knew that there was a good man inside that body. She'd seen it in the way he'd protected her, in his determination to find his brother. She was not going to let hate take this man. Not this way. He deserved better.

Hadn't he told her that the opposite of hate was love? That the trick was to convert hate to love? That was his brother's specialty?

Screw Cameron-the-unhelpful. She knew love. Yeah, Jarvis was too crazed to respond to poetry or candlelight, but he was a man, wasn't he? Men were *never* too insane for sex. And since men and women always confused sex with love, it might just work.

It was time to bring out the girls.

She pulled back from him and ripped her shirt off. His eyes were unseeing, blindly staring past her at some demon she couldn't see, the one coming for him. She tugged her jeans off, her hands shaking. More skin, more skin. He needed skin.

His sword was pulsating with purple and black smog. He screamed again, sweat streaming down his temples. The veins were standing out on his neck, and he was the epitome of power, of strength, of fury.

He was everything she needed right now, and she was keeping him. But first, she had to get him naked, and she had to do it before he accidentally killed one of them.

"Okay, nappy time, big guy." She waggled her fingers at him, tapping him with just a wee bit of powder. Enough to give her two minutes.

He shuddered and sagged to the floor. The chains kept his heavily muscled arms stretched awkwardly above his head, tweaking his shoulders horribly.

The silence was deafening in the small room. She swallowed, suddenly nervous about what she was going to do. Did she really have that much faith in him, and in her?

She thought of the way he'd kissed her so desperately in the woods, how he'd come back to himself after their connection. It had happened again and again. Yes, he'd never been like this, but they'd never taken things as far as they could.

The connection between them was beyond the explainable, but she'd felt its strength and power in every fiber of her spirit. This would work. They could do it. He would never walk away from her, and she wasn't going to abandon him.

She wiped her clammy hands on her bare thighs and then reached for the chain buckled around his wrist.

"Don't prove me wrong, Jarvis. I don't want either of us to die."

Then she unhooked his chains.

~~~

"It's okay, Jarvis. Everything is okay." Reina frantically stroked Jarvis's chest as he struggled to regain consciousness. She expected him to leap to his feet in another rage, but his heart rate calmed and his breathing quieted. He was still out.

She still had time.

Desperate now, knowing she had only seconds, she tugged his shirt over his head. His muscles were bunched, and a light smattering of dark hair covered his chest. A few scars, probably from a time before he became immortal under Angelica's care. The rest of him was flawless. A warrior who had healed every injustice done to him. No evidence, except those in his heart.

He shifted under her, and his face contorted as if he were fighting demons inside his head. Which, of course, he was.

The sands were falling too quickly through the hourglass.

She pulled off his boots and tossed them aside, then went for the button of his jeans. Unfastened, unzipped, disrobed. Not nearly as elegantly as the words implied, but hey, naked was naked.

She bit her lip as she studied his massive body strung out over the floor. Should she re-chain him before he woke up?

No. He'd been imprisoned his whole life, and she knew that taking choices away made everything worse.

She would have to trust that she could do it.

She let out her breath and straddled him. As her thighs wrapped around his hips, she shuddered at the feel of so much skin against hers. It felt right, so right. Despite the purplish discoloration spreading out from his palms to the rest of his body, of course. "Okay, Jarvis, let's make this happen."

His head flew back, his body convulsed, and a terrifying bellow ripped through the air.

"Yikes!" She threw her arms around his neck, anchored her legs around his hips, and hung on as he bucked and raged. "Hey! I'm naked, for heaven's sake! You better start appreciating it, because I haven't taken the time to get naked with a man since I watched my third sister die!"

She fisted his hair, yanked him close, and kissed him again.

He struggled to get free, but he didn't have his full strength yet, and he couldn't get away from her loving affections. She kissed him harder, and she shuddered when her nipples brushed over his bare chest.

In her dreams, her reentry into the world of sex was supposed to happen after her life was settled, with a lovely man who cherished her, in which the lovemaking was a candlelit, peaceful, nurturing experience that filled her bruised heart with joy and love.

Not a ride on a mechanical bull trying to buck her off.

His arms suddenly went around her, yanking her down, and then he was kissing her back. Desperate, frantic, but without the force she knew he wanted to inflict on her, because he was still too drugged for full engagement. Which meant she had time to break through before he was too strong for her.

"You're in control, Jarvis." She kissed his throat. "You're not hate—"

He grabbed her hair and yanked her head back. He nipped her throat, edging that line between pain and pleasure. Well, on the plus side, at least sacrificing her body to save her sister and the world felt good, right?

He went still suddenly. She looked into his pitch black eyes, and she realized he had just returned to full consciousness, and only the beast was present.

But there was agony in his eyes, a deep-rooted terror of losing control. Her heart lurched for him, for that feeling of having everything that mattered spiraling out of control. She lived with that fear every day as she watched her family die, and she knew how much it sucked. She stopped pretending she'd gotten naked in some completely altruistic need to save him from himself.

She was doing it because she was the one who needed his touch. She needed to see his humanity return and know she'd done it, to know she'd made a difference to someone she cared about. She needed to save someone she loved at least once. She needed to succeed, and she needed it to be with him.

He kissed her again, almost violently, and she realized that it was no longer her choice. She'd offered herself up to the monster, and he'd accepted the gift.

His hands moved to her waist with astonishing speed, anchoring her on his pelvis. He plundered her mouth as he settled her deeper onto his lap, his fierce groan of pleasure licking at the heat already pulsing through her belly. His erection hardened beneath her, and excitement tingled between her thighs, curling into her belly.

One move, and he would be inside her, plunging deep, taking her, making her his.

Oh, dear God. Was she really going to do this? Wasn't there something inherently flawed with the premise of making love when one of the partners was insane and under the influence of hate? Did he even know it was her?

She pulled back. She couldn't do it.

"Reina." He caught her face between his hands and she saw the smallest fleck of blue in his eyes. He was coming back. Because of her? *Because of her*.

"Don't leave me," he said, his voice raw, throaty, barely recognizable. "I need you."

The entreaty in his eyes nearly broke her heart. A man like him asking for help? "I'm here."

His eyes flashed with a lethal darkness that made her skin grow cold, and then he grabbed her behind the neck and pulled her down. His kiss was instant fire, racing through her body. His lips were hot, his skin was burning, his muscles rigid. The internal battle was waging, but he was hanging on, fighting for survival.

She abandoned all hesitation and kissed him back. His response was instant, powerful, and intense. His fingers dug into her skin, leaving marks. His mouth closed over her nipple, a hot, wet assault of brutal, soul searing need. His desperation for her was ripping at her in every kiss, in every touch of his hands. She felt the hell slagging at his mind, sensed the demons he was trying to outrun. He was seeking refuge in her touch, in her kisses.

This is what she'd wanted. This is what she'd craved. She was meant for him, for this, to be his salvation, to make a difference in his world. To use her love to temper the blackness within him. *I'm here for you, Jarvis.*

She wrapped her legs around him as he attacked her breasts, and he groaned, a deep-throated sound of satisfaction as his hips began to pump, his erection slamming against her, building, preparing for the ultimate invasion.

His body was so hot, his muscles rock hard, sliding beneath his skin as he drove against her, as his mouth consumed her, kissing her again, so deeply, so fiercely she could hear the crash of their teeth, feel his tongue so deep she felt like he was a part of her, taking over, owning her.

His possessiveness was evident in every thrust of his body, in each demanding kiss, and it stoked fires in her that had no business responding to domination by a male who would soon explode, ripping her heart from her soul.

But she was so empty inside, a gaping well of fear and loneliness, and his fire was filling the chasm with warmth, with belonging, with something that made tears slide from the corners of her eyes as she clutched at his shoulders. He gave her light and hope, filled her well with renewed energy. She scrunched her eyes shut. *God, no, Reina. Don't get sucked in emotionally—*

But it was too much, too intense, and she felt herself falling, succumbing to the hot desire pulsing through her, to his intense yearning and need for her.

She didn't want to resist. She wanted to fall under his spell. The strength in his body, the fierceness of his soul... it was intoxicating.

He grabbed her hips again and lifted her up.

She stared down in the turbulent depths of his eyes as he positioned her. His gaze was riveted to her face, as if she were an anchor he was holding desperately onto. She met his gaze, losing herself in the man fighting to surface.

She felt him pressing at her entrance, and a feeling of absolute rightness pulsed through her. This wasn't a raw slap-and-tickle to save the world. This was Jarvis, and they were connected in ways neither of them even understood. This was right, this was their moment, no matter how it had come about, or what happened afterward.

"Yes," she whispered.

He thrust. Nothing gentle, nothing seductive, just one powerful move and he was deep inside her. *Oh, dear God.* It felt so right.

Jarvis went utterly still, and a feral growl ripped out of his throat.

She knew what he meant. She kind of wanted to growl herself—

Then he started moving, and she forgot about anything but their connection, the feel of his body sliding into hers as if this was what they'd come to this earth to do. She moved her hips, and then he was sinking deeper. Faster.

She gripped his shoulders, bowing her head as she fought against the wave trying to take her. Trying to hang on for as long as he needed.

"Reina. I need to see you." His voice was still raw, desperate.

She lifted her head and met his gaze. His face softened. "You're okay. I'm not tainting you."

She nodded at the fear in his eyes. "You can't poison me. It's okay."

"It's okay," he repeated, as if trying to convince himself. His gaze was fixated on her as he ground deeper and faster, until she couldn't think, couldn't do anything but hang on and succumb to the sensations rolling over her.

Fire began to lick down her limbs, igniting each inch of her until the sensations exploded inside her, overwhelming her soul and her body. She screamed his name and his deep roar mixed with hers, his body convulsing as he drove again and again, as if he was stripping himself of everything in his soul and turning it all over to her for safekeeping.

He groaned and fought it, as if he couldn't trust himself to let go, to allow it to happen.

"I've got you," she whispered. She wrapped her arms around him and cradled his head to her heart. "Everything's going to be okay."

His body went rigid beneath her, his hands dug into her hips, his body did one final shudder, and then he bellowed as the orgasm took him over the edge. She clung to him as they both rode the vibration tearing through them again and again, until it stripped them both of every bit of life they had in their souls. He gave a final lurch and collapsed back onto the floor, dragging her down on top of him, his breathing raw and harsh on her neck.

Too exhausted to fight, she sank into his embrace, into the protective circle of his arms as he tucked her against him and pressed his face to her throat.

The storm was over. Who had won?

Chapter 16

WHEN REINA FELT THE SOFT BRUSH OF JARVIS'S LIPS OVER her hair, she had her answer. She knew that hate had been defeated, at least for the moment.

"You give me peace, Reina Fleming," Jarvis whispered softly. "Peace I never thought I could have."

And with that one comment, her tension released, and tears filled her eyes. They'd done it.

"Reina?" Sudden worry lined his face. His whiskers were prickly, making him look rugged and untamed, but his long eyelashes framed eyes that held enough blue to keep the black at bay. He traced his thumb over her cheek so tenderly it made more tears form. "How do you feel? Are you okay?"

Reina cupped his wrist, holding his hand to her face, loving the tenderness of his touch. "Oh, no, I'm fine."

"You're fine." He repeated the words with a breath of awe, of disbelief, of wonder. He traced his finger over her cheekbone, as if she were some fragile treasure he was afraid of breaking. "I really don't affect you, do I?"

She laughed. "Well, I wouldn't say *that*…"

He smiled and kissed her again, but this time it was tender, soft, none of the brutality and desperation of before. A flirt. "I've never been able to do this before."

"Do what?" She was afraid to move, afraid that the moment of intimacy would disappear. It had been so long since she'd felt treasured, but being in his arms, feeling his kiss… it was a moment she would always hold dear in her memories.

"Indulge." He feathered kisses over her eyebrows. "Touch."

She closed her eyes as he trailed his fingers down her spine, lightly drifting over her buttocks. "That feels good."

He laughed softly. "Yeah, you could say that." He nuzzled her neck, her throat, her breasts, his kisses so gentle and seductive, like a hot wind blowing over her ultra sensitive skin. "You brought me back, Reina. I have no idea how you did it." He paused. "You don't have any idea of your strength, do you?"

His words reverberated deep inside her. They touched upon the person she'd wanted to be, but had never succeeded at being. But she sensed his belief in her, his certainty that she was some indomitable force that could knock down any obstacle. Which was just sort of absurd, you know, given how everything had come out at Symphony Hall. Oh… right… She'd forgotten about all that…

Jarvis tangled a lock of hair around his finger. "What's that look for, rock star?"

"My sickle broke." She rubbed her hand over his chest, enjoying the feel of his toned muscles. Touching him felt so good. Like he was hers, to do with whatever she wanted.

Jarvis rubbed his jaw, his brow furrowed as if he were trying to remember. The lines around his mouth were deep, but his expression was calm and focused. Determined. The warrior was back in residence, which was good for everyone involved. "Did I break it?"

"Sort if. You were trying to be the hero, which was very sweet. You were trying to kill Augustus for me." She sighed. "So, yeah, we've still got the same problems as before, only worse. I don't have a sickle, and your brother is turning out to be a bit of a selfish jerk who won't help you—"

"Cam!" He swore under his breath, set her to the side, and jumped to his feet. His body was lean and lithe as he strode across the cell and grabbed his jeans. But the raw marks on his wrists from the chains were a brutal reminder of what he'd just been through, and where he was headed. "We've got a problem."

His tone was all business and distant, and she stiffened at his sudden departure. Yes, yes, she understood they were in the middle of war, but at the same time, it hurt to have him so easily dismiss her. Hadn't he felt that tenderness and that connection? Apparently not. Apparently, it really had been just sex for him, which sucked, because the way her heart was aching at his withdrawal made her fear that it had been a lot more than sex for her. "Which problem are you referring to?" She grabbed her own pants, trying not to feel completely naked and exposed, which was kind of hard when she *was* naked and exposed.

Come on, Reina, pull yourself together. She needed to grab her bra, get some clothes, focus on the mission. He empowered her, he believed in her, but that *didn't* mean she had to start really caring about him, right? Of course right.

Except she knew she had. Way too much.

—⁂—

Jarvis still couldn't believe it as he replayed the conversation with his brother in his head. His memories from the time when he'd snapped were returning, a bit foggy, but at least he could recall them. "Cam's the assassin that I'm helping you find a victim and investors for."

Reina turned sharply, her lacy thong dangling from her fingers. "I know."

"And he's fired up about it." Jarvis had barely registered the discussion at the time. He should've grabbed his brother and bailed right then. But he hadn't. *Shit.* He'd been so worried about Augustus killing Reina that he'd deviated from his *one* purpose in life: to protect the world from hate by containing himself and protecting his brother. He grabbed his boots and shoved them onto his feet, glaring at Reina. "I could have saved him, but you distracted me."

"Me?" Her hands went to her hips. "For your information, we all sacrificed to get you out of there. Did I stay to try to take Augustus? No. Did Blaine drain himself to protect you long enough so you could escape? Yes. Did Nigel stay behind to try to save your brother? Yes. To help you." She stalked across the room and poked him in the chest. "So, do *not* ever use that attitude with me. I do not distract you. I help you, for heaven's sake!"

He stared at her, warring between admiration for the fact she stood up to him and shock over what she'd just said. "Save Cam's life? What happened to him?"

"You deflected a pink star into his chest when you were going mad."

"Jesus." He didn't remember that at all. He grabbed his phone to check on his brother, but before he dialed, he saw a text from Nigel. *Crisis averted. But your brother got away. Love is powerful shit, man. I like you better. We're tracking him now.* "He's missing, but okay." He strode toward the door of the cell. "We have to go after him—"

"We won't find him." Reina tugged her jeans over those legs that had been wrapped around him only moments before.

He stopped, unable to stop himself from staring. Shit, he didn't want to walk away. He wanted to grab her, bury himself in her, and never lose that feeling of peace again.

Reina paused, her jeans halfway up her thighs. "Don't look at me like that."

He walked over to her and ran his hands down her bare arms, and lightly kissed her. "Thank you," he said quietly. "You gave me a gift I'll cherish for the rest of my life."

Her eyes glistened. "Don't be nice," she said. "I can't deal with it right now."

"Why not?"

"Because you're going to die!" she burst out.

She was right. He didn't have the right to ask her to care, not after all she'd been through. Even if she made him want to get down on his knees and beg for her heart, ask for the chance to have someone see something in him other than hate. For someone to care when he was gone.

But he couldn't do that to her. It would have to be enough to know that she could care, if he forced it. If she let herself do it.

"We have to focus," she said, her voice strained.

"I know." Regretfully, with a sense of loss beyond anything he'd ever thought he could feel, he grabbed the waistband of her jeans and tugged them up over her hips. "We'll go find Cam and—"

"Now that Death knows you're after him, he'll hide Cam." She moved out of his reach and fastened her jeans.

He flexed his fingers against the urge to haul her back over to him. "You know all his hiding places—"

"No one knows his hiding places." She pulled her shirt over her head and tugged it down, shutting him out from the last intimate view of her body. "We'll have to get Cameron at the festival. We'll work on my stuff in the meantime."

Jarvis picked up his scabbard and slung it over his back, forcing himself to focus on their situation. "No. I'm not letting it get that close—"

"Death won't let Cameron kill until the festival, because it will decrease his value if it's not a virgin reaping." She slipped her feet into her shoes. "Waiting until then gives us time to put everything in place to save my sister, so we both win. My issues matter too, you know."

She did have a point, but his brother wasn't the only problem. Jarvis held out his hands. They were a dark brackish purple. "I can't afford to wait."

She pressed her lips to his palm, and the tension eased from his body, like always. "I'll help you ward it off."

"It can't be stopped."

She pushed his hand away with a noise of frustration. "I am well aware of my horrific track record when it comes to staving off death, thank you so much. But I don't have the emotional energy left to fight for your life, so I give up trying to keep you alive. I can't deal with it."

Something collapsed inside him. "You're giving

up on saving my life?" She'd never given up on her sisters, and he wanted that same kind of belief in him. That he could somehow beat his rap, which, of course, he couldn't, but shit. Did *she* have to abandon all hope as well?

But she nodded resolutely. "I'm going to let you die—" Her voice cracked and she cleared her throat. "I'm just going to help you hold it off long enough for us both to get what we want." She gave him a challenging look that didn't hide the anguish in her eyes. "You believe in love, right?"

"Hell, yeah, I believe in love." He'd spent the first six years of his life watching Cam bring light, laughter, and love to everything around him. He would kill a flower. Cam would bring it to life. Oh, yeah, he knew the power of love. "Just not for me."

Reina clasped his hand and set it over her heart. "I'm saving my sister because I love her. If you honor love the way you say you do, you will fight for love in every form, not just your brother."

Oh, well, now, that was just unfair. Strategically brilliant as well.

His job, as the Guardian of Hate, was also to protect his brother and the love he safeguarded. And Reina was love. He knew that was why she could withstand his hell. Which meant it was his duty to safeguard her and her issues as well, as she'd just so cleverly pointed out.

Shit. Everything she said made sense. It was asinine to spend the next forty-eight hours chasing shadows in hopes of finding his brother, when they knew exactly where he was going to be at midnight on Friday night.

He could keep Blaine and Nigel on the hunt while

he set the trap for the festival and entrusted his sanity to Reina. It was the smart plan, and he knew the only reason he could think clearly enough to realize it was because she was touching him so tenderly.

When he saw the relief in her eyes, he knew she'd figured out his answer before he'd even said it. "Hey." He caught her under the chin, needing her to understand exactly who he was. Not able to live with himself if he disappointed this woman. For hell's sake, he was already going to die on her, and he didn't have to be a genius to know how badly that would wreck her, no matter how much distance she claimed to have between them. But he needed her to understand the truth about him, to know exactly what his loyalties had to be. "If it comes down to a choice at the end, your sister loses. You lose. Do you understand? I have to make that call."

Her smile faded. "And if comes down to it, I'll sacrifice your brother."

"And poison love?"

"No." She released his hand and stepped away from him, taking her space back. "I don't believe love is dependent on the survival of one suicidal Cupid." She tapped her heart. "I've got enough in here."

He almost believed she was right. If she didn't, she would never be able to survive him without being affected by his negative energy. "What about the people who aren't like you? Who do need my brother? The ones who will have no resistance or protection when I explode? Are you willing to risk them?"

"Yes." She met his gaze. "Love comes from within for everyone."

"I'm not willing to take that risk."

Something flickered in her gaze, something he couldn't read. "It is time, Guardian, for you to believe in something other than hate." Then she pushed open the door and walked out.

He stared after her, feeling like he had just missed something important. Something that had been eluding him his whole life.

Something he didn't have time to worry about.

He grabbed his T-shirt and sprinted after her, swearing he would do everything in his power not to betray the woman who had risked everything to bring him back from the edge, but knowing in his gut that he would do it if he had to.

And with that realization, the self-hate began to fester inside him again. As he ducked under the doorframe, he knew the end was coming.

Fast.

———

Jarvis palmed Reina's back as he hustled her up the stonewashed stairs to the Our Lady of Help Catholic Parish, according to the carved words over the archway. The stonework was intricate, huge stained glass windows flanked the massive iron front doors, and a gorgeous white steeple stretched up high into the orange and pink dusk sky.

On the left side of the front door was an ancient sign listing the priests who had been in residence a hundred years ago. On the right was an ivory box with a thin slit, from which protruded a delicate lacy material.

Reina eyed the frock. "That seems a little decadent for a Catholic church."

"Former church." Jarvis plucked the lace out, and Reina realized the box was actually a dispenser for lace scarves. "The building is now a bar called the Grotto of Sweet Loving. Come here." He expertly wrapped the scarf around her neck, his touch deft and skilled, as only a graduate of the Den could boast.

"What are you doing?"

He tied a lace scarf around his own neck. "It's a way to show we honor them."

"Honor who?" The moment Jarvis had taken ownership in making this festival happen on his terms, he'd hauled ass down the highway to this spot. He'd been on the phone the whole time, relaying to his team her suggestions of possible places Death could have stashed Cameron. His frenzied pace hadn't left time for explanation other than that it was time to find the investors.

"The Tribe. This is their favorite bar."

She froze. "The Tribe of Peace and Goodwill? The vampires who have sworn to become harbingers of peace, love, and harmony by declining to kill, maim, or mindroll anyone? The ones who are so deviated from their true calling as vampires that they often snap with minimal provocation and kill anyone who happens to get too close to them?"

"Overrated. Only the lower vampires subscribe to that philosophy. The leaders think it's a crock and they're working hard to instill the appropriate bloodlust back in them." Jarvis shoved open the door. "The floor is yours."

She didn't move. "I don't really have time to be drained right now."

Jarvis laughed softly, took her hand, and pulled her inside. "Neither do I, babe, so let's get this right. These guys have money, and they have someone who drives them nuts. I think we can make this work."

"Or we can die. Always good to have several options." Reina stopped as over a hundred ashen faces turned toward her. The Bible reading groups went silent, the flute players stopped fluting, the poetry reading in the corner went on hold, and yoga-meisters on the right all dropped out of downdog to stare at her.

The only sound was the rhythmic chanting from a group who were sitting on bamboo mats, eyes closed, palms resting skyward on crossed legs.

Not a single vampire was in black. Every color of the rainbow, but no black or gray or white. Pinks, yellows, blues, aqua, green… a veritable cacophony of brightness.

And then, in that silence, all the vampires began salivating, a hundred pairs of red eyes fixated on the scarf around her throat. "Um, Jarvis? They don't look entirely at peace with their chosen lifestyle—"

"We just startled them. Kinda like throwing raw meat to a bunch of wolverines without feeding them first. They'll calm down in a second." But he pulled out his sword.

Nice to be with a warrior.

"They're sensitive to my negative energy," he said quietly. "I need to stay grounded."

And not so nice to be with one who could trigger a feeding frenzy of hate.

"Lord Hate?" A young vampire wearing jeans, a tie-dyed shirt, and a silver peace necklace peered around the corner of the altar. "Lord Hate!" His face lit up, he leapt down the stairs, and he raced down the center aisle. "You came!"

He took a flying leap at Jarvis, and the warrior barely

had time to catch the kid before he was wrapped up in a teenage bear hug. Jarvis looked so confused and unsettled that she almost had to laugh. "How's Rocco, Sylvan?" Jarvis asked.

His voice was so concerned, Reina smiled. So she wasn't the only one in the world who could bring out Jarvis's softer side. Seeing him holding the youth and listening to his answer so carefully was very sweet.

"Oh, man, Rocco's in bad shape." Sylvan tugged Jarvis toward the altar. "You gotta come see."

Jarvis allowed the boy to lead him, even though she knew he didn't have time for visiting the boy's friend. Again, a sweetheart. Dammit. She didn't need to be liking him right now.

"Where's Damien?" Jarvis asked. "I need to talk to him."

"Damien's with him. Rocco's dying, man." The youth's eyes suddenly filled with tears. "He doesn't want to live."

Reina recoiled at Sylvan's words. "Who's dying?" she demanded. What was with her ability to attract dying beings into her life? She couldn't handle any more of them, thank you very much.

The kid looked over at Reina with a startled expression, as if he'd just noticed her. His gaze dropped to her breasts, and then he scrambled backwards. "It's a girl," he shouted. "It's another girl! Run away! Run away!"

Yes, of course. A completely typical reaction by a teenage boy to the appearance of a female.

Jarvis caught him by the collar and arrested his escape with gentle ease. "Sylvan, this is Reina Fleming. You don't need to fear her. Reina, meet Sylvan. He's a little skittish around women."

Sylvan was skinny, with baggy jeans that were a little too saggy, a shock of red hair, freckles, blue eyes, and sadness in them that she'd seen too many times in her own. She loved him immediately. "Hi."

Sylvan stared at her without speaking, pressing back against Jarvis's chest as if the man of hate could save him.

Jarvis lightly set him aside. "Don't touch me, kid," he said gruffly. "It's not smart."

"What?" Sylvan shot him a look of panic. "Why?"

"There's no hate in Sylvan's eyes," Reina said. She could tell Jarvis cared about the boy, and it wasn't fair that he should deprive himself of reaching out to him. "I think he's okay."

"No one is safe." Jarvis stepped back, and she saw the self-disgust on his face. She also noticed him reached up to ruffle the kid's hair, and then force himself to drop his hand before he made contact. A man who had spent a lifetime holding himself back from connection with others. "Where's Damien?" he asked again, his voice strained.

Sylvan shot Reina another wary look before pointing at a white door tucked in behind a red velvet curtain. "He's in there."

Jarvis nodded at Reina to follow, and then he glanced over his shoulder. She did the same, and then was shocked to see the bar's patrons had converged at the bottom of the altar steps. They were all leaning forward in a disturbingly predatory way and there was a fair amount of drool dripping off their pearly whites.

"See?" Jarvis tightened his grip on his sword. "Vampires don't respond well to me."

"Not all vampires have difficulty with you." Reina

nodded at Sylvan, who was casting a hero-worship look at Jarvis as he pushed open the door.

"Give him time." Jarvis took one last survey over his shoulder, and then followed them inside. "I got to him once already."

He locked the door behind them.

Call her pessimistic, but she didn't feel like that was going to be quite sufficient if things got ugly.

Chapter 17

"LOVE IS PAIN, BOY, AND YOU'VE GOT TO SNAP OUT OF IT," Damien was saying as Jarvis walked into the sunlit room.

The sight of the boy on the canopy bed was not what he'd expected. Rocco was so pale that only his eyebrows and lips were noticeable against the white sheet. Damien was sitting in a foldable chair, staring intently at the boy. The boy was dying. Jarvis knew that instantly. "Damien."

The older vampire's face lit up. "You came!"

Jarvis snorted. "It's not a smart man who looks that happy to see me."

Reina hurried over to the bed, startling Jarvis. She knelt down beside Rocco and touched his forehead tenderly. "He's like ice." Her voice was so full of concern for this stranger that Jarvis's throat tightened. How was it possible to be as loving as Reina? How could she really exist?

"Don't touch him, lady!" Sylvan grabbed a pencil from a nearby table and brandished it like a dagger. "Get away from him!"

"Don't threaten her." Jarvis yanked the kid back with a growl. "She's not like other women, kid. She's all good." As soon as the words were out of his mouth, Jarvis knew he meant it. Despite all he'd learned about women being ruthless, evil, and untrustworthy, he'd put his life in Reina's hands without hesitation. In fact, he kinda already had.

Her worry about Rocco was evident in the gentleness

of her touch, in the kindness of her voice. Reina was bent over the dying vamp, her hair falling over her shoulders as she whispered to him. She didn't even know the kid, and she was there, giving her heart to him. She wasn't like the women he knew. She wasn't like anyone he knew. She was beautiful. She was sheer, angelic radiance, and he knew his world was forever changed because she'd been a part of it.

She looked up then, as if sensing his perusal. He smiled, and she smiled back, her eyes lighting up in a way that made something inside him melt just a little bit.

"You've come to make Rocco hate the girl? His father returns tonight." Damien leaned back in his chair. His eyes were shadowed, his body gaunt.

"If he hangs around me long enough, he'll hate everyone." Jarvis trailed his hand over Reina's hair as he passed her on his way to the window, as if the breeze could take away his stench. "I've got an offer for you."

"I knew it!" Sylvan beamed at him. "You're going to help! I knew it!" He raced toward Jarvis. "High-five, man!"

"Stop! Don't touch me!" Jarvis pointed his sword at the kid, stopping him in his tracks, trying not to notice the crestfallen expression on the youth's face. "It's not you, it's me," he tried to explain. "I'm the problem."

Sylvan shook his head, his face starting to glow again. "No, dude, you're awesome. You're the most powerful being in the universe, and you're here to help. You're a god, man. A god."

Reina looked up, and he saw her smile. "Keep telling him that," she said. "He doesn't believe it."

Sylvan whirled around, fingers curved into claws. "Get away from Rocco, woman!"

Typical kid. Thought he had it all figured out, and he had it all wrong. Had his faith in the wrong damn place.

Damien set his hand wearily on the youth's shoulder. "Sylvan. Take a walk. I need to talk to Lord Hate."

"No! I won't leave." Sylvan broke free and raced to stand beside Jarvis. He folded his arms over his chest, checked out Jarvis's stance, and then mimicked it perfectly, down to the distance between his feet and the angle of his hips.

Something shifted in him at the sight of Sylvan imitating him. "I'm hell, kid. Trust Damien."

"No." Sylvan folded his arms and moved closer to Jarvis.

"Let him stay," Reina said. "He seems to be unaffected by you, and every time he speaks, Rocco's eyes roll back in his head. Rocco knows he's here."

Sylvan tossed a suspicious look at Reina. "You're just saying that so we'll stop watching you, and you can stake him."

"No more hostility toward her," Jarvis warned. He set his hand on the kid's shoulder before he could remember not to. "I trust her, and you will respect her or you will leave."

Sylvan looked up at Jarvis, then over at Reina, and indecision flashed on his face. Finally, he gave a reluctant nod. "Okay."

Okay. Just like that. Jarvis had spoken and the kid had ditched a lifetime of lessons about how women weren't to be trusted. Shit. He didn't know what to make of that. Didn't these people get that he was the bad guy?

Damien shoved back from the bed, walked across the

room, and poured himself a glass of milk from a small fridge. "You have a deal," he prompted.

"Yeah." Jarvis gave up ditching Sylvan. He could knock the kid out if he went over the edge. He nodded at Reina. "Reina's the one who can make the offer."

Both vampires turned toward Reina in surprise. "The woman?" Sylvan sounded disgusted. "We can't trust a woman!"

Jarvis flicked the kid in the head, and then he spoke to Reina. "Have you heard of the Sisterhood of the Fairy Tale Hero?"

Reina nodded. "Of course. It's an organization of women who have Princess Gatherings and believe that the men of today aren't as manly and heroic as the ones in the fairy tales." Her gaze flicked to Sylvan. "They are particularly irked by the vampires who refuse to follow their calling of being violent, blood-sucking warriors, thereby depriving women of their birthright to tame real men."

"They're a bunch of witches," Sylvan snapped. "This girl, Sarah Dutton, met Rocco at a fairy picnic, and she totally seduced him. They went out a bunch of times, and he fell in love with her. So, I double dated with them, you know, 'cause she had this friend who had this great rack…" Sylvan paused to catch his breath and Jarvis could feel the heat rising from Sylvan, his anger, his fury.

Instinctively he put his hand on the kid's head, then pulled away. *Seriously, Jarvis*? Trying to ease a hot-headed reaction with his touch? The kid needed Reina, not him.

"And then, after dinner, we were on the beach and

getting all up close and personal, you know, the way chicks like, and then Sarah whipped out this mug of blood and threw it all over both girls."

Reina sat up. "She was *trying* to get you to attack her?"

"Yeah, man!" Sylvan moved closer to Reina. "Totally disrespecting that we aren't that kind of vamp, you know? And Rocco almost snapped, and then I got him down, and he was pissed at her for not respecting him. I mean, trying to get us to bite them! We don't even know them! It would have been empty, meaningless, blood sucking, and that's just crap. Can't do that, can't go there, you know? It's got to be blessed by the Holy Spirit and be all about love and eternal commitment and shit. You know?"

Reina raised her brows. "Um, yeah, okay, I guess blood sucking would be best done that way—"

"Damn right!" The pencil snapped in Sylvan's hand. "I got him out of there, and I thought we were good, but then she got so pissed at him for refusing to rip her throat out, and she broke up with him by text. Rocco didn't think she meant it, I mean, seriously, they'd been dating for like two months, and she'd ditch him just because he wouldn't give her the action? Is that right?"

Reina shook her head. "No, of course not. You deserved to be honored for your choices about who you are."

Sylvan blinked. "Really?"

"Of course, really." She was rubbing Rocco's hand in a gesture so tender it made Jarvis think of how she'd done the same to him. He wanted her back by his side. Touching him. "So, then what happened?"

"We don't have time for this," Damien interrupted.

"We do," Jarvis said quietly. "This is part of the deal."

Sylvan moved closer to Reina, as if entranced by her

willingness to listen. Of course he would become captivated by her. What male could possibly be immune to her aura and her spirit? "So, then, she wouldn't talk to him. Wouldn't return his calls. Nothing. He went to see her, and she asked if he'd attack her, and he tried, he really tried, and he even got his fangs to extend, and then he couldn't do it. So she staked him. Said that if he loved her, staking him would make him attack."

"And he didn't?"

"Nope." Sylvan sighed and looked at Rocco. "She left him to die. I found him, brought him back here, but he's given up. Can't live without her, can't be the man she wants him to be." His voice broke, and he went down on his knees in front of Reina. "Can you save him, ma'am? Can you?"

She looked at Jarvis. "You can, can't you?"

He shook his head. "I'm not inflicting myself on anyone."

"What is going on?" Damien slammed his empty milk glass down on the dresser. "Who's got the deal for me?"

Jarvis nodded at Reina. "Make the offer."

She stared at him, and then comprehension dawned. She turned to Damien. "I work for Death, and we're launching a new Reaper this weekend. We're looking for investors who would like to sponsor the event." She hesitated, and Jarvis could see her discomfort with the rest of it. "And we're seeking recommendations on souls to reap."

Damien blinked. "You're asking me for money to pay you guys to wipe out the Sisterhood? You guys do contract work? Shit, I had no idea. I thought we all just died when we died."

Sylvan frowned. "You'll kill the Sisterhood? That's not right." He leapt to his feet. "No one should kill or inflict harm on others. Ever!"

Reina blanched, and Jarvis's heart softened for her. Reina was never going to be the brutal hard ass she had to be to make this happen. Fortunately, he was fucked up enough not to have the same limitations. "Here's the deal, kid," he said. "Everyone dies at some point, and the Afterlife is a bang up place for eternity. Death manages the processes and keeps a balance." Well, Death kept a cash stash in his pocket, but Jarvis didn't think now was the time to mention it.

"People fear death," Reina said. "And there's no reason to, really. The Afterlife is really wonderful."

And with those words, Jarvis got it. He understood why Death wanted to use Cam, why Cam wanted to do it. "And since the new Reaper is the Guardian of Love, everyone whose soul is reaped by him will experience the love and inner peace that's been eluding them their whole lives. They will go into the Afterlife with purity in their hearts."

Reina looked at him. "No more taking five hundred years to rid your heart of the stains from being in the physical world. Instant peace."

"Instant peace," Jarvis repeated. Like the kind Reina gave him, only it would last forever.

"It makes such sense," Reina said, staring at him with understanding on her face as well. "It takes away the fear."

"World peace." Holy shit. It did make sense. In a completely fucked up way, of course, but it still made sense.

"So what?" Sylvan got in Reina's face. "Death is still death, and just because it's this ultimate high doesn't mean it's right to pull the trigger early. You can't do that! It's wrong!"

"It's all right, kid." Damien leveraged himself off the desk. "Sometimes you gotta stand up."

"But you're part of the Tribe! We believe in peace and—"

"Survival." Damien ran his hand through his hair. "People abuse us, knowing we won't strike back, and now that the Sisterhood has their claws onto us, we won't be safe. They'll be jumping us at intersections and staking us at red lights just to get us to become their fairy tale heroes." He gestured at Rocco. "These two are my best altar boys. They believe in our philosophy in their deepest of hearts, and look what they get for it."

"No." Sylvan stomped his foot. "We can do this with love, the right way! The world can be at peace. We'll have a vigil for Rocco." He ran for the door. "I'm getting my friends. We can do this without violence. I know we can!"

The door slammed shut behind him, leaving the three adults alone.

Damien sighed. "I appreciate the utopian view of the youth, but I can't let more boys suffer like Rocco. Women like that can't be allowed to run around staking young boys before they're old enough to handle it."

"They need to be protected. Killing off the Sisterhood would do it." Jarvis saw Reina's indecision. Her discomfort with the whole notion of what they were talking about. Hello, woman? They weren't actually going to allow Cameron to assassinate anyone, even murderous fairy tale princess wannabes. "Reina."

She met his gaze. "What?"

He gave her a look of impatience, and her face

cleared as she realized his point. That they weren't actually going to do it. "Oh, right. Great." She stood up. "It's three billion dollars, and it'll be done by Friday."

"Three billion?" Damien pulled out his checkbook. "That's a bargain."

She raised her eyebrows. "You have three billion dollars at your disposal?"

"Of course." Damien's pen flew over the paper as he filled out the check without hesitation. "We got the church in a deal with the Vatican."

"So?"

"So, how much money does the Catholic church have?" Damien ripped out the check. "They share well when threatened with vampires on their holy turf." He winked at her. "We might not believe in ripping the throats out of dainty young maidens without provocation, but we've got no problem taking money from an organization who tries to convince the world that we belong in hell." He set the paper in her hand. "My boss is going to love this idea," he said. "How is this going to work?"

Reina took the check, turning it over in her hand, as if unable to believe it could be that easy to solve her problems. "We've rented out Foxboro Stadium Friday night. How many seats do you want?"

"Three boxes for the royalty, and then maybe a couple thousand for the others."

"Done." She tucked the check in her pocket. "It's been lovely doing business with you, and I appreciate the opportunity to reap on your behalf."

Damien grinned. "I must say that I'm really pumped to see the Guardian of Love at work. It's really a monumental moment for all of humankind. I'm impressed as hell with the idea."

Jarvis felt his good humor disappear. "It is top secret," he said. "No one can know Love is involved, or you forfeit your money."

Damien swore. "Then I need to retrieve Sylvan. He'll share that information freely." He glided for the door, and then turned. "But if Rocco isn't on the hate parade by the time I get back, I'm stopping payment. Take care of him, Lord Hate."

The door slammed shut before Jarvis could reply. "Fuck that—"

Reina caught his arm. "Don't you get it? Rocco has given up hope. Hate gives him something to live for—"

"Then he's better off with a visit from Cam." He grabbed her hand and laid it over his heart. "Can't you feel that? It's black in there, sweetheart, and it's a hell of a way to live."

She splayed her hand on his chest. "Rocco can't get to love from where he is. Give him hate. Not enough to kill her. Enough to give him a reason to live."

He pulled her hand off. "I'm *hell*, Reina. You don't understand how bad that is because you can't feel it. I'm an insidious poison and—"

"Stop it!" She shoved at him. "Stop talking about yourself like that. You *guard* hate. That doesn't mean you *are* hate. Give Rocco a jump start, and you'll see that there are times when a little negative emotion is a good thing, even if it's not where you ultimately want to end up. You said yourself that hate can be transmuted into love, but apathy and depression can't get translated into anything!"

He wanted her words to be true. To believe he was some great balance in the universe, that this shit inside him wasn't wrecking him. That an explosion that would decimate the emotional well-being of the world wasn't ticking away inside him.

But that would be denial, and there was no time for that. Denial didn't change the truth.

Only action would.

Rocco coughed, and he looked over at the boy. At his pale features, at the hopelessness on his face. The kid looked like shit.

"He's dying because of love," Reina said softly. "Give him some hate and a reason to live."

"It's not a reason." He shoved his sword into his scabbard, pissed as hell that he couldn't help this kid. He hated leaving Rocco like that, but he wasn't going to inflict himself on anyone, despite Reina's delusion that he simply wasn't that bad. "Let's go find Augustus. Part One finished. Part Two, and we'll have this festival in line."

"No!" She folded her arms over her chest. "I will not leave him here to die when you can save him. For God's sake, Jarvis! I'd have given anything to have the ability to save those I love from death, and you could do it right now. How dare you walk away from that? How dare you reject that gift?"

"Gift? You think it's a fucking gift? Fine. You want a gift. I'll give you a gift." He stalked across the room, grabbed Rocco, and swung the kid over his shoulder. "I'll have Nigel bring him to the festival on Friday night. Once I find my brother and knock some damn sense into his brainwashed head, I'll have him infuse Rocco with some warm and snuggly feelings so he can feel better. Happy now?" Hell, that was actually a brilliant idea. So much better than leaving this poor love-struck sod to disintegrate into the mattress.

Reina made a sound of exasperation. "He needs *you*, not your ego-maniac brother who suffers from such delusions of grandeur that he thinks he can save the world by killing it."

He yanked the door open. "Don't malign my brother."

"He's the one who should be maligned, not you."

Jarvis whirled around and stalked back to Reina. She lifted her chin as he neared. "Don't diss him." If love wasn't worth admiring, then what the hell was he?

"Protecting your brother is not what gives you value," she snapped. "And quite frankly, I'm getting a little tired of you being so melodramatic about what a bad guy you are."

"Are you deluded, woman? I'm *Hate*."

She rolled her eyes. "For God's sake, I can't reach you, you bullheaded cretin." She snatched her car keys out of his hand and stalked out the door.

He scowled as he shifted Rocco and headed after her. It was time she stopped arguing and accepted what he was, and what he wasn't. He might not like it, but at least he accepted it.

He stepped out into the hall and saw the roomful of vampires salivating at the sight of Reina stomping her way through their midst, muttering about obstinate and asinine warriors.

"Dude," a younger vampire muttered. "If I was going to break my vows, that chick is the one I'd do it for—"

Jarvis whipped out his sword and had the tip of the

turbulent, purple blade at the kid's throat before the youth could finish his thought.

The boy's eyes widened, and his friend grabbed his arm. "Dude," he whispered. "That's the Guardian of Hate. He'll blow your vows for good—"

The kid's eyes flared red, and Jarvis swore as the room filled with the sound of popping corn. He turned to see fangs popping free left and right. Eyes turning red, and they were all fixated on Reina. "Yeah, welcome to my world, Reina. I'm like sunshine every time I walk in the door."

She looked around, and he saw the sudden tension in her shoulders. She slowed her walk, easing slowly toward the door, clearly trying not to make any quick moves.

Jarvis had no such qualms. He broke into a run and sprinted for her. Caught her around the waist a split second before a roomful of vamps pounced like kitties on a catnip mouse. He swept her out of the way, put his sword into action, and headed for the door.

Reina held on tightly as he fought to get them out.

"Nice effect I have them, eh?" He couldn't keep the smugness out of his voice. "Still think I'm a gift?"

But when he saw her sadness, he didn't feel quite as smug anymore.

Which just pissed him off even more.

Which was good, because being a little insanely violent helped him take down another five vamps.

Which was bad, because as God was his witness, he was damn tired of feeling pissed off and insane.

Maybe he'd offer himself up as Cam's first victim. As long as he was going to go, wouldn't it be better to experience a moment, just one freaking moment, of love before he died, instead of going out in an explosion of all the blackest parts of his soul?

He dismissed the notion before he'd even finished the thought. What kind of crap was that? He'd fought off death for a hundred and fifty years. He sure as hell wasn't going to offer himself up to it now. He was hanging on for as long as he could.

He sprinted to the car, threw his cargo inside, and gunned the engine, hitting the road as the gang of vamps spewed out into the dusk. He glanced in the backseat and saw Reina holding Rocco's head in her lap, her face full of love and concern. Hellfire and damnation, what he'd give for one moment in that light.

"We can't go after Augustus yet," Reina said.

He peeled around the corner toward his place. He should have known she wouldn't be able to pull through. "Hey, babe, I know you don't want to—"

"No. My sickle was destroyed." She patted Rocco's head and then climbed back through the seats. In an automatic move, almost unconscious, she plucked his hand off the gearshift and held it between her palms.

His tension eased. Just a bit. He wanted to haul her onto his lap and breathe her in, but there was no time. He'd never craved anything the way he craved Reina's touch. It felt good, but at the same time, it was unfathomable torture to have her that close and not be able to take her. "So, we get another sickle from your boss." Excellent. It would give him a chance to check out the property for his brother.

"No." Reina traced the lines on his palm. "He won't give me another one. He put me on leave, remember? I need to get one from someone else."

"Where else are you going to get a sickle designed for harvesting souls? Death's got corner on that market—" Then he realized what she was saying. "You want to hit up the original Grim Reaper?"

"He must have spare ones lying around that will work for me." She massaged his palm with her knuckles, as if she could dig out the hell that stalked him. "Death has to send him pictures and a snail mail letter on the first of every month to show he is adhering to the terms of their agreement." She held up her phone, showing a contact page for the Grim Reaper. "I write the letters, so I have his address. He doesn't live far from here."

Jarvis whistled under his breath. "I've heard he's a crazy bastard. He'd kill you in a minute."

"I know." She turned off her phone and put it away. "It's the only way."

"I'm going with you." No way was he letting her face the Reap unprotected.

She smiled at him, relief evident in the way she squeezed his hand. "Thanks."

Thanks. *Thanks?* That word made him want to be the man he'd never be. A man who actually deserved a smile and a nod of appreciation. Not the man who was going to rain all over the parade of every living being in existence. "Then let's do it."

Chapter 18

"I DON'T WANT TO WAIT UNTIL FRIDAY." THE GUARDIAN of Love sashayed into Death's office, clasping his new twenty-four-carat bow under his arm, and wearing nothing but a quiver of arrows. Cameron's body was pale, as if he hadn't been exposed to sunlight in a couple centuries, he had a sizeable paunch, and his endowment needed a serious infusion of testosterone.

He'd also had his hair highlighted a brassy gold and invested in extensions, so his tresses floated down his back. The kid had clearly not used Death's high-class in-house services for his makeover. He was perverted, cheesy, road trash all the way.

This wasn't the man who people would want to be their last experience in this physical world, let alone invest vast sums of money in. "Where are your clothes, for God's sake?" Death demanded.

Cameron leapt up onto a red velvet chair, set his foot on Death's desk, and tossed his head so the bleached out straw masquerading as hair cascaded down his back. He fished an arrow out of the quiver, fixed it into the bow, and then took aim at the smoke detector in the corner of Death's office. He didn't fire; he just held the pose. "How do I look? Dead ringer for all the ancient paintings of me, aren't I?"

"Those paintings are of a cute little cherub. Once you hit age six, the naked thing can get you arrested." With

Cam's foot up on the desk, it put his dangly bits way too close to front and center. "For God's sake, boy, cover yourself up."

Death shoved his chair back and tossed one of the dishtowels from his espresso corner at the Guardian. It landed right on its target, but Cameron wasn't perky enough, and after a moment, it dropped uselessly to the desk, right on top of the monogrammed pen set Angelica had given Death on his first day of business. He treasured those pens so much he'd never even used them. And now…

Sigh.

Cameron laughed, a loud bellow of mocking humor. "You need me, old man, so you must let me do as I wish." He sank down in the velvet chair, his naked ass wedged into the cushions that Death had had specially imported from a secluded gnome monastery in upper Mongolia. Shit. He really loved those cushions.

Cameron tucked one foot under him, pulled his left knee up, and rested his chin on it. He was wearing the most idyllic expression of peace Death had ever seen. "It's been so long since I've felt like this," Cameron sighed dreamily. "I'd lost my meaning in life. But you've brought me back."

Death saw the lack of turbulence in his blue eyes. And better yet, there was a spark of energy, of fire. "I'm glad to hear it, my boy. You had me worried."

"I know." Cameron began to twirl his bow like a baton. "I haven't wanted to be naked in almost a hundred years. It feels great to feel the wind over my skin."

"Yeah, well, you might want to consider a thong."

"Why?" Cameron tossed his hair again. "People think

of me in my naked glamour, armed only with a bow and arrow. Why deprive them of such beauty and the fulfillment of all their dreams?"

Death rubbed his jaw. "Well, you do have a point. Half the job is people's expectations." He gestured at the rolls of fat nearly covering Cam's manly regions. "But if you're going to go naked, you need to get into shape, man. If you're going to represent love, then women have to want you, and men have to want to be you."

"You really think that's why they all like me? Because of my washboard abs?" Cameron raised an eyebrow, revealing a surprising sharpness to his wit. Naked glee wasn't the only thing returning to life with the Guardian of Love.

"People are superficial," Death said. "They respond to beauty, money, and power. Women especially. It's what they want."

"No, it's not." Cameron plucked another arrow out of his quiver. It had a gold tip with a double heart logo that looked suspiciously familiar.

"Is that one of my cuff links?"

"Yep. I had one of your welders turn it into a razor sharp point. It's my new signature—"

"No." Death plucked the arrow out of his minion's hands. "That's mine, and if you ever, *ever*, go through my private things again, I will cut out your entrails and feed them to the hell's hounds skulking around my backyard. Got it?"

Cameron's eyes widened. "Wow. You've got issues, don't you?" He leaned forward and propped his elbow on the desk. "So, tell me, Prentiss, why does a man who makes a living ending lives have hearts all over his walls, a pink bedspread, and a twenty-foot mural of Cupid both on your bedroom ceiling and in your office? And was it just me, or does every *single* piece of your man-jewelry have that double heart logo engraved somewhere on it?"

Death's hand went to the scythe under his desk and his fingers closed around it. "Be very, very careful, young man. You are not so important to me."

Cameron grinned. "Did you not get enough of your mama's love when you were a kid, Prentiss? Because I cover all types of love, you know. Romantic love, motherly love, and brotherly love, and everything in between." He pulled out another quill, this one unabashedly sporting the ring Death had plucked off his dead father's hand just after Gramps had inadvertently knocked him off. "Allow me?"

Death began to slide the scythe out of its brackets. "That was my father's."

"Well, by all means, take it back." Cameron extended it helpfully toward him, and Death reached to snatch it—

Cameron twisted it suddenly and jammed it into Death's palm.

Death swore and jerked his hand back. "Don't you dare—"

An overwhelming sense of peace and calm settled over Death. His chest felt warm and full, and he had a sudden urge to stretch out on his floor and start singing "Somewhere Over the Rainbow." His palm was glowing a rose pink, almost the same shade as his bathrobe. Twin, intertwined hearts pulsed in neon pink, as if they had been tattooed in his skin.

Death raised his palm and pressed his lips to his hand. "My sweet baby—"

Cam started giggling.

The feeling of oh-so-sweet-love vanished instantly, replaced by sheer humiliation and the rawest sense of loss he'd ever experienced. That amazing sensation had been a fraud! He jerked the scythe free and had it at Cam's throat instantly. "You toyed with me—"

Cameron tapped the blade cheerfully, his eyes sparkling. "Not at all. I simply gave you a small taste of what I offer. Imagine if I gave you the full dosage? I just pricked you."

Death frowned. "This is what you do?"

"This is what I do." Cameron leaned forward. "You see, my good man, I don't need to be handsome or rich or even funny. I simply need to be me, and I fulfill everyone's dreams exactly as I am." He bowed with a flourish. "Love at your service. Nothing else is needed."

"You just touch people and they love you?" What kind of racket was that? Death sat back down. "But you're out of shape, arrogant, and naked with a small penis." For hell's sake, Cameron didn't have a castle, wasn't the richest man in creation, didn't wield the ultimate power, and he still got every being on the planet to love him just by poking them? Hell. Death had taken over the wrong damn business, hadn't he?

Cameron grinned. "And to think I was so self-absorbed in my misery that I forgot about all this for so long." He held out his hand. "I owe you thanks, big guy, for bringing me back. You've got my loyalty, and we're going to make a killing."

Death slid the scythe back under the desk. "I didn't fully grasp the extent of your powers." He'd just wanted to keep the sorry bastard from depriving the world of love. But in the process of the only altruistic duty he'd undertaken in his life, he'd stumbled onto a gold mine.

Cameron grinned and mimed shooting his arrow into the painting of the original Grim Reaper that was part of the landscape behind Death (another condition of the sale). "So, yeah, I don't want to wait until Friday night. Let's make this happen now."

Death shook his head. "We need to be strategic. I don't want to rush."

Cameron leapt up and began to pace the room. "Well, I gotta get going on it. I'm on a high, and I don't want to lose it. Gotta ride this wave." He breathed on his bow, then defogged it with a lock of his hair. He spun it around, and Death could see his own reflection in the gold.

Shit. Since when had he started to look so pale and worn out? Compared to the energy cascading off Cameron, Death looked like one of the souls he'd just harvested.

"See, man, this is the deal." Cameron vaulted over the chairs and frog-landed right in the middle of Death's desk, knees up, feet flat, hands on the desk—which was just not an attractive pose for a naked man. "I haven't felt this alive in so long. I thought I was broken. I thought I was useless. But when I got to Symphony Hall, and all hell broke loose around me, it triggered something. Seeing my brother with his hate—"

Death jerked upright. "Your brother? Jarvis?"

"Yeah, the dude's like this major downer right now." Cameron side-hopped and stretched out on his side across the mahogany desk. He propped his head up on his hand, cocked a knee, and grinned. "This is a seductive beach pose, is it not? Imagine a beautiful maiden stretched out beside me." He began stroking the air in front of Death's face. "I would touch her like this, grazing my hand over her breasts and—"

"Hey." Death caught his hand. "What was your brother doing?"

"Trying to pry me out of your grasp, of course."

He should have killed the Guardian of Hate after all. Who knew he'd be so persistent? "And were you tempted?"

"Only by the hellaciously attractive Reaper who distracted Jarvis long enough for me to shoot arrows at every cop and reporter, except the one with the biggest TV camera, of course." Cupid winked. "Let's just say that public fornication reached new heights outside the Elton John gala tonight. Check out channel seven. They'll have some excellent footage."

"The Reaper who was with Jarvis?" It must have been Reina. "What was she doing?" If that woman had gone against his wishes, she was fired on the spot, no matter how much love she had oozing from her pores.

"It appeared she was trying to save Jarvis from his hate-monster, rescue her sister from some over-sexed orgasm factory, while trying to reap some dude who smelled like rotting bananas." Cameron sighed dreamily. "I would have loved to hit up the sister and her lover with a couple arrows. They would have melted pavement. I'm going to have to find them and give them a jump start. I could get off just watching those two."

Death rubbed his jaw. So, Reina had been rescuing her sister and trying to harvest Augustus at the same time? That was kind of impressive, actually. That wasn't the easiest of multi-tasking.

Who knew. Maybe after the sister had kicked the bucket, Reina would actually become competent enough to promote… He started laughing at the thought. There was no chance Reina Fleming was going to become a full Reaper.

He couldn't allow it. She was simply too soft. In fact, he was going to have to let her go once Cameron was on board (a good boss could only delegate full Reaper power to so many people, right? Can't dilute the talent). Too bad, but one of the costs of business. The money always came first, and now that he knew how lucrative Cam was going to be, there was no room for ordinaries like Reina. The gal would have to move on.

But Jarvis was not so easily trifled with. "Did you kill your brother by any chance? Or did Napoleon? Speaking of which, where is the old man?"

"He was trying to choke Angelica's location out of the banana hammock guy." Cameron swung around and sat cross-legged on the desk.

Death was going to have to get a new desk.

"And no, I didn't kill my brother." Cameron rolled his eyes. "I couldn't be bothered. He was going insane and wanting me to sully myself by touching his hate. Hello?" He fluffed his locks. "Does this look like the mane of a man who would soil himself? No, he can go do what he likes. I am above him."

That meant Jarvis was still at-large and coming after Cameron. Death was well acquainted with the Guardian of Hate from the warrior's years of incarceration. He was formidable, determined, and quite talented. If he wanted his brother back, he would get him, unless Death cemented his bond with the Guardian of Love first. There was no way in hell Death was going to lose out on this gold mine. "You're right."

Cameron cocked his neck to the side, and a sharp crack echoed through the office. "Of course I am, but what are you referring to?"

"There's no reason to hold you back from world peace. From your new role as an assassin. We'll find someone for you to reap before Friday. I wouldn't want you to backslide from your happy place." It was time to cement Love's role before Jarvis showed up and screwed it up. Death was sure he still could arrange a substantial financial windfall even if he moved up the date.

"Really? Today?" Cameron whooped, leapt off the desk, and began to skip around the office.

"Yes, I'll make a few calls and have something in place in the next few hours."

"I'm so excited!" He grabbed his bow and began shooting arrows all over the office. "Yay! I'm alive! Do you hear me, world? I'm coming to save you!" He threw back his head and let out a catcall of total glee.

Death yanked the bow out of his hand.

"Hey!" Cameron lunged for it, and Death backhanded it into a gap in the wall. The golden bow slipped through the opening and was gone.

"My light! My life!" Cameron pressed his face against the crack. "Mirabelle, my dear love! Come back to Daddy!"

"Mirabelle isn't coming back until you get your-self new arrows that do not involve my logo or my belongings." Death yanked an arrow out of his framed, autographed copy of "Ode to the Afterlife," written by Henry Wadsworth Longfellow upon his relocation to the land of posies and champagne. On the tip of the arrow was the monogrammed penis ring Death had commissioned when he was eighteen. There was still space on it to add the initials of the woman he would wear it for. He shoved the ring into his pocket. "It's non-negotiable. Find a new tip for your poles, or it's off."

Cameron opened his mouth to protest, and then he must have seen something in Death's eyes. "Okay, yeah, fine. I can live with that, buddy. You have a need, and I'm there with you."

Some sort of happy feeling bloomed inside Death at the idea of being buddies with the being that encompassed love in all its forms, and then he scowled. "There are no friends in business."

"Oh, well, gee, Mr. Grumpy. Lighten up—"

"Go to my design department and have them come up with a new logo for you. We need something worthy of the combined efforts of your powers and mine. It has to be brilliant, unique, and utterly memorable." He raised his brows and leaned back in his chair. "You can handle that, I presume?"

"You bet! Can it be gold? I love gold."

"Of course."

"And can I get matching wrist cuffs?" Cameron held up his arms. "I've always wanted wrist cuffs. There's something so gladiator about that, you know? Those were real men."

"Yes, yes." Death waved him off as he started typing on his computer. "I'll find someone for you to reap and some investors. Be back here by four o'clock with new arrows and clothes."

"Aye, aye on the arrows. Not a chance on the clothes." Cameron strode toward the door, wiggling his hips with just a trifle too much flourish given the cellulite bouncing around back there. "I can't deprive the world of their fantasies, you know." He snatched two arrows out of the door and tossed them at Death. "Just so you know, those arrows are still laced with love for the next few hours."

Death caught them easily in one hand. "So?"

"So, if Miss Pastry Chef comes by, be careful what you sit on." Cameron winked. "Or don't be so careful. Your call."

"Don't insult me. I'm the most sought after male in existence." Death threw the arrows into the corner. "I can get a woman to fall in love with me on my own. I would never stoop to an arrow."

Cameron poked his head back in the almost closed door. "Then why, my good friend, are you still alone?"

———···———

There was nothing like seeing one of your fellow torture victims to make everything feel hunky dory. Or at least it made the fast track toward explosion seem a little less lonely.

Keeping Rocco anchored on his shoulder, Jarvis held the door to his penthouse suite open for Reina.

Nigel was sunning himself on the patio, wearing nothing but a bandana around his throat. Scars raked across his abdomen, and there was a new painting of a red and gold phoenix emblazoned across his chest. The sun was making the gold sparkle as if the bird was

actually taking a siesta on the chest of a psychotic warrior with sensitivity issues. "Hey, painter boy, we're
home. Is dinner ready?"

Nigel rolled to his feet with the grace of a tiger. "You
bring the vamp with you?" His eyebrows shot up when
he saw Reina, and he immediately filched his hard core
leather pants off a nearby lounge. "Sorry, Reina. Didn't
realize he was bringing girls home with him already."

"Girls?" She shot Jarvis a curious look. "No, just me,
this time."

"I don't bring any girls home," Jarvis muttered.
"You're my first, for hell's sake." Not that it mattered.
Seriously. It wasn't like they were dating. But he wanted
to make it clear anyway, you know. Just 'cause.

Reina said nothing, but he saw her mouth curve in a
small smile. She was possessive of him? Huh. He didn't
really mind. Felt kinda good, actually.

But for good measure, he glared at Nigel anyway as
he strode into his place. No need for the artist to interfere in Jarvis's personal life. Then he saw Nigel's concerned expression and his annoyance faded. "I'm fine,"
he muttered.

"Are you?" Nigel took Rocco from Jarvis and slung
him over his shoulder. "We need you. Don't be an ass
and get yourself killed. The boys would cry."

Jarvis ground his jaw. "They'd party."

"Yeah, sure they would." Nigel gave him a long
look. "You fight this mother fucker off," he said quietly. "We're not letting you go down now that you're
free. Just so you know." Before Jarvis could answer,
he began walking down the hall. "I'll take a look at the
kid. Stay here with Reina and find motivation to stay the

fuck alive." Nigel disappeared down the hall to the guest bedroom where they'd set up a sick bay.

Jarvis stared after them, unsettled by Nigel's words. What did Nigel mean, they weren't letting him go down? No way should his team be risking themselves to save him. Yeah, true, it was their code, but there were limits. Hell. He was going to have to dodge them and go solo, wasn't he?

"They care about you," Reina observed, sounding pleased.

Jarvis scowled and walked over to the fridge to get hydrated. "They're loyal teammates."

"No, it's more than that." She was studying him. "They know how dangerous you are, and they still care about you. You do realize that you couldn't have so many people wanting you to live if you were nothing but hate, don't you?"

He handed her a water bottle. "Let it go, Reina."

Her mouth tightened as she took the drink, and he felt bad for rejecting her overture. But it was the right call. Her words made him want things to be different, and he couldn't afford that.

Reina turned away, giving him her back. "Your place is interesting."

She had her hands on her hips and was surveying his penthouse suite. Her shoulders were back and there was a determined jut to her chin. She wasn't going down, and she wasn't going to abandon him. Shit, he wasn't going to go solo, was he? He had Reina with him, a woman he couldn't contaminate. He didn't have to be careful with her. He could simply be himself. She might not be a warrior, but she was his weapon, that was for damn sure. He needed her, and he couldn't afford to piss her off enough to make her bail on him. So, he managed a decent smile of acknowledgement to her comment about his place, and he capitulated to meaningless, polite conversation as a silent apology for rejecting her overture. "I don't like my place. It doesn't feel right."

Or it hadn't. Not until Reina had been standing in the foyer. Suddenly, the skylights and floor to ceiling windows seemed to brighten. The wood floors seemed to be a richer color. The black leather couches looked softer.

"There's something wrong with it. I'm glad you feel it." She studied the room more carefully, her forehead wrinkled in a cute little frown as her feet sank into his plush carpet and she turned in place. "This place has no passion," she said. "It's empty. Cold." She cocked her head. "You need passion. A fire in the soul."

He snorted as he grabbed a beer from the mini-fridge one of the boys had set up in his living room. Water wasn't cutting it. "Screw that. I got enough shit in my soul already."

"Not that kind of passion," Reina said thoughtfully. "Positive, energizing passion. Love."

Jarvis paused at her words. Thought about it. Was that what he needed? It actually sounded appealing… oh, who was he kidding? "That's not my avenue."

"It is." She ignored him and walked over to the painting he'd hung over the couch. It was a stark black and white modern art painting of who knew what. Just lines and shit. "This is how you see yourself."

Jarvis took a swig of the beer, surprised by how much he liked seeing her leaning on his couch. A woman in his home. Felt right. Made his place feel better. "It's a painting."

"No, it's you." She trailed her finger over a thick, jagged black line, and Jarvis could almost feel his skin prickle as he imagined that same finger running down his arm. "Did you pick this out?"

He shifted, suddenly uncomfortable. "I just picked it randomly."

"No." She trailed her finger down another black line. "See all that black? And the white? That's you. The black is your hate. The white is your soul. Fighting each other. Struggling for supremacy. Who wins? This painting is about conflict."

Jarvis frowned at the decor. The jumble of black and white lines were jagged and sharp. Bold. Angry. White lines dominating black ones. Black ones cutting off white ones. Suddenly, he saw it as she did. A battle. Good versus evil. Toughness and conflict. Nothing at ease. Nothing peaceful. "It's just a painting." But even as he said it, he wanted to take it down. Burn it.

"Art is never just art. It always means something to those who respond to it." She grabbed the edges and lifted it down. "This is bad energy. You don't need it. It has to go." She tucked it under her arm. "I've learned that it helps to put positive energy into my life. Sometimes it's all that kept me going."

Jarvis could have stopped her from interfering in his life. But all he felt was relief when she carried it out onto the patio and set it out of sight. The wall looked empty now. Barren. But better. He realized suddenly that the painting was why he'd never sat on his couch. It had loomed over him, and now it was gone. It was better.

Reina walked back inside, carrying a large piece of paper. "Nigel was drawing this outside. This is what you need." She held it up, and he saw it was a drawing of a large green field, populated with pink and yellow flowers. All different shades of pinks and yellows.

He frowned, not liking how it reminded him of the forced decor in the Den. "I'm not a flower guy."

She ignored him and propped the painting on the back of the couch. "This feels better," she said. "I couldn't handle that other one. This reminds me of the backyard of our house growing up. I used to play out there with my sisters. We used to try to catch butterflies." She held up her hand to him. "Come feel this art," she said. "Come feel the difference."

"We have to go—"

"For one minute," she said. "This is important. Come here."

Grumbling, but drawn by a need to accept any excuse to touch her, Jarvis walked up beside her and let her take his hand. She gestured to the painting. "Can you see us? Playing there? Laughing?"

"No—" Jarvis had a sudden vision of Reina cavorting through the fields with butterflies. Lighthearted and free, before life had dealt her a tough hand. "Shit. I can."

"What else do you see? For yourself?"

He frowned and studied the art. "It's just—" Then he stopped. He suddenly remembered the field that he and Cameron used to go to, when Cameron would show him how the butterflies liked to dance. "I would stand completely still, and my brother would shoot me with one of his arrows. After he did it, the butterflies would land on me."

Her eyes widened. "Really?"

"Yeah. It only lasted for a few minutes, but I still remember how their little feet felt. So light, almost like a breeze." He pointed to a yellow flower. "That's what color they were. Yellow." He hadn't thought of that in centuries. "The butterflies landing on me made me feel like I wasn't a monster," he said.

Reina squeezed his hand. "You aren't."

He didn't feel like arguing. Not this time. He just kept looking at the painting and remembering that day. "Thank you," he said quietly.

She raised her brows. "For getting rid of that other painting?"

"For making me remember the butterflies."

She smiled and touched his face. "Good memories are worth keeping."

He set his hand over hers and tried to imprint her tender smile into his mind. "Yes, they are." He leaned forward and kissed her lightly. "You have given those back to me. My old ones, and you've given me new ones."

She smiled. "And you've given me good memories as well. It's been a long time."

"Too long." He hugged her then, just wanting to hold her while he thought about butterflies. Butterflies. Hah. The boys would laugh. But it didn't matter. Reina was taking him places that just felt good. He took her hands and squeezed lightly, searching for the words to say, to explain how she made him feel. He didn't know where to start, but he needed to try.

Chapter 19

JARVIS HESITATED AT REINA'S EXPECTANT STARE. SHE WAS beautiful. How could his words do justice? "Reina—" He stopped. Unsure what to say.

She touched his face, her smile kind and welcoming. "Tell me, Jarvis. It's okay."

He nodded, searching for the right words. "Reina—"

"Jarvis!" Nigel's shout interrupted him. "Get in here!"

Jarvis swore at the reminder of what they were facing. Shit. He squeezed Reina's hand regretfully. "We gotta go."

She smiled with resignation, and she held onto his hand. "I know we do."

Together, they headed down the hall and into the sick room. It felt different walking in with Reina by his side. It felt less dark, less dire, less hopeless, which was exactly what he needed. She'd been right to take that moment for them. To bring them both into a better place. He could feel that he was further from detonation than he had been. Never had he valued inner peace before, but he understood its power now.

Jarvis kept holding her hand as he walked up to the bed Rocco was resting on. The youth was the color of the all organic, humanitarian-endorsed, angel-blessed cream that Nigel poured into his coffee every morning. Rocco's T-shirt was hanging off him, as if he'd lost more than a couple handfuls of muscle since he'd tossed living to the wind. He was giving off no energy, as if his soul had already checked out.

Jarvis had seen men in this state plenty of times when he'd been in the Den, and he knew where it would end. With a visit from one of Death's Guides. Why had he bothered to grab the kid anyway? He had enough trouble keeping alive those who wanted to live to waste time on those who had already packed it in.

But he knew why he'd snagged the kid. It was because Reina had wanted him to do it, and she'd gotten in his head the idea that maybe, just maybe, he could make a positive difference for someone instead of being responsible for death and mayhem. "You think you can heal this kid?"

"I don't know." Nigel was sitting beside him, frowning as he rested his hands above the kid's heart. "He's in bad shape."

Reina was already pulling back the sheets. "Let's get him under the blankets. He's so cold."

Jarvis smiled at her instinctive desire to help someone in need. Whether it was his bad interior design that was sapping his energy, or a young kid suffering from a broken heart, she was there, offering her support. Never failing. He lightly brushed her hair off her shoulders. "Sweetheart, he's a vampire, so he'd be like a block of ice even if he wasn't willing himself into the Afterlife."

"So, we need more blankets, then." Undeterred, she doubled over the comforter as Nigel leaned over the kid.

"Pascal's still sleeping it off in another one of your guest rooms," Nigel said. "I stashed the other five we rescued in my place. They're all in bad shape. I don't know if they're going to make it. Christian resurfaced and he's up there with them playing nurse." Nigel passed his hands over Rocco's forehead, and his palms began to glow a pale pink. "I put in some porn movies for Pascal, so hopefully all that bumping and grinding will get through his coma and jerk him back."

Reina looked up. "You use porn as a medicinal aid?"

"Sure." Nigel winked. "You know what men are like. We see the world in shades of sex and violence."

Reina's gaze flicked curiously to Jarvis. "At the same time?"

"Not me." Nigel looked offended. "Sex is a beautiful, magical experience that embodies love, poetry, and angels flitting around."

"Really?" Reina leaned a little closer to Nigel, a small smile curving her mouth. "That's such a lovely image."

"Hey." Jarvis sat down on the bed between Nigel and Reina, shouldering his friend to the side. "You give the rest of us a bad name when you talk like that. Make the rest of us sound like insensitive clods."

"You are an insensitive clod." Nigel rubbed his palms together, then held them over Rocco's heart.

"Stop it, Nigel," Reina snapped, putting her hand protectively on Jarvis's thigh. "Jarvis just likes to pretend he is, and when you make comments like that, you just encourage it."

Reina had taken his side against the artist warrior who represented everything she was? Jarvis was on board with that. "I don't need to be defended."

"Of course you do." She patted Jarvis's shoulder, and he kinda felt like purring and arching his back. "You need to be defended from yourself."

"Too many nights spent with disenfranchised souls

has messed with your perceptions, woman." Nigel was chuckling. "No one can see any good in Jarvis except his own mother."

A dark shadow appeared in the corner, thick and black. "My mother died when I was born," Jarvis said quietly.

"Exactly. She had no time to realize you weren't lovable—"

Reina smacked Nigel in the head. "Don't be an ass. I've dusted you once, and I can do it again."

Nigel raised his brows at Reina. "You're getting violent on his behalf? What? You love him or something?"

Jarvis tensed.

"Of course I do." Reina bent over Rocco again, her hair shielding her face.

The room started to spin. Jarvis's hands got cold. Cold? He hadn't been cold since the day he was born.

"You do?" Nigel looked shocked.

"Well, of course, I do. He's a good man with a good soul. He should be loved." She pointed a finger at Nigel. "And you love him too, so don't try to deny it."

Sensation rushed back into Jarvis, and his fingers started to burn again. Of course he qualified for loving. Reina's all-encompassing love included every freaking creature that lived, breathed, thought, or talked. She hadn't been referring to that *other* kind of love.

Course not.

Nigel chuckled. "Of course I love him. Doesn't mean I can't see that he's an insensitive brute with no emotional depth whatsoever—"

Rocco groaned suddenly, and Nigel stopped talking. He closed his eyes and laid his hands on the youth's chest. "Mother fucker," he whispered. "He's going out now."

"No!" Reina leaned over Rocco. "No woman is worth dying over! Hang on!" Tears spilled over as the boy's body began to convulse. "Don't you dare—"

"Hey, babe." Jarvis rubbed his hand over her back. He had no business putting her in this situation. Her soul was far too raw when it came to people dying around her. "Let me take you out of here—"

"No! He needs help, can't you see?" She laid her cheek against Rocco's. "Come on, sweetie. You can make it. You can fight it." She was starting to tremble, and the icy cold emotion of raw, debilitating terror was cascading off her. "He can't die. He's so young. My sister Bertha was sixteen, just like him and—"

He knew then that Rocco was not just a vampire to her. Rocco was all the people she'd loved and lost. She was reliving it again, and it was his own damn fault for sucking her into it. Jarvis gathered her in his arms, careful not to break her contact with Rocco. "You're not alone, sweetheart." He let the heat from his body fill her, blanket her, comfort her. "We're still going to save your sister. I swear we will." He stroked her hair, feeling completely out of his comfort zone. How the hell did he ease her pain? He wasn't someone who eased pain. He caused it. He broke souls. He made people's worst fears come alive within them. And it didn't bother him. It really didn't. It never had.

Until now.

Until this second, with Reina emanating fear so deep he could almost feel it past the boiling heat of his own body.

For the first time in his life, he wanted to be his brother. He wanted to be able to heal. He didn't want to be able to kill a dozen demons with one sweep of his sword. He wanted to bring peace to the heart of one amazing woman who had spent her life trying to save her world and failed every time.

And he had no fucking idea how to do it.

He leaned forward, until his lips were right next to her ear. Her dangling heart earring swung lightly against his lips. "I swear by all that's holy and way the hell out of my reach that I will find a way to save your sister. *You will not lose her.*"

She didn't look up, didn't stop shaking, didn't stop whispering words of encouragement to Rocco, but she reached up with one arm, wrapped it around Jarvis's head, and held him to her.

He stayed right where she wanted him, his cheek against the side of her face, her fingers gripping his hair so tightly, as if he was her lifeline. As if he was actually, somehow, someway, giving her comfort.

He wouldn't have moved from that spot for all the gold in the entire world.

Nigel's palms began to glow and the air began to hum. "I need more energy. Now."

Jarvis shook his head. "My energy's so tainted right now. If you channel my vibe, it'll blow his head off and yours—"

"Jarvis." Reina touched his face. "Please," she whispered. "You can help."

Hell. How could he turn that down? He couldn't. Not when she was suffering like that. "Fine."

He stepped back, pulled out his sword, and began whipping it in a circle over his head. The air began to hum, his blade glowed, and the atmosphere began to crackle. Dark shadows grew on the walls, dancing, laughing, crawling closer. Taunting him.

Interesting. The specters were a new twist. Wasn't thinking it was a good sign.

He pried his gaze off his stalkers and focused on the trio on the bed. Nigel healed with energy, and Jarvis could harvest it and dispense it. Normally, he wasn't tainted enough to wreck his friend, but now? He was no bundle of whimsy, that was for sure. He let the energy travel into his body, and his hand began to pulse. "You sure about this?"

"Shit," Nigel said. "I think we lost him—"

Jarvis slammed his hand onto Nigel's bare shoulder. His palm was so hot, Nigel's shoulder caught fire, and black smoke exploded into the air.

"Jesus, man." Nigel gasped as his hands began to glow. "You weren't shitting me. You need to take a bath in angel dust or something."

Jarvis started to pull back. "I'll stop—"

"No, no! Keep it coming." Nigel's hands were glowing black now, and smoke was pouring out of his palms into Rocco's chest. The kid was jerking and twitching, and Reina was trying to hold him still.

The gaping wound in the kid's chest began to close. Jarvis realized Rocco's lips weren't quite as blue anymore, and his face had the faintest beige tinge instead of being sheet white.

Holy crap.

It was working.

He was saving a life.

Shock and awe. No other words. Jarvis renewed his commitment to his sword, turning up the energy harvest.

He shoved it all into his friend, hoping like hell that Nigel would be able to transform that much negative energy into a healing force.

Rocco unleashed a high-pitched shriek of agony. "Cut it off," Nigel shouted suddenly. "Cut it off!"

Jarvis jerked his hand off his friend, stilled his sword, and stepped back. Shadows were dangling from the ceiling, and the air was thick and turbulent. His handprint was burned into Nigel's shoulder, and his teammate's muscles were trembling.

"Get out of here," Nigel ordered. "Now."

Jarvis swore when he saw Nigel's face turning gray. Shit! "Let me take it back—"

"I need it, but I can't take any more," Nigel ordered. "You're bleeding shit everywhere. Get out!"

There was a scream from the room that Pascal was stashed in. Jarvis was bringing the whole place down. There was no time to make it to the elevator. Without hesitation, he sprinted for the balcony.

"What are you doing?" Reina's frantic shout barely reached him as his foot hit the railing and he launched himself into the air off his thirty-fifth floor penthouse.

As he began to fall, he heard Reina's shout. "Can he fly?"

He didn't need to hear Nigel's answer.

He already knew he couldn't.

Discovering that the agonizing pain that jerked Natalie out of her happy-place-coma was actually a gold-tipped arrow in her butt was... well... a little freaky.

Natalie fisted the shaft she'd just pulled out of her

backside. It had no blood on it, was made of a light pink steel shaft, and it had a golden tip that appeared to be made out of a large signet ring with a double heart on it. She stared blankly at it. "I just have no context at all for knowing what this is."

"Natalie! Are you okay?" Trinity knelt beside her.

"Hi, Trin." She held up the arrow. "Did you do this?"

"Shoot you with an arrow? No." Trinity examined it. "Why? Should I try it? Would that help?"

"But if you didn't do it, who did?" No one else was present, and they were twenty feet beneath ground in a cement dungeon with no windows and impenetrable bars… Oh… "I'm in jail? I'm that bad?"

"You were, but your little catnap seems to have mellowed you a bit. We need to keep you away from certain boys, sweetie." Trinity scanned the room. "Okay, so that's just a little bizarre that someone shot you with an arrow down here. Does the Godfather carry loaded?"

"The Godfather?" At the mention of the sexual dynamo who had already rocked her world about a dozen times, Natalie was hit with an incompatible mix of total lust, bubbling warmth, and indescribable terror. "His name's Matt. Matt LeFlandstrom."

"Matt? That's way too ordinary. He should be named Vlad the Impaler." Trinity hovered closer. "So, is he armed? Does he have a tracking device on you?"

"I don't think so." A soothing warmth began bubbling at the spot where she'd been hit with the arrow. Natalie smiled as a peaceful sensation soothed her. Trinity's face took on a golden hue, as if she were a little Buddhist statue of friendship. She touched her friend's skin, but it was soft warmth, not hard metal. "Are you turning into gold?"

"No." Trinity helped Natalie sit up. "How do you feel, sweetie?"

Natalie shook her head, and the motion felt effortless and light, as if she were floating in space. "There's a weird buzzing in my ears and I'm seeing in shades of gold."

Trinity frowned. "Really? Is that normal for you in that condition?"

"I don't know. I've never been in this condition." Natalie tried to stand, but her legs were shaky, and she fell back down. Excitement shot through her. "Did you see that! I'm weak! I'm weak! I'm healed! I—"

"Your sister dusted you." Trinity's face was apologetic. "I'm so sorry, hon, but it's just the residual effects of the dust."

"How do you know? Nothing has ever made me weak before." Natalie slammed her fist into the back of the chair. The chair didn't break, and pain screamed through her hand. "Oh, dear lord! That hurt!" Tears filled her eyes and her heart began to swell with the most amazing feeling of love. "Nothing has hurt me in weeks." Her chest began to pulse, almost painfully, and she bent over, trying to catch her breath. "Oh, my God. I'm healed. I'm not going to die."

"I came as fast as I could!" Gina Ruffalo, the soulswitching candidate and sous chef extraordinaire, raced down the cement stairs carrying a gigantic gun. "I brought the elephant tranquilizer I filched from the zoo last month. Is it time?"

"No!" Natalie beamed at her. "I'm healed."

"What?" The gun fell limply to Gina's side in visible devastation. "You are?"

Natalie's heart thumped with appreciation for the guardian angel who had been her only hope. "Oh, Gina, we'll find a way to get you to heaven. I promise. It'll be no big deal to find someone who's dying and who is willing to trade bodies, you know? You'll be reunited with Phillip and have that wedding night you never had before he broke his neck falling off your sex hammock—Ow!" Her butt was suddenly burning, like a thousand hot razor blades were jamming in her backside.

"What's wrong?" Trinity grabbed her arm. "Tell me what's wrong!"

"My butt's on fire." Natalie knuckled her padding. "Something's happening to me."

"Let me see—" Trinity tried to roll her over, and the pain shot through Natalie.

"Don't!" She shoved Trinity away, and her friend flew across the cell and crashed into the cement wall. "Oh, *no*. I'm strong. Dammit! How can I be strong?"

"You're still dying! This is awesome!" Gina yanked open the cell door, leapt inside, and slammed it shut. She punched a code into the keypad, and there was she sound of loud clanging as the pistons slammed shut. "We're trapped in here with you until Reina comes back. This is it, girls." She hoisted the gun onto her shoulder. "Say when, chica. I'll knock you into the land of sweet dreams until Reina gets here."

"No, no, no, not yet." The pain vanished from her backside again, and Natalie was suddenly filled with the most lovely feeling. Of total joy. Of peace. Of appreciation. She beamed at Gina. "Even though I met you only a few months ago, you are my best friend ever, to trade your body with mine. I love you so much."

Gina winked. "No sweat, hot stuff. I'm glad to be of assistance."

"And you." Natalie whirled around to where Trinity was struggling to her feet. "You're my best friend, too. I'm so sorry I hurt you." She threw herself at Trinity, knocking her friend over again with a giant hug. "I love you, Trinity!"

"I love you, too," Trinity gasped. "Nat, you're getting awfully strong. Are you still afraid of dying?"

The words, the question, made something go queasy in her belly. "Oh, no. I'm feeling all warm and fuzzy, actually. No fear at all." The happy feelings began to infuse her even more, getting stronger and stronger. She whirled toward Gina. "Hit me up. Now."

"Done." Gina raised the gun and fired it.

The dart hit Natalie in the shoulder.

She waited.

They all waited.

She didn't fall down. "Do it again!"

"Again? It's an elephant dosage," Gina said. "It'll kill you."

"It can't kill me. I have to die in a more dramatic way. It'll be fine—"

"Oh, my love!" A male voice filled the room, and Natalie whirled around.

Her heart filled with delight when she saw Vlad the Impaler standing halfway down the staircase. He was wearing the same tux he'd had on the night before. It was wrinkled and dirty, and he was missing one shoe. His hair was disheveled, stubble encased his jaw, and he had a golden arrow broken off in the front of his thigh. He looked *beautiful*. "Matt!"

He beamed at her and held out his arms. "I've missed you, my love!"

"Shoot her!" Trinity shouted.

There was a loud crack, and Natalie was vaguely aware of something slamming into her hip, knocking her back.

"My love! You've been shot!" Matt's face paled, and he vaulted down the stairs.

"I'm okay!" She jumped up. It was so marvelous to see him. She felt like her life had just come to meaning. To purpose. "I'm so happy to see you!" Natalie reached the bars and flung herself against them. Matt caught her and hauled her close. The metal bars pressed against her breasts as she shoved her face through the bars.

His lips met hers instantly, and she felt like her world had just exploded. She gripped his shirt as he showered kisses all over her. "I love you, Matt."

"Oh, babe, I love you, too." He grabbed her hand and pressed it to his heart. "I never thought I would feel like this. I feel so alive. I feel like there is someone out there who cares, who loves me despite all my flaws."

Trinity yanked Natalie back. "Hey, testosterone boy, if you make love to her now, she'll die, and you'll lose her. Is that what you want?"

Matt's brow furrowed slightly. "I don't want to kill her." He backed up.

Natalie screamed, her whole body aching for him. "Don't leave!"

His face was panicked now, terrified. "I can't live without you, my love. I would be devastated if I killed you."

"I can handle it." Natalie shook the bars, frantic as he began to move away. He couldn't leave her, couldn't walk away, couldn't abandon her. "I need you!"

Matt was standing at the base of the stairs, gripping the railing, head bowed as if he were trying desperately to summon the strength to walk away. And as she watched, he took a step, and then another and another— "Matt!"

He spun around, sweat trickling down his temples. "What is it, my love?"

Natalie gripped the bars, her throat so tight, so desperate. "If you love me enough to walk away, then don't you think you love me enough to keep from killing me when we make love?"

He stared at her.

"That logic is way too sound," Trinity muttered. "Gina! Hit her again."

"Again?" She cocked the gun. "I hope you're right."

Natalie was reaching for Matt when the dart thudded into the back of her head. "Enough already!" She yanked it out and hurled it at Gina, then grabbed the one in her hip and unleashed it at Trinity. Both darts hit their marks square in the chest.

"We'll be fine." Trinity yanked the dart out and dropped it to the floor as Gina did the same. "The tranquilizer has already been released into Natalie. There won't be enough left to affect us." She pulled out her phone. "I'm calling Reina, though. It's time for her to sleep with her boss for the promotion. No time left to do it the old-fashioned way."

"I'll knock out the sperm factory." Gina bent to pick up the gun. She positioned it on her shoulder aimed right at Matt… And then she yawned.

Natalie smiled. "I love you guys, but you don't know what's right for me. I do."

"When you're sane you do, but right now, not so much." Trinity jerked her head sloppily at Gina, in a not-so-subtle attempt to tell her to shoot the good guy. She tapped the speaker on her phone, and the ringing began to echo in the cell.

"I've got it." Gina pulled the trigger, promptly tranquilizing the flat screen television on the wall. "Whoops."

Trinity swung her head around to look. "Oops."

"Hello? Trin? What's going on?" Reina's voice echoed out in the cell.

Trinity stared blankly at her phone. "Reina? Did you call me?"

"No. You called me. What's going on?"

"I think—"

Natalie blew on the back of Trinity's head. Her friend swayed, the phone dropped to the floor with a clang, and then she tipped over. Asleep.

"Wow, Nat." Gina gave her a bleary-eyed thumbs up. "That was really cool."

Natalie blew her a kiss, and Gina immediately tipped over and was asleep by the time her head landed on the well-worn pink teddy bear that Natalie had slept with every night of her life.

Until tonight. Tonight she would sleep with Vlad the Impaler.

Natalie turned back toward the entrance, and of course, her lover was still there. Waiting. Natalie strode over to the bars. "How many times will you make love to me if I can open these up?"

He ripped off his shirt, revealing a buff, toned body.

"I've never made love before," he said. "I've only had sex. This time… it's making love, and I'll make love to you as many times as my heart wants to tell you it loves you. A million, maybe? For starters?"

The most delicious warmth rippled over her, and she yanked at the bars. For a moment nothing moved, and then Matt walked up, took her face in his hands, and lightly kissed the tip of her nose.

Strength surged through her, the bars moved aside if it they were overcooked noodles, and then she was in his arms.

And this time, there was no one to stop them.

Chapter 20

Jarvis might not be able to fly, even on his best days.

But he could land.

He hit cement easily, executed a textbook tuck and roll, followed by a round-off and two handsprings to absorb the excess momentum, and came to a graceful stop right at the entrance to the alley where he'd left his vehicle.

He hated to give Angelica any kudos, but his gymnastic talents had come in handy on more than one occasion. Shit. Maybe the chick knew what she was talking about—

He staggered as the full force of the Mean and Nasties smacked him, and he reeled as the purple shadows batted at his face. Since when were the hate goblins corporeal? He decapitated the lot of them to the sound of giggling that no grown warrior wanted to hear from the death shadows chasing him.

More came out of the ground, squeezing out of the cracks in the sidewalk, bulging out of blades of grass. He felt them piercing his skin, eating at him. Black smoke began spiraling out of his fingertips, filling the air with noxious fumes.

A couple passing by began to argue and then shout at each other. The cars began to honk. A dog howled. A cat squealed and hissed.

Shit. This couldn't be good. He was contaminating the world.

"Jarvis!" Reina, looking like an angel in her blue jeans and white T-shirt, sprinted out the front door of his building, past the very proper doorman who was, thanks to Jarvis, currently berating the sweet old lady from the first floor for daring to outlive his own grandmother. "You're alive!"

His throat was thick, too thick to talk, so he just held his arms out. *Come to me, babe*.

Reina, bless that loving heart of hers, threw herself into his embrace without hesitation. Her kiss was like magic, the soothing of magical touch, of peace, of sanity. He stumbled back toward the car, gripping her like she was his lifeline to sanity.

Oh, wait, she was.

Yeah, it was so not manly to rely on some sweet thing to stay sane, but what male could really control the monster inside? Wasn't that what Angelica's point had been? Maybe there was some truth to the notion that the warrior shit was all well and good, but in the end, a man needed a woman to bring out his soft side.

Hell, now was as good a time as any to give it a try, right?

Reina's lips were warm, her tongue daring and a little saucy as she played with his teeth, her hands enfolded in his hair as he yanked open the driver's door with one hand. He set himself in the driver's seat without breaking contact and she straddled him, her knees on either side of his hips. He pulled her down on top of him and kissed her, drinking in the tenderness of her kiss, the softness of her body.

"You're going to drive like this?" she whispered against his mouth.

"No." He worked his hands under her shirt and shuddered at the feel of her bare skin beneath his touch. "I'm going to make love to you like this."

"What?" She pulled back, her flushed cheeks a stark contrast to the surprise in her eyes. But not fear. There was excitement and anticipation in her expression, revealing a woman who had just realized how badly her man needed her and was thrilled by that discovery. "We're in a car! In public! People will see—"

He cupped her face with his hands. "I need you right now. I need to feel your body against mine. We don't have time to go upstairs, or even to take two minutes to get physical." He tightened his grip, unable to keep the raw need out of his voice. "But I have to make time, because I need to get connected to you. I need to feel your soul wrap around mine and ease the pain."

Her face softened, and she touched his face. "Jarvis—"

"We're in an alley. No one comes back here. And if they pass by, they'll just see two fully clothed adults kissing in the front seat. They can't see what else is going on out of view." He pulled her down and kissed her mouth, working it until she began to kiss him back. Every muscle in his body was trembling with the need to be with her. "Two minutes of your soul and your body," he whispered. "That's all I need."

Longing flared in her eyes, and she leaned toward him ever so slightly. Calling to him, to them, even while the old Reina, the fearful Reina, tried to be heard. "But—"

He gripped her hair and pulled her close, his fingers twisting in her silken locks as the darkness pulsed inside him. Fighting to get free. "I can't live without you," he whispered. "Let me make love to you. Not on the edge of insanity, like before." He pressed his mouth to hers, a tender, soft kiss. "Let me feel what it's like to make love. To experience that tenderness. I need to go there, and I need it with you." His skin was hot, too hot, and he felt bad shit churning inside him.

It was trying to take over, trying to taint his mind, and he didn't want to go there. He knew his time was getting near, and before he died, he wanted to experience the peace that he knew only Reina could give him.

He had to experience it. He couldn't go another moment without it. So, he took over the moment. Took over her choices. Kissed her with the passion and depth and tenderness he'd never been able to do before she'd given him the gift of human contact.

Reina leaned forward, pressing her breasts against his, in an unspoken acknowledgement of her own need for him. "But if someone sees us—"

"Sweetheart." He kissed the side of her neck, whispered in her ear. "I'll keep watch for anyone. You're safe with me."

Reina pulled back then and looked at him. Her blue eyes were dark with passion and need, and she looked like she was almost ready to cry. "I'm always safe with you, aren't I?"

He nodded. "I would never let anything happen to you." He slid his fingers in the back of her hair, no longer able to talk. He needed to touch her. To connect. So, he pulled her close and kissed her. Harder. Deeper. Yet with a tenderness he hadn't ever felt before.

And this time, Reina finally capitulated to her desires and his and kissed him back with a commitment that made his heart soar. She accepted her own need for intimacy and connection. She stroked his shoulders with a tenderness that made his whole body shudder.

Hands that soothed. Not hands that hurt. A gift.

He caressed her back, her hips, drank in the feel of her womanly curves, loving the differences between their bodies, the gentleness of her being. Something deep inside him, something soft that was buried beneath the monster within, fought for acknowledgement, struggled to surface in response to her touch.

He kissed her deeper, needing more, and she kissed him back every bit as passionately. It was intense and power-ful, driven by need, but it wasn't blind physical need. It was a burning in his core, in a part of his soul that had never been fed, and he was desperate for more, to access that part of him, to feel that warmth spread through him.

But the beast tangled with it. Striving for supremacy. Not allowing defeat of its hold on the throne. But as Jarvis kissed her more deeply, as he shed her jeans and unzipped his fly, as he felt the skin of her thighs settled across his, he felt that flickering warmth inside him take a stronger hold. Still small. Still subordinate. But solid. Glowing. Holding on to the connection with Reina, and the tenderness of her touch and her kiss.

He needed more. Had to be inside her. Had to com-plete the connection. He palmed her hips, stroking her soft skin as he lifted her over him.

"Yes," she whispered. She met his gaze, and then she smiled, so tenderly, so affectionately. An expression of pure, non-judgmental love directed at him, only for him, from her heart and soul into his.

He thrust deep, one movement, and then he was sheathed deep inside her. She shuddered and leaned her forehead intimately against his, her gaze not leaving his as he moved inside her. He saw in her face pure tenderness, sensuality, and a need for who he was and what he could give her, the same emotions pulsing so deep inside him.

Together, connected in their bodies, in their souls, and their spirits, they moved, passion building, need escalating, connection tightening, until he couldn't think of anything but Reina. He couldn't feel anything but her body around his, her breasts against his chest. He sought out her mouth and felt the world shift as their lips connected.

When she cried out at the peak of her passion, his own answering orgasm hit him hard, rolling through him like a beautiful sunshine beating down at his soul, and he felt peace settle over him. True peace. The kind he'd never felt in his life. The kind of peace that only Reina could give him.

She sagged against him, her arms wrapped around his neck, holding him so intimately, as if she'd never let him go.

For a moment, neither of them spoke. They simply breathed in the moment, the connection, the bond.

Then he heard voices, and he tensed, jerking his head up to look past her. She tensed against him as he watched a group of teenagers stroll past the end of the alley. One glanced over, and Jarvis felt the beast roar to life. *Don't look at my woman.*

He swore and leaned his head back, bracing himself as the poison careened through him like an angry, swollen river trying to destroy everything in its path.

One minute. That was all he'd gotten. One damn minute of relief.

Reina studied him, her face pinched with concern. "Are you okay?"

"Yeah, sure." He slipped his hand underneath her shirt, and he sighed at the feel of her bare back under his palms. He moved his hand around and cupped her breast. Dear God, *yes*. Her skin was so soft, a breath of life he could get nowhere else. She was his salvation, and he drank it in, trying to fight back to that place of peace she'd taken him to, but it was elusive, flitting out of his grasp. He tucked his face into the curve of her neck and inhaled her scent. The lavender and vanilla imbued his pores and his soul, but the relief would not come back. "I'm not having a good day, babe."

Reina sat back on his thighs, her knees on either side of his hips. She held his face in her hands and searched his gaze, her blue eyes so genuine and careful. "You did it," she whispered.

He couldn't tear his gaze away from hers. "Did what?"

"Rocco's going to be okay." She smiled, her eyes dancing with so much love he could feel the warmth of it in his own heart. "You gave him the strength to continue. You saved his life."

"I gave him hate—"

"Which is more powerful than apathy. Sometimes you have to get angry first, before you can get happy. People don't understand that, but it's true. You gave him anger and hate, and that's a reason to live." She smiled and brushed her thumbs over his cheeks in a gesture so tender it made something burn in his chest. "You're a gift, Jarvis. You saved his life."

Who the hell was tender with Hate? Didn't she understand who he was? But he was glad she didn't. He treasured the fact that she saw him as something other than a big, black ghoul. He took her wrists in his hands and squeezed affectionately. "You're insane."

She smiled. "No, I've just seen everyone in my family surrender to death. Watching Rocco find the courage to fight to survive was the greatest gift you could ever give me."

His heart began to thud, a slow, laboring beat at her warmth, at her complete belief in his value. "Sweetheart, you can't make other people fight. They have to make that choice, and if they choose not to, it's not your fault."

She cocked her head. "Like how you're choosing not to fight your explosion?"

He scowled. How had the conversation turned to him? "That's different. That's how I end. It's been a given since the day I was born."

She leaned forward until she was resting her forehead against his, mimicking her position when they'd been making love. "I want you to fight," she whispered. "Why do I want you and Natalie to live more than either of you want yourselves to live? Why?"

The thickness to her voice touched something inside him, and he wrapped his arms around her, holding her tight. "Sweetheart, you need to ditch the love and start drinking in some of my hate. If you hated me, it'd be a hell of a lot easier."

"Hate?" She lifted her head to stare at him. "Are you kidding? I'd rather have a part of my heart die with you and my sister than soil my love with hate just to protect me from pain." She laid her hand over his chest. "Love is good, Jarvis. You just need to let it in."

He sighed with frustration. "I'm not hard-wired for love. You need to stop making me into something I'm not."

"Jarvis—" Her phone rang, and she pulled it out of her pocket. "Oh, it's Trinity." She answered it. "Trin? Hello? Hello?"

Jarvis fisted her hair, absorbing the silkiness of those locks. He tunneled through her tresses and, almost absently, began to braid it. His mind began to refocus, to think about what they had to do next. The interlude was over. The final battle was approaching. And now, by the grace of Reina's soothing presence, his thoughts were clear enough to strategize.

Reina rested the phone against her cheek. "She's in trouble."

"What's wrong?" He finished one tiny braid and started on another, a smaller one this time. Narrower than his fingers, but somehow he was able to manipulate her hair with a finesse that had always eluded him with knitting needles.

"I don't know. She didn't say anything, but I could hear noise in the background. We need to go to my house and check on her—"

"No time." Jarvis had his plans, and it was time move. Regretfully, he shifted Reina to the passenger seat and helped her put her pants back on, even though a part of him wanted to tumble her into the backseat and go back to that place she'd taken him.

That moment was past. Now was time for reality. "We'll have Blaine go check on her." He zipped himself up and then took her hand. "We need to get that scythe from the Grim Reaper." He pressed her palm to his lips. "I swore I'd help you save your sister, and I meant it.

We're going to make this happen for you. Your sister's going to live, and Cam's going to save the world from me. Got it?"

She nodded, but he could tell she was barely listening as she settled into her seat and pulled her hand out of his. "I think maybe I should go see the Grim Reaper alone," she said.

"Absolutely not." He shot a surprised look at her as he started the truck. "Why in the hell would you even suggest that?" As if he would allow her to go into that den of iniquity without protection.

"Every time your stress level goes up, you go closer to the edge. Fighting my battles is shortening your life span." She strapped on the seat belt, trapping herself on the other side of the car. Away from him. "So, drop me off and—"

"No chance." How sweet was it that she wanted to protect him? Completely insulting as to his warrior talents, of course, but instead of getting offended… shit… it made him feel good. She was willing to trade her best chance of saving her sister to let him live a little longer?

His throat tightened for a split second, and he leaned over and planted one on her. No mouth had ever tasted as good as hers did, right in that second. "You are a treasure."

She studied him. "How can you have so much faith in everyone else, but not in yourself?"

"I've got tons of faith in myself. I know exactly what I'm capable of." He pulled out into traffic, his grip tight around her hand. "I'll kick everyone's ass to hell and back before I die."

"That's not what I meant."

"I know." Yeah, he knew she was asking why he didn't try to beat his own rap. Reina made him feel like there was chance he had a shred of decency in him, and he'd never felt that way before. Damned if he didn't like it. But at the same time, he knew it was a false hope. He was what he was, and he'd accepted that long ago.

She had more fire and more heart than he could ever hope to have, and a part of him wanted to pull her into his lap, dive into bed with her, and never emerge. Just bury himself in the peace she gave him and pretend he was worthy of her.

But he didn't have that choice.

───※───

Reina glanced over at Jarvis as they hurried up the stone steps of the gorgeous brownstone on Commonwealth Avenue. His skin had a faint purplish hue, which, on him, was rocket sexy, even if it was terribly disheartening at the same time. He was being trailed by a horde of black shadows, like he was the pied piper of all things ominous and deadly.

Jarvis glanced over at her, and his expression softened. He brushed his hand through her hair, his fingers playing with the braids that hadn't fallen out yet.

When had she stopped thinking of him as a monster? When had she started noticing the lines in the corners of his eyes, as if he'd once smiled, and his skin still remembered how to do it?

Now that she thought about it, she couldn't really remember when she'd smiled much either. Well, there were smiles, and there were *smiles*. The latter was what counted. The kind that started in the heart and swelled up and out until there was no choice but to expose those pearly lights to the sunshine.

Two non-smiling death mongers. What a perfect couple they made.

Jarvis hit the buzzer, snaked his hand around her wrist, and yanked her against him. She melted into his body and pressed her face against his chest. His heart was racing, as if it were immersed in some great fight for its life (go figure), and his skin was so hot she was surprised his shirt hadn't caught fire. But she could smell the faint scent of woods, of man, of humanity. In there, underneath his destiny, was a real man.

A man who held her tightly, as if he would never let her go. A man so unlike the brother he was risking it all for. "What is the deal with you and your brother?"

Jarvis pressed the buzzer again. "What do you mean?"

Reina hesitated, not sure whether to pry. "Why is he so mad at you? I mean, you're trying to save him, but he won't help you."

"I haven't seen him for a hundred and fifty years." Jarvis sighed and leaned against the wall. His face was drawn, his hands nearly black. "I was six. He was five. Angelica had heard of the Guardian of Love, and she'd decided that he would be a great addition to the Den."

Reina raised her brows. "Of course she would."

"So, she came after Cameron." Jarvis's face hardened, and she could see the pain as he began to drift back to the past. "We were playing hide-and-seek in the woods. It was easy for me to find him because the animals always gravitated toward him and gave him away. He could never find me." His fists tightened. "I was hiding in the trees when Angelica passed beneath me. She was heading right for Cameron, and I heard her talking to one of her apprentices about harvesting Cameron."

Reina saw the anguish in his eyes and knew what he had been feeling. That moment of knowing that someone you loved was about to die, and you were all that stood between them and death. "And so you stopped her."

"I tried. I dropped out of the tree on top of her with my sword. Hit her right between the shoulders." He shook his head, as if trying to shake away the memory. "The hate took her, and she focused it on me. Hated me with a fucking passion."

Reina could imagine what Angelica became when infused with hate. "She tried to kill you."

"No. She decided to hurt me." His voice was flat, but she saw the bead of sweat on his brow.

Her heart tightened. "You were only six."

"I was only six." Anger laced his voice. "I couldn't beat her. Never could."

Reina slipped her arms around his waist and rested her cheek on his chest. His heart was thundering, as if he were back in that moment, fighting for his life again.

He wrapped his arms around her and buried his face in her neck. "I knocked her out. Had my opportunity to escape." His body tensed, and his voice changed. Softened. "And then I saw Cameron watching. He was in a tree, sitting there butt naked, in plain sight."

"She would have taken him if you'd left."

"My job as the Guardian of Hate was to protect him at all costs." He held her tighter, as if he was using her to block the memories. "It's what I am here for. My dad and I had discussed it many times. Cameron's safety took priority. We both were to sacrifice ourselves for him. And if one of us died, the other would close ranks and protect him."

Reina lifted her head to look at him. "So, you let yourself be taken, knowing that your father would never come looking for you?"

"Yeah." That was it. Just a simple word. Flat. Emotionless.

The intentional emptiness of that word was enough to tell her how much it still burned at him. What kind of boy was taught to accept a life of torture, who believed that that's all his life was worth. "That's a choice no six-year-old boy should ever have to make." Or an adult. No one should ever have to decide they were worth less than someone else.

"No." He released her. "I accepted it with honor." He turned away and jabbed his finger into the doorbell again. "But he got fucked up while I was gone. I left him behind and he's in trouble. That's why I have to save him. Because I betrayed him once already. There should have been another way to handle it the first time."

"Are you kidding?" She pulled him back to face her. "He betrayed you! He let you take the hit for him and then didn't honor your sacrifice. You didn't fail, Jarvis. He did. We are all responsible for ourselves. It's not your fault that he chose his path of arrogance."

"I left him. He's not fit to be left alone—"

"You are a hero," she said. "You're the one people will admire and remember. You faced hell, and you turned out to be the one with the soul of gold, not him." Her body vibrated with the truth of those words, and she knew she was right. He had given his life for his brother, and he was still planning to do it.

She took his face in her hands and went up on her tiptoes to kiss him.

He frowned. "What is that for?"

"For being the man I knew you were." No wonder he understood her need to save Natalie. Because he lived by the same code of ethics, and he had the same loyalty. They'd both failed, and now it was time for them both to win.

Jarvis said nothing, but he hugged her tight and buried his face in her neck. Holding her, as if her embrace could change the life they'd both led. In that moment, she almost felt like it could. "We can do this," she said quietly. "We can do it right this time. Save Natalie and Cameron. Make it turn out right."

"I know we can." Jarvis lifted his head and searched her face. His eyes were almost black, but the blue flecks were strong and vibrant: the man looking out from the doom trying to take him. "You give me hope, sweetheart. Hope of things I've never dared hope for before."

Her chest started to beat more quickly at the intensity of his expression. Did he believe he could live, after all? Was he willing to fight that battle? Was it possible that he could stop fate? "Like what?"

He opened his mouth to answer, and then a loud crack blistered through the air.

Chapter 21

REINA AND JARVIS WHIRLED AROUND AS ANOTHER CRACKLE sounded, and she realized it was the intercom coming to life. Not another police invasion or a pink star on the way to them. "Who's down there?"

Jarvis rested his cheek against her hair and closed his eyes, as if he were trying to hang onto the intimacy for a second longer. "We're here to see the Grim Reaper."

But even as they stood there, she felt the tension return to both their bodies. The moment was over. Reality was back.

"He's busy," the voice said. "Go die somewhere else." And then it disconnected.

Reina sighed. Normally, being hung up on by the Grim Reaper, who was living behind a reinforced building with a skull and crossbones over the door and marble statues of naked, decapitated men on the front porch, would be daunting. But honest to God, she was too strung out to be daunted. "Jarvis?"

He gave her a grim smile. "Aren't you glad you didn't leave me at home?" He pulled out his sword, gave a manly flourish, and then he slammed it into the door lock. Purple steam began to hiss out of the lock. The door began to bubble, and little fissures began to run down the sidewalk.

"Boom." Jarvis tucked her against him and turned so his body shielded her from the door. She snuggled against him and tucked her face into the curve of his shoulder.

The door exploded with such force that it flattened two lampposts and a fire hydrant on the other side of the sheet. Not to mention half a dozen specters.

"Nice shot."

He shot her an absentminded grin. "Thanks." He dusted off the carnage. "After you?"

"Such a gentleman." The lobby of the single-family townhome was black and white marble, with depictions of horrible, awful deaths of ancient beings covering the walls and ceilings. Loud clanking was coming from a room to the right of the magnificent, curved stairway. "Back there."

She darted across the floor, Jarvis on her heels, and she threw open the double French doors that were almost identical to the ones in the Castle.

Standing inside an office similar to Death's was a man at least eight feet tall, with broad shoulders and dark hair cut in a military buzz cut. He was naked except for a leopard print thong and a full body tattoo that had various faces in expressions of extreme agony, pain, and death.

He was up on a ladder, yanking books off the wall and hurling them to the floor as he frantically searched for something. "Dammit! Where the hell is it?"

"Excuse me, sir?"

The Grim Reaper whirled around. He was wearing jet-black eyeliner and eye shadow, blood red lipstick, and a base foundation of mouse gray. Ruining the ensemble was a pair of geek glasses with large tortoise-shell frames in olive green. "If you can find my cloak, my robe, and my wig in thirty seconds, I'll give you anything you want."

"Wig?" Scythes lined the walls of the office, all of them with little brass nameplates in front of them. Clearly, she and Jarvis had come to the right place for scythe requisitioning. Rock on!

"Twenty-five seconds and I'll make all your dreams come true." The Reaper began yanking books off again. "I hid them from my three-year-old great-great-great-great-nephew and his penchant for scissors, and now I can't find them."

"Wig it is." Reina opened a cabinet, only to find assorted bottles of preserved brains. "Oh, wow." She shut the door.

Jarvis pulled out his sword. "Did you harvest souls wearing it?"

"Of course I did. It's the real thing—"

Jarvis began whipping the sword around his head, and the air began humming. The Grim Reaper turned and stared at Jarvis. "What the bloody hell are you?"

"Talent." A statue of Lord Grim began to vibrate, and then a small, hidden door in its belly opened and out flew a ratty black robe and what looked like roadkill with long hair.

"He's afraid of my statue. Of course I would hide it there!" The Grim Reaper raced down the ladder. "How did you do that?"

"Everyone hates you, right?"

"Yes, of course. That's the point."

"I have a knack for finding hate. Your stuff is tainted with it." Jarvis sheathed his sword as the Reaper yanked on his robe.

It got stuck in his thong, and he fought to untangle it. Reina hurried over and helped free the burlappy material from the velvet soft leopard print. "Here you go."

"Excellent." The Reaper threw the wig on and grabbed a stack of bobby pins off his desk. "Do you know how to keep these suckers on? I just cut my hair last week, and I haven't used the wig since. I need to make sure this stays put and no bobby pins show."

"I've got it." Jarvis strode across the room and grabbed the box. "Sit."

The Grim Reaper plopped his well-toned butt on a velvet topped stool as Jarvis fiddled with the straggly black locks. Her warrior let out a sigh of what sounded like contentment as he pried open a bobby pin with his teeth.

"Do you do nails, my dear?" The Reap pointed at his desk. "Black. The Sally Hansen Insta-Dri. I don't have time for the real stuff."

She grabbed the bottle and hurried over. "I want a scythe."

"A scythe? Hah." The original Lord of Death laughed as he held out his hands for the mani. "You'll die if you use one. They are enchanted and can be used only by the gifted."

"I'm gifted." His nails were lumpy and knotted, mis-shapen and well over an inch long, curving into some-thing akin to claws. "I'm not sure how much help nail polish is going to be."

"Oh, these are fake. My real ones are perfect, but I can't have perfect nails at the Sisterhood of the Fairy Tale Hero's Annual Testosterone Awards, can I? I have a reputation to uphold."

The Sisterhood that had staked Rocco? The one Damien had given her a check to eliminate? Those girls got around. Reina stroked the black liquid over the lumpy nail. "What are the Testosterone Awards?"

"Oh, my dear," the Reap said. "They're very, very important if you're a man. The competition is fierce, and they consider only men who are lethally dangerous to the women they date, who are incredibly handsome and compelling, and who have a tender side that only the right woman can access."

Reina glanced at Jarvis. "Have you ever been nominated?"

He didn't look up from bobby pin central. "Six times. I had to decline. Couldn't get out of the Den to attend the awards ceremony."

"Six times?" The Reaper regarded Jarvis with new interest. "And who are you?"

"The Guardian of Hate."

"Why didn't you say so?" The Reap slapped Jarvis on the butt. "I could have used you when I was in business." He pointed to an array of testicle-shaped plaques on the far wall. "I won for a hundred and twenty consecutive years. Eventually, they had to pass a term limit of thirty years, or else no one would get a chance. They invite me back every year to present the award, and I must look appropriately horrific, you know?"

"Of course." Reina accidentally swiped a cuticle and frantically wiped it off before the lord of all things hellacious noticed.

"And today my personal handmaiden quit. Her boyfriend was jealous of her being intimately involved in my life, and he said it was me or him. So she left!" He shook his finger at Reina. "Imagine leaving such a coveted position for sex! Sex!"

Reina immediately thought of the Godfather, and she started brushing the polish on more quickly. "I'm Reina Fleming, the Guide who sends you Death's reports each week, and I really do need to borrow a sickle or a scythe—"

"Reina Fleming?" The Reaper did a full inspection of her. "Surely you aren't that attractive while you're working, are you? What man would be scared of a woman with those breasts— Ow!" He held his head and glared at Jarvis. "You stabbed me."

"Then don't look at her breasts."

Reina smiled at Jarvis's muttered threat. He was willing to stab *the* original Grim Reaper with a bobby pin for staring at her breasts. Something warm began to bubble inside her. "Actually, I'm totally hellish when I reap," she lied. "But I need a new scythe."

"Never. I don't loan them out." The Reap's phone rang and he answered it. "Out of the Darkness Suicide Hotline, can I help you?"

That was his retirement? Keeping people from killing themselves? Irony didn't even begin to describe the enormity of that inconsistency.

"Oh, yes, certainly. Put him on." The Reap covered the mouthpiece. "I apologize for taking this call, but my staff is busy preparing the limousine for my arrival, and others have gone ahead to make sure my red carpet is sufficiently luxurious."

"No problem." Reina finished his nails and set down the polish. She watched Jarvis as his fingers flew through the hair, as bobby pins flashed and then disappeared into the ratty mess.

For the first time in a long time, his brow wasn't furrowed, and the shadows perched on the wall were playing poker instead of looming at him. The sword on his hip was still pulsing purple and black, but his broad shoulders weren't as rigid as they usually were.

He looked at peace. "Jarvis?"

"Hmm?" He didn't look up, didn't bother to take the bobby pins out of his mouth.

"Perhaps you were right that knitting isn't your calling. But maybe something else is."

"There's no peace for me, sweetheart, but I appreciate the thought."

"What about doing hair?"

He looked up, his expression one of true horror. "I am not a stylist."

She held up one of her tiny braids. "You're really good at it—"

"I kill people. That's how I get relief," he snapped. "Jesus. A hair dresser?" He shook his head and went back to work.

"Hello, Joel." The Reap's voice was suddenly dark and raspy, and chills raced down her arms. "This is the Grim Reaper."

He was breathing heavily in a fantastic Darth Vader imitation. "I am so pleased you are about to kill yourself. I am going to come to you with my scythe and rip your screaming soul from your pathetic little body, and then you will be mine. A thousand years of acid poured on your manly bits, leeches on your testicles, and my assistant will pluck out your facial hair one whisker at a time."

He winked at Reina. "I will gnaw the meat from your bones while you are still alive and—" He grinned and tossed the phone on his desk. "He hung up screaming. I feel so validated."

Reina frowned. "That was an interesting approach to a suicide hotline. Scare the suicidal so badly that they become too terrified of death to kill themselves."

The Reap stretched his long legs. "I cannot have these people thinking death is better than living." He nodded at Reina. "Go get me one of those gold balls from the bowl on my desk, darling, will you?"

"But life after death is often better than the life they had while they were alive." Reina hurried over to the desk, still trying to think of a way to talk the Reap into giving her what she wanted.

"Well, of course it is, but they don't need to know that. Death must be terrifying or no one would bother to fight it out and accomplish anything in real life. Where would all the great inventions be if people realized that if they just chopped off their heads, life would be wonderful? Total anarchy in society. Can't have it." He held up his black fingers and made a scary face. "Argh! Run away from Death, little boys and girls! I'm coming for you—"

He burst out laughing, and tears started to run down his face, smearing his makeup. "You should see some of the people I've scared. Grown men and women actually wetting their pants! I have to say, I miss that, I really do. I don't miss the grind, but I miss seeing everyone so debilitated with fear and screaming my name in anguish." He pointed to a carnation red skull on a pedestal in the middle of the floor. "Please put the ball in there, if you will be so kind."

"Don't you think that's a little manipulative? Trying to terrify people into being productive members of society?" She dropped the ball into the skull, then jumped back when smoke exploded and screams filled the air. "Is someone in there?"

"Oh, no, no. Those are recordings of assorted victims. I made a collection of my favorite ones. Each time I successfully manipulate someone into a debilitating fear of death, I put a ball in the skull. Helps me keep track." He frowned suddenly. "Haven't you heard that recording? I left a copy with Prentiss so he could play it at reapings and terrify people."

Um... time to change the subject, because Death most certainly did not whip out the ol' iPod when he harvested. Reina pointed the scythe hanging above the skull. A brass plaque beneath it was inscribed with the words *Ivan the Terrible, d. 1584. Wet pants three times and sobbed like a baby. A+.* "Did you really make Ivan the Terrible cry?"

"Oh, yes, yes." The Reaper beamed at her. "I toyed with him for an hour, just because it was so lovely. You may admire it." He flicked his hand toward it, there was a clicking noise, and then brass chains lowered the scythe. "I turned off the booby traps. It's safe now, comrade."

"Thanks." Reina carefully lifted it down. It was much heavier than the lightweight, metal composites that Death now employed. She did a test swing and nearly dropped it. "Does it work?"

"They always work. They've all been blessed." The Reap looked at his watch. "I'm late! I hate it when Prentiss gets there first! Just because he held the title for three decades and leveraged the title into an assortment of sexual liaisons does not mean that he's more of a Fairy Tale Hero than I am, despite what he may think."

Reina tightened her grip on the staff. "Prentiss? You mean Death?"

Jarvis stepped back, pride evident on his face. "You're all set. No one will know it's a wig, and you could get caught in a hurricane and it won't budge."

"Fantastic." The Reap snatched his cloak off the back of the chair. "Prentiss is bringing some new Reaper, and I must be there to make sure the new hire is up to snuff."

Jarvis went still. "What new Reaper?"

Death was moving up Cameron's debut? Reina looked at Jarvis's grim face and knew he'd come to the same conclusion.

"I don't know. All he said was that it was an appropriate choice given that the Godfather was receiving the Testosterone Award and would be killing his true love on stage in front of everyone."

Reina's chest tightened. "The Godfather? Killing his true love? Tonight? What are you talking about?" He was going to kill Natalie tonight? On stage? The number of things wrong with that scenario were just too many to list. What was wrong with the Sisterhood, anyway? Showcasing a murder as popular entertainment? Seriously?

"Apparently, the Sisterhood has been trying to locate him for weeks, and they finally found him. He's on the scent of a woman, which makes him utterly inconsolable until he kills her, so they're making it part of the ceremony. I think it's brilliant. That's what the award is about, anyway: men who are a danger to their women." He peeked at his reflection in a gilded mirror. "My makeup is ruined! I can't go like this! I am far too hand-some!" He whirled around. "Hate Man, do you know how to do makeup, too?"

Jarvis shook his head. "No—"

"I do," Reina interjected.

"Thank the good lord above!" The Reap glided across the room and snatched a gold silk purse out of the ward-robe. "My boots. I almost forgot!" He grabbed a pair of battered, thigh-highs out of the closet. They were caked in crusted blood and dried flesh… or was it the product of ground turkey breast and Elmer's glue? "Get in the limo. We'll do it on the way."

"Get us inside the door with you," Reina said quickly. They had to get inside. It was all going down now. D-day had come ahead of schedule, and there was no time for strategizing.

"And let Reina borrow the scythe," Jarvis added.

"No, no, no!" The Reap threw his hands on his hips. "I can't—

Jarvis held up a bobby pin. "What is done can be un-done just as easily. Those bobby pins know that I'm their master. You want to walk in there with pretty boy hair?"

"And I know how to use boot polish," Reina added. "I'm really good at buffing to a shine. That Perdue ground turkey isn't going to make it to the event. And you look really pretty. Your fair skin is glowing and you have such lovely blue eyes."

The Reap's face contorted with fury. "You are both scum."

Jarvis tapped his sword. "Thank you."

The Reap broke into a grin. "You're welcome! I love scum! Come on, then!" He grabbed a monstrous scythe off the wall and slung it over his shoulder, nearly taking out the doorframe. He marched over to the wardrobe and pulled out two more black robes and wigs. "If you're coming in with me, you need to look the part. There can be no beautiful people stepping out of my limo." He tossed them at Reina and then grabbed another scythe and handed it to Jarvis. "Hold this for Reina. Don't try to use it," he warned. "Only those who have been properly blessed can use it without blowing themselves up."

Jarvis's fists closed over the steel. "Wouldn't want to blow myself up," he muttered.

Reina glared at him. "That's not funny."

His face softened and he touched her hair. "Sorry, babe. I forget it bothers you." He lightly kissed her forehead.

The Reap hurried them out the door. "So, Hate Man, you want to be my new handmaiden? You're great with my hair, and we could work on the handsome thing. Some plastic surgery could deform you nicely. What do you say? You in?"

"We'll see. Got some things to take care of first." Jarvis took Reina's hand as they all sprinted down the stairs.

How cute was that? A public statement that they were together? In front of the Reap? Damn it. How come all the good ones died?

A black stretch Escalade limo was purring at the curb. On its side were black and gold letters that said *The Grim Reaper*, along with copious ancient drawings depicting brutal moments of death. On the back door was a large gold star that said *Lifetime Achievement Winner for the Testosterone Awards*. Her warm and fuzzy feeling toward Jarvis was replaced with the sobering reality of where they were going. To the place where it was all coming together. Her sister. The Godfather. Cameron. Death. They had no plan, no time to prepare, and it was happening now.

The moment where it all was lost forever, or not.

She slipped in next to Jarvis, and he threw his arm around her and hauled her up close as the Reaper climbed in after them, sweeping his robes out of his way with a flourish that was a little too threatening for comfort.

The car began to move.

"Where's the ceremony?" Jarvis asked.

"Fenway Park. They needed the seats."

Jarvis pulled out his phone and dialed. "Blaine, it's—" He listened for a moment, then said, "Meet us at Fenway Park. Bring Gina inside. It's going down tonight."

The Reap unzipped his makeup kit and handed it to Reina. "What's going down? Do you do have a nefarious plan? Because I like the Sisters. They honor me and are terrified of me. They have a PR department that's fantastic, and they've done great things for my reputation."

Ignoring the Reap's babbling, Reina pulled the ash gray Estée Lauder foundation out of the bag. "What's going on, Jarvis?"

"Blaine found Trinity and Gina. They're okay, but Natalie and the Godfather are gone."

"The Sisterhood has them." Reina looked at the Reap. "Can you give me full soul harvesting powers? The ability to move souls out of a body?" And into another?

"Oh, no, no, not anymore. I can't even do it myself these days." He punched a button on the door, and a lighted makeup mirror rose out of the center console.

Then she had no choice. She had to force Death to

promote her. Now. She let out her breath, then took out her phone. It was time to play the last card.

Heaven help her.

Chapter 22

IN THE SHADOWS OF THE OLD STATE HOUSE AND ALL ITS magnificent history, Augustus stood over the whimpering assassin who used to be his greatest competition. He raised his pink star to thrust it mercilessly into the throat of Napoleon—

"Damn it!" He flung the star into the cement where it lit up with pink fireworks. "Seven hours of combat with you and I still feel no love for killing? Do you feel inspired by our battle? Because I don't."

"I'm pissed, actually, that I can't kill you until you tell me where my wife is." Napoleon was trying to stem the fountain of blood cascading from his right side, staining the white tux shirt that was already torn and soiled.

"I could have killed you at any moment, but I was waiting for that moment of glee. But nothing." Augustus thumped his chest with frustration. "There's this great weight in here. This hopelessness. A cavern of emptiness."

"You want meaning in life?" Napoleon picked up one of the many magicked daggers that Augustus had so easily knocked aside. He flipped it in his hand. "Find a girl."

"I have many girls desperate to be impaled by a man of my stature." Augustus stared bleakly at the blade. If Napoleon launched it at him, he wouldn't even bother to duck. He was simply too bored and uninspired.

"Not sex. You gotta find love," Napoleon said.

Augustus snorted. "Love? You're kidding."

"Hell, no, man. I was like you. Out there, making all this money, killing seven or eight beings per day. I was at the top of my game. Everyone loved me. All the governments bought me dinner at the fanciest restaurants, kids calling me all the time to set up internships, women throwing their bras at me."

Augustus sat up. "Your friends were turning on you at a moment's notice? You lived in solitude because no one was worthy to stand in your shadow?"

"Exactly." Napoleon slid the blade over his jaw, trimming the beard that was haunting his gaunt face. "I was at the pinnacle."

Augustus leaned forward. "And you weren't happy either? I'm not the only assassin to lose the love for the job?"

"Hell, no, man! I actually was gonna kill myself."

"No!"

"Yeah." Napoleon laid his hand over his bleeding side again, and this time it began to seal off. "I was going through my weapons stash to find the best spell to kill myself with, the one worthy of me, because, you know, I couldn't die by a poisoned apple or some shit like that, right?"

Augustus nodded. "I'm going to use a star made of pink diamonds. Six hundred and sixty-six carats. I've been saving it for myself."

Napoleon set his hand on Augustus's shoulder. "I had a spell to be eaten from the inside out by condoms. That's how I was going to go."

Augustus blinked at his opponent. "What?"

"It's a hell of a spell." Napoleon got a distant expression, as if remembering a special time in his life. "And a couple months ago, when I was trying to find the condom spell in my warehouse, I came across the first spell I ever taught Angelica. An illusion trick to make the socks stuffed in her training bra look real. My heart came alive the moment I saw those socks."

Augustus inched closer, desperate to hear more. "You fell in love with the socks?"

"Hell, no, man, with her." Napoleon grinned dreamily. "Those heart stockings made me remember how much I loved her. I knew right then that I had to bring her back into my life. And ever since then—" He shrugged. "Life got meaningful. Big time."

Well, that was the most unhelpful advice ever. "I've boned every eligible female in the physical world, and a bunch who weren't," Augustus sighed. "No sparks. Nothing. I've tried them all."

"Maybe you weren't ready. It wasn't until almost three hundred years after I'd killed our daughter, abandoned my wife and grandson, and fornicated my way through thousands of assassinations that I realized I'd done it all out of love for my wife." Napoleon suddenly threw his knife so quickly Augustus didn't even see it coming before it plunged into his chest.

"What the hell's that for?" He yanked it from his ribs and nearly doubled over from the agony. "I thought we were bonding."

"Sorry, mate." Napoleon punched him on the shoulder affectionately. "But I want my wife back. Talking about her made me realize it was time to take control."

"Well, you can't have her!" He coughed, and rainbow

bubbles drifted out of his mouth into the air. "What'd you lace this with anyway?"

"Black magic spell. I call it Leprosy on Speed." Napoleon pulled a heart sock out of his breast pocket and laid it across Napoleon's knee. "You'll die in five minutes unless you tell me where she is."

"But if I die, you'll never find her."

"I've located every target I've ever agreed to kill. I'm like a bloodhound with hands." He leaned forward, and Augustus saw the ruthless determination. "I will find the woman I love, and it can be either over your dead body or your live one. Your choice."

Oh, come on. Like the old fart had any chance of bluffing his way out of this one. They both knew he needed Augustus alive to find the love of his miserable life. But even knowing that his nemesis had just played his last card and blown it wasn't remotely satisfying.

Clearly, Augustus had no heart left. It was time to capitulate. "I wish you the best of luck." His fingers were turning a shade of green that was really quite putrid. Augustus leaned back, clasped his hands behind his head, and stared at the sky. At the stars. He was tired of fighting. Why bother? He knew the Afterlife rocked. Why not just go? "I accept death."

"What? You can't just accept death! You need to be so desperate to live that you tell me where my wife is so I will spare your life!" Napoleon grabbed his shirt and hauled him upright. "What about that woman you're supposed to meet? Maybe it's Reina Fleming! And you're going to die without finding out?"

"Reina?" Augustus rolled the name over his head. "Reina Fleming, woman of my destiny," he mused.

"No, no. There's no magic there." Then he remembered that angelic face beaming at him as Reina had argued with him. "But you know who was really interesting? Her sister."

"Ah…" Napoleon's grip loosened and he got a hopeful look on his face. "Natalie? She's a decadent little thing, isn't she?"

"She's got a zest for life that's quite awe inspiring."

"So, maybe it's Natalie!"

Augustus contemplated her cherubic face. "Nah. She's not my type." His phone rang and Augustus glanced down at it. "Speak of the devil." He sighed and picked it up, noticing that his fingernails were starting to flake off. "Reina Fleming. You got tired waiting for me to kill you, didn't you? Well, you're just going to have to keep waiting because—"

"I'm going to Fenway Park in ten minutes," she interrupted. "Come take me out."

Augustus watched his little pinkie slough off and land on the curb. "You bore me. I'm going to die now on my own. Good-bye."

"Wait! Don't!"

He sighed. "What now?"

"You really want to die? Then let me kill you. It's the only way to save my sister."

"Yes, yes, she's dying. I already know that." He noticed that his left foot had fallen off and was now sitting beside his leg. He raised his eyebrows at Napoleon. "Interesting spell."

Napoleon shrugged modestly. "It has good showmanship value."

"The Godfather's going to kill Natalie tonight,"

Reina shouted. "Can't you do one decent thing before you die and let me kill you?"

"Tonight? The Godfather?" Augustus shot upright, sudden fury rushing through him. "That's not acceptable! Where is she?"

"Fenway Park. Be there in ten."

"Five. I'll be there in five." He shoved his phone in his pocket, whipped out a star, and held it at Napoleon's throat. "Heal me now, peon!"

Napoleon grinned. "I think you have a crush on the girl."

"I do not! The Godfather usurped one of my most important clients, giving an ecstatic death to someone who was supposed to suffer egregiously. It took me years to repair the damage to my reputation. I will not let that bastard destroy the one woman on this planet who has an inner fire deserving of deification!"

"You want to kiiisss her," Napoleon chanted. "You want to huuuggg her. You want to looooove her."

"Natalie's an angel child, not a love whore! She's a beacon of glimmering light. She cannot have her death soiled by that bastard orgasming his dirty soot all over her." It felt fantastic to want to destroy the Godfather! He hadn't cared about anything in so long. There was a spark of life inside him after all. Revenge killing was a beautiful thing! He leapt to his feet and whistled for his horses to bring the carriage around.

But his lips flew off and landed in a puddle of engine oil.

"So, shall we go wife hunting then? I hear the Godfather works fast. You don't have much time." Napoleon brought out a dagger with a white blade that looked like it might be handy for reversing a body-falling-apart spell. "What's it gonna be, old man? You going to pass up on exacting revenge on a bastard by saving a girl you idolize, or are you going to let yourself die some pathetic, wimpy loser?"

"I am on fire!" It was time for orgasms to be vilified! Augustus tossed an orange star at Napoleon. "Angelica's in the null-zone in my mansion. You need—"

"Your mansion?" Napoleon frowned. "I already checked that."

"The null zone, you dimwit! Am I really going to put her somewhere where magic will work? You can't sense her because you're magic! Take the star with you, use it to open the liquor cabinet, and then follow the directions." He ripped his shirt open and bared his chest. "Save me now! I don't have time to waste."

"Stab yourself with this." Napoleon tossed him the weapon. "You screw with me, and I'll finish the job. Your penis will be the next appendage to fall off."

Augustus slammed the blade into his heart and nearly screamed at the pain ("nearly" being the operative word—all he really did was give a manly sneer of disdain). Then his left foot dropped off and he fell to his knees. "You lied!"

"Relax, hot stuff. It takes time to reverse. You'll still be on your knees by the time I find out if you're telling the truth about Angelica. It'll be easy to finish you off if you're lying." Napoleon saluted him, wove some archaic and unintelligible figure in the air, and then vanished.

Augustus yanked the blade out and tried to whistle again. No lips rendered him useless. His horses continued to graze on the sparse grass peeking up between the cobblestones. "Hey! Snowball! Carmen! Come on, girls!"

They didn't move.

"Shit."

He began to crawl.

Yeah, call Jarvis cynical, but the fact he could barely feel Reina tucked up against him because his skin was burning so badly could not be a good sign.

"These things are annoying as hell." The Reap batted another flying specter out of his way. "But they're fantastic for image building. Who did them for you?"

"They're mine." And he wasn't all that happy to find they'd followed him into the limo and were caking the windows with their smut.

"Can I borrow them?" The Reap closed his eyes as Reina affixed the second set of falsies on him.

"Be my guest, if you can pry them away from me." Because it could really be that easy to ditch his destiny.

The Reap held up his scythe. "Anyone want to come with me? Hop on."

They circled closer to Jarvis. He shrugged. "Can't help it. I'm a ghoul magnet."

"Well, then, you must stay by my side. No one will know they're for you." The Reap eyed him with a calculating expression. "I'll double the money. Come work for me, Hate. I think we'd get along so well."

"I'll think about it." A man did need a career, after all. You know, if he wasn't going to blow up. Odds of that? Not looking so good. Not even with Reina snuggled up against him and stroking his chest. What would he be like if she wasn't touching him? He didn't even need to ask. He knew.

He'd be dead.

"Finished." Reina sat back. "I can't believe you want to cover up your gorgeous lashes with false ones that are sparse and mutated. Don't you think that would be a great tactic to have these luscious eyelashes such a contrast to the darkest hell you offer?"

"No, no, there can be no sign of humanity." The Reap peered into the mirror. His face was steel gray, he appeared to be missing half his teeth, and his face was pinched and drawn with sunken cheeks and eyes. "I look great! I'd scare a vampire right out of his grave. You're fantastic, my dear. Just in time, too," he said as the car began to slow down. "We're almost here." He gave Reina a pair of cheek kisses that made something not so soft and fuzzy shift inside Jarvis.

"Wouldn't do that if I were you," he muttered. "I get testy when another man touches her." He pulled her onto his lap, so they were chest to chest.

She draped herself over him, and pressed her lips to his neck. "You're sweating."

"Hot." He closed his eyes, focusing on the coolness of her skin. "We gotta find Cameron."

She rested her cheek against his. "I don't want you to die," she whispered. "I want you to stay with me."

I do, too. As soon as the words jumped into his mind, an unfamiliar emotion flared inside Jarvis. Something that had nothing to do with darkness and hate and destruction. It was a feeling he'd never experienced before. He was stunned by the magnificence of the sensation. By the faintest hint of soul-deep peace, the utter stillness of his spirit. Then it filled him with warmth… not the burning fire of hate… something richer, purer, like the feel of the sunlight on his face in the morning when he was a kid, when he used to sneak out at dawn to watch Cameron play with the fawns. He reached for the light with his mind, tried to catch it—

The window beside Reina exploded in a shatter of glass. She was ripped out of his lap. Jerked out the window.

And then she was gone.

———

Reina shielded her head as she was hurled through the air. She smashed into a street vendor, sending his T-shirts flying off his cart.

"Hey! Watch out! Those are specially ordered for tonight's award ceremony!" the man yelled at her.

"Sorry!" Yanking a *Green Monster for the Testosterone Award* T-shirt off her face, she rolled to her feet as a teenager in overalls, a straw hat, and freckles leapt across the road. He landed in front of her, crouching like a frog. His tongue flipped out, like a lizard or a teenage boy going in for his first French kiss.

Or a deedub trying to scent chocolate.

He smiled, revealing two pigeon-toed canines and a chipped incisor.

Her blood went cold. She'd never forget the tooth imprint she'd found on her sisters. It was him. The one who had killed their family. He was back, just as Natalie had said. "Tell me what you want," she pleaded. "Anything, I swear it. I'll give it you, just save my sister."

"Save her?" He gave a low laugh that made her skin prickle. "Baby, I'm here to make sure she dies. One more kill and I'll be able to graduate. And you're not going to screw it up. Five hundred years in high school is two hundred years too long."

"Screw it up?" Reina stared at him, realization dawning. "So it'll work! That's what you're saying?"

"It might, and that's why you're going to have to stop messing with her." The deedub approached with the cocky swagger of a teenager who could get anything he wanted. "I hate to do this, because you're not a sweet, but hey, a guy's gotta do what a guy's gotta to do." His teeth flashed and his gaze fixed on her throat. "My dad's going to cut off my inheritance if I don't graduate this spring. Can't have that, now can I?"

"I don't have time for this, you ingrate." She waggled her fingers and dust shot out of her hands—

He slapped a gas mask over his face a split second before it hit him in the face. "You really think I'm dumb enough not to research who I'm going to kill? Come on, woman, don't underestimate me just because I'm gorgeous."

And to think her scythe was just sitting in the car. It so would have come in handy right now—

She forearmed him as he dove for her throat. His teeth slammed into her arm, and she had a split second to rejoice in the sensation of her forearm cracking underneath the force of his bite when pain ripped through her abdomen.

Oh, yeah, forgot about the raptor claws—

She grabbed for her stomach, and he grinned. "You just forgot to protect the throat." And then he came at her with an openmouthed, full teeth assault—

A tower of raging black flames slammed into

the deedub, sending him spinning sideways. Reina scrambled to her feet as Jarvis, utterly consumed by the purple and black fire, thrust his sword into the deedub's heart. The creature screamed, his skin turned black and wrinkled, like he was having a party in raisin-ville, and then he vanished.

A small, purple rock remained behind, stuck to the tip of Jarvis's sword. It was glowing and misshapen, like volcanic rock that had escaped a bad science experiment.

"Oh, God," she whispered in horror. "Look at you."

Jarvis was encased in flames. He was a blackened ghoul, a haunted demon. He was covered in the shadows that had been stalking him, glommed on to him like paper-mache. He held up his hand to her, palm up, an entreaty, silent begging for help. She didn't hesitate. She ran for him, was almost to him, and then he exploded.

Chapter 23

REINA WATCHED IN HORROR AS PURPLE ROCKS BEGAN TO rain from the sky. Thousands of fragments like the one that had been at the end of Jarvis's sword. Littering the earth. Lodged in awnings. Busted through car windows.

One rolled to a stop right in front of Reina and she laid her hand over it. Searing hot. She picked it up, closed her eyes, and sent all the love in her soul into it. "I know you're in there," she whispered. "Please come back. Come back for me. I love you."

The minute the words were out, she knew it was true. Knew that she'd fallen. Of course she had. How could she not? He was a man of such courage, who had held himself together against all odds for so long, a man who had stood by her even at cost to himself.

Rescuing her had been stupid of him to do. Of course it would have sent him over the edge. He'd known that, hadn't he? And he'd done it anyway, so she could live.

This was a man who claimed not to be able to feel anything but hate? Hello? Could he be more wrong? She held the rock to her chest, and she felt her skin sizzling. "I'm not giving up on you," she said. "Come back to me. Now!"

"For hell's sake, woman, drop it!" The Reap ripped the stone out of her grasp and flung it across the street. It clunked to a stop against the curb. "Look at your hands."

She saw she'd burned nearly all her skin off. She hadn't made that rock cool off. It had been utterly resistant to her love. *Jarvis was truly gone*. "Oh, dear God." She gripped her chest, assaulted with a sudden emptiness, a numbness, and a raw, eviscerating horror.

"Mourn him, my dear." The Reap dropped her scythe on the sidewalk in front of her. "Death is a horrible, awful fate, and he's writhing in agony right now—"

"Shut up!" She grabbed the scythe and swung it at his head. "Don't play that crap on me! I know it's not true. He's in a happy place—"

"He's Hate, my dear. It's different for him." The Reap blocked her blow with ease. "He really is suffering. If you listen closely, he may still be close enough to the physical world for you to hear his screams. And by the way, you do look like hell when you're reaping. Very tortured. See you inside, death girl!"

He turned and loped across the street and into Fenway Park, his cape billowing behind him. "I imagine his skin is being ripped from his body right now," he called out as he disappeared inside. "Pain, pain, pain—"

"Go away!" The scythe slipped from her fingers and Reina sank to the street, pressing her face in her hands, unable to stop the flood of loneliness. Of agony. The hollowness of her chest. She knew the grief and shock was coming. Been here before. Again and again, and again. And now, again.

But this was worse. The world was spinning away from her, grief hammering at her from all sides. She could see the anguish on her mom's face when she'd taken her daughter's hand and told her good-bye, because she wouldn't be sane enough to say it when she actually died. She could smell the acridness of the blood oozing onto the wooden floor as her sisters lay bleeding from that initial attack. The wail of the sirens as the ambulances cut through the night, too late, too late. The utter silence of the house after her family had been taken away, leaving her behind, all alone. The oppressiveness of those walls, the furniture, so full of love, now empty.

It was alive again, closing in on her. Suffocating her.

It hurt too much. She couldn't go through it again. Couldn't survive it. Sobs racked her body, and she hunched over, holding her stomach.

A loud horn screeched, and someone yelled. She covered her ears, trying to shut it out, but then more wails ripped through the night. People shouting. Fists thwacking flesh. "Everyone shut up!" But the intrusions continued assaulting her. People were arguing up and down the street. Cabs honking at one another. A woman in an evening gown was in a fistfight with a homeless man. So much anger. So much fury.

So much hate.

Oh, *no*. Jarvis's pebbly remains were poisoning the world, exactly as he'd predicted. His own worst nightmare. He'd fought so hard to protect others, and he'd failed. So close, he'd been so close, and he'd failed because he'd sacrificed himself and the world for her.

She was the one who'd let him down. She'd forced him to help her instead of going after his brother. She'd been so consumed by the potential loss of her own sister that she'd failed to appreciate his own struggle, his own goals, the man he was.

He'd known his fate, he'd faced it, and he'd accepted it. A man who'd had only fifty years of life, but stretched it to a hundred and fifty. He'd given it everything he had, and he'd taken the hit at the end so he could save her life. Jarvis had lived his whole life with passion instead of hiding from it, like she had.

A scream echoed through the night that Reina recognized instantly as her sister. *Natalie*. Reina whirled toward Fenway Park. Her own misery had kept her from being there for Jarvis, and now she was going to miss her chance with Natalie, too? Screw that.

She could fight with courage, too, just like he had. He'd faced his last moments with determination, using his last efforts to save her. Was she really going to dishonor his choice by curling up into a ball of misery, instead of taking action and making the best of whatever she could do?

What had living in fear gotten her? More loss. More fear. More failure. Yeah, not working so well to hide, was it? She could keep it up, or she could try to honor the legacy he had left behind. She could fight with all the life she had left in her.

She could be the woman Jarvis had always believed she was, and she knew that's exactly who she wanted to be. His spirit was with her, by her side, cheering her on, and she wasn't going to disappoint him. "This is for you, Jarvis."

She grabbed the scythe and started to run toward the building. *Natalie. I'm coming for you*.

But Natalie wasn't the only one she was coming for.

She was going after Cameron, too. For Jarvis. She was going to win everything for him. For the man she loved.

"I can't believe you finally kicked the bucket."

Jarvis groaned at Death's familiar voice, but he was

in too much agony to open his eyes. His body felt like it had been shredded and then fed to a bunch of hungry pit vipers. And he knew what that felt like. "Go shave your legs. I'm not dead."

"Close enough, my friend. You crossed the line."

Yeah, right. He'd had this conversation with Death more than a hundred times. "Nothing's changed. I'm not going." Then he lifted his head and looked around. He wasn't in the street outside Fenway Park. He wasn't in the Reap's limo. He wasn't in the Den.

He was in a heart-shaped room decorated in more shades of white than Jarvis had thought existed, and he'd aced Color Composition 402 back at the Den. There was a plush white couch, a snowball white wood table with matching chairs, an ice sculpture of two swans necking, and several paintings of what appeared to be snowstorms. Yeah, so not thinking this was Kansas. "I don't suppose this is the green room at the Testosterone Awards, is it?"

Jarvis!

"Reina!" At the distant sound of her voice, Jarvis shoved himself to his feet, surprised to find that his body felt lighter than it had in centuries, as if he'd ditched a thousand weights. He saw an opening in the white-washed wall that had a large gold-gilded heart above the archway, and puffs of smoke were billowing out of the doorway. "Reina!" He sprinted for the door, hit the mist, and rebounded onto his ass. "What the hell?"

"I need to cleave your soul first." Death was sitting on a black bench, the only item of color decorating the room. He was wearing a tux, a red boutonniere, and a gold crown emblazoned with the words *Lifetime*

Achievement Winner: Testosterone Awards. "You can't take the body with you."

Had the awards started? "I have to get to Cam—"

"Sorry, my man, but the only place you're going is the pearly gates of heaven." Death jerked his finger at the cotton candy cloud emanating from the heart-shaped doorway. "It's the service entrance. More efficient to carry souls in that way, so you don't get bogged down with the red tape and bureaucracy."

Jarvis stared at the cotton ball parade. "I can't be dead." Then he noticed his palm was pristine. No black stains on it. No shadows stalking the walls. This time, the lightness in his body took on new meaning. The hate was gone.

"Oh, you're dead, and it's about time." Death slipped a collapsible scythe out of the sleeve of his tux. "I've done your bedside vigil more times than I've been laid in the last hundred and fifty years, and I get laid a lot."

Jarvis!

He whirled around at the sound of Reina's desperate call, her agony and despair feeding a frenzied need for him to find her. "Reina!"

There was no answer. *Shit*. He fought to remember what had happened, but his mind was blank. "Where is she?"

Death looked severely disappointed. "You don't remember?" He leaned forward, his forearms resting on his thighs. "Come on, man, you gotta know."

"I was in the car." Jarvis fought to clear his head. "With Reina and the Reap. And a deedub grabbed her—" He suddenly remembered Reina getting attacked, that hellacious feeling when he'd been sprinting toward them, terrified beyond anything he'd ever felt before, a sheer, raw panic that he'd be too late, too late, too late—

He grabbed Death by the lapels. "Is she okay? Tell me I wasn't too late!"

Death broke into a huge smile. "That's my boy! Yes, yes, she's fine. You capped his ass with great aplomb and timing."

"Mother fucker." Jarvis's knees gave out and he fell to the fluffy white carpet like some pansy. He braced his palms on his thighs, barely able to hold himself erect, the relief was so great. "She's okay."

"Well, for now. Augustus is on his way to get her. Can't imagine she'll survive that."

Jarvis jerked his head up. "You set her up to die, didn't you?"

"Not at all. I thought there was a faint possibility she could bring herself to kill him. Obviously, I over-estimated her." Death's disdain was apparent, and fresh fury rose in Jarvis.

He stumbled to his feet, lunged at the old man, and slammed his hands around his throat. "Reina Fleming is an amazing, courageous woman, and the fact she can't kill is a testament to the hugeness of her heart and the love that guides her." His fingers tightened, and red marks appeared on Death's neck. "If you had any humanity in your soul, you'd see her for the light she is."

Death raised his eyebrows, apparently unfazed by the assault. "If she's so fantastic, why'd you leave her?"

"I didn't leave her! I died!"

"You gave it up."

"I gave it up? What is wrong with you people? Hate wins! You can't stop it—"

"You bore me." Death sounded disappointed as he unfolded his scythe. "Time to say bye bye, warrior."

"It's not permanent yet?" Jarvis grabbed for his sword, found nothing.

"Haven't you ever heard you can't take it with you? Includes swords." Death gripped the scythe, and Jarvis ripped it out of his hands.

He had it at Death's throat before the beast could move. "I'm better with weapons than you are," he said. "Send me back."

"No." Death waggled his fingers at Jarvis, and black powder shot out of it, knocking Jarvis flat on his back. Immobilizing him like a mummy.

Shit. That's right. Death had pulled that on him before, hadn't he? Always smart to forget what your opponent can do. Jarvis tried to summon the hate that had knocked aside the stun gun moment the last time… but he had nothing this time.

"I couldn't delegate your harvest to one of my Guides. I'm too impressed with you, and I wanted to do it myself. I made them put the awards ceremony on hold just for you. Congratulations, and welcome to my world—"

Jarvis! Reina's desperate voice cut through the inertia pinning Jarvis to the floor.

Death swung the scythe and Jarvis rolled to the right, leapt to his feet, ripped a swan ice sculpture off a white marble table, and upended it into Death's family jewels. "You don't get to have me."

"Mother of pearl! How did you break my hold?" Death grabbed for his crotch and went down like a boner at the sight of Angelica. "That's a brilliant tactic.

The only chance you had to take me down." Then his face turned green and he rolled over, moaning. "But I'm going to kill you when I can move again."

Jarvis grabbed the matching swan off the table and stood over Death. "I'm going back home."

"You're not going back. You crossed the line. You're mine. You're done."

Jarvis heard the finality in Death's words, and he felt a tugging from the direction of the white cloud. The tractor beam of heaven. It was true. He was really dead.

Stunned, he let the swan fall from his hand. It shattered across the floor. He'd gone and died, and he hadn't finished his mission. His brother. The world. *Reina.*

She was on her own now. She had to harvest Augustus? She'd never be able to do it. He'd sworn that he'd help her. He'd *promised.* And he'd gone and turned himself into vulcanized rock.

Rock that was destroying the world right now.

He leaned against the table, too stunned to move. It had never occurred to him that he'd fail. Not really. Not once she'd shown up and cut through his shit. He'd thought she could hold it off long enough to do what he had to do.

But he'd let down his brother. Betrayed the world. And worst of all, he'd failed Reina. Not just by not saving her sister, but by *dying* on her. He slammed his fist into his palm. He shouted an unearthly bellow of anguish and devastation, the evisceration of his soul.

Jarvis! Reina's voice was filled with tears now, and his body went cold. "Reina!"

"She can't hear you, you nitwit. But she can feel your life force bleeding out of you. Terrible to be on the living side of that sort of experience, but I suppose she's an expert at it now."

Jarvis swore as her agony hit him. She was in so much pain. He was killing her. She'd suffered so much, and he'd made it worse.

Death worked his way to his feet, still hunched over, one hand on his nuts, the scythe in the other. "Let's get it over with. On your knees, warrior. Die with honor."

With honor. For what? For letting down everyone that mattered, because he wasn't man enough to fight off the hate? Yeah. It was time for him to blow this joint. He dropped to his knees and bowed his head. "Do it." He wasn't worthy of honor.

"Excellent. A fine way to go out." Death took a backswing, and then a white dove flew out of the puffy doorway and landed on Death's shoulder. He dropped the scythe with a shout of glee. "Mom!" Death lightly kissed the bird's beak and nuzzled her feathers. "I miss you so much, Mama. I come here almost every day searching for you. I'm so happy you came out today!" He beamed at Jarvis. "Say hello to my mom. Isn't she beautiful?"

Jarvis stared numbly at the feathered creature. "Your mom's a bird."

"No, dumbass, she's a person. But everyone in heaven gets the ability to change into doves to travel. It's a perk of getting the good Afterlife." Death jerked his thumb toward Jarvis. "You'll be flying around before you know it, too, big guy. Never thought you'd get heaven, but who knows how this shit works?"

"How I got heaven?" Jarvis looked at the white fluffy door again. Scanned the room. No other entrances or exits. Just that one white door. "I'm... I'm going to heaven?"

"Well, duh, what part of 'pearly gates' did you not understand?"

"You've got to be kidding." *He was going to heaven?* But he was hate. He was bad shit. He was a monster.

Then he thought of the way Reina always looked at him. As if he were more than that. He'd thought she was naive. Blinded by her cheery world view. But as Death was his witness, she'd been right. Heaven didn't lie. Heaven didn't get duped, and heaven was inviting him in.

He was good. Good? Him? But it was impossible—

Death's phone beeped. "I've got to run, Mama. The Godfather is almost finished killing off that girl."

Natalie. Reina couldn't save her by herself. "Reina," he whispered, his voice hoarse. "I'm so sorry."

Death cheek-kissed his mom. "Later, Mama, I miss you." Death sighed as he watched the bird fly off, then he turned and picked up his scythe. "Okay, warrior man, it's time—"

Jarvis realized he couldn't feel Reina's anguish anymore. The emptiness hit him like a tremendous void. Like someone had ripped his soul out and strung it up by its fingernails. "Where is she?"

Death began to swing the scythe. "She cut you off. She's got a sister to say good-bye to, an assassin to fight off, and assorted other obligations. No time for a broken heart."

"A broken heart?" Jarvis leapt across the room and pinned Death up against the wall. "A broken heart? Because I died? Because she loves me?"

Death went still, so still, his staff clutched in his hand. "You tell me."

Jarvis closed his eyes and reached out with his senses. The way he used to do with his sword when he was trying to sense hate, fear, and terror. This time, it was just him, and he wasn't sure how to do it. He pictured Reina, the laughter in her eyes, the smoldering passion in her eyes when he'd finished making love to her, the way she'd held his face to give him peace, the tenderness of her touch. Something swelled inside him, something he'd never felt before, and he *knew*. "She loves me," he whispered. And not the way she loved everyone else. She *loved* him.

"Very nice, my boy."

Jarvis opened his eyes to tears glistening in Death's eyes.

The new Reap pulled out his handkerchief. "You did it. You let love reach you. Do you realize how powerful that love must be?" He blew his nose. "I swear, it just gets you right here." He thudded his ribs.

Jarvis's own chest hurt like he'd never hurt before. The pain of being impaled by Blaine's blade during "Maim a Warrior, Stab a Friend" day at the Den was nothing compared to how he felt right now. Heat was burning in his chest. Stinging his eyes. It was fire, and it was energy, but not hate. It was something different, something that breathed life into his very pores.

"I can't send you back, my boy. But true love is a rare gift to be cherished. If you can get back to her, I'll let you go."

Jarvis blinked. "I can go back? How?"

"Same way you've done it every time before. By sheer force of will."

"But I'm dead—"

"Not until I separate your soul from your body." Death sheathed his blade. "You've never been this far over the line, and I've never seen anyone recover from this, but if anyone can do it, it would be you." He took Jarvis's face in his hands, and his face was solemn. "I live for the fairy tale endings," he said. "Make me happy." Then he kissed Jarvis's forehead, stepped back, and vanished through the wooden table.

Jarvis braced his hands on the table and reached out with his mind to the one man who could help him. A being more gifted as a healer than anyone he'd ever met. The man who had helped him back from the brink every time. *Nigel. I gotta get back to the girl. Help me.*

There no response. Just a cold void.

Nigel had to be there, fighting over his body. Nigel always knew when one of the team needed his healing. He would be there. Jarvis was sure of it. *Nigel!*

Again, just a barren emptiness. Jarvis realized what the problem was. Without hate, he had no energy to tap into. No passion. No fire. He was powerless. Without hate, he was nothing.

He threw back his head and roared with frustration. "Reina!" All the times he'd come back, and now, when it really mattered, he was stripped of the power to do it.

He grabbed the table and hurled it across the room. It cracked against the wall and shattered, fragments shooting across the room. One wooden leg impaled itself in the heart plaque above the door. It severed the heart right down the middle, kind like how his own body felt right now—

Then he studied the mist swirling around his feet. Mist that was open to him because somewhere inside him was something worthy of heaven.

Because of his heart? Love and hate, two sides of the same emotion?

His pulse began to skyrocket. Was it really possible? No, it wasn't.

But even as the words chanted through his mind, he sat on the floor. Crossed his legs. Folded his hands in front of his chest, just like he'd done so many times in Meditation for Warriors. But this time, instead of searching out the storm inside him and trying to ease it down, he sent his mind to his heart, into his emotional center.

For a long moment, nothing happened. Just a frigid gap in his chest.

He whispered Reina's name, pictured her face, heard her voice, felt the fullness of her presence fill his soul.

And then his heart began to beat, truly beat for the first time in his life.

Chapter 24

REINA YANKED UP THE HOOD OF HER BORROWED CLOAK, gripped her scythe, and raced into the ballpark. "I'm with the Grim Reaper," she shouted to the guards as she ran past them.

They didn't bother to look up from their canasta game.

She bolted up the nearest ramp and emerged from the tunnel into the reserved seats. The stands were full of cheering women dressed in their most beautiful finery. The stadium lights were glaring, and luxurious cascades of maroon velvet were draped over the seats and floor. Dozens of crystal chandeliers were suspended from temporary wiring, and the Boston Pops orchestra was set up behind home plate. Banquet tables adorned the outfield, and a massive, round stage was rotating in the middle of the infield. The hotdog and pretzel sweat-shops had been transformed into a night of glitz, glam, and murder.

On the stage were her sister and the Godfather. They were behind an almost sheer curtain that put them in shadow, but it was clear they were naked and getting it on. Six women in black evening gowns were standing in a semi-circle around the soon-to-be-murder scene, their faces somewhat strained with the effort of not dropping to the floor in writhing ecstasy. The scoreboard in right field was listing the accolades of the Godfather, while a woman in a sparkly silver gown read off it.

The Reap was standing off to the left, arms folded, looking huge and terrifying as he glared down at everyone.

"Oh, oh, oh!" A woman beside Reina clutched her abdomen and went down, writhing in delight. "Kill me now! That's my sixth orgasm!"

"My abs are going to be killing me tomorrow!" another shouted.

Reina tore down the stairs, vaulted over the railing, and sprinted across the infield. "Natalie!" She was almost to the stage when something hit her from behind, sending her sprawling into the grass.

A tall woman in a strapless gown and serious biceps pulled her to her feet. "Got another overload! Take her into one of the padded rooms," she shouted as more bouncers descended. "Strap her down so she doesn't hurt herself."

Reina jerked her hand free and sprayed death dust over all of them. They all dropped as Death stepped out onto the stage. He was followed by four men in chains and Cameron, who was stark naked, wearing only a golden bow, a quiver strapped across his chest, and long flowing hair. He surveyed the crowd with great delight and bowed deeply.

"These women to my left are the winners of the Kill Your Love with Love auction that took place during the foreplay session," Death announced. "Here are their true loves, who they have commissioned to die." He gestured to the men who were looking quite pleased to be on stage in front of thousands of screaming women. "Now, we shall see the newest incarnation of death: Death by Love!"

Reina sprinted toward the stage again. "No! Cameron! Don't do it! Jarvis—"

Another group of bouncers tackled her, locking her hands uselessly behind her back. "Let me go!"

"Death by Love?" The Reap whirled toward Death. "That violates everything we stand for!"

Death ignored the Reap. "I present victim number one."

The man was led forward, and he noticed Death. And the Reap. His eyes went wide and he started screaming.

The crowd went silent.

"He fears death, but this will change," Death said. "No longer will anyone need to fear—"

The Reap slammed his scythe down on the back of Death's head.

The women on the stage shrieked, and Death dropped to his knees, holding the back of his head. "Give it up, you archaic remnant from the past!" he shouted. "It's my business now!" He slung his own scythe toward the Reap's throat.

The cloaked ghoul blocked it with a clang of metal that reverberated over the sound system. Muscles flexed, macho grunts, speckles of blood. Women leapt to their feet, cheering, applauding, and hooting. Shouts of "Fairy Tale Hero" rang out.

The bouncers turned toward the stage, riveted by the ancient macho battle, forgetting they were supposed to have Reina under lockdown. She leapt back up and fought her way past the admiring throngs toward the stage.

Cam was flexing, but no one was paying him any attention. His puffy face began to contort with anger. Apparently, the Guardian of Love didn't like being ignored. Great. Because all they needed was to get him on the offensive as well. Love was one of the most vicious motivators of heinous crimes, and from the look on Cam's face, he wasn't that far away from that point.

"Hang in there, Cameron," Reina shouted. No way was she going to let Jarvis's brother fail to be the man Jarvis wanted him to be.

No one paid her any attention as she leapt up on the stage. She hurried over to the screen hiding her sister and ripped it back. The Godfather had his manly death bullet in his hand and he was guiding it right to the target zone.

Steam was rising from Natalie's skin, and her eyes were rolled back so there was nothing but white. Reina unleashed dust at the Godfather, and he didn't even hesitate. Just brought his hips back to slam them home. "No!" She swung the scythe and broadsided him in the side of the head. He flew across the stage, sailed off the edge, and disappeared to the infield.

Reina dropped the scythe and fell to her knees beside Natalie as her sister writhed in unfilled sexual torment. "Nat, Nat, it's me! Come back! Think of…" Something so non-sexual it was disgusting. What? What? What? "Think of having sex with a werewolf after he's eaten your dog!"

Natalie made a gagging sound.

"And um… your tenth grade chemistry teacher?" What was his name? "Mr. Porcheesy? With the huge gut? Remember when we accidentally walked in on him in the men's bathroom?"

Another gagging sound, and Natalie's blue eyes rolled back into sight. They were still glazed but visible. Making progress.

"And—" God, she couldn't think of anything else disgusting enough.

"My New Year's Eve date last year." Trinity skidded

to her knees beside them, her face red from exertion. "The one with a dozen tentacles where his boy toy was supposed to be. Remember how he gave us all a show?"

Reina hugged her friend. "You made it!"

"I'd never let you down." Trinity set a bag of ice between Natalie's legs. "Didn't know if this would help, you know? Sort of the cold shower theory. Where's Augustus? Is he here yet?"

Reina scanned the stage, but there was no sign of the stinky assassin. "He said he'd be here in five minutes." She pulled out her phone and dialed. "No answer. He needs to get here soon!"

Trinity glanced over at Death. "It might be time to sleep with him to get the promotion, girlfriend."

Reina's stomach churned as she looked over at the handsome, wealthy bachelor clad in his designer clothes. "Sleep with him? That's just gross."

"There are times for morals in the workplace, and there are times to engage in every subversive and manipulative and illegal tactic to get what you want. Now is one of those times."

"No. Augustus will be here. He has to be—"

Gina ran up, sank down by Natalie's head, and pulled her onto her lap. "Hang on, girl, we're almost there." She looked at Reina. "We have to make the switch. She's dying right now!"

"I know, dammit! I know!"

Trinity patted her shoulder. "Just close your eyes and imagine Death is actually Jarvis. Then you'll be able to sleep with him."

Reina's chest ached at the mention of Jarvis, and she knew she would never be able to sleep with someone else, not even to save her sister. "No. I'll just ask him to do it. I'll trade something else."

"Something else? All he values is sex and money, and you don't have any of the latter—"

"I have to try." Reina turned toward the battle that was still ensuing. "Death!" She started to run toward him, and Cupid leapt in her path. His eyes were blazing with fury, his skin was flushed with rage, and he was wielding a golden sickle with double hearts imprinted on the blade like he knew how to use it.

The all-powerful Guardian of Love was pissed, and he was going to take it out on her. Screw love. This Guardian had death in his eyes. Hers.

"Get the rest of the rocks. Hurry up."

The sound of Nigel's calm voice was like the angels shining down on Jarvis. He wrenched open his eyes to see Nigel leaning over him, his hands glowing like a couple of neon fireflies.

Nigel was wearing a bandana decorated with pink flowers, and blood was streaked down his face. "Welcome back, buddy."

"We need to get inside. I need to get to Reina." Jarvis started to sit up, and Nigel pushed him down.

"Not done yet. Healing takes longer when you're not juicing me."

Blaine sprinted up to them, his hand full of purple rocks. He was on fire, flames licking away at his body. "The minute I turn the flames off, I hate the world." He dropped his load on Jarvis's gut, and Jarvis winced at the pain. "You're one bad shit, man. I keep setting everyone on fire to clean them up. The place is an unholy mess."

Jarvis sat up, gingerly this time. He had arms, a chest, and a lumpy torso but his legs were still a pile of purple pebbles. Around them was total chaos. People were shouting at each other. Fistfights. A taxicab in the window of a bar. Shit. What had his explosion done to Reina? "I gotta go."

"Give me a sec, pretty boy." Nigel moved his hands over Jarvis's leg, and heat began to pulse. The rocks began to melt together, turning back into limbs. "This isn't like regrowing an arm. This takes finesse, expertise, and phenomenal talent, so give the master room to work a miracle."

Blaine squatted. "The boys have the last of the stones. That's all we can find."

"The boys?"

Rocco and Sylvan came running up, holding more rocks.

"He blew a total land mine," Rocco said. "Found these three blocks away." The youth's face was flushed (well, it was off-white, which was ruddy as hell for a vamp). His chest was healed, and he was wearing a headband made of flowers. And he had a knife at his hip. The kid was alive and fighting.

And Jarvis had done it. Jarvis had really saved his life with hate, just as Reina had predicted. "Holy crap." He needed to tell her that she'd been right. That he was the man she'd thought he was. "Heal me now, Nigel!"

"Patience, big guy," Nigel muttered. "A little help from you would be nice. Either that, or shut up."

Sylvan dropped the rocks near where Jarvis's knee was starting to take shape. "Welcome back, Lord Hate. It's great to see you again."

"I'm not Lord Hate—" But even as he said the words, Jarvis felt the heaviness of his body, of his heart, and he knew he was truly back. Magnificent didn't even begin to describe how good it was to feel the weight of the end of the world pulsing through his veins.

Sylvan held up Jarvis's sword. "Would you like this?"

"Hell, yeah." He took his sword and began whipping it over his head. He sucked in all the heat energy in the area, absorbed all the hate, the anger, the fury. Drew it in from people, from cars, from plants, from the four men surrounding him. Channeled it until his sword was pulsing with it.

Then he jammed it into Nigel's shoulder.

"Now that's what I'm talking about." Nigel crowed. The healer's skin turned black, smoke rose from his hands, and black light exploded all around them.

When it faded, Jarvis was healed. Legs, feet, torso, and his family jewels. He was back. Black palms at all.

"Reina! I'm coming!" He was on the move before anyone had recovered enough to blink.

This was one second chance he wasn't going to blow.

Cameron's eyes were blazing with fury, and his body was shaking with rage. He slammed his palm into Reina's chest, knocking her to the ground. "You ruined my matchmaking between your sister and the orgasm king!"

She scrambled backwards. "Cameron! You can't murder. It will destroy love—"

"You destroyed it already. They were in love, and you killed him." He reached into his quiver and pulled out an arrow. "Screw the paid victims. You're my first death. You don't deserve to live."

Reina threw dust at him, and he unleashed his own powder at the same time. Their particles collided and dissolved in midair, and he jammed an arrow into her thigh. She yanked it out, but even as she threw it away, a sense of peace came over her. Of love.

Somewhere in the depths of her mind, she was vaguely aware of someone screaming, of the feeling that this serenity was wrong. But as she stared up into Cameron's face, she couldn't make herself care.

For the first time in her life, there was no ache in her heart.

"Reina!"

She saw her sister writhing on the stage. Trinity and Gina struggling to contain her. Behind them, one tanned hand reached over the edge of the stage. Then another one. And then the Godfather's bloody head appeared. Inching his way back. Through blood. Through carnage. To her sister.

"I'm going to lose her," she whispered. "I'm going to be alone." But the thought didn't cause pain. She just felt love for her sister, for the times they had shared. Her mind drifted to Jarvis, and she smiled. What a lovely man.

"Feels good, doesn't it?" Cameron squatted beside her, his long hair brushing his knees. "Tell me how wonderful I am. Tell me that I'm a god." He put the microphone in front of her. It squealed. "Tell me how you feel right now."

She marveled at the way his golden highlights glistened in the stadium lights. She brushed her fingers through his hair. "I feel good."

He brought the microphone to his own mouth. "I feel good," he repeated. "And now I'm going to kill you. How do you feel about that?"

Something tweaked deep in her mind, something shouted at her to fight, but she couldn't break the hold he had on her body, on her mind. The feeling of peace and love was too all-consuming, as if she'd been searching for it her whole life.

But she knew she didn't want this kind of peace. It wasn't the answer. This love was disempowering, robbing her of her ability to truly care about and fight for those she loved. She'd take the pain of loving and losing over this artificial void all day long! *I don't want it!*

Death and the Reap were still fighting, and there were pools of blood on the stage. She looked over at her sister, who was fighting off Trinity and Gina as they tried to pull her away from the approaching Godfather. Behind them, pulling himself along like a snake shedding his skin, was Augustus. He'd made it! But wow… he was not having a good day. No arms, no legs, just a body, slithering, but his gaze was fixed determinedly on Natalie. He was going to save her? He was going to save her!

Then Natalie flung up her arm in ecstasy, clipped Augustus, and sent his disintegrating body flying off the stage and out of sight.

The one time you want a hit man to be up and running, he has to go and have his body fall apart. What was up with that? There was no one to help her break free of Cameron's hold. No one except herself. Not good odds—

Cameron stood up, and she jerked her attention back

to the naked murderer. "She smiled! I, the Guardian of Love, can take the fear of death away! I rule!" He lifted his hands in a grand flourish. "Applaud!"

The place erupted into cheers.

"It is time!" Cameron said, pulling out his sickle. "Behold, the transformation of love into a killing machine." Dust drifted down over Reina's face, and a milky white mist appeared above her hair. Her soul. Coming out to play. Drawn by the powder.

He raised the sickle over his head to resounding cheers. He was going to cleave her soul while she was still conscious.

Fight, Reina, fight! She tried to move her hands. To scream. But her body didn't respond. She just gazed up with him with an inane smile.

And then the blade came down.

Jarvis broke through the crowds of cheering women just as Reina rolled to the side, barely dodging his brother's sickle as it crashed to the stage beside her head. Cameron slammed his foot on her throat, pinned her down, and reared back to deliver the killing blow.

Jarvis hurled his sword with unerring aim. It plunged right through the heart of the man he'd sacrificed his whole life to protect.

Cameron looked up, his face stunned. "Jarvis?"

"What are you doing?" Nigel shouted. "Are you crazy? Killing love?"

Jarvis vaulted onto the stage. He grabbed the handle of his sword but didn't remove it. He paused to think of Reina, to open his heart to her, to allow his feelings for her to sweep through his body. When his chest got so full he could barely breathe, he reached for the heat energy in his brother's body. The love that was the other side of hate. He tugged gently and it came willingly.

Jesus. It was working. He focused on his sword and began to harvest energy with full force, until he'd sucked every last bit out the man who'd been entrusted with it. His sword flashed red, then white, then pink, then became a fiery red caked with blackened ash.

"Dude. You blow." Cameron still looked shocked. "You're supposed to protect me, not kill me."

Jarvis slid his sword out of his brother. "You betrayed those who gave you Guardianship."

"Me? You're the one who stabbed me!"

Jarvis looked at his palms. The black stains were mixed with pink now. Holy crap. He'd done it. He held up his hand to show his brother. "I didn't kill you. I took love from you." And it had survived. It was alive inside his blackened, poisonous body. Because Reina had changed him. Her faith had changed him forever.

"You took my love?" Cameron leapt to his feet. "It's mine! You can't take it! I own love—"

Blaine knocked Cameron out with a light tap to the temple. "Shut up."

"Jarvis?" Reina was on her knees, staring at him in disbelief. "But you're dead."

"Hey, babe." He crouched beside her and his whole body came alive at her nearness. "I came back. Told you I'm hard to kill."

She touched his face, and his soul vibrated in response. "You're really alive? And you're the Guardian of Love now?"

"Hell, yeah, sweetheart. I'm the whole shebang now." He laid his hand over hers. "Yeah, I came back for you, and you showed me how to—"

"Reina!" Trinity screamed. "Help!"

They turned to see Natalie and the Godfather going at it. Full-on naked tango. Natalie was screaming and her body was on fire.

"Oh, God. I'm too late," Reina gasped. "I can't switch them—"

"Death can," Jarvis interrupted.

But the most powerful being in creation was on his back, trying desperately to hold the Reap's blade off his throat. And it was clear he was losing the battle.

"Make the Reap love." Reina gripped his forearm desperately. "You can do it."

Shit. He probably could. Jarvis grabbed the bow from his brother and loaded it. "You love Death," he whispered. Then he shot it.

The arrow hit cleanly in the Reap's ass, and he leapt off Death. "Young buck! I almost killed you! I apologize profusely!"

Jarvis was stunned. He'd just created love? Not hate. *He'd just created love*. His heart began to lift, and lift, and lift—

Death scrambled to his feet, his face ashen with the realization of how close he'd just come to death. "Nice work, Swain—"

"Switch their souls!" Reina commanded as she ran toward Death. "Switch my sister and Gina! Now!"

Death looked sharply across the stage, and Jarvis saw him analyze everything that was going on. He glanced at the Reap, who was now on his knees using his cloak to polish Death's shoes. He looked Jarvis in the eye, then he flicked his hand toward the women.

Natalie shrieked again, and then she was dead.

Chapter 25

REINA'S SOUL SHRIVELED WHEN HER SISTER CONVULSED and went still. "Natalie!" She started to run toward her, but Jarvis caught her around the waist.

"Look." He pointed at Gina, who was now slumped in a pile on the ground, her back toward them. All Reina could see were her hunched shoulders and rounded back.

She gripped Jarvis's hand, hanging for support as she looked between the two women. "Nat?"

Gina's shoulder moved.

"Natalie?" Hope seized her heart, but she didn't dare move. Didn't dare jinx it.

"I did it again!" The Godfather let out a horrific bellow and scrambled backwards. "I am a demon! I killed her!"

"Hey, big guy." Nigel caught his arm as he tried to throw himself on Cameron's sickle. "Suicide's a little extreme, don't you think? Chill out. Borrow my sketch pad."

Gina rolled onto her side and opened her eyes. They were Natalie's vibrant blue ones. Natalie's face. Natalie's hair. Gina's clothes, but Natalie's face.

Reina gaped at her, then looked back at the woman beneath the Godfather. Gina's dark curly hair. Gina's paler complexion. "But—"

"Our souls define us," Jarvis said quietly. "Natalie's soul was switched with Gina's, and their external appearance is changing to align with the soul within."

"So, they got switched? Nat?" Reina inched nearer, afraid to hope, afraid to believe.

"It's her." Jarvis gave her a light push. "Go to your sister, sweetheart. It's over."

Natalie grinned, her tears sliding down her cheeks. "It's me, sweetie. You did it. You really did it!"

Reina knelt beside her and searched those familiar blue eyes in a body that was still wearing Gina's clothes. "How do you feel? Did you take the poison with you?"

Natalie shook her head. "There's this great silence inside me, like this other being that's been in my body all these years is gone. It's just me."

"Oh, Nat!" Reina threw her arms around her sister and hugged her. Unable to let go. Unable to stop the flood of tears. "I love you," she said.

And she really did, in a way she'd never before allowed herself to love. Her whole body was vibrating in a way she'd never felt, not even when Cam had shot her with the arrow. She'd thought she loved in the past, but she'd been holding back, hamstrung by the fear of loss. But right now, in this moment, she was letting herself truly love her sister. She'd proclaimed love all this time and she'd been a fraud.

But not anymore.

Trinity crawled over to them, sweat pouring down her face. She said nothing. She simply wrapped them both in a hug and held them.

It was over.

—∿∿—

"You're shitting me. You're the Guardian of both now?" Nigel studied Jarvis's sword, which was still pink and black. "How come you're not destroying yourself?"

"Because love is stronger than hate. I'll keep myself under control now. No more explosions." Jarvis's throat was thick with emotion as he watched the three women embrace. He could feel their love, and he'd never felt it before. Nothing like this. He was used to feeling hate. Not love.

It was unsettling as hell, and there was a gaping emptiness cleaving his chest in half.

Because he'd blown it.

He'd had the chance with the girl, but he'd been a stupid bastard and rejected her faith in him. He'd died on her instead. He'd betrayed her, failed her, and abandoned her. She'd recovered and moved on, put her love into those who hadn't let her down.

"Tell her." Blaine set his hand on his shoulder. "You look far too pathetic and weepy staring at her like that. Recite her a poem or something."

"That's quite a moment. All that tenderness. I need to paint that." Nigel pulled out a paper and a sketch pad. "Black and white will have to do."

Blaine nudged Jarvis. "Just do it."

He wanted to, but his feet were stuck to the ground. He didn't know what to do. How to handle it. The emotions flooding him were too unfamiliar. Too confusing. All he knew was that he wanted to hold her forever. He couldn't think past that.

Reina turned toward him, then she smiled. She held up her arms. To him.

"Sweet Mother Mary. That's for me." He couldn't believe it.

Blaine slapped him on the back. "Go get her, big guy, before she smartens up."

Jarvis took a step, and then another, and then he was sprinting across the stage. He caught her in his arms and hauled her against him. He buried his face in her neck and greedily breathed her in through every pore in his body. Vanilla, strawberries, and that scent that was just her. He tangled his fingers in her hair, desperate to hold her. To never let her go. "You brought me back," he said, his voice hoarse. "I came back for you."

She pulled back, searching his face. "What do you mean?"

"God, woman. Don't you understand?" He framed her face with his hands. "You showed me that there's love in me, that there was something redeemable. You brought that side of me to life. I used it to come back and to harvest my brother's love. It's you, babe, it's all you. You made me the man I never thought I could be."

She frowned. "So, you're not hate anymore?"

"Oh, I'm hate. But I'm also the Guardian of Love." Shit. He was going to have to spell it out, wasn't he? But he didn't know what to say. Desperate for her to understand, he grabbed her hand and pressed it over his heart. "This beats for you. No one else. For you."

Her face lit up with the most magical smile he'd ever seen. "That's love, Jarvis. You love me."

The words felt like sunshine beaming down on him. "Yeah, yeah. I do."

She stood on her tiptoes and lightly kissed him. "I love you, too."

"Like you love everyone?" He knew the answer, he was sure he did, but he had to hear it. Because his woman loved every freaking thing on the planet, and she'd already told him before that she'd loved him the same way she'd love her damn dog.

He didn't want to be her dog.

She smiled. "No, not like anyone else, you goof. Just like you."

And in that moment, he became the man he'd been trying to be his whole life.

A warrior who was stronger than hate.

A warrior who knew that his most powerful weapon wasn't his sword.

It was his heart.

When he bent to kiss her, he was so psyched to kiss his woman that he almost didn't hear the cheers and the chants of "Guardian of Hate for the Testosterone Award" from the packed stadium.

But he did hear them. How could he not? After a lifetime of being tortured by women, hated by many, and burdened by the knowledge he could destroy the world in a single moment of weakness, he was now loved by a goddess, kissed with tenderness, and hoisted as a hero?

Sometimes, it just felt good to be a man.

With Reina snuggled in his arms, now was one of those times.

"Dude, that's some kind of trust you got going on," Nigel said. "I'd never let a woman blindfold me."

Jarvis grinned as he allowed Reina to lead him down the sidewalk. He still couldn't get over the freedom of being able to stroll down the street without worrying he might accidentally brush against strangers and trigger a fistfight. Yeah, the hate was still brewing, but he was getting pretty good at calling on the love to balance it.

Cameron was on a walkabout, pouting that world peace was no longer on his agenda. The love spells he'd cast on Natalie, the Godfather, and Reina had disappeared the moment Jarvis had harvested his love, and Cameron was rockingly pissed about it. Jarvis was planning to let him stew until he was well-cooked, and then he'd try to bring him back toward the decent kid he once knew.

Which meant, for now, Jarvis had only one agenda, and that was to enjoy the hell out of every moment, every experience, and every touch with the woman who had loved him into salvation. "You need to meet the right woman, Nigel."

"No woman is that right," Nigel scoffed. "Hell, man, doesn't the blindfold remind you of the time that Angelica—"

"Stop." Reina's voice was firm. "You aren't in the Den anymore, Nigel. Stop torturing yourself."

"I wasn't the one who did the torturing," Nigel muttered.

Jarvis scented chocolate and was tempted to sneak a peek under the edge of the blindfold. "Are we going to your store?"

"Next door."

Jarvis tried to remember what stores had been adjacent to hers... no clue. Last time he'd been there, he'd been tunnel-visioning for a woman to save his brother, not window-shopping.

"Okay, in here," Reina said. "Let me get the door."

"This is the big surprise?" Nigel started laughing. "You've got to be kidding, Reina. There's no way he's—"

"Shh! Don't give it away!" There was humor in Reina's voice as well, but it was also filled with warmth.

Jarvis couldn't stop his shit-eating grin as he followed her inside. He couldn't get over how good she made him feel. If she was giving him pompoms, he might even sign up for cheerleading lessons.

Cool interior air blasted him, and he smelled chemicals. And pomegranate. And lavender. He sensed the energy of dozens of people, all of it warm and positive. A shitload of love in that room. What the hell?

Nigel was laughing his ass off. "Wait 'til you get a load of this, Jarvis. Holy shit, never trust a woman. Isn't that what I said?"

"Nigel!" Reina scolded. "You can wait outside if you're not going to be quiet." Her fingers gently worked at his blindfold. "Ready?"

For some odd reason, Jarvis's heart began to race. He caught Reina's hand just before she loosened the blindfold. "No one has ever given me a present before."

"Then it's time." She dropped the blindfold.

For a moment, all Jarvis could see was a roomful of people. Blaine, Trinity, Death (who had finally pried the Reap off his shoes when Jarvis had cut off the love spell). Also present were Rocco, Sylvan, Damien, and a dozen others. Christian was noticeably absent, confining himself to sick bay management. He'd been looking more gaunt and becoming more withdrawn with each passing day since they'd rescued him, and they were going to stage an intervention if he didn't start improving soon. They were all worried about him, and Jarvis didn't like the fact he hadn't made it here.

Napoleon wasn't there either. He'd shown up at

Fenway Park minutes after the event had cleared out, pissed as hell and searching for Augustus, but all they'd been able to find of the missing assassin was an ear and three toes. Napoleon had bellowed something unintelligible about betrayal and taken off to find Napoleon, and they hadn't heard from either assassin since. Angelica was still incarcerated, and that was the important thing.

Jarvis saw Natalie was standing to the side. Fear still haunted her face, and he knew she wasn't healed. Not emotionally, and he knew what that was like.

The Godfather had vanished that night, and no one had seen him. The press was buzzing about the disappearance of the world's most dangerous bachelor, and Jarvis had caught Natalie double locking the doors on more than one occasion.

Even anti-female Nigel had noticed her fear, and he'd left a sketch pad and new box of colored pencils by her door one morning with a note that said simply, "Try these." Nigel had denied responsibility, but Jarvis recognized the brand and knew the truth. And from the way Natalie watched Nigel, he suspected she knew he'd done it as well. Not that it had changed anything. She was still giving off the cold vibrations of fear, and nothing was able to take that edge off.

Folks he didn't know were also crowded into the store. Men, women, all of them grinning at him. He finally looked past all the people and saw there were mirrors on all sides, and barber chairs, sinks, shampoo bottles. He frowned. "Where are we?"

"Look up, you goofball." Reina squeezed his hand and pointed to the wall.

In delicate gold script across a black and pink wall were the words, *Design by Jarvis*.

An enormous knot formed in his throat and he couldn't talk. Couldn't speak.

"It's a hair salon," she said, her face creased with a smile that illuminated the room. "Yours."

His. Holy crap. He fisted his hands and his throat ached, even as he forced himself to shake his head. "I'm not a stylist—"

"No, you're not. You're an artist whose venue is hair." Reina gestured at the crowd. "Meet your staff. Poached from all the best salons in Boston. They're horrifically expensive, but Damien donated some of the money for the botched assassination of the Sisterhood because you saved Rocco."

"I'm a minority owner," Death said. "I expect results."

"So am I," Natalie said. "You have to sell our chocolates in here."

"And the *piece de la resistance*." Blaine swept a black and pink checkered sheet off a stylist chair. A black leather seat. The letter *J* embroidered in pink sweeping font across the back. Arms designed to look like his sword, and a black serpent crawling up the supporting pole beneath. "Your chair, Lord Hate."

His own chair? "It's…" Shit. He didn't even know what to say. "It's magnificent."

"I know. We had it specially designed for you." Reina clapped her hands. "Try it!"

Stunned, unable to believe what she'd done for him, Jarvis walked across the floor and ran his hand over the leather. Soft. Of course. He traced the silken threads of the *J*. He braced his hands on the back of the chair and looked in the mirror. He imagined someone sitting there, entrusting themselves to him. He envisioned taking their hair in his hands. Creating a masterpiece in his mind. Turning it into reality. Designing. Creating. Art. Limitless potential.

Peace settled over him. This was where he belonged. This was his calling. He knew it. This was his salvation.

Reina peeked around his arm, a little frown knitting between her eyebrows. "You don't like it?"

Jarvis turned and buried Reina in his arms. "Thank you," he whispered, too overwhelmed to do anything but repeat the words. "Thank you."

She squealed with glee and hugged him. "I know you can't knit," she said, "but I know how much cross-stitching helps Blaine and painting helps Nigel. Hair is your thing, sweetheart. And now you can do it."

He kissed her then, and he made sure to show her exactly how far his creative talents went.

The catcalls as he hauled her against him?

Didn't bother him one bit.

Nothing did.

Because he'd finally found his place.

He wasn't only the Guardian of Hate.

He wasn't only the Guardian of Love.

He was, quite simply, a man who had found his way to love.

Acknowledgments

THANK YOU TO MY AMAZING EDITOR DEB WERKSMAN, FOR her enthusiasm, guidance, and vision. And thank you for everyone at Sourcebooks for all their hard work that make this book possible, especially Susie Benton, Danielle Jackson, Liz Kelsch, and Cat Clyne. Thank you also to my agent, Deidre Knight, for everything. Thank you also to my family for all their love and support. And thank you, with all my heart, to Mark, for showing me my way. You are my light, my soul, and my love.

About the Author

Nationally bestselling author, Golden Heart® award winner, and four-time RITA® Award nominee, **Stephanie Rowe** is the author of more than twenty books. A former attorney, she resides in New England.

Now Available from Sourcebooks Casablanca
and Stephanie Rowe

Kiss at Your Own Risk

WHEN THE BLACK SKULL AND CROSSBONES CARVED into Alexander Blaine Underhill III's left pec began to smoke, he knew tonight wasn't the night he was going to get his newest cross-stitching tapestry finished. His escape from the Den of Womanly Pursuits, the hellhole he'd been imprisoned in by a black witch for the last hundred and fifty years, was about to get complicated. "Look pretty, boys, we're going to be entertaining."

"Shaved two days ago. Good enough?" Nigel Aquarian was sprinting beside Blaine, his shitkickers thudding on the stainless steel floor of the Hall of Embroidery. He was wearing only dark leather pants and a pale pink rose tattooed on his left cheek. His palms had turned to blackened charcoal, and burning embers were sloughing off onto the floor. "Forgot the cologne, though. Never remember to smell nice after I party with starving piranhas." He held up the pinkie finger he'd had time to grow back only halfway. "I hate fish."

Blaine leapt over a breeding pit for vipers that was blocking his path. "Spiders are worse."

Nigel grimaced. "Bet the witch is good with spiders."

Blaine refused to revisit that particular hell in his mind. "Toughened me up. It was fun."

Nigel shot him a knowing look. "Yeah, I bet it was."

One hundred and fifty years at the non-existent mercy of Death's grandma, Angelica, had given new meaning to the definition of hell. The black witch was diabolical in her quest to become the most powerful practitioner in history, and she wasn't exactly the nurturing type when it came to her experiments. Ruthless evil bitch from hell was probably a better way to describe her. But after a century of planning their escape, it was finally *hasta la vista* time for Blaine and his boys.

Blaine flipped a grin at one of the security cameras he'd disabled only moments before. "Hope you miss us." He was so jonesing for a little *mano a mano* to make her pay for all she'd done, but his brain was the one thing she hadn't managed to mess with, so he was hitting the road instead of gunning for a battle he couldn't win. Embarrassing as hell that one grandma could kick the shit out of four badass warriors. Not going to be posting that on his online dating profile when he got out.

Green and pink disco lights began to flash, and the screams of men being tortured filled the air.

"The fire alarm? Come on, guys. Can't you two keep the smoke in your pants for five minutes?" Jarvis Swain sprinted up beside them. A checkered headband was keeping his light brown hair off his face, and he was streaked with sweat and blood from the spar he'd been winning when Blaine had pulled the trigger on the escape. For Jarvis, a practice session ended only when his opponent was on the bleeding edge of death. He was clenching his samurai sword in his fist.

"Nice pants." Nigel nodded at the yellow tulip cross-stitched on the hip of Jarvis's badass martial arts outfit.

He raised an eyebrow at Blaine. "Is that your delicate touch, Trio?" His question smacked with friendly insult.

Blaine ignored Nigel's sarcastic reference to his pedigree. Far as he was concerned, everyone he was related to could go to hell. Hoped they already had, in fact.

He looked over his shoulder to check on the progress of the most important member of their team, Christian Slayer, but the Hall of Embroidery was empty. "Where's lover boy?"

"He detoured for his girlfriend when we passed through Flower Appreciation." Jarvis hurled his sword at a small black box tacked onto the seventeen-foot high ceiling. "He caught her scent, said she was nearby, and took off to get her." The blade hit cleanly, sparks exploded, and the alarm went silent.

Without breaking stride, Blaine leapt up and grabbed the sword. "We're in the middle of a daring escape from our own personal torture chamber, and he's taking time to get a girl?"

"That's what he claimed," Nigel said. "He can't lie worth shit, so I tend to believe him."

They continued to haul ass toward the door at the end of the hallway. Freedom was less than fifty yards away. "Well, damn." Blaine hurled the sword blade-first at Jarvis's heart. "That's really sweet of him."

Jarvis snatched the sword out of the air easily, his hand unerringly finding the handle. "You think?"

"Sure. It's not every man who will strand his team in a war zone so he can go rescue a girl." Still running hard, Blaine pulled out a pair of small blue balls from a sack strapped to his hip. "Of course, I'm going to have to kick the hell out of him for doing it, and there's no way he's going on future missions with us, but I admire that kind of choice."

The three men he'd handpicked to escape with were the only residents of the Den of Womanly Pursuits he'd trust with his life. He didn't take loyalty lightly, and neither did his team. Yeah, Christian's detour showed that honor could be a liability, but Blaine was down with that kind of cost. Anyone who refused to leave someone behind had his vote, no matter what the repercussions were.

He heard the muted pitter-patter of little feet skittering around the corner behind them, and he swung around to face their pursuers, spinning the blue balls in his hand. Instinctively, one hand went to the long tube he'd strapped to his hip. Just checking to make sure the one cross-stitching project he was taking with him was still secure.

It was.

"Personally, I think he's lost his sense of perspective." Nigel planted himself at Blaine's right shoulder and extended the burning embers of his hands toward their oncoming pursuer. "Getting laid has completely compromised his ability to think clearly. I'm thinking celibacy is the way to go. You boys in?"

Blaine snorted. "Sex can be good for the brain. Depends on the situation." Blaine's blue balls caught fire, and he swiveled them in his palm. He wanted to toss those suckers at the bastards on their tail, but he'd blow Christian to hell if he were in the middle of the pack. Where was the slacker?

"How would you know whether a man's brain gets fried when he gets laid?" Jarvis asked. "When was the last time you got some, Trio?"

"A real man doesn't discuss his conquests." Blaine

caught the faint scent of kibble and he stiffened, hoping he was wrong about what was after them. Yeah, a good battle was fantastic for achieving inner peace, but some things really were the stuff of nightmares.

Jarvis barked with laughter. "A real man keeps a journal and reads it to his sex-deprived buddies. Last action we got was the stick figures Nigel painted on the bathroom wall with toothpaste."

They'd all agreed long ago that the forced intimacy with Angelica didn't count as sex. Some things had to stay sacred.

Nigel shot Jarvis an annoyed look. "Don't knock my artistic talents. You're just jealous because you can't knit your way out of a weekend of torture with the witch."

"I choose to suck at knitting. Being subjected to another of her experiments makes me tougher." Jarvis began to whip his sword over his head in a circle. The air crackled with the energy he was generating. "You're the pansy, choosing to make beautiful pictures so she's happy with you and lets you skip out on the torture."

"I like to paint." Nigel's unapologetic tone was a truth that Blaine knew they all felt. Anything they could do to get through another hour, another day, under the blonde despot's reign was a victory. Nigel was lucky she'd chosen painting for him, because the lightweight actually dug it.

Counted cross-stitch hadn't exactly been a mental haven for Blaine.

His team was comprised of the only four men left from the batch of thirty boys kidnapped and brought to her realm that night a hundred and fifty years ago. Most had died. A few had been rescued. Jarvis and Nigel had hoped to be saved for a while, but Blaine had never bothered.

Even as a four-year-old, he'd known no one would come for him. He'd heard his own parents make the deal with the sorceress. Still remembered sitting there at the top of the stairs, clutching the wolf he'd just finished carving for his mom's birthday. The clunk of the animal hitting the wood floor, the snap of its leg breaking off, as he'd sat there in stunned silence, listening to his own mother hand his soul over to the devil.

He'd been no match for Angelica when she'd come to get him, and the thick scar down the length of his forearm was proof. He rubbed his hand over the mark, the last injury he'd gotten before he became her plaything and developed the ability to heal from anything.

That scar was his reminder never to trust a soul with anything that mattered to him. The day she'd dropped him on his ass in that cellar was the day he'd decided to save himself. There were times when his thirst for freedom had been the only thing keeping him going. Lying there, his life bleeding out, the witch standing over him… his refusal to die a prisoner had often been the only thing strong enough to pull him back from the edge of death.

His resilience had made him one of Angelica's favorite playthings.

And now he got to win. Rock on.

"I hate knitting. My hands are too damn big for all those little knit/purl things." Jarvis flexed his fingers as he moved beside Blaine. Shoulder to shoulder to shoulder, in strict formation. The witch tried to emasculate them with womanly pursuits so she could control them, but she'd also wanted her warriors to be tough as hell. She had no idea how far they'd taken it.

Today was her lucky day. She was about to find out.

"Knitting is about finesse, not the size of your hands." Thick black smoke flowed out of Nigel's palms. "It seems to me that you have a mental block about it."

"Nigel does have a point, Jarvis." Blaine focused his energy into his chest. The skull and crossbones mark burst into flames, and he opened himself to the pain. *Bring it on.* "I've seen you do some good detail work with the knitting needles when you're in the zone." The flames licking at his chest were orange. Not hot enough. He thought of the last time he'd been alone with Angelica, and what she'd done to him. Fury rose hard, and the flame turned blue-white. Now that's what he was talking about.

Then their assailant arrived. The first of the schnoodles rounded the corner, teeth bared, ears pinned. Blaine tensed as it erupted into frantic yapping. *Dammit.* He'd wanted to be wrong.

It could have been the demons.

It could have been the pit vipers.

But no. She'd sent the schnoodles.

Their odds of making it to freedom had just gone to hell.

"Seven days until you're murder free!"

"Nothing like jinxing me to add to the challenge," Trinity Harpswell teased (okay, maybe there was a little bit of seriousness, aka panic, there as well as teasing). She raised her water and clinked it against the wineglass of her best friend, Reina Fleming. It felt a trifle premature to be celebrating breaking the black widow curse, but she was down with trying to stay positive. She'd made it this far, right? It was all about having the faith. "I can make it a week, don't you think?"

Trinity was wearing flip-flops and a black pencil skirt so narrow that she was reduced to a penguin waddle when wearing it. An outfit chosen specifically to make it difficult to sprint after unsuspecting prey if the curse decided to have its merry way with her morals, ethics, and basic human values.

She was so not loving that feeling of spiraling out of control. That moment when the lights got too bright, when her heart started to race, when her mind was screaming at her not to do it, and somehow, someway, she couldn't stop herself yet again. The black widow curse was decidedly ruthless in its drive to get her to fall in love and force her to send the guy gallivanting off to the Afterlife. Not the stuff teenage dreams are made of, for sure. Or the dreams of twenty-nine-year-old single gals either, actually.

"Of course you're going to make it." Reina was wearing a sparkly red cocktail dress and strappy sandals. Her auburn hair was in an updo, and her eyes were dancing with the thrill of life, as they always were. Her positive, uplifting spirit had buoyed Trinity so many times, and she treasured her friend. "You've made it almost five years. What's another week?"

"I don't think the curse is going to let me go without a fight. Something's coming. I can feel it." Trinity leaned back in her chair, not quite able to keep the worried tone out of her voice. "I had this dream last night that I was walking through the Boston Common, and this marching band of really nice guys came by and they wanted to buy me dinner and then I killed them all." Her stomach churned at the memory. "And they were all dads. And now their kids have no dad and their wives are all single moms and—"

"Stop!" Reina tossed a roll at her. "For heaven's sake, girl, you need to get a grip. You aren't going to orphan any kids or take out an entire fleet of guys. You're not that bad!"

"You don't live in my body. I can feel this darkness pulsing inside me. All the time. It's freaky." A flirty giggle caught Trinity's attention, and she glanced over at the table beside them.

A twenty-something couple was just arriving. The woman was wearing a beautiful off-white dress, and the man flashed dimples at her as he pulled out her chair. The gal beamed up at him as he guided her into the seat, his hand light on her back with the tenderest of touches. They both smiled, and then he bent and brushed his lips over her cheek.

Trinity propped her elbow on the table, chin in her palm, and sighed. "Okay, that's the sweetest—"

"Hey!" Reina grabbed Trinity's arm.

Trinity tensed and looked at her friend. "I did it again, didn't I?"

"You have *got* to stop noticing nice guys." Reina pointed at herself with her first two fingers. "Focus on me, killer girl. You know it's no good for you to be looking at love. It gets you all worked up, and then I have to sit on you to keep you from killing the poor guy."

Trinity almost laughed. "Somehow I don't think you sitting on me would stop me if I was really caught in the thrall."

"I know. You're crazy girl when you fall in love." Reina twirled her goblet between the tips of her fingers. "You know, I have to say I'm completely impressed you've gone this long without killing. You've done good, girl."

The words released some of her tension, and Trinity felt a sudden thickness in her throat. "Thanks. I appreciate it."

Reina sat back in her chair and faked a sigh of exasperation. "You do realize, however, that if I ever thought you'd make it this long without knocking anyone off, I'd never have decided to become your friend."

Trinity grinned. As one of Death's most promising young talents, Reina spent her time around all things dead, which is why she'd been so attracted to Trinity when they'd first met. "Yeah, well, I'm glad you misjudged me."

Reina winked. "Me too. Your angelic ways might not be helping my career, but you still rock."

"Amen to that, sister." Trinity might have baggage, but carting people off to the Afterlife didn't exactly make Reina one of the most popular girls on the block either. Most human and Otherworld beings could sense her aura of death, and they naturally shied away from her, some without even understanding why they were doing it.

Admittedly, Trinity had been a little wigged by Reina when the feisty stranger had shown up at her apartment door armed with a chocolate cake and an offer to be friends, but in the end, it had been too much to resist bonding with someone who knew what she was like and still dug her, even if Reina did have a vested interest in capitalizing on Trinity's mistakes.

A perfect, enduring friendship between a couple of freaks.

Reina leaned forward. "So, your black widow curse expires Sunday night at seven fifteen, right?"

"Assuming I don't kill anyone between now and then, yep." Trinity had etched that date in her mind five years ago, when she'd forced herself to visit her last true love in the morgue, her ice cream cone still lodged in his carotid. She'd stood over his mint chocolate chip scented body and vowed to him that she would break the cycle, that no one else would fall victim to the blackness coursing through her veins. The black widow curse was a fickle creature, and if Trinity could go five years without killing, the curse would leave her.

She had no clue how she'd been lucky enough to acquire the curse. No one did. She'd been kidnapped as a baby for six months, and when the police had found her in a pet store snuggling in a pile of puppies, no one had known what had happened to her.

Until she'd turned sixteen and fallen in love for the first time. It hadn't taken Trinity and her parents long to figure out what had happened, and the Internet was rife with all the info she needed to find out exactly what was wrong with her and how to break it.

Diagnosis: Evil killer bitch. (Sigh.)

Treatment: Abstain. (Yeah, so easy. Not. Way harder than giving up caffeine and chocolate. You don't believe? Pick your worst habit and try to break it. Not so easy, eh? And you're not even compelled to do it by some wicked, supernatural force.)

Worst-Case Prognosis: Forever a murderer if she killed five times. (Up to four now. The first couple of years had been tough...)

Best-Case Prognosis: Forever free if she could go five years without killing anyone. (One week left.)

She was down to d-day, and she knew her curse wasn't going to let her go easily.

"So, not that I don't fully support killing, you know, as Death's assistant, but as your friend, I really want you to succeed." Reina twirled her wineglass between her thumb and finger. "I talked to Death and got him to offer up his cabin in Minnesota. We could take a girl's week and watch bad movies and avoid men."

"Oh, wow." Relief rippled through Trinity at the thought of escaping. "That sounds so good."

"Fantastic." Reina grabbed her iPhone and started dialing. "I'll just call him and let him know. Don't want any of his harem girls hanging around when we get there—"

Trinity set her hand over the phone. "I can't duck out on this, Reina."

Reina pried Trinity's fingers off her mobile device. "Why not? Running away is a basic human reaction when pure, unadulterated hell comes looking for you. People try to flee from me all the time. "

Trinity raised her brows. "And does it work when they hide from you?"

Reina shrugged. "Well, no, but I'm really persistent."

"And the curse isn't?"

"Mmm… true. But this is different. I mean—"

"No." Trinity leaned forward. "I need to prove to myself that I'm stronger than the curse." If she could resist temptation while under the dictates of the curse, she would be able to believe in herself, to know there was something worthy in her soul. "I need to know I'm not some evil killer who uses the curse as an excuse to do bad things."

Look for Stephanie Rowe's next
paranormal romance

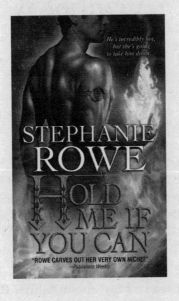

Available from Sourcebooks Casablanca
January 2012

Strange Neighbors

BY ASHLYN CHASE

HE'S LOOKING FOR PEACE, QUIET, AND A MAYBE
LITTLE ROMANCE...

Hunky all-star pitcher and shapeshifter Jason Falco invests
in an old Boston brownstone apartment building full of
supernatural creatures, and there's never a dull moment.
But when Merry McKenzie moves into the ground floor
apartment, the playboy pitcher decides he might just be
done playing the field...

What readers say about Ashlyn Chase

"Entertaining and humorous—a winner!"

*"The humor and romance kept me entertained—
a definite page turner!"*

"Sexy, funny stories!"

978-1-4022-3661-7 • $6.99 U.S./$8.99 CAN/£3.99 UK

The Werewolf Upstairs

BY ASHLYN CHASE

SHE SHOULD KNOW BETTER...

Attorney Roz Wells is bored. She used to have such a knack for attracting the weird and unexpected, but ever since she took a job as a Boston Public defender the quirky quotient in her life has taken a serious hit. Until her sexy werewolf neighbor starts coming around...

Roz knows she should stay away from this sexy bad boy, but she can't help it that she's putty in his hands...

What readers say about Ashlyn Chase

"Entertaining and humorous—a winner!"

"The humor and romance kept me entertained—a definite page turner!"

"Sexy, funny stories!"

978-1-4022-3662-4 • $6.99 U.S./$8.99 CAN/£4.99 UK

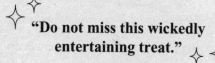

Wicked by Any Other Name

BY LINDA WISDOM

"Do not miss this wickedly entertaining treat."

—Annette Blair,
Sex and the Psychic Witch

STASI ROMANOV USES A LITTLE WITCH MAGIC IN HER LINGERIE shop, running a brisk side business in love charms. A disgruntled customer threatening to sue over a failed spell brings wizard attorney Trevor Barnes to town—and witches and wizards make a volatile combination. The sparks fly, almost everyone's getting singed, and the whole town seems on the verge of a witch hunt.

Can the feisty witch and the gorgeous wizard overcome their objections and settle out of court—and in the bedroom?

978-1-4022-1773-9 • $6.99 U.S. / $7.99 CAN

Hex in
High Heels

BY LINDA WISDOM

Can a Witch and a Were find happiness?

Feisty witch Blair Fitzpatrick has had a crush on hunky carpenter Jake Harrison forever—he's one hot shapeshifter. But Jake's nasty mother and brother are after him to return to his pack, and Blair is trying hard not to unleash the ultimate revenge spell. When Jake's enemies try to force him away from her, Blair is pushed over the edge. No one messes with her boyfriend-to-be, even if he does shed on the furniture!

Praise for Linda Wisdom's Hex series:

"Fan-fave Wisdom… continues to delight."
—*RT Book Reviews*

"Highly entertaining, sexy, and imaginative."
—*Star Crossed Romance*

"It's a five star, feel-good ride!" —*Crave More Romance*

"Something fresh and new."
—*Paranormal Romance Review*

978-1-4022-1819-4 •$6.99 U.S. / $8.99 CAN

DEMONS
ARE A
GIRL'S BEST FRIEND
BY LINDA WISDOM

A BEWITCHING WOMAN ON A MISSION...

Feisty witch Maggie enjoys her work as a paranormal law enforcement officer—that is, until she's assigned to protect a teenager with major attitude and plenty of Mayan enemies. Maggie's never going to survive this assignment without the help of a half-fire demon who makes her smolder...

Praise for Linda Wisdom

"Hot talent Wisdom does a truly wonderful job mixing passion, danger, and outrageous antics into a tasty blend that's sure to satisfy."
—RT Book Reviews

"Entertaining and sexy... Ms. Wisdom's stories have something for everyone." —Night Owl Romance

"Wickedly captivating... wildly entertaining... full of magical zest and unrivaled witty prose."
—Suite 101

978-1-4022-5439-0 • $7.99 U.S./£4.99 UK

Catch of a Lifetime

by Judi Fennell

"Judi Fennell has one heck of an imagination!" —
Michelle Rowen, author of *Bitten & Smitten*

WHEN HE DISCOVERS WHAT SHE REALLY IS,
○ ○ ○ ○ THEY'RE BOTH IN MORTAL DANGER... ○ ○ ○ ○

Mermaid Angel Tritone has been researching humans from afar, and when she jumps into a boat to escape a shark attack, it's her chance to pursue her mission to save the planet from disaster—but she must keep her identity a secret. For Logan Hardington, finding a beautiful woman on his boat is surely not a problem—until he realizes his life is on the line...

○ ○ ○ ○ ○ PRAISE FOR *IN OVER HER HEAD*: ○ ○ ○ ○ ○

"A charming modern day fairy tale with a twist. Fennel is a bright star on the horizon of romance." —Judi McCoy, author of *Hounding the Pavement*

"Fennell's under-the-sea suspense will enchant you with its wit, humor, and sexiness." —Caridad Pineiro, *NYT* and *USA Today* Bestseller, *South Beach Chicas Catch Their Man*

978-1-4022-2428-7 • $6.99 U.S. / $8.99 CAN

I Dream of Genies
Judi Fennell

He needs to change his luck, and fast!

Matt Ewing would gladly hunt down a fortune in lucky pennies if he thought it would help save his business. But for all his hoping, Matt's clueless when his long-awaited lucky charm falls in his lap in the form of a beguiling genie. He just can't believe that this beautiful woman could be the answer to his prayers…

She's been bottled up for far too long!

Spending 2,000 years in a bottle would make any woman a little stir-crazy. So when Matt releases Eden from her luxurious captivity, she's thrilled to repay him by giving him the magical boost he needs…

But for all her good intentions, Eden's magical prowess is a little rusty and her magical mistakes become more than embarrassing. And though Eden knows falling in love will end her magic and immortality, she can't help be drawn to the one man who wants her just for herself…

WITHDRAWN